SPLURGE

AND THE THEATRE OF MAGIC

Splurge and the Theatre of Magic

Copyright © John Hayes 2008

ISBN 978-184426-500-8

First Published 2008 by
UPFRONT PUBLISHING LTD
Peterborough, England.

Printed by Printondemand-Worldwide Ltd.

SPLURGE

AND THE THEATRE OF MAGIC

by

John Hayes

**UPFRONT PUBLISHING
PETERBOROUGH**

For

Kaya and Ashanti

"O brave new world
That has such people in't"" – Miranda –

(The Tempest – Act 5 – Scene 1)

Chapter One – A School Trip

Splurge had never been to a theatre, not a proper one that is. He remembered going to a pantomime once in the village hall, when he was about seven. Puss in Boots it was called. He wasn't that impressed. It seemed to be a lot of people dressing in funny clothes and saying silly things and singing silly songs. It was not at all like the story that his teacher had read to them in class.

It was, therefore, with a degree of resignation, apprehension and definite misgivings that he now viewed his first real theatre visit. At least he had the consolation of not being alone in his anticipated boredom and misery, as the whole of Miss Edison's class was going, which meant that his two best mates, Dash and Blip, would be there to share the same discomfort.

It was educational to see a real live play instead of reading it in a book. That was Miss Edison's view at least and, as she was their English teacher, at the village school, in Wolverton (where Splurge and his friends lived), her views counted. On the other hand there were some advantages to such an excursion – an afternoon away from school for a start, and maybe the chance to wander around the shops. That was Splurge's view. He rarely got the chance when his mother took him with her on one of her shopping expeditions to Traffield. That's where this play was being performed. He couldn't remember the name of it – MacDonald or McDougal – some name like that. It was Scottish anyway. He remembered that much. When his teacher had mentioned Shakespeare, he switched off - not his cup of tea at all. He preferred History or Geography, and not too much of them either.

Anyway, at the moment, the whole class was lined up outside the theatre, while Miss Edison went inside to sort out the tickets. Mr. Turnbull, a young student teacher, was left to keep an eye on the class. That's when it all went wrong – or right, depending on one's point of view. For Splurge's two friends, Dash and Blip, it would go pretty well, but for Splurge, it would be something altogether different.

"We're going to be here for ages," Splurge muttered to Dash.

"Why don't we sneak off? Nobody will notice. We could go round the shops, and get back in time when the rest of the class come out," his friend replied.

Dash made it sound very plausible, but Splurge was not so sure. "What about Mr. Turnbull? He's bound to be at the back and check everyone in."

Dash screwed up his eyes as he simulated some sort of thought process. "A diversion. That's what we need."

"Can we go to the cake shop? There's one just round the corner. I noticed it as we walked from the bus stop." It hadn't taken Blip long to focus on his favourite pastime. "I'm hungry."

"Can't you leave your stomach at home, just for once?" Dash was less than sympathetic to Blip's needs.

"Never mind that now. Look! Everyone's going in. Let's hang back. Mr.Turnbull won't notice. Then we make a run for it." Splurge had worked it all out. "We'll go round the side of the theatre, just in case anyone comes looking for us."

"Don't you think that we'll get into trouble if they find out that we're not in the theatre?" Blip didn't sound too sure.

"Naw." Dash, however, was sure.

"You want the cake shop, don't you?"

Splurge's suggestion was enough for Blip.

So it was decided. The three friends were poised to experience a couple of hours of unfettered liberty among the glitter and sparkle of Traffield's shopping malls. Though in actual fact only two of them would sample the delights of their truancy, for Splurge was to be catapulted into an entirely different world.

It all happened as they made off quickly around the back of the theatre. Dash took the lead with Blip close behind.

Splurge lingered for a brief moment to make sure that the rest of the class had gone inside the theatre, then followed Dash and Blip. As he turned the corner of the theatre, he could see no sign of his friends, though he thought he could hear their footsteps. He couldn't imagine where they could have got to because it was only a narrow alley between the theatre and the next buildings, which looked like a row of small shops. He stopped and looked up and down the passageway. There was no way out at the other end, so they must be around somewhere. He was on the point of going back to the front of the theatre, in case they had decided to join the rest of the class after all, when he noticed a large steel door at the side of the theatre. It was slightly ajar.

They were having some sort of joke, he supposed. He tentatively pulled at the door, which despite its size, swung open quite easily. He was tempted to call out but didn't want to alert any doorman or other official who might be lurking about looking for stray boys. Stealthily he crept inside. It was dark and smelled old and musty. He supposed that's what all theatres were like.

He had only taken a few steps when he heard a low, rasping squeal, which ended in a loud, metallic clang. The steel door had swung closed. He stumbled back to it and felt for some kind of handle, but could find nothing. Immediately he thought that his friends had lured him here and closed the door on him. Some joke! He hammered on the door and called out, but it was so thick that he could barely hear the sounds himself, as his voice had become all muffled in the thick, cloying darkness.

He was trapped.

For a moment, Splurge was seized with a sudden heart-thumping panic. How was he going to get out of this place? He took a few faltering steps and bumped into something. It was hard and box-shaped and he was sure to have a huge bruise on his shin. He would have stumbled around it but something was stopping him.

"We've been waiting for you."

A strange, mechanical sort of voice came out of the blackness and echoed all around him. At first, Splurge was startled, then realised that it was probably Dash or Blip messing about. He would teach them a lesson. Slowly and stealthily he crept towards the sound. But he had taken only a few steps when suddenly he fell headlong into something. What it was, he couldn't tell, because he kept on falling and falling into a never-ending darkness.

Chapter Two - The Theatre of Magic

Splurge was an unusual name for a boy but it turned out to be a sensible one. His parents, Mr. and Mrs. Edwards, had originally named him from his six uncles, Sidney, Percy, Leonard, Ulysses, Ronald and George. Despite having six names to choose from, there was always going to be a difficulty in deciding which one to use. The trouble was that his parents didn't want to offend any of the uncles by calling their son one name before another. Using their initials seemed the fairest way of resolving the problem. Splurge himself was grateful for the arrangement, as he didn't fancy any of the names. Names should fit a person, he believed, and he had passed this idea on to his two friends, Derek Ashton and Brian Lipton, who became Dash and Blip respectively.

With freckled face and unruly mop of brown hair, Splurge was like any average boy, if there ever was such a thing as an average boy. Like most average boys, he got into trouble with an alarming frequency, though he himself would never see it as trouble, more as adventure. But he had to admit that at times his thirst for adventure could lead him into danger – like now.

He had no idea what had happened to him or where he had landed though he reckoned it must have been on something soft because he couldn't feel any aches or pains usually associated with such a fall. He stood up to make sure. Nothing broken or sprained, he decided. But where was he? And what about that voice?

He didn't have much time to consider because suddenly, out of nowhere, a hand grabbed him, and though he tried to resist, the grip was much too strong. In fact several pairs of hands had grabbed him. They pinched and tore at him with a ferocity that made him cry out with pain. He struggled as best he could but it seemed as though a dozen metal clamps had gripped him. Worse, however, was not being able to see his tormentors. There must be several of them, he reasoned, but it was so dark, that he couldn't make out even the vaguest of shapes.

Just as he was about to give up and let himself be led to wherever these hands were taking him, he found himself free.

As he rubbed his arms, where the pinching had been at its most savage, he staggered about trying to get some sense of direction. Before he had taken many steps, however, there was light everywhere. At first Splurge had to shield his eyes because of the brightness but when he did examine his surroundings, he was surprised to find that he was in a theatre. But it was not the theatre he was supposed to be in, with the rest of his class. This one was different. Firstly it was much smaller, and so was everything in it, from the stage and curtains, to the seats. He looked around, half expecting to see a crowd of small people to go with this small theatre. There was nobody. Nor were there any sounds of people, nor any kind of noise – just a dead silence. Splurge had an uncomfortable feeling that something was not quite right.

While he was trying to sort out everything in his head, he was startled to hear a voice ring out. It was a sharp but reedy voice, which seemed to come from a long way away.

Splurge looked around, again half expecting to see somebody. But there was no one in sight. This strange, little theatre was completely empty.

"Hurry! Hurry! The curtain is about to go up." The voice rang out once more, this time with a distinct air of impatience.

Splurge was unsure what to do. Was the voice speaking to him? He took a hesitant step towards the nearest row of seats.

"Get a move on. The performance is about to begin. Take your seat." The voice sounded even more impatient.

That must mean me, thought Splurge, because there was nobody else here, so he began to ease himself into the first seat of the row.

"Not there!" the voice snapped. "In the middle. The better you will see. You must be able to see everything quite clearly." There was a pause before the voice spoke again. "Good." It had somehow known that Splurge had now managed to squeeze himself into a seat in the centre of the row.

The seat was small but surprisingly quite comfortable and Splurge awaited the next development with a certain amount of trepidation. Everything had happened so quickly that he was not at all sure that he was really here. However, he could still feel the bruises on his arms where he had been so roughly manhandled. It must be real, he reckoned. But what was it all about? And who were these mysterious beings, which so far hadn't shown themselves?

His questions looked as though they were about to be answered, because suddenly it went dark. For a moment, he wasn't sure whether he was about to be grabbed again, and he sank as deep as possible into his seat. It would have been quite ineffective, however, as it was so small and offered no protection. Before he could start making plans for some sort of defence, there was a loud trumpet blast, which almost deafened him. At the same time the curtains opened.

Splurge sat up in his seat and watched with a trance-like fascination as a myriad coloured lights and small explosions danced about the stage. No sooner had his eyes grown accustomed to these dancing lights than they disappeared, to be replaced by another curtain across which was emblazoned, in large, twinkling, gold letters, THE THEATRE OF MAGIC. At the same time a voice, this time deep and hollow, boomed out.

"Welcome to our grand presentation!"

Splurge, although not as scared as he had been, was still a little concerned, and the questions began to return. He had an uneasy feeling about this place. It didn't seem real, and he still hadn't seen anybody. It could all be done by machinery, or even by a computer, though the bruises on his arms soon dispelled the latter theory.

The banner faded until the stage was dark. Then there was a sudden explosion, which lit up the stage and produced a big cloud of orange coloured smoke, causing Splurge to jump up in alarm. As the smoke faded, several tall figures, shrouded in some kind of shimmering blue costumes, materialised. They glided noiselessly towards the front of the stage and held out their arms.

Splurge sank back into his seat. He wished he could have sunk right into the floor, because these figures were pointing at him. He had a quick look around in case somebody else might have slipped into the theatre, but he appeared to be the only audience. All he could do was to watch in a dreadful fascination. If he could have moved, he would have done so, and quickly, but he felt glued to his seat. What did they want with him?

Just as he thought that he might be dragged upon the stage, the figures began to fade. In a twinkling they were gone and Splurge was left to ponder whether he had actually seen them after all.

The stage grew dark again and, for a moment, he was left in what seemed like a black void. It was probably only dark for a second or two, but it was enough for him to feel a little anxious. Just as he was considering hiding under the seat, there was the sound of a big drum coming from the stage. There were still no lights but the drumbeat became louder and louder – boom – boom - boom. With a final crashing boom, the stage was suddenly lit up in a brilliant array of coloured lights.

Whatever Splurge had been expecting could not have prepared him for what he now saw, which was the strangest assortment of figures he could have imagined.

Almost hidden behind a large drum, tiny arms could be seen frantically wielding drumsticks and occasionally poking out a small round face, as if to judge the effects of the noise it was making. This figure took the centre of the stage and at each crash of the drum, another figure would trot out from the side of the stage and stand beside the drummer. Each one gave a small bow. Splurge wondered if they were children, for they were small, and like the drummer, had childlike faces. But they couldn't be children because their arms and legs didn't move the way they should. Their movements were jerky and unnatural as though they were on strings, with someone else manipulating them. That was it! They were puppets. This must be a puppet theatre attached to the main one. He felt a lot better now that he had solved that mystery. But no sooner had he congratulated himself at coming up with the obvious explanation, than the figures on the stage began to sing. It was an odd sort of singing, all high pitched and squeaky. Something like cartoon characters, thought Splurge. But that wasn't what caused him to change his mind. They were all singing together, and that was something that he didn't think even the best puppets could do. The song wasn't important. He could hardly understand it anyway. If they were really puppets, there had to be a lot of people somewhere behind the stage, or wherever they hid themselves. Not possible, he thought.

Then, as though to emphasise their versatility, the doll-like figures began to gambol and somersault about the stage in a wild frenzy of activity, with a variety of coloured lights exploding about them at the same time. Again, no puppet could do that without becoming seriously entangled.

Splurge was puzzled. He had supplied his own explanation and as quickly discounted it. Now, he didn't know what to think. All he could do was to sit back and wait for the next strange event to happen. It didn't take long.

With one big crash of the drum, and after an extra bright flash of light, the stage was suddenly plunged into darkness once more. As Splurge began to wonder what was coming next, he felt a tug on his arm. Startled, he looked around to see two of the strangest persons he had ever come across.

Even close up, Splurge still couldn't make out what sort of creatures they were. They might have been human but they were very small, a little more than half his size, (though Splurge was tall for his age). Their round, bald heads, large, round eyes and tiny mouths gave them a doll-like appearance. Yet they were definitely not dolls. Nor were they like any kind of person he had seen before.

"Come with us." The one who had tugged his arm spoke in a flat, hollow voice, which sounded strangely loud, considering the size of the speaker.

Splurge hesitated for a moment.

"You must come with us," said the other one, in a similar kind of voice. At the same time it reached forward and grabbed Splurge's other arm.

"Hey!" Splurge yelled. "You're pinching me!"

They ignored his discomfort and continued to pull at him till he was clear of the seat.

"Alright, alright! You don't have to be so rough. I'll come with you, only stop pinching me." Splurge recognised the grip of these two tiny creatures as the same as he had experienced earlier.

As he was being led, or rather pulled along towards the stage, Splurge scrutinised the two creatures that had hold of him. Their doll-like faces betrayed no emotion as they resolutely pulled him up to the stage. They had no difficulty in doing this for they had long arms and great strength. No doubt of that, thought Splurge, as he could imagine the bruises already welling up on his body. He found it difficult to understand how they could be so strong for their size. They were really quite small. Perhaps they were some sorts of mechanical toys. He couldn't tell much from their clothes, which were identical and looked like some sort of smock or overalls. Robots! That's what they were.

Suddenly pleased with himself for having at last discovered a logical explanation, he almost forgot the rough handling from the two that had hold of him. He was sure that he would soon meet the person who was behind this whole performance.

The two creatures, whatever they were, had now reached the stage. Because of their short legs, it had taken longer than he supposed, although they were hurrying. Splurge could have covered the distance in a dozen strides. At the same time, the lights dimmed and he couldn't see how they were to get up there. He was sure that he had seen some steps at the side of the stage, but they weren't there now. However, he needn't have worried about it, because suddenly he was thrown upwards by these two creatures onto the stage, where he landed with a crash.

Dazed and confused, he staggered to his feet and tried to make some sort of sense of this new situation. He knew that he was on a stage, but it didn't look like it. It was more like a large room; at least he thought it was. He couldn't be sure because his head was swirling about and ringing with noises.

"I see you made it at last."

The voice seemed to come out of thin air, and Splurge looked vainly around in the expectation of seeing someone. But there was no one there. Splurge sighed. They were at it again, he thought. Why must they play games? "Stop playing games," he suddenly called out.

"Sorry about that."

A head appeared out of the blackness and glided slowly towards Splurge, who stood transfixed with a mixture of fear and curiosity.

Chapter Three – Mysterio

The head stopped in front of Splurge, who thought he would be forced off the stage in an attempt to avoid it touching him. Before he could recover from his astonishment, the head spoke.

"There. That's better."

The figure of a tall, dark-haired man, with a small, neatly trimmed black beard, had suddenly materialised and proceeded to kick at something on the floor. The man was dressed in black and around his shoulders a small, red lined cape. "How did you like my entrance?" He smiled a strange, mysterious smile as if daring Splurge to say something by way of praise.

"I know how that trick is done," said Splurge smugly. He had seen it on television, so he was quite sure that this strange, bearded figure was nothing more than an ordinary magician. Before he could utter another word, the man disappeared, except for his head, which now bobbed about like a balloon.

"Do you know how this trick is done then?" Without warning, the head suddenly shot upwards into the blackness above the stage, laughing as it did so. "Want to see some more?" the head called down to Splurge.

Splurge could only gape at this strange spectacle. He certainly hadn't seen anything like that on television. The voice called down to him again.

"Why don't you join me?"

Before Splurge could reply, he suddenly found himself floating upward towards the blackness above the stage till he was level with the head.

"You know how this trick is done then?" The head gave Splurge a mocking smile.

Splurge wasn't taking much notice, as he was more intent on trying to stop himself from being sick. Though he was upright, floating in the air above the stage made him feel as though he was being churned around by some whirlwind, and he was desperately trying to come to terms with the feeling. Then, without warning, he was back on the stage, having landed with a bump, which sent him sprawling. Beside him was the tall magician.

"So how do you like my theatre?" The magician spread out his arms and the whole theatre was lit up in a bright golden light.

Splurge rubbed his head, still not used to the swirling about in mid-air and the unceremonious landing. "Your theatre?" was all he could mumble.

"Here." The magician took off his cape and threw across the stage. Before it had landed, a small doll-like creature appeared from out of nowhere and caught it. Immediately the strange creature disappeared in a puff of blue smoke.

Splurge never knew what to expect next. Whenever he thought that he was beginning to get used to this strange new world, the simplest things would suddenly surprise him. "Who are you?" he asked. "And where am I?"

The tall figure of the magician drew himself up till it seemed that he was even taller. "I am Mysterio," he said in a loud, booming voice, which made Splurge's ears ring. "And you," he pointed a long, menacing finger at Splurge, "are my guest. Welcome to The Theatre of

Magic." He accompanied this statement with an elaborate bow.

Splurge could never tell whether this Mysterio was serious or having some sort of joke at his expense. There was always a sense of menace in his words. Splurge didn't trust him, or anyone who could arrange for him to be floating in the air. He was a magician all right – a real magician. On the other hand, if he was supposed to be a guest that should surely mean that he was entitled to some sort of consideration. "Thank you very much for me being a guest and all that," he mumbled, " but why am I here? And how did I get here?"

Mysterio said nothing but stared hard at Splurge. His eyes were like dark spots of piercing light (that's how Splurge saw them) and they seemed to burrow into his very soul. "You are here because you didn't want to go to the other theatre. How you came to be here is only for me to know." His eyes relaxed. "After all, if I told you, you would be coming here all the time." He allowed himself a slight smile. I'm only surprised that your friends didn't accompany you."

"What about my friends? Do you know what has happened to them?"

"I only know what is in The Theatre of Magic," Mysterio said, somewhat enigmatically.

Splurge reckoned that he wasn't going to get too many answers from this Mysterio character, so he would have to try to work things out for himself. It was pretty certain that Dash and Blip were off somewhere round the shops so he needn't worry too much about them. It was himself that he had to worry about. If he didn't get out of this theatre, he would miss the coach back to Wolverton. He wondered how long he had been here. "How do I get out of this place?"

"Why would you want to leave? You have barely seen anything of my theatre" As he spoke, Mysterio pulled a top hat from somewhere out of his cloak and snapped it open. He then proceeded to pull from the hat a variety of objects.

Splurge was mesmerised by the swiftness of the trick, for in no time there was a pile of objects littering the floor of the stage. A strange assortment they were, ranging from a string of sausages to tiny model soldiers, which scuttled about the floor like marauding insects. Splurge had to move to avoid being overrun by them. But a wave of the hand from Mysterio was enough to halt them in their tracks and send them scuttling back to the ever-increasing pile of objects coming out of the hat.

"Well? How do you like that? Real magic. And there's much more where that came from. Wouldn't you like to see more?"

Splurge nodded dumbly. He knew that he should leave this place and join the rest of the class in the proper theatre but the lure of more spectacular magic was too much for him. There were still questions though. "If I stay, can I get out later? And can you teach me some magic?"

Mysterio laughed aloud and the sound echoed and re-echoed around the small theatre, till Splurge thought that it would go on forever. "I will show you such magic that will make your head spin. I can even make your head spin, if you wish." He gave another loud guffaw, which grew into a low, deep rumble, which even shook the stage with its vibrations.

Splurge would have been suitably impressed, except that he was too busy trying to keep his balance, as he was sure that the whole theatre was about to collapse. He was beginning to realise that this Mysterio was no ordinary magician. Perhaps it wasn't such a good idea to have him as a teacher, though he would like to learn something, if only to impress Dash and Blip.

Meanwhile, the hat continued to produce objects, which tumbled onto the ever-increasing pile on the stage. Splurge noted no one item was the same as the other (except for the soldiers, of course). He caught a glimpse of a frying pan, with two eggs sizzling away in it, to be covered almost immediately by a large, fluffy cat. It looked real enough and he began to worry about whether it would get burned by sitting on top of a frying pan, which was obviously hot enough to fry eggs. He needn't have been concerned because with a wave of his hand, Mysterio suddenly made them all disappear, except for the hat, which he put on his head.

"You liked that trick?" Mysterio chuckled. "Not too difficult when you know how. I will teach you how to do it if you like."

Splurge shook his head. He couldn't help thinking about that cat sitting on top of two fried eggs. "I would like to learn a little magic but something that I could manage without hurting anyone or anything," he muttered.

"Ha, ha! So you want to impress your friends." Mysterio paused and took a step towards Splurge till they were face to face. "Listen, my young friend. If you want to learn magic, then learn magic, not some parlour trick that any child could perform."

Splurge felt stung by the allusion to his age. He was practically twelve and he saw himself as almost grown up, but, nevertheless, he was still hesitant about learning anything from this Mysterio. You could never tell where it might lead. He could become so good that Mysterio might keep him here as his apprentice. "I wasn't thinking of parlour tricks," he mumbled.

Mysterio gave him a strange smile and turned to the side of the stage. As he did so a crowd of the doll-like creatures came rushing out and lined up in front of him, just like soldiers on parade.

"Can I ask you a question?" Splurge wasn't sure that he would get an answer but he just had to find out. "What are they?" He pointed at the strange little creatures, which seemed not to notice his interest.

"Who, not what. They are not things. They are beings, like you and me. Well not exactly like you and me, but you would do well to treat them with respect. They are the source of all magic." Mysterio turned to the tiny creatures and gave them an elaborate bow; he then turned back to Splurge. "I have discovered that a little courtesy goes a long way – especially with the Quargs."

"Quargs? What...who are they?" Splurge stuttered over his question, as one of these Quargs had suddenly appeared in front of him and gave him a curious stare.

"Quargs arrange all the magic. They do the manufacturing and organising you could say."

Splurge was so disconcerted by the Quarg staring at him, and he didn't pay much attention to what Mysterio was saying. He just mumbled something unintelligible in reply.

Mysterio took off his top hat and waved it about. "The trick with this hat, for example, was mostly their doing. All I had to do was to think of something, anything, and they would provide it." He seemed on the point of performing another top hat trick but changed his mind, and put it back on his head. "If you are to be a great magician, you will need the Quargs."

"I...I...I don't want to be a great magician." Splurge was still stumbling over his words, being quite unnerved by the Quarg still staring at him.

"Oh you will, you will. Wait till you've been backstage. You won't be able to resist the lure of the theatre. You will want to perform the greatest magic in the world, next to mine of course." Mysterio beamed at him, like a benevolent uncle.

"Um...um," Splurge wanted to say something about the Quarg staring at him. He was half afraid of what the creature might do. He had already had a sample of their strength and was unwilling to risk a further manhandling. He smiled weakly at the Quarg, hoping that he, or she, or it (each one looked the same and the way they dressed didn't give him much of a clue), would take it as a friendly gesture. The Quarg didn't change its expression but continued to stare at Splurge, its big round eyes unblinking, like a dog waiting to be taken for a walk.

"I see Hodges has taken a fancy to you. You're lucky. It doesn't happen very often. They're usually not keen on outworlders, unless of course they are great magicians like myself," he added with a smirk.

"Hodges?" Splurge thought he had heard incorrectly. The name didn't seem to fit this Quarg creature at all.

"Oh yes. Their own names are much too unpronounceable. So I renamed them. They didn't seem to mind. In fact it was surprising how quickly they adapted to them. Almost instantaneous."

Another Quarg had come out from the side of the stage and went up to Mysterio, who had to bend almost double to listen to the small creature as it whispered something to the magician.

Splurge couldn't overhear what was said but had an uncomfortable feeling it was about him, for the tiny Quarg kept looking in his direction as he spoke.

When the Quarg had finished, Mysterio straightened his back, giving a slight groan as he did so. "That's the only drawback with these Quargs – their size. Sometimes it is difficult to hear them unless one stoops to their level." He rubbed his back as he walked across to Splurge. "Wilkins has asked me if you are another magician," he said in a low voice. "So I told him that you were my pupil, so to speak." He turned back to the Quarg and smiled. "He seemed happy with that explanation."

"Your pupil!" Splurge exclaimed. "I'm already a pupil, at a proper school. Besides, suppose I don't want to be a magician?"

Mysterio chuckled. "Oh but you do. All boys want to be magicians, or at the very least be able to practise some elementary magic. I'm sure you are no exception."

Splurge was in a quandary. He didn't want to admit that the idea of becoming a magician was tempting, but he knew that his main concern had to be getting out of this place. He was also a little worried about these Quargs, especially the one, Hodges, who was still staring at him. They might not want to let him out of this theatre, especially if they thought he was going to be a magician.

And there was another question he wanted to ask this Mysterio, but before he could say anything, Wilkins, had joined Hodges and between them they took hold of Splurge and began to lead him towards the rear of the stage. This time, he was glad to note, they were not so rough, although their grip was still quite firm.

"Where are they taking me?" Splurge called out to Mysterio.

"You are privileged. They want you to see their workshop. It's quite something, I can tell you."

"Can't you tell them that I've got to get out of here? People will be worried about me. They'll come looking."

"Oh, I doubt it. The first act of the play upstairs has only just started. Still a long way to go yet. Plenty of time for you to learn some real magic." Mysterio was walking alongside Splurge and occasionally would flick something out of the air and turn it into a small animal, like a squirrel, or mouse, or even a bag of sweets. He would then make it disappear with a pop and a small puff of orange smoke. "You will like the Quargs. They are very obliging, if you know how to handle them."

Splurge wasn't much comforted by Mysterio's casual attitude to these Quarg creatures, and he wasn't much looking forward to having anything more to do with them than he could help.

Before he knew it, Splurge had been shepherded into the darkness, somewhere at the back of the stage. He wondered whether he ought to resist these Quargs and try to break away from them. If he was quick and could take them by surprise, he might be able to get out of this weird place. But before he could form any sort of plan, he felt himself flying through the air, and landing with a thump, to be picked up by the two tiny creatures, Hodges and Wilkins.

Splurge wondered whether the Quargs had guessed his intentions. He couldn't tell, because their expressions were impassive, betraying no sort of emotion. Not that it mattered much, for he suddenly found himself in the strangest place he could have imagined.

Chapter Four – The Quargs

The two Quargs, Hodges and Wilkins, who had been leading Splurge, left him standing at the doorway from which several wooden steps led down to an unusual world.

His first impression was one of a giant workshop, inhabited by scores of tiny people, working away at long tables, where puffs of coloured smoke would erupt, accompanied by flashes of light, making the whole room sparkle. There was so much to see, that he couldn't take it all in at first.

Quargs were scurrying all over the place and already Splurge had lost sight of Hodges and Wilkins. It wasn't surprising because they all looked the same to him. Even their clothes were the same, some sort of smock and short trousers, which revealed tiny legs. The only difference between them, that he could detect, was their colour. He hadn't really noticed at first, probably because the stage lights had made them look the same. But here, in this workshop, he could now tell that they were all of different colours. Well not so much different colours as different shades of the same two colours – blue and green.

Splurge was not sure what was expected of him so he decided he would wait till one of the Quargs directed him, as they were sure to do, he reckoned. Meanwhile he had to think of some way he could get out of this theatre. He could see, however, that it would not be easy, not with so many of these creatures flitting about. Although they all appeared to be busy, he couldn't shake off the feeling that they were keeping a close eye on him. As far as Splurge was concerned, the feeling was mutual, because he was just as determined to keep an eye on the Quargs – and that magician. As the thought crossed his mind, he suddenly noticed that several Quargs had ceased working to stare at him. He couldn't really tell, but he thought that they were smiling. That was another thing he found difficult to fathom about these creatures. They appeared to have no real facial expressions. One look was much the same as another, totally bland and empty. Nevertheless, he did have a feeling that they were trying to show that they were pleased to see him. Splurge supposed that it was a welcome of sorts, and perhaps he should be grateful for that, especially after the rough treatment he had already received from some of them.

"Ah, I see that they have taken you to their place of magic. You are indeed privileged." Mysterio had suddenly appeared beside Splurge.

"I wish you wouldn't keep doing things like that," Splurge muttered.

"Like what?"

"Appearing and disappearing like...like"

"Like magic." Mysterio chuckled. "You will get used to it. Wait until you can do the same."

Splurge wasn't at all sure that he wanted to keep disappearing. You could never tell with that sort of magic. Things could go wrong. He remembered once when his Uncle George (his mother's brother), had tried to perform a trick with a ten pound note belonging to his father. The note ended up in so many pieces that it couldn't be put together again. His father wasn't best pleased. However, Splurge didn't want to give up the chance of learning some small bits of magic, something that he could manage. "What do I have to do then?" he asked, trying hard not to show too much enthusiasm.

"They will show you." Mysterio waved a hand towards the Quargs, all bustling and hurrying about like a lot of robotic ants. Those who had paused to stare at Splurge had now joined the busy throng.

Splurge had been watching them and was a little puzzled. "What are they actually doing? They all seem to rushing about quite a lot, but I can't see that they are doing anything." He turned to Mysterio who could only offer him another enigmatic smile.

"A bit like people from the outworld, I daresay. Only with Quargs, even if you can't see what they are actually doing, their work is serious. Remember this is a theatre of magic and, like most theatres, a lot of work is done behind the scenes. All sorts of things have to be arranged; tried out; tested and sometimes thrown out if they don't work."

Splurge nodded in understanding, though he wasn't really sure that he did understand. He knew little of how an ordinary theatre worked, never mind a magic one. He then thought of something else. "Why do all the Quargs look the same? And how can you tell the difference between them?"

Mysterio raised his big, black eyebrows till they almost joined with his sleek, black hair. "Not very observant are you? Surely you can see that they are different in colour if nothing else. The blue ones are the males and the green ones are female."

"What about the children? They all look the same size to me. Don't they have any children or do they keep them somewhere else?" Splurge had a young sister, so he was naturally curious about whether these creatures had the equivalent of girls. He could never get on with girls. They tended to be bossy and somewhat illogical, and they scared him at times.

Mysterio laughed aloud, so much so that he sounded as though he was choking, and at the same time the floor began to shake.

Splurge couldn't see what was so funny. "I thought that was a perfectly reasonable question," he said. It was his turn to frown.

Mysterio quickly stifled his laugh and became serious. "In the world out there maybe, but Quargs are just – Quargs. There are no children. There might have been a long time ago but after the great catastrophe..." Mysterio paused and gave Splurge a strange, piercing look. "It's best that you not mention anything about children to the Quargs."

"Why?" Splurge sensed that there was something more behind the history of the Quargs, and his natural curiosity began to overcome his suspicion of them.

"Just don't mention anything about their past," said Mysterio. "Just concentrate on the present - and your future," he added darkly.

Splurge was suddenly nervous. For a brief moment he had forgotten about escaping from here.

Being a boy, Splurge was naturally curious about everything around him, and sometimes the urge to go exploring and poking into things was too strong to ignore – even when it led him into trouble. At the moment he was torn between getting out of this theatre and finding out more about the Quargs. He had already realised that they were strange, almost scary, creatures, but now, with an unexplained history behind them, they had become much more interesting.

"Well? Shall we go and meet them?" Mysterio took Splurge by the shoulder and propelled him down the few steps to the floor of the giant workshop.

Before he had the chance to object, Splurge found himself among the Quargs, who were now bustling and scurrying about in an even greater frenzy of activity. If they had wanted to impress him with their industry, they had certainly done so, though he still couldn't see exactly what they were doing. They were all busy constructing things, but what, he couldn't tell. As he wandered along the rows of busy Quargs, he tried peer over their shoulders to find out exactly what they were making. As soon as they became aware of his interest, however, they quickly made some kind of magical pass and everything they had been working with disappeared in small explosions of colour.

"Amongst other things, the Quargs are very secretive," Mysterio explained. "They don't like anybody to see their work until the finished product, then they will gladly demonstrate their cleverness for you."

Strange creatures, thought Splurge.

"You think so?" Mysterio turned to him, with a smug grin on his face. "Have you never been eager to show off your cleverness before you have made sure that something works?" His eyes twinkled as he spoke.

Splurge felt uncomfortable. He still remembered that model plane which had done one loop before smashing into next door's greenhouse. He blushed at the memory. But how did this magician know? "Can you read minds?" he asked suddenly.

Mysterio chuckled. "Boys' minds are easy to read. Their heads are usually full of nonsense anyway."

Splurge would have argued that point with Mysterio but he felt a tug on his arm. He turned and saw a Quarg staring at him, with big, round, unblinking eyes.

"Hodges?" He couldn't be sure because they still all looked the same to him. They were of different colours, it was true, but it would take him ages to recognise the subtle shades of blue and green.

The Quarg nodded.

Splurge felt a certain sense of achievement in recognising one of these Quargs, though he knew it was more down to guesswork than anything else.

"Come," said Hodges firmly, and took hold of Splurge's hand.

Splurge was surprised to find that touch of the Quarg was not unpleasant. He felt a slight tingle as the tiny hand curled round his fingers and pulled him gently along the floor of the workshop towards a door at the far end. As he passed the rows of Quargs busily working away at whatever they were doing, he could hear small popping explosions, and glimpses of brief flashes of colour. "Where are we going?" he asked nervously. He was half afraid to ask too many questions, though there were many he would like to have asked. He kept thinking about those two who had dragged him onto the stage and was only too well aware of how strong these creatures were.

"You must see Jonesy. He will teach you."

"Er..um..yes but you see.." Splurge was stumbling over his words, not sure how his lack of enthusiasm would sound to a Quarg.

Hodges stopped so suddenly that Splurge almost fell on top of him. He looked up at Splurge and wrinkled his brow, or where his brow would have been if he had one. "There are to be no questions. That is what the Master says. You are to be a great magician. We shall teach you. Me and Jonesy." The Quarg's thin, piping voice held no threat or warning of what might happen if Splurge objected, but somehow conveyed a certainty that it would be as he had said.

Splurge was not happy at the prospect of becoming a magician. It sounded fine on the face of it, and in other circumstances he might have jumped at the opportunity. But here, in this strange, little theatre, he wasn't so sure. His priority had to be finding a way out somehow, though how he was going to achieve it he couldn't see at the moment. He could only hope that an opportunity would present itself before too long. All he could do now was to go along with whatever Mysterio and these Quargs had arranged for him.

The tiny Quarg paused before the door. Having let go of Splurge's hand, he gave a tentative knock. There was a sound from within and the door swung open.

Splurge wondered why it was necessary to have doors if the Quargs were so good at magic.

"Magic isn't everything," Hodges suddenly said.

Splurge was taken aback. Could everyone read minds in this place? That was something that he would like to learn. Could be very useful, especially at school.

"Only few possess the art of seeing minds. Not for you. You are to be great magician. Greater than the Master." Hodges then strode through the doorway, not waiting for Splurge.

Splurge thought he had better follow; though he hoped that this was not the beginning of a long traipse around everywhere. The thought had occurred to him, that although the theatre itself was quite small, the rest of the place was beginning to look decidedly large. Was this another example of the Quargs' magic, he wondered? Could they really expand space to suit themselves or was it the work of Mysterio? Splurge was having difficulty in separating the two. Perhaps he had better follow Hodges and see what happens. He was sure to be in for more surprises. Since being dragged into this theatre had had nothing but surprises, most of which were not all that pleasant. He wasn't to know that when he walked through the doorway he would receive his biggest surprise yet.

Chapter Five – Jonesy

The room was dim, but Splurge could clearly make out the form of Hodges who was standing before what appeared to be a large wooden chest. There seemed to be nothing else in the room, not even windows. More light was needed, he thought, and subconsciously began to grope around for a light switch, not that he really expected to find one. This place was full of magic, after all. If he were a real magician, he would just wave his arm like so.....

Splurge almost fell over in his astonishment. As he had waved his arm, so the whole room was suddenly lit up in a bright, pink light. He quickly glanced around. Where was Mysterio? This was the sort of trick he would pull. But there was no sign of him. If it wasn't him, then it must have been the Hodges, Splurge reasoned. But when he looked across at the tiny Quarg, he could see that it was much too interested in that chest to be bothering to do any magic. He wondered. What if.... but the idea was absurd? Surely he couldn't... No. It just wasn't possible. Nevertheless he would try it - just in case. Almost self-consciously he raised his arm and slowly waved it, at the same time wishing that he could change the colour of the light – pale blue would be a good shade.

If Splurge had been astonished before, it was nothing to the mind-blowing amazement he now experienced. Did he really change the colour of the light by just waving his hand? No. Impossible. He couldn't believe it. It was just coincidence. It must be. Perhaps he ought to do it once more, to be really sure. So, once again he waved his arm. This time he decided on green.

Green it was.

Splurge was dumbfounded. He could do magic without even knowing how. That must be some kind of record, he reckoned. Another try maybe, to be absolutely sure. He raised his arm again and was about to wish for another change of light when he was suddenly halted by a strange, rasping voice from the other side of the room.

"When you've had enough of playing about with the light perhaps you could spare me some of your valuable time."

If Splurge had expected that the voice belonged to another Quarg, he was to discover how wrong he was, for there, at the other end of the room, (which was not very large) was the strangest creature he had ever come across.

Splurge's jaw dropped. Even in the green light, (which he realised was not so good for distinguishing detail), he could see a large, round figure, more like a huge football, with tiny legs and arms sticking out. This creature was sitting like a king on a small throne-like chair, which was draped with some sort of velvet material.

At first, Splurge was reminded of Humpty-Dumpty, in shape if nothing else. But it looked anything but a nursery- rhyme character, for as he approached, he could two large, bulbous eyes glaring at him and a wide, narrow mouth, which constantly twitched. As the creature's mouth twitched, so it dribbled onto the front of his shirt, at least Splurge guessed it was some sort of shirt. It was difficult to tell what sort of clothes this creature was wearing because he was so round.

While Splurge was trying to take in the details of this odd-looking character, Hodges had suddenly appeared in front of him.

"We must change the light back," the tiny Quarg croaked, and with a flick of his hand, the room was bathed in a bright, white light.

Surprised though he was, Splurge could not help but stifle a smile, when he saw that this creature, had a long, drooping moustache. Somehow the sight of it seemed to drain away any feelings of disgust or alarm he might have had at seeing him for the first time. He could also see that the creature was bright purple in colour. Now he was reminded of a giant grape – with a moustache.

"This is Jonesy," said Hodges. "He will teach you everything. I will help."

Splurge wanted to ask Hodges some questions about this Jonesy, but wanted to do it quietly, so Jonesy wouldn't overhear. You could never tell with these strange creatures. They may look harmless, or even funny, but he had already learned that they could be quite rough. What sort of creature was this Jonesy, for example? Not a Quarg, certainly. But a rasping sound, like someone with a bad cough, interrupted his thoughts.

"So we have another candidate." The giant purple grape, growled, wheezed and spluttered, all at the same time. His tiny arms, much too short for his rotund form, tried to reach up to where his nose should be, in order to wipe it with a cloth that had magically appeared in front of him. He gave up, and was content merely to wipe the dribble from the ends of his moustache.

"Candidate?" said Splurge, nervously. Sounded suspiciously like an exam to him. This wasn't school and he wasn't going to be fooled or bullied into any sort of schoolwork.

Hodges explained.

"A candidate is one who is to learn the ways of magicians. Already, by being in the presence of Jonesy you may have learnt some magic." The thin, piping voice of the Quarg sounded a little sceptical.

"Suppose I don't want to learn the ways of magicians?" Splurge couldn't get rid of the feeling that he had been somehow manipulated into a classroom, even though it looked nothing like the classrooms he was used to.

"You have no say in the matter," the giant, purple grape form of Jonesy spluttered again. "You were brought here to learn, so that you will become the new Master. Even greater than our present Master." The effort of speaking seemed to have been too much for Jonesy, for he suddenly had a ferocious bout of coughing, spluttering and wheezing, all mixed up in one loud rasping sound.

Splurge wasn't at all surprised. With such a monstrous figure like that, it was a miracle that he could do anything. But he wasn't happy about what Jonesy had said. "What do you mean? Brought here?"

Jonesy looked at Hodges, then they both looked at Splurge. (The rotund Jonesy had stopped spluttering and wheezing). However, they didn't seemed inclined to say anything to him.

Splurge wasn't having this. The idea of being able to do a bit of magic was one thing, but to have been kidnapped and taken to school, for that's what it amounted to in Splurge's estimation, was something else. "You mean, I've been kidnapped?"

"We do not know what is 'kidnapped'," said Hodges, without any emotion showing on his face.

Splurge frowned. He wasn't sure about these two. Were they trying to fool him or were they as innocent as they looked? He couldn't make up his mind. In any case he wasn't altogether happy at the situation. He had to get out of here, and quickly. How he was to achieve an escape, he had no idea. So far, nothing he had seen seemed to offer him any opportunity. He wanted to examine this room a little closer but he had to keep his intentions strictly to himself, especially as it seemed that everyone in this theatre could read minds. That was going to be the biggest drawback – mind reading.

"You will learn all things, even how to see into minds," Jonesy suddenly rasped. "Hodges will teach you how to contrude your own mind, so that others will not see into it."

"Contrude?" Splurge had never heard that word before, but then he guessed that there would be many words from these two that were going to be incomprehensible to him.

"You will learn how to stop your thoughts from going into other minds." Hodges explained.

It still wasn't very clear to Splurge, although he had a vague feeling that his teachers had said something like that to him, except they had definitely wanted thoughts to go into his head.

"You will not find it so bad," Jonesy wheezed. "Even you, a young one, should be able to master the elementals before you perform."

"Elementals! Perform!" It was Splurge's turn to splutter. "I...I...can't perform – elementals, whatever they are. I've got to get back home and my class. They will be wondering where I am. People will be looking for me. They will send the police and..and..." Splurge was lost for words.

It seemed to make no difference to the two other characters in the room. Both Hodges and Jonesy looked at him without any sign of sympathy or understanding.

"And what are these 'elementals' anyway?" Splurge continued, and would have carried on asking questions and displaying his annoyance, but the giant grape-like figure of Jonesy began to roll about on his chair, in an effort to get down from it. For a moment, Splurge was so fascinated at the sight, that he forgot what he was about to say. If he fell, wondered Splurge, would he go splat on the floor, like an overripe fruit?

The question remained unanswered, because with much grunting, wheezing and coughing, the huge, round figure of Jonesy finally managed to land without mishap. Though Splurge half expected him to bounce several times before he became still.

"I don't bounce," growled Jonesy.

It seemed to Splurge, however, that Jonesy had turned a paler shade of purple, either from his efforts in getting down from his chair, or the fact that he had read Splurge's mind and it was his way of showing embarrassment.

Though he was in fact very round, Jonesy was not that tall. Indeed, as he waddled up close to Splurge, it was obvious that he was only slightly taller than the average Quarg (who all seemed to be exactly the same height).

"Listen to me," Jonesy rasped, "if you want to get out of here you had better pay heed to what we teach you." He glanced at Hodges as he spoke, as though wanting some sort of confirmation that what he was about to say would meet with his approval.

The tiny Quarg merely turned his head, but said nothing.

"Good." Jonesy nodded in understanding.

Telepathy, thought Splurge. That's how they communicated. He didn't know why they bothered because it wouldn't have mattered that much if they had spoken aloud in front of him. What could he do anyway? It looked as though he was trapped here, for a while at least. Perhaps he had better go along with whatever they had arranged for him.

"You must now come with us," said Hodges, as the Quarg took him by the hand.

Splurge half expected that it would be another of those vice-like grips but Hodges was strangely gentle and yet forceful at the same time.

The Quarg led him over to the wooden chest, which he had been examining earlier. Jonesy waddled slowly behind them, puffing and wheezing at the same time.

Relinquishing his grip on Splurge, Hodges, with a flick of his wrist, opened the chest and leaned inside.

So precariously balanced on the edge of the chest was the tiny Quarg that he looked as though he might easily tumble into it. Splurge thought that this could be a chance for him. The rotund Jonesy would never be able to match him for speed if he decided to make a run for it. He would have to take a chance on any magic the giant purple grape might perform to stop him.

Unfortunately for Splurge, the opportunity never arose because Hodges emerged safely from the chest holding a strange object. "Take this. It will help you to learn quickly." He then placed into Splurge's hands what appeared to be a pot of paint.

Splurge was puzzled and slightly amused. "What do I do with this then?" He grinned. "Have you just brought me here to paint the walls or something?"

"No!"

A loud voice rang out. So loud that it vibrated around the walls of the room making it seem as though an earthquake was taking place.

At first, he thought that it was Mysterio playing one of his games but when he turned round to discover the source of that voice, he was more shocked than surprised.

Chapter Six – Jonesy's Secret

Splurge had no words to express his feelings of amazement and horror. There standing in front of him was the most formidable person, or thing, he wasn't sure which, he had ever seen or could have imagined. But the amazing thing was that it was Jonesy.

This was no longer the round, giant purple, grape-like figure, but a tall, sinuous creature, which looked like a cross between a giraffe and a hippopotamus. If it still hadn't retained its purple colouring, and drooping moustache, Splurge would have been more than a little scared of this creature. It looked fearsome enough, but he couldn't help thinking that it looked like a bit of magic that had gone wrong. He was tempted to laugh, but thought better of it. You could never tell with such strange creatures. He looked at Hodges to see if he would show any surprise.

The tiny Quarg merely shook his head, like a disappointed teacher.

"I told you not to do that one." The thin, piping voice sounded almost angry.

The curious, purple figure swayed and tottered looking as though it might fall over at any moment.

Splurge didn't know whether to move or not, because it kept swaying one way then another. Transfixed by the strange sight though he was, he felt that he was owed some sort of explanation for this sudden metamorphosis. He turned to Hodges. "What's happened to him?" He spoke quietly, not wishing to say anything that might annoy this new Jonesy.

"Jonesy is trying to get back," the Quarg said simply.

"Get back where?" Splurge asked.

"Back to being what he was."

On the whole, Splurge couldn't see that one form was better than the other, apart from the fact that he had almost got used to the round, giant grape-like shape. "You mean being..." He spread his arms around trying to indicate an overly large, round person.

For once Hodges expressed some indignation. "No. No. No," he tutted. "He wants to get back to being a Gromilly."

Splurge couldn't keep up. "What on earth is a Gromilly?" he asked, daring to brave another outburst of tutting from the tiny Quarg.

"It is a secret," Hodges said, so quietly that Splurge could hardly hear him.

Splurge pondered, wondering if it was really worthwhile to try to find out this secret. As far as he was concerned, the whole place was a secret. He was still for getting out if he had a choice. As he glanced at the monstrous figure of Jonesy, still swaying and tottering as if trying to overcome some invisible obstacle, he couldn't help thinking, however, of what a Gromilly might look like. Would he, or it, be like a Quarg? He somehow doubted it. Nothing that size could shrink so small. Anyway, he was still not sure whether he could regard Quargs as being in any way human. And he was definitely sceptical about Jonesy as a Gromilly, or anything else for that matter.

"It is going to be some time before Jonesy changes. He doesn't always get it right." Again, Hodges was displaying some signs of emotion, for he let out what sounded like a sigh.

Splurge was nonplussed. He couldn't make up his mind about these creatures. It was beginning to look as though at least one of them was not devoid of feelings. He wasn't sure whether this was a good thing or not.

"Well I can't wait here all day for Jonesy to change, or whatever he is going to do," said Splurge, who was suddenly conscious of time passing. "I have to get out of here – soon." He tried to sound as forceful as he dared because he was still a little scared of upsetting these tiny people.

"I will teach you while Jonesy changes," Hodges said,

this time without any trace of emotion. "Come with me." He took Splurge's hand and led him once more to the chest. The pot of paint had somehow mysteriously vanished.

There was that same tingling sensation as the Quarg took hold of him and for a brief moment, Splurge again wondered if Hodges and the others were, in fact, some highly sophisticated robotic creations. The sensation in his hand had been very like static electricity, the sort of thing associated with something metallic. He looked hard at the tiny Quarg, as it reached once more into the chest, trying to see if there was any sign – a button or a switch – something like that, which might give him a clue. But there was nothing that he could see. Maybe he would have to ask him right out and was on the point of doing so, when Hodges straightened up.

He looked pleased with himself, for there was the merest hint of a smile on his lips.

Splurge couldn't be sure. He had given up trying to interpret the facial expressions; such as they were, of the odd creatures he had so far come across.

"This is what you need," said Hodges, quite solemnly.

Splurge could have laughed out loud but managed to stifle the urge.

The Quarg had pulled out of the chest a dusty, old top hat that would have easily slid over Splurge's ears, together with some kind of wooden rod. With some furious shaking and rubbing, Hodges tried to get rid of most of the dust and grime which both these objects seemed to have accumulated whilst in the chest.

Splurge supposed the wooden stick was a wand of some sort and the top hat – well - he couldn't help grinning. "Do rabbits come out of that?" He pointed to the hat. "And with a wave of my magic wand..." He never finished because Hodges, suddenly threw both objects at Splurge.

After some juggling, Splurge managed to grab hold of both items and took a closer look. They were indeed what he had thought them to be. At close quarters the hat looked distinctly old and shabby, and still very dusty, for every time he tried to smooth it out, a small cloud of dust was sprayed into the air. The wand was no better. Splurge had seen more likely pieces of wood on sale in cut-price shops at Halloween.

"Take them and perform magic. They once belonged to a great magician," Hodges intoned, like some high priest. "You too will be a great magician. I will help you." As he spoke he gave a quick glance across at Jonesy, who was still struggling and writhing in an attempt to change into whatever he was going to change into.

Splurge was still strongly tempted to laugh, but again suppressed the urge. "How will these make me a great magician?" He indicated the top hat and wand, with a disparaging shrug. "All magicians use these things, usually not very good magicians at that. You don't have to be very good to pull a rabbit out of a hat. That's not real magic. Not like Mysterio can do."

Hodges was not put out by Splurge's lack of enthusiasm. "You will start with something simple. I will show you," the Quarg said imperturbably.

Splurge was not altogether convinced that Hodges would show him how to do real magic and was a little taken aback when Hodges pointed to the tottering figure of Jonesy.

"Your first lesson will be to turn Jonesy back into a Gromilly."

Splurge gasped. "How am I going to..to," he stuttered. "I don't even know what a Gromilly looks like. How can I do.. do..that sort of magic?" He stuttered again.

Hodges looked at Splurge. His eyes flickered and his face became a slightly darker shade of blue. "You will do it. I have shown you." His voice had suddenly become shrill and high pitched.

Splurge wondered if this was how Quargs showed their temper, though he didn't have long to think about it because Hodges had seized Splurge by the arm and turned him in the direction of the hapless Jonesy.

"Point at him with the wand and you will see," Hodges said, still in that shrill voice, which seemed to have grown more strident and ear piercing.

Not wishing to upset the Quarg any further, Splurge pointed the wand at Jonesy but with little enthusiasm, and even less confidence, that he would be able to perform some sort of magic.

The result was not at all what he expected.

Jonesy, who had for several minutes been struggling to assume some sort of normal shape, suddenly began to shrink.

"Hold out your hat," Hodges shouted, more like his normal self.

Splurge did as instructed, and was astonished to see the shrinking shape of Jonesy become gradually vague and misty, like the steam from a kettle. At the same time, it began to move towards the upturned hat, and in no time it had disappeared. Splurge looked inside the top hat but could see nothing. He turned to Hodges.

"What happened? Where has Jonesy gone? And how did I do it?"

Hodges didn't answer. Instead he rushed forward, took the hat and wand from Splurge and dashed from the room back to the workshop.

Splurge was both puzzled and somewhat awe-struck. He had obviously performed some sort of magic, but hadn't a clue as to how he had done it. And where had Hodges gone? And why? A whole heap of questions began to flood into Splurge's mind; questions to which he was determined to get some answers. And as far as he could see the only person who was capable of doing that was Mysterio. But where was he?

Bang! Crash!

Purple smoke suddenly exploded in clouds all around Splurge, accompanied by loud, deafening sounds. He coughed and spluttered and tried to fan the smoke away so that he could see what had happened.

"A bit too much, I'm afraid. Sorry about that."

There, standing before him was Mysterio, apparently unconcerned at the discomfort his entrance had caused Splurge.

"Wish you wouldn't do that," Splurge gasped.

"Well, I am pleased. You have passed your first test."

"First test?" spluttered Spurge.

"Oh yes. There are more, of course. But you have begun well. Come. Follow me." Without waiting to see if Splurge was following, he strode out of the room, through the workshop and up the steps to the stage.

Splurge didn't know what to do. And what were these tests? "I haven't been told about any tests," he called after Mysterio. "I'm not supposed to be here. When can I leave? And what on earth is a Gromilly?"

There was no reply for Mysterio was gone ahead.

Splurge had no option but to follow this weird magician, wishing all the time he knew how he had become entrapped in this theatre, and more importantly how he was going to get out. He sighed. "Things always happen to me. Why not Dash or Blip?" As he approached the doorway to the workshop, he heard the low humming sounds of activity and lots of voices murmuring. Then it struck him. Quargs don't make sounds like that. He quickened his steps until he was back in the giant workshop, and sure enough there was much activity but little noise. Where was this humming sound coming from then? It sounded like a lot of people talking. Suddenly his heart gave a jump. Someone else must be in the theatre. Now he had a chance to get out.

Chapter Seven – First Performance

When he had passed through the workshop earlier, Splurge had seen much activity but no sign of anything that the Quargs had made. Now, to his astonishment, there were all sorts of contraptions and gadgets lying on the long tables, with Quargs standing by each one as though awaiting some sort of inspection or approval. It was like wandering around the toy section of a giant department store. There was so much variety and colour that he could have spent the rest of the day just looking at these strange and wonderful things.

Boxes of different shapes and sizes would open of their own accord as he passed. They were all colours and, as they opened and closed, the colours would change. He stared at one, which actually dismantled itself into pieces before reassembling itself into an entirely different shape and colour. Splurge couldn't help but be fascinated but then his attention was drawn to a gadget that seemed to be producing and endless stream of coloured scarves, which rolled themselves into a ball then burst into a bunch of flowers. These quickly disappeared to be replaced a string of sausages, again of different colours, which then turned into a tiny toy train. He could have spent ages watching these magical toys, but a Quarg at another bench who was bouncing what appeared to be coloured tennis balls as if testing them took his attention. Usually there would be nothing remarkable in that, except that as each ball bounced it changed colour. The Quarg first bounced a blue ball, which turned red as it hit the floor only for it to keep changing to a different colour at each bounce. If that was unusual, it was nothing to the next trick. After several bounces with the ball, the Quarg replaced it on the bench to pick up another ball, much the same as the one he had been using. This time, much to Splurge's continued amazement, as the ball bounced it divided itself into two, both different colours before returning to a single ball. This the Quarg did several times, and each time the ball bounced it divided into two then four till finally there seemed to be a dozen or so balls all bouncing in time to the Quarg's direction. Splurge could really have watched them all day and some part of him realised that he would never have seen such things in shops outside. He wished that Dash and Blip could see them, because he knew that they would never believe him when he told them about this place.

While still staring goggle-eyed at these magic balls, Splurge felt a tug on his arm and a Quarg, a bright emerald green one, indicated something on the next bench. It didn't look to be anything special, for it was merely a hollow tube, made of some sort of metal by the looks of it. The Quarg, who being green was therefore a female, gestured that he should pick it up.

Since being in this place, Splurge was very wary of these Quargs. He was never sure what they were up to.

However, this female Quarg, sensing his reluctance, picked up the tube and pointed out that it was hollow by holding it up to her face and staring at him.

It was definitely hollow because Splurge could see the large, round eye of the Quarg at the other end of the tube. It was a bit scary, he thought, seeing a disembodied eye looking at him like that.

Then she indicated that he should put his arm into the tube.

Still a little wary, Splurge tentatively took hold of the tube and gingerly put his hand into it. Expecting at any moment to have it either mangled by some hidden mechanism, or to feel something slimy and squelchy, he took his time. He wanted to be able to pull out his hand quickly at the first sign of anything like that. But there was nothing. Splurge was relieved. Then he began to wonder what was so special about this tube. He withdrew his hand and looked at the Quarg.

The Quarg repeated her instruction. This time she indicated that he should put his hand all the way through the tube.

It should be easy enough, for it was wide and long, sufficient to cover the length of his arm like a piece of armour. So again, he put his hand inside the tube, slowly and gently. Not feeling anything he pushed it all the way through till it poked out at the other end.

Then he had the fright of his life.

Instead of his hand sticking out of the tube, he saw a hideous, scaly claw. With a loud yell he quickly pulled his hand out, half expecting that it might get stuck because of its misshapen appearance. But to his immense relief, he saw that his hand was perfectly normal. No scratches, cuts – or scales. He put the tube back on the bench and rubbed his hand to make sure. For a moment, he thought that his heart would stop beating. He turned to the Quarg. "Wha...what happened?" he gasped, as he continued to rub his hand.

The Quarg said nothing but picked up the tube and held it out to Splurge.

Did she really want him to do that again? "No way!" he shouted and shook his head vigorously to emphasise his distaste for such an idea.

But the tiny Quarg would not be denied, and went up to Splurge and took hold of his arm. Her grip was not rough, but firm, so firm and Splurge could do little else but submit to having his arm replaced in the hollow tube.

With much trepidation he pushed his arm through the tube, as slowly as he dared, all the time fearing what he might see come out at the other end. He wanted to shut his eyes so he wouldn't have to look at that scaly claw again. Females were all the same, he decided. You just couldn't trust them.

To his surprise, however, and again much relief, he saw his own hand come out at the end of the tube. He wiggled his fingers about to make sure that it was his own hand. He turned to the Quarg and grinned in embarrassment, for he realised that this was a magic tube. Of course, he should have known.

The Quarg nodded and pointed to the tube. She wanted him to do it yet again.

Splurge wasn't sure. Once was enough, but his curiosity was now aroused and once more he slipped his hand inside. This time, to his further amazement, he saw that his hand had become a pair of scissors. Sure enough when he pulled his hand out and replaced it, it had returned to being a normal hand. He then tried it several more times and on each occasion his hand had become something different, always returning to his own hand when replaced a second time. He liked this magic tube, and could just imagine the looks on the faces of Blip and Dash. Then he remembered. He had been so taken up with this tube that he had forgotten that he should be looking for a way to get out of this place. He was about to put the tube back onto the bench when the Quarg pushed it into his arms.

"It's yours," she said in a soft voice, quite unlike that of the other Quargs. "You will perform great magic." She blinked her eyes, as if trying to smile.

A Quarg who smiled? Now that was something special. It was the first time that Splurge had seen any sort of real emotion displayed by these tiny creatures, and it slightly unnerved him, though he didn't know why.

"Take these." The Quarg gathered up several of the coloured boxes on the adjoining bench and thrust them at Splurge, along with two of the magic balls.

As soon as he took hold of them, they automatically collapsed into separate pieces, with the balls conveniently nestling somewhere within the collapsed boxes, which proved to be much easier to carry.

"Use them well. You will be a great magician. I will help you." She almost smiled again.

Splurge was too dumbfounded to make any reply, except a mumbled 'thanks'. He had wanted to say something more to this female Quarg but couldn't think of the right words. He merely grinned and turned away, but struck by an afterthought, he turned back to the Quarg. "What is your name?"

The tiny, female Quarg, seemed to hesitate. "My name is Meela," she said quietly, "but the Master calls me Smith."

"Thank you Sm..Meela," said Splurge, who was beginning to think that maybe some females weren't so bad after all.

He had to find Mysterio and Hodges, so his arms full of magical gadgets, he hurried as best he could, towards the steps at the other end of the workshop. Maybe, he thought, that if he had to give some sort of performance, he wouldn't be quite so badly off now. It seemed that everybody was there to help him, though he didn't feel particularly confident. At the top of the steps, he looked round to see if Meela was still there, but she was lost amid the scores of other Quargs, still busily constructing their magic appliances. Splurge would like to have seen more of such things and made a mental note that he must visit this place again – if he had time. His priority was still to get out, and back to somewhere he understood.

"Ah! There you are!"

The booming tones of Mysterio welcomed him back onto the stage, which had been transformed into some sort of old-fashioned street, with gas lamps and strange looking shops, with bottled glass windows. Splurge had expected to see an audience but the curtains were drawn.

"Your first performance, eh?"

Splurge nodded and looked around for a place to put down the various items that Meela had given to him. He would feel a lot better if he could use his arms. He wanted to get all this business over and done with as soon as possible so that he could have a chat with Mysterio. It seemed that he was the only one who would be able to help him. That's if he would help him. Splurge knew that he was bound to make a mess of his performance and perhaps then they might let him go.

"You will need these." Hodges had come out from the side of the stage and handed Splurge the battered top hat and wand. The other gadgets fell to the floor in the process. "Remember, Jonesy is inside there," he pointed to the hat. "He will help you." With that he scuttled back into the shadows.

Though he expected to give a bad performance, Splurge was, nevertheless, a little apprehensive. He had never appeared on a stage before. In fact he had never appeared anywhere before in front of an audience. They would be watching his every move and laughing at him. The thought frightened him more than the idea of Jonesy turning into something horrible. And what sort of audience would be out there, Quargs or some other strange creatures?

"Time for the curtain to go up." Mysterio was at his side and smiling as if he knew something that Splurge did not.

"What do I do?" Splurge whispered nervously, staring at the curtains. "I've never been on a stage before."

"Nothing to it, my boy. Just make magic."

"But I don't know..." Splurge turned round but Mysterio had gone.

Splurge would normally have been trembling violently but he was much too confused by everything. He just stood in front of the curtain, not knowing whether to stand still, turn around or just run off the stage. What was he supposed to do? He had now begun to tremble in anticipation and the curtains in front of him began to look dreadfully ominous. How he wished that they would never open. If he had had more time to practise or do something or.., he didn't know what. And he still hadn't found out about the elementals. It was sure to be a disaster. All he could do was to wait and hope.

He almost jumped in fright as a loud blast of trumpets sounded in his ears. The whole of the tiny theatre resounded to the noise and he was sure that the place would disintegrate in a blaze of sound.

Then slowly, the curtains began to open.

Splurge was about to give his first performance in The Theatre of Magic.

Chapter Eight – Splurge the magician

As the curtains gradually opened, the trumpet blast subsided and there was a heavy silence in the theatre.

Splurge could see nothing of the audience because of a brilliant light, which now shone upon him. He fancied that he heard some subdued muttering from beyond the light but couldn't be sure. Maybe that was the humming he had heard earlier, or it might have been his imagination beginning to play tricks with him. He looked towards the sides of the stage, hoping that he might catch sight of Mysterio or one of the Quargs, who would perhaps offer some sort of help. But he could see only blackness. It was as if he had been shut in a large box, open at one end, and that end was towards this invisible audience. If he had felt afraid before it was nothing to what he was now feeling. He was positively terrified.

"Pick up the balls," a rasping voice whispered.

Startled, Splurge looked about for the source of the voice but could see noone.

"Look in the hat," the voice rasped again.

Not wishing to appear foolish, Splurge turned away from the audience and peered into the hat. At first, he could see nothing but then after a second or two of hard staring, he could make out what appeared to be a pair of small eyes. Whether there was a mouth underneath them, he couldn't tell. It was enough of a shock to see these two bright pinpoints shining up at him from the darkness of the hat.

"Pick up the balls and bounce them," the voice from inside the hat rasped again. "Show them to the audience first," the voice further ordered.

Splurge was not sure what he ought to do. He was still trying to come to terms with the voice in the hat, which sounded very much like Jonesy's. He gave a nervous glance at the audience, which he couldn't see because of the bright light shining on him. Although he had heard nothing from them, he supposed that they still must be there, and if he didn't do something soon, they would start booing. Yet he knew that he was no magician and they would more likely laugh at him when he tried to do any magic. He wasn't sure whether he preferred laughter or the booing. It didn't matter either way. He just wished that he wasn't here.

"Pick up the balls!" the voice hissed angrily.

Well, he supposed, it was worth a try. Carefully he put the hat down and reached for the balls, which had somehow become stacked on top of one another. He didn't question as to how this could be but used both hands to pick them up and, in accordance with his instructions from the hat, showed them to the audience.

Immediately, there was the sound of applause.

If that's all it took to please the invisible audience out there, thought Splurge, then he shouldn't find it too difficult.

He had three balls in his hands, red, blue and green, which he began to bounce one at a time, hoping that they would perform as they had done in the Quargs' workshop.

Sure enough, as each ball was bounced by Splurge, the colours changed, the blue to orange; the green to red, and the red one to purple.

At each bounce and colour change, Splurge was sure that he heard the audience gasp with wonder and amazement, or it might have been wishful thinking on his part. At any rate, he was beginning to feel more confident and he wondered if now would be a good time to do another trick. He would try a few more bounces first, he decided, to see if the balls would multiply, as he had seen them do before. Was there a magic word or phrase, he wondered, which would make them double or triple? He couldn't be sure if the Quarg, who had been demonstrating the magic balls had said anything. Then he remembered. They didn't need to. They were all telepathic. Though he wasn't sure how it worked with objects. Anyway, he would give it a try. He didn't have anything to lose. He put two of the balls on the floor and bounced one, hoping that it would do something other than change colour.

Splurge wasn't prepared for what happened next.

As the ball hit the floor it suddenly exploded in a flash of blue smoke and there standing before him was the figure of a Quarg. It was Hodges. At least, he thought it was Hodges. Splurge hadn't yet been able to distinguish, with any certainty, between the Quargs.

"I am here, master." The tiny Quarg bowed low and then straightened himself and tilted his head backward to stare Splurge directly in the face.

It was Hodges. Splurge could, at least recognise voices.

"What are you doing here?" Splurge whispered fiercely.

"I am here to do your bidding," Hodges intoned impassively.

There was no murmur or any other sound from the audience that might have suggested that they were either surprised or shocked that a Quarg had suddenly appeared on stage.

It took Splurge a few seconds to realise that the audience probably thought that it was all a part of the magic display.

"Look in the hat," Hodges said, still in the same flat tone.

Trying to look as though he knew what he was doing, Splurge picked up the top hat and looked into it briefly. There was the same pair of beady eyes staring out at him. He expected a voice but there was no sound, no words of advice or instruction - just those eyes.

"Put it on your head." It was Hodges, who had sidled up him, and made another bow before retiring to the side of the stage.

Still acting as though he knew what he was doing, Splurge put on the hat, which promptly fell over his ears and shut out most of his vision. He quickly took it off, not bearing to think about Jonesy, the Gromilly, which had been lurking in its depths. Immediately there was a distinct sound of applause.

Splurge strained his eyes to see the audience and wondered why they had applauded. If that's all it took to make them clap then he might think of doing it again. But with Jonesy inside the hat, he decided against it. He gave a small bow and then realised why they had clapped him for what had seemed such a silly thing.

His own feet had changed. No longer were they normal size but had somehow grown into two large, boat-like shapes, which turned up slightly at the toes. Splurge was immediately reminded of a clown and glanced quickly at his clothes to see if they had changed. But, apart from his feet, everything seemed to be as before. As he tried to recover from the shock of the change, the ends of the boots suddenly opened up and sprayed coloured confetti over the stage. This immediately brought another round of applause from the unseen audience.

Splurge could feel himself going red. It was one thing to be a magician, but a clown was something else. Even as the thought crossed his mind, the boots disappeared and his feet were back to normal. For a moment he wondered if he had imagined it, but was again distracted by another burst of applause from the audience. Perhaps now would be a good time to try out the tube. He was about to reach down for it when Hodges, who once more surprised him by his unexpected appearance, suddenly thrust it into his hands.

"A good choice," the tiny Quarg intoned, and then stepped to the back of the stage.

Trying to remember exactly how the Quarg, Meela, had performed the trick, Splurge showed the audience the empty tube and then put his hand inside. This was the moment of truth. Already he had misgivings and was conjuring up all sorts of horrors, which would protrude from the other end of the tube. Slowly and deliberately, and trying hard not to show his nervousness, he slid his arm all the way inside, hardly daring to look at what might appear at the other end.

A stifled gasp from the audience seemed to indicate that something had gone wrong, as indeed it had, for wriggling about from the other end of the tube was his own hand. Splurge couldn't understand it. That wasn't supposed to happen and he gave a quick glance around to see if Hodges was on hand to give him some advice or help. Girls! He knew it. That Meela had tricked him. He quickly withdrew his arm and received another shock.

There, at the end of his arm, instead of his hand was a large balloon. Splurge stared in horror. Even though he guessed that the trick had somehow worked in reverse, how was he going to get this huge balloon back into the tube? For the first time since being on the stage, he began to panic.

The audience obviously thought that it was all part of the magic, because there was a sudden burst of applause.

Splurge tried an uncertain bow and made it seem that everything was as it should be, even though he knew that it wasn't. How was he going to get out of this one?

Suddenly there, standing in front of him was the tiny figure of a Quarg. It was Meela.

Ignoring the audience Splurge waved the balloon in front of her face. "What happened?" he wailed. "It all went wrong." Though he hadn't intended to, it sounded as though he was blaming this tiny, green Quarg for his predicament.

Meela just flickered her eyes and handed him something. "I said I would help you," she said solemnly.

Splurge looked at what the Quarg had handed him. It was a small pin. Of course! Why hadn't he thought of it? But he was still unsure what might happen if he burst the balloon. Would he lose his hand altogether or would something else appear in its place? There was only one way to find out.

While he was trying to make up his mind (and pluck up the courage), Meela had left the stage and was now lost in the darkness behind him.

"Here goes," he muttered to himself. Still conscious of the audience somewhere beyond the light, Splurge made pretence of a magic pass, which ended as he stabbed the balloon-like hand with the pin.

There was a sudden loud plop and a series of sustained 'aahs' from the audience. Splurge's balloon-like hand had become a beautiful, white dove. He looked in disbelief. But before he had got over that shock, the dove changed into a large eagle, which strove to pull away from Splurge. He hung on for dear life, expecting at any moment to whisked off his feet, or at the very least have his arm torn off in the struggle. The audience still gasped their 'aahs', seemingly unaware of Splurge's plight.

Just as he thought it couldn't get any worse, the eagle became a frying pan, with several sausages sizzling away in it. The weight of the pan dragged his arm to the floor.

"Wave your other hand," a tiny voice rasped.

Splurge had forgotten all about the hat and Jonesy. He gave a slight nod in its direction and waved his other arm. With a loud plop, his hand was back to normal. The pan and sizzling sausages had disappeared, along with the eagle, dove and balloon. Still trying to make some pretence of knowing what he was doing, he gave an elaborate bow, which immediately brought forth a loud burst of applause from the audience.

As he straightened himself, he couldn't help feeling some pleasure (as well as enormous relief) that the trick had finally come to a satisfactory conclusion.

But what should he do next? He began to look around for either of the two Quargs, Hodges or Meela, but they were nowhere in sight. He could try Jonesy, he supposed, but he was not so sure about that strange creature. Could never tell what he might do or suggest.

While he was desperately trying to think of something, he was almost shaken out of his skin by a loud blast of trumpets, as the lights in the theatre came on and the curtain slowly began to close. It seemed that his first performance was at an end. But it left him with another mystery. Now he could see beyond the light, which had been shining on him throughout his performance, he saw that there was noone in the audience. Every seat was empty. Who then had been applauding his tricks? Was it another example of Mysterio's magic? Or maybe the Quargs themselves had arranged it. He didn't know what to think, but one thing was certain. If he was going to perform more magic on this stage, or any other come to that, he would make sure that he was better prepared.

The curtains were now completely closed and Splurge was about to gather up all the paraphernalia of his act, when he thought he heard a strange noise. He listened hard and it seemed to be coming from the other side of the curtains. It sounded just like people leaving the theatre, chatting, laughing and banging seats. Splurge couldn't resist the temptation to have a peep through the curtains. A minute ago, there had been nobody there, so where had all the noise come from? He crept up the spot where the curtains had come together and carefully pulled them apart, just enough for him to get a glimpse of the audience, an audience which seemed to have somehow reappeared. What he saw, however, was not what he had expected.

Chapter Nine – Magicians Galore

Splurge stared through the curtains but couldn't believe what he was seeing. There was an audience after all and he now understood why it had kept disappearing. They were all magicians. He knew this, because lots of them were dressed in the same way that Mysterio dressed, with black cape and top hat. Some, however, he noticed, were a little more colourful in their appearance, and preferred to wear ornate turbans, or strange, conical hats. Some even wore long robes, which glittered with all manner of devices such as stars and moons. They must be magicians because each carried a small wand. Occasionally, one of them would get worked up over some point he was discussing with a fellow magician, and his wand would swirl about in his hands sending showers of coloured sparks everywhere. Noone seemed to mind. In fact, Splurge saw one magician casually gather the flying sparks in his hand and stuff them under his hat. He would have liked to see more such demonstrations but his attention was suddenly drawn to one magician in particular.

The theatre slowly began to empty, which was taking some time, because despite its size it seemed to be able to contain more people than there had been seats, and those seats were tiny. They were certainly not Quargs but grown up human beings by the look of them. How they had managed, Splurge had no idea, but he supposed that as they were magicians, and probably good ones, they would have had no trouble in arranging something so simple.

That one magician, however, was not disposed to join his fellows, as they made their way out. He sat in the middle of the theatre staring at the curtain – staring at Splurge, who quickly withdrew his head.

"Your first performance but not your last." A voice suddenly boomed out behind Splurge. It was Mysterio, who clapped Splurge on the shoulder. "I must congratulate you on a first rate job."

"If I hadn't been helped by Jonesy and the Quargs I would have made a right mess of it," Splurge muttered. "I'll never get the hang of this magic lark, I don't care what you say."

"You were quite…" Mysterio paused as he tried to select the right word, "effective."

"I was effective alright. I messed up one trick and nearly lost my arm, and that stupid hat turning me into a clown." Splurge wasn't going to let Mysterio pretend that he had been any good, because he knew otherwise. "Did you watch any of my performance?"

"O course, of course," Mysterio boomed. "I was out there," he pointed to the curtains, "giving you moral support. They thought you were very good." He added in a confidential whisper.

Splurge was not to be mollified. "I made mistakes. You know I made mistakes, and with all those magicians out there, watching. And what about that one who just sits there staring at the stage – staring at me? What does he want?"

Mysterio stroked his beard and looked thoughtful. "Hmm. Perhaps you are right. It is best that you know from the very beginning that magic, real magic, is not come by so easily. It requires patience and hard work, which means much practice."

"I know that, but you didn't have to put me in front of all those real magicians, did you?"

"I didn't. When they heard that you were performing, they were anxious to see what you could do. I couldn't stop them."

Mysterio didn't sound entirely convincing, and Splurge couldn't help thinking that he was up to something. "You could have stopped them if you had wanted to. You just wanted them to see me for some reason of your own." He sighed, an exasperated sigh. "I've had enough of this place. When am I going to get out of here?" Splurge wanted to have a good moan but there was still a niggling curiosity at the back of his mind. He still wanted to know more in spite of himself. "And who is that magician out there?" he asked more forcibly.

Mysterio allowed himself a small smile. He knew that Splurge was still intrigued by this theatre and the magic, in spite of his desire to leave. "There's no-one there," he said smoothly, and waved towards the curtains, which suddenly swished open.

Sure enough the theatre was completely empty. Once again, Splurge was baffled. Where had that lone magician got to? And why was he sitting there just staring? He tried to remember what he looked like but there was nothing special about him as far as he could recall. He wore the usual top hat, and dark cape, but as to his features, Splurge couldn't be certain. He might have had a beard, or dark hair, but nothing in particular had made any impression on his memory. As he tried to think back, two or three Quargs came running onto the stage and gathered up the various gadgets he had used, including the boxes, which he hadn't used, interrupted his thoughts. It might have been much better if had used the boxes. They would have provided a safer form of magic, which perhaps, would have been easier to perform.

"Your first performance was better than you think, or perhaps deserve," said Mysterio as, with another small wave of his hand, he scooped up the dusty hat in which Jonesy was still residing, together with the wand, and thrust them at Splurge. "But if don't believe me," he continued. "Come and meet some of your fellow magicians."

"What...er... now?" was all Splurge could stammer. He had been taken by surprise at the invitation and wasn't so sure that he wanted to face other magicians, who were bound to quiz him about his performance.

"They are waiting in the foyer to offer their congratulations. You really ought to meet them. You could learn a lot and make some useful contacts. You might need them some day." Mysterio winked knowingly as he said this, but Splurge was none the wiser.

I might need them some day, he thought to himself. What does that mean? Splurge believed that he had had enough of magic for one day. He supposed that some of it was interesting, even fun, but he had learnt that too many things can go wrong. Then it suddenly hit him. What about the other theatre - the one where he was supposed to be, with Blip and Dash, and the rest of his classmates? Surely the play must have finished by now. But he wasn't given any time to consider further because Mysterio had suddenly grabbed him by the elbow and was rushing him off the stage.

"Why do I have to meet them?" Splurge muttered.

Mysterio ignored Splurge's discomfort and continued to propel him along towards a passage Splurge hadn't noticed previously.

Before he had time to ask more questions, Splurge found himself in a brightly lit foyer. It was much the same as the one he had seen in the real theatre where he was supposed to be with his class, except that it was much smaller. It was made to look even smaller by the fact that it was crowded with people – all of them magicians.

The hubbub and general chatter suddenly ceased as Mysterio entered with Splurge.

"Found another one, have you?" One large, round man said in a tiny voice, which belied his size. "Will this one be any good?"

"You know that if I say he will be good, it should be enough for you," said Mysterio, in a sharp voice.

The big, round magician went pink and gave a small deferential bow. "If you say so, Master."

"I do say so," Mysterio snapped.

The big, round magician said no more and was content to lose himself in the crowd, which hemmed around Mysterio and Splurge as if they were famous pop musicians.

Mysterio, Splurge noted, was given plenty of room as he moved among his fellow magicians, some of them even giving him a low bow and murmuring 'Master' as he passed. But apparently not all of them were so disposed towards him, for one magician, came thrusting through the crowd to confront Splurge and Mysterio with a glare which would have lit all the lights in the theatre.

"So you're still trying, eh Mysterio?" The intruder snarled. "You think that you can control everybody and everything. Well you are mistaken. I'll..."

Before he could continue, Mysterio held up his hand. Immediately this irascible magician was silent, though his eyes continued to glare.

Splurge recognised him as the same magician who had been sitting in the theatre at the end of the performance and staring at the curtains. He had seemed somewhat sinister to Splurge then, but now, close up; he could see that he was quite unlike the other magicians, in that he wasn't entirely human. He wasn't a Quarg because he was much bigger, but he did have that kind of doll-like appearance but without any of the gentle roundness of the Quargs. What really set him apart from the other magicians, who were now pressing in much closer, was that he was a dirty, pale purple in colour, unnaturally so, as though his original colour had been changed in some way. This was made more obvious by the fact of several large, unsightly protuberances on his face, which were a deeper purple in colour.

Mysterio didn't seem at all put out at the obvious rudeness of this strange person. (Splurge was beginning to wonder if he was in fact a magician after all). "Nothing changes does it, Broga. You are still the unruly, ill-disciplined and extremely rude pupil whom I banished from my theatre. A pity because you could have been good." He shook his head in a kind of mock regret.

This Broga still remained silent, though Splurge could see that he longed to make some reply to Mysterio. The other magicians had also crowded in closer, anticipating of some sort of contest between the two of them.

From what he knew of Mysterio and what he had seen of Broga, Splurge didn't reckon that there would be much of a contest. Already Broga had been struck dumb by a mere wave of the hand. That was a trick that Splurge wished he could perform. He could think of one or two people on which he wouldn't mind working that sort of magic. However, he was intrigued by the animosity shown by Broga. Surely Mysterio was too powerful to have enemies. He had seen how the other magicians had treated him, with respect and awe. Yet this one magician seemed unafraid of Mysterio, and Splurge wondered why. He didn't have much time to speculate because other magicians were crowding them and attempting to either to talk to Mysterio or to Splurge.

Splurge tried to stammer out a few words as questions were fired at him like a machine gun.

"When did you begin your magic?" one tall, silver-haired magician asked.

Before Splurge could reply another had thrown out a question, then another and another, till there seemed to be an endless stream of questions.

"How long have you been with Mysterio?"

"Has he passed on his secrets to you?"

"Are you to be the new Master?"

"When will you take over?"

"What about Broga and the Quigs?"

The last question suddenly brought about an unexpected silence.

"Enough questions!" a voice boomed out. A space had appeared around Mysterio and Splurge, as the other magicians backed away.

Mysterio looked stern, even angry, and Splurge wondered if it had anything to do with that last question. Who were the Quigs? Was this Broga a Quig? Just as he was beginning to understand this place it seemed that there was still more mysteries to be unravelled. He wished he could get out of it all. It was getting too complicated.

"I have done you all the courtesy of introducing a new member to our ancient order and all you can do is to bombard him with pointless questions."

"Pointless questions? Pointless questions?" Broga's voice had returned and he pushed to the front of the crowd, who were more than willing to give him room. "They are anything but pointless, and well you know it," said Broga with a sneer, which made him look like a disappointed goblin.

"Do I have to seal your lips again, Broga?" Mysterio said quietly, but with a hard edge to his voice, that even made Splurge shudder.

Broga didn't appear to be overawed. "You can do what you like here in your own theatre, I daresay, but you can't shut me up forever. You know the price if you do. I warn you, Mysterio, the Quargs are mine and I will see that they remain so." As he spoke his voice became high and shrill till the last words were almost screamed out. He was about to turn away but suddenly pointed a long, lumpy finger at Splurge. "And the same goes for your lackey!" he shrieked. With a puff of black smoke, which left everyone coughing and spluttering, Broga was gone.

He was just like a bad-tempered fairy, thought Splurge. What could this Broga do to him? Yet on second thoughts if Broga was a magician, maybe not as powerful as Mysterio, he was certainly more powerful than himself. That thought didn't comfort him one bit, and he had a feeling that here was someone who was going to cause him a lot of trouble.

The spectacular departure of Broga had brought the short meeting to an abrupt end. What Mysterio had hoped to accomplish by introducing him to a crowd of magicians, odd ones at that, Splurge couldn't imagine. There were a lot of questions for which he needed answers, though it seemed that Mysterio wasn't in the mood for questions.

Without a word of explanation to the crowd, still eagerly awaiting some sort of statement from the

'Master', Mysterio brusquely pushed his way through them, propelling Splurge along at the same time.

Once back on the stage, Mysterio seemed to relax a little, though he still looked anything but pleased. Would this be a good time to ask some questions, Splurge wondered?

"Wilkins! Hodges!" Mysterio barked out.

Before the echoes of his voice had died away, the two Quargs were in front of him. Their expressions betrayed no annoyance or any other emotion at being summoned so peremptorily.

"Broga was there. I thought I gave express orders that he was never to be admitted to this theatre."

The two Quargs said nothing but stared stonily in front of them, not even catching the eye of Mysterio.

Splurge realised that this was definitely not a good time. He wondered, however, if he might get some answers from the Quargs, though he had gained little information from them so far. It was worth trying, because he needed answers soon, specially if he was ever going to escape from this theatre. Then he had an idea.

Chapter Ten – Meela's Problem

While Mysterio was talking to the two Quargs, Splurge decided that he would take a chance and slip away. If he was going to find out anything about Broga and the Quigs then he reckoned that he needed to talk to someone who was likely to help him. The only person he could think of was Meela. She may be a Quarg but she had been the only one of them who had, so far, shown any kind of sympathy towards him, even it was only in the form of a doubtful smile.

Trying to be as unobtrusive as possible, Splurge eased towards the back of the stage, where it was quite gloomy. Neither Mysterio, nor the two Quargs, seemed to notice him, and he soon found himself at the door of the workshop. He listened for a while, hoping that there would be no Quargs still working in there. After all, they must have a rest sometime, though he couldn't really be sure about these strange people.

As he stood undecided, he felt a tug on his arm. At first he thought he had been discovered by Mysterio but was surprised to see that it was Meela, the very person he was looking for.

"I wish to speak to you," she said in a low voice.

"And I want to speak to you." Splurge's spirits rose as he realised that this could be a great opportunity to get some questions answered. "Is this a good place to talk, do you think?"

"Come." Meela took Splurge's hand and pushed through the door to the Quarg workshop.

Though the place was full of Quargs, they were busily working away as usual, and took no notice of Splurge or Meela as they passed amongst them.

Splurge couldn't resist taking a quick glance at what was being constructed on the benches but the Quargs were much too secretive to allow him to see anything of interest.

"Here." Meela had stopped before a doorway into a darkened room.

Splurge at first thought it was the same room in which he had met Jonesy, but when Meela waved her hand, the light showed that they were in fact in a long passage. There were doors ranged along either side of this corridor and Splurge fully expected that Meela would go through one of them. Instead she pulled him to the end of the passage where she let go of his hand and promptly disappeared.

Splurge looked around but could see no trace of the tiny Quarg. The passage was not so dark that he couldn't discern a soft, green light coming from somewhere ahead of him. "Meela," he called softly, not wishing to raise his voice in case he should be heard by anyone else.

There was no reply but a slight shuffling sound behind him caused him to turn and behold Meela, who was carrying the shabby top hat and wand.

"You will need these," she said.

Splurge took the hat and wand from Meela, wondering how she had managed to get back to the stage to recover them. Now he had them in his hands he was not quite sure what he was expected to do with them.

Trying not to make it too obvious, he took a quick look inside the hat to see if Jonesy was still there. It seemed to be empty, but you could never tell with Jonesy. "What am I supposed to do with these?"

"Come, we don't have much time." Ignoring Splurge's question, Meela took his hand and plunged ahead towards the green light.

The green light turned out to be no more than seepage from underneath yet another door, which opened in front of them without any magical wave of the hand from Meela. The green light immediately changed to a soft amber glow as soon as they entered. The door closed behind them with a dull but solid thud, which sounded very final.

Splurge felt as though he had been trapped and had a sudden misgiving that he had been so keen to ask questions. Perhaps he shouldn't have bothered, after all.

"We are not trapped. This is the only place we can talk and not be overheard by the others," Meela said, as she released Splurge's hand and went wandering off.

Splurge had forgotten about the Quargs' ability to read minds. It was something he wished he could learn.

"You will in time," a tiny voice squeaked from somewhere nearby.

Splurge would have been more alarmed if he hadn't realised that it was Jonesy in the hat.

"What are we doing here, Jonesy?" Splurge whispered.

"Have patience," the voice squeaked in reply.

"Where's Meela got to now?" Splurge muttered to himself. "I wish everyone wouldn't keep disappearing like that." That was something else he would like to learn. It could come in very handy, especially at school. He looked around at this new place, but couldn't really tell if it was another room or not for there was nothing beyond the amber glow. It seemed to fill the air like a coloured fog.

"I have spoken to the others."

Meela was standing beside him and Splurge gave a sudden gasp of fright.

"I wish you could let me know when you are going to do that," Splurge muttered.

"We don't have time," said Meela, with the faintest suspicion of a smile on her face.

Splurge felt himself going red. He liked Meela. She had been the only one so far to display any kind of emotion. He regretted that he had been so brusque with her. "Sorry. I didn't mean to be so rude but it is a bit difficult trying to get used to everyone here coming and going like that. It's a little unnerving to say the least."

Meela nodded and flickered her eyes, which shone brightly, lighting up her whole face. "I understand. I will try to remember." Then suddenly her face returned to the more usual stony look of a Quarg. "Now we have to..." she hesitated, "ask your help." Her large, round eyes flickered as though she had just been asking a great favour, for which she expected to be turned down.

Splurge thought for a moment. Helping a Quarg ought not to be a problem in itself, though with their multitude of talents, he couldn't see that they needed much help from him. What really worried him was the thought that the more he got himself involved in this place, the less likely he was going to get out of it.

"Before I agree to help you, perhaps you could answer me a couple of questions."

Meela stared at him in such a way that Splurge felt that he ought to agree to help without argument. "Who is the magician Broga and who, or what, are Quigs?" Splurge could have sworn that Meela had turned to a paler shade of her normal emerald green colour.

"You might well ask such a question," Jonesy's voice piped up from the hat. "But I will let the Quarg tell you."

Meela, however, just hung her head as though she was too embarrassed to explain.

At least, it seemed so to Splurge. But he couldn't really be sure because Quargs, he had noticed, were not particularly prone to showing their feelings. "There's no need to feel shy or anything like that." He felt a little awkward because he was never quite sure how these Quargs would react, especially female Quargs.

Meela looked up at him and blinked. "I have a problem," she said simply.

"I will help if I can, but I don't see how. I'm not a magician. I can't even do the simplest tricks without making a mess of them."

"You are a magician, whether you like it or not," a voice rasped from the hat.

"You will be a great magician, better than the Master," said Meela.

"Why not go to Mysterio?"

"He cannot help. Besides..." she hesitated, "I don't want the Master to know of my problem because it could put him in danger."

"Danger!" Suddenly Splurge felt a twinge of alarm. Problems were all very well but when they involved danger, he had to give such things special consideration. "What sort of danger?" he asked warily.

"It is to do with my problem and those questions you asked." Meela looked Splurge straight in the eye and said nothing for a moment or two.

Splurge waited for the tiny, female Quarg to say something more, as it was a little unsettling to have those big, round eyes focussed so intently on him. "You mean about...about Broga and the Quigs?" he stammered nervously, as he sensed that any danger was likely to come from that particular magician. He also sensed some secret was about to be revealed – a secret belonging to the Quargs. It was then that he suddenly remembered Mysterio's caution about not mentioning anything about their past.

Meela nodded. "Broga is a bad Quarg and a bad magician. He will harm you if he can," she said solemnly as though it were nothing more than a forecast of rainy weather.

For Splurge, her words only confirmed his fears. He had met this Broga and could well believe what Meela had said, was true. "What about...?" he began but was cut short by Meela.

"Mysterio cannot help. He is the Master and must prepare."

Splurge wanted to ask what Mysterio had to prepare for, but he reasoned that perhaps he'd be better off not knowing because he had a feeling that it had something to do with his own future. Perhaps he had better ask something else. "Wh...wh...why..." he stuttered nervously, "is this Broga a bad Quarg?" Splurge sensed that he was about to be privy to a Quarg secret and didn't want to upset Meela before she had explained.

"Broga is a bad Quarg because he took all the young ones." Her eyes flickered as she spoke. "He was once a Quarg, who used to serve the Master, as Wilkins and Hodges now serve. Broga thought he was better than the Master. But his magic was not good enough and it made him angry." Meela paused and cast her eyes to the floor as though not wanting to say any more.

"He looked pretty angry when I saw him and I guessed that he and Mysterio didn't get along," Splurge said, trying to encourage Meela. "But if you don't want to tell me any more, that's okay."

"It is difficult for me, because... because..." Meela paused again, and blinked as if she were trying to hold back her tears.

Splurge didn't think that Quargs could cry and he was a little surprised to see that Meela was showing all the signs of being tearful. Maybe it was because she was a girl. He hoped that she wouldn't cry. He never knew what to do when ordinary girls cried, never mind Quarg females.

However, Meela's tears, if she was capable of crying, did not materialise. Instead, she stopped blinking and resumed the normal Quarg stare. "It is difficult because I may not speak against the Quargs, and Broga is a Quarg."

Splurge couldn't help interrupting. "But he's not the same as you or Hodges, or Wilkins. He's a different colour for a start. And he's not as...as nice as you." He wished he had not made that last observation for he could feel himself going red.

Meela took no notice of Splurge's remarks and continued with her explanation. "Though we may not speak against Quargs, I believe Broga is different. He has hurt us by taking away all the young ones."

"Why did he do that, and how did he do it, and what are you going to do about it? And why didn't Mysterio stop him?"

Splurge had fired the questions so rapidly that Meela's composure was momentarily shaken. "You ask many questions. It would be better if you listen and you will learn."

"I'm sorry," Splurge mumbled. He didn't want to upset Meela, now he was on the verge of finding out something of their history. At the same time, he found it difficult to rein in his curiosity.

Meela resumed her story in the usual Quarg manner, without emotion and without emphasis. "Young Quargs are called Quigs and Broga took them to punish the Master, because the Master would not let him do the forbidden magic."

Another question popped into Splurge's head. This 'forbidden magic' now intrigued him.

"I will explain forbidden magic later," said Meela as she read Splurge's unspoken question in his mind. "First you must understand something about Quargs. We live for a long time and it is not unusual for a Quarg to live to a thousand of your years. We do not know exactly but there is a time when a Quarg is no longer useful to the Master."

Splurge wanted to ask another question, this time about Mysterio's age, but restrained himself in the hope that Meela would explain later.

"Broga will not be satisfied till all Quargs are his, and I do not want to go with Broga." Meela paused and looked at Splurge, her large, round eyes blinking, as though expecting him to come up with an answer.

To Splurge, it was simple. "Don't go with him," he said.

Meela hung her head, and Splurge could only guess that she was not happy with his answer. Though she did not show any open expression of emotion, he was pretty sure that Meela was upset.

"It sounds simple to me. You don't have to go. No-one can make you, not even this Broga."

Meela shook her head. "It is not Broga who wishes me to go, it is the Quarg Corum."

Splurge scratched his head in puzzlement. "What is a Quarg Corum?" he asked, trying to keep the exasperation out of his voice.

"The Quarg Corum are Quargs who believe that the magician Broga will give back the younger ones if I go and work for him."

Splurge thought that he had heard of such a situation before, either from a book, or maybe a film. He wished he could remember, as it might have been useful in providing him with a solution. "So that's your real problem," he murmured. "But why does he want you? When do you have to go and what can I do? I am no magician. What about Mysterio? He is the one you want."

"You ask many questions. Is that the way of the outworlders? A Quarg will ask only one question at a time, and receive one answer before the next question. All questions are different and require different answers."

Splurge thought that much was obvious, but he still needed his questions to be answered. Mysterio puzzled him the most. He couldn't understand why he hadn't done something about this Broga.

"I have said that the Master cannot help in this because he must prepare. When it is time, he will tell you. Only you can help us, because the Master will give you his power."

Again, Meela had read Splurge's mind but her answer had given him little comfort. It did explain, however, why Broga had regarded him with such a strong dislike. "So what do I do now? I don't have the power at the moment and am not likely to get any while all this trouble is going on."

"You will help me, because I will help you. So will Jonesy," said Meela, as though it was the simplest thing in the world.

Splurge frowned. He had a strong feeling that he was being manipulated and he could see himself ending up in more danger than before. "When will I be able to get out of this theatre? I can't stay here forever. People will be looking for me."

"Do not worry about other outworlders. They will not look for you."

The way Meela spoke these words made Splurge shiver. There was something different in her tone of voice, which sounded hard and determined. Though he sympathised with the plight of Meela and the Quargs, he couldn't help thinking that it was all a waste of time. And he wasn't altogether happy about the idea of nobody looking for him. In fact he felt quite miserable at the thought and wished he had now gone into the proper theatre with the rest of the class. Dash and Blip, probably wouldn't have gone swanning off round the shops on their own. He heaved a great sigh. "Why does it always happen to me?" he muttered.

"You will help us." Meela stated it as a fact rather than a question. "If you do not help us, then the Quigs will be lost forever – and I shall be lost forever."

Splurge wondered if the last statement was to evoke some sympathy from him. If it did, it only partially worked, because at the moment he felt like reserving all his sympathy for himself. He sighed again. But looking at the tiny figure of the female Quarg, he had to agree that she looked frail and vulnerable and he couldn't see her, or any other Quarg, competing against Broga.

"There must be something you can do. You have lots of magic and stuff. Even if I am to be a great magician as you say, I am not one at the moment, far from it. So I don't see how I can be of any help to you."

Suddenly the top hat in Splurge's hand began to tremble and then shudder violently, almost causing Splurge to drop it. "You have the greatest weapon of all magicians, if you know how to use it," the voice of Jonesy rasped angrily.

"Me? A weapon?" Splurge was confused and intrigued at the same time.

"Yes, you fool. The greatest weapon of all."

Splurge rapidly tried to think of what would likely be the greatest weapon anyone could possess, but his mind wouldn't go beyond thinking of guns, bombs, and invisible cloaks. What could be the greatest weapon anyone could possess? And would he know how to use it?

Chapter Eleven – Splurge Learns To Contrude

Splurge was about to ask for more details regarding this weapon he was supposed to possess, when Meela suddenly grabbed him by the arm and pulled him out of the room.

"We cannot stay," she intoned. "Hodges is looking for you."

So what, thought Splurge. He didn't have to jump every time the Quargs wanted something.

"He only wants you to be a great magician," Meela said, as once more she read his mind

Splurge said nothing but wondered how he could prevent the Quargs, and anybody else for that matter, from getting inside his head and seeing his thoughts. It was very disconcerting to say the least. "Okay, I suppose we'd better go and find him," he said, with obvious reluctance in his voice. Clutching the battered top hat, and with wand hastily stuffed in his jacket pocket, he hurried along with Meela, who despite her size, could move quite quickly. "I don't know what I can do about your problem though," he muttered.

"You will find a way. I know it," said Meela.

"I'm glad you're so confident." Splurge himself was anything but confident. Moreover, he was having serious doubts about this business with Broga. He just couldn't see Mysterio allowing such a thing to happen. Then a thought suddenly struck him. Maybe it had all been arranged for his benefit, as a sort of test or something. He hoped not. The experience on the stage had been bad enough so he certainly didn't fancy tangling with a master magician like this Broga. The more he thought about it, the more likely it sounded. There was only one way to find out, and that was to ask Mysterio directly, face to face.

Splurge had been so intent upon trying to work out some sort of solution that he had not really taken notice of the journey back through the passage, and was surprised to suddenly find Meela and himself in the large Quarg workshop. The size of the place still puzzled Splurge, who could not see how such a large room could exist in such a tiny building.

Then Meela let go of his arm and promptly disappeared among the scores of other Quargs, who were still busily working away at their various magic contraptions. They didn't register any surprise at Splurge being among them but carried on working as if he wasn't there - at least all but one.

"I have been looking for you," said Hodges in his usual flat, unemotional tone.

Something in his manner, however, made Splurge a little wary, almost nervous. You definitely couldn't tell with Quargs.

"You have been with the green one," Hodges continued.

Splurge pretended to be a little obtuse. "Green one? I'm sorry, but I don't know what you mean." He had a feeling that there was something not quite right in the Quarg society and he wondered if Hodges was one of those who wanted Meela to give herself up to Broga for the sake of peace. Or was he just plain jealous? It wasn't obvious in his totally expressionless face.

"The green one called Meela. You must not see her. She belongs to Broga and will bring great harm to all Quargs if she does not go to him. You must not stop her."

Hodges spoke with as much feeling as if he had been reading out a shopping list. At least that's how it sounded to Splurge, and he couldn't understand how Hodges, more than the other Quargs, could be so cold-blooded about it. He wanted to ask the Quarg more questions but he knew that he would get very little explanation. He would have to tackle Mysterio about it. Whatever he decided, it had to be fairly soon. Yet he felt that he owed it to Meela to do something, even if he wasn't a properly trained magician.

"Come," Hodges ordered peremptorily, and took hold of Splurge's arm and dragged him out of the workshop, up the steps, and onto the stage. "You must learn more magic," said Hodges, and proceeded to arrange the stage, with some frantic arm waving into some sort of shop.

Splurge guessed that it probably wasn't a real trick, but some mechanical device that just moved the scenery about. It looked magical though.

He didn't have time to appreciate this new setting, however, as suddenly he was confronted by the imposing figure of Mysterio, who had decided to forsake his usual black cape in favour of a strange assortment of clothing. The most eye-catching item had to be a long, bright red coat, reaching almost to the ground. Perched on his head, like a basin, was a round hat, which sported a small whirling propeller. This took Splurge's attention more than the green and blue tie, which kept alternating the colour of its stripes. "You look like a clown," he said at length. "And you've got clown's shoes." He pointed to the large protruding shoes, which kept letting out a strange squeaking sound every time Mysterio moved, as though he was stepping on some small creature.

Mysterio gave a bellowing laugh, which as usual, reverberated throughout the stage and the whole theatre. "I thought it about time that you learnt some more magic – this time from me." He was about to make some sort of flourish as though still wearing his cape, but suddenly realised that he was no longer suitable dressed for such gestures. Instead he attempted to strut about the stage but forgot he was wearing those ridiculously large shoes and almost tumbled to the floor.

Splurge couldn't help sniggering, and fought to control an explosion of laughter. For most people it would look comical, but for the master magician, Mysterio it was even more so.

Whether he heard, or even noticed Splurge's amusement, didn't seem to matter to Mysterio because he immediately, with a wave of his right hand, had changed the large shoes for a pair of smart looking riding boots.

Splurge wasn't sure whether this was a change for the better or not. He still looked somewhat odd, the clown-like appearance notwithstanding.

"That's better," Mysterio muttered to himself, and stamped about the stage for a while as he got used to the new footwear. He then turned to Splurge. "We are what we wear," he said. "Now you see a clown, without the shoes of course, they were much too uncomfortable, and you expect a clown to be funny and not to make magic." He raised his eyebrows, which Splurge had only just noticed were exaggeratedly bigger and bushier. "And you would expect a magician to make magic and not be funny." As he spoke he turned about and 'hey presto' - he was dressed in his usual black clothes and redlined cape about his shoulders.

Splurge had now witnessed too much magic to be particularly impressed by Mysterio's games. He sighed an exasperated sigh. He was fed up with this theatre of magic business and just wanted to get out of here. Surely the play in the proper theatre must be over by now. People would be looking for him. He also wondered about Dash and Blip and whether they had got back to the rest of the class before they discovered that he was missing. He tried not to think about it too much because it was beginning to look as though he had enough problems to deal with already.

"Right. Where shall we begin?" said Mysterio, as he slowly approached Splurge, eyeing him with a thoughtful look. "I am told that you will be a greater magician than myself, and these Quargs know what they're talking about." He paused and knit his brows. "Do you think you can become greater that myself? Is that really possible?"

Splurge was nonplussed. He wasn't sure what Mysterio was getting at.

"Hmm." Mysterio stroked his chin in a thoughtful manner as he eyed Splurge. "I hope so."

Splurge was even more baffled. "I don't understand what you mean," he said.

"You will. You will," Mysterio said, "but first we must make sure that you learn more magic." As he spoke he pointed to various items, which lined the stage and beckoned them towards him. These items consisted of the contents of this make-believe shop into which the stage had been converted, and, with a click of his fingers, they flew unerringly into his hands or at his feet.

Splurge hadn't been sure what sort of shop it was supposed to be but by the look of the items that came whizzing through the air, he supposed it was some sort of grocers.

Packets of tea, tins of biscuits and an assortment of cakes and loaves of bread had now assembled themselves either in Mysterio's hands or around him.

Splurge wondered if they were real or only cardboard imitations. He had had that experience once before, when the local sweet shop had its window smashed by a large tree during a gale, and all sorts of things were strewn on the pavement outside, particularly bars of chocolate. He remembered vividly how he and his two friends, Dash and Blip, had rushed around to the shop as soon as they heard the news, hoping that there would be some useful salvage items. They were disappointed when they discovered that everything that had been scattered around were just dummy bars. He supposed that the food, which had been summoned by Mysterio was the same.

"Hmmm, nice," commented Mysterio, in between mouthfuls of biscuit which he taken out of one of the tins, and was busily chewing it.

Splurge frowned. Mysterio was always doing things like that. It was easy for him to read minds and he seemed to take a certain pleasure in showing off his skill, which annoyed Splurge.

"I can show you how to contrude your mind so that it can't be read."

Splurge shook his head. "I don't understand that word. I have never heard it before. What does it mean?"

"Contrude is the opposite of intrude. It is a way of blocking your thoughts from prying minds. If you are to replace me, that is probably the most important thing you should learn, otherwise other magicians could get into your head and that wouldn't do. No, it wouldn't do at all."

"What do you mean, replace you?" Splurge almost choked on the question.

Mysterio pretended not to hear Splurge's question and turned to the side of the stage and immediately Hodges appeared carrying some sort of instrument, which he handed to the magician. Mysterio bowed to the tiny Quarg, who disappeared into the gloom at the side of the stage. "The secret of contruding your mind is simple enough. If you have the wit to see and understand." He looked searchingly at Splurge and slowly shook his head as if doubting that Splurge could do it.

Splurge was still nettled at Mysterio's reference to him as his successor but he was, nevertheless, intrigued at the thought of being able to block his thoughts from Mysterio and the Quargs, and anyone else for that matter. "I can do it," he muttered defiantly.

"Good," said Mysterio, and his eyes sparkled with a demonic delight.

He looked a bit like a devil at the moment, thought Splurge. He just hoped that he wasn't going to pull out any of his devilish tricks.

"All you need to make your mind impervious to anyone else is an aid, something that you can do over and over without even thinking about it. Like a click of the fingers, for example; or a wave of the arm, though that is a bit too elaborate. I would stick to something simple. Well? Can you do that?" He gave Splurge a small, mocking smile.

Splurge frowned in annoyance. "Course I can," and to prove the point, he clicked his fingers. He wasn't sure that it would work, however, and he did it again just in case.

"It will work," said Mysterio," but you must have the will to make it so."

"It didn't work then. I think it's just a load of rubbish. There's more to it than that. Some sort of magical thing that you haven't told me about."

Mysterio laughed aloud, but not so much as before and there was no accompanying reverberation. "Magic? Yes there is magic. There is magic in all things. There is magic all around, even inside you, and mostly in the outworld. That's where the real magic is. You just have to look for it."

Splurge considered what Mysterio had said, and as he tried to come to terms with this idea of magic everywhere, he subconsciously clicked his fingers. At the same time he tried to think of likely places where he might find magic in his village.

"There! You have done it. I could not read your mind. All I saw was a dense mist." Mysterio sounded delighted, as though he had pulled off some stupendous piece of magic.

Splurge was not sure whether to be pleased or not. In fact he was not that sure that he had managed to block out his thoughts. Mysterio could just be pretending to make him feel good. "You mean that was all I had to do. Just click my fingers. I don't believe it."

Mysterio chuckled. "You are wise not to be deceived by mere gestures. There has to be something else. There has to be willingness for it to happen. You must believe that you can do it. In the outworld you probably never had to think about such things. Most outworlders have difficulty seeing what is before their eyes let alone seeing the thoughts of others. Here it is different, as you have discovered."

Splurge pondered on what Mysterio had said. "So, all I have to do is to want it to happen, then it will?"

"Exactly!" Mysterio clapped his hands like an excited child. "And if you can realise that then you will have achieved much progress. More than I had originally hoped for."

Splurge wasn't sure whether to take that as a compliment or not. In any case, he felt a lot better about not having his mind read by these Quargs.

"You realise, of course, that the same thing applies to magic. If you want a thing to happen in a certain way, you have to really want it. That's the first step. The rest is just..." Mysterio paused and raised an eyebrow. "Shall we say the rest is just practice."

Splurge also raised an eyebrow. He was pretty sure that it wasn't as easy as that. Not that he fancied too much practice anyway. He just wanted to be out of here. He looked hard at Mysterio to see if he had read his thought. But, apart from a silly grin on his face, the master magician showed no sign that he had penetrated Splurge's mind. There were still plenty of questions to be answered, however, but Splurge reckoned they would wait for a while. Meanwhile, he was anxious to try and put this newfound freedom into practice against the Quargs. Somehow it seemed to disturb him more that they could read his mind, than when Mysterio did. It was odd that there wasn't one of them around when he wanted them. Perhaps they already knew that he had learned how to contrude his mind, as they called it. Never mind, he thought. It would wait. They were sure to be popping up when least expected.

Mysterio, who took off his cape and with a small flourish threw it to the side of the stage, interrupted Splurge's musings. When only inches from the floor, however, Wilkins suddenly appeared and caught it. Before Splurge could find out whether his mind could be read, the Quarg had vanished into the darkness of the side of the stage.

"Now for your next lesson," Mysterio boomed.

There was that word 'lesson' again, thought Splurge. Too much like school.

"You have learned how to block your mind, but that is easy compared to sending your thoughts to others, particularly the Quargs. You will have master that art, otherwise you will be able to perform very little magic." He paused and pointed to the side of the stage where he had thrown his cape. "You saw Wilkins take my cape. So how did he know I was going to throw it there?"

Splurge shrugged. He wished Mysterio would get on with whatever he was going to show him.

"Because I told him to be there and be ready for anything." Mysterio stared at Splurge, his dark eyes glittering, as though he had just explained all the mysteries of the universe.

Splurge wasn't particularly impressed. Before he might have been, but if he had given the matter any real thought, he could have worked that much out for himself.

"Most of magic that we perform in this theatre depends upon such preparation." He gave Splurge more hard stares, as if by staring he could implant the lesson into Splurge's mind.

"That's pretty obvious," said Splurge.

Mysterio allowed himself a sly grin. "But did you know that when I summoned Wilkins, he was at the other end of the workshop." He let a smile broaden his features as he noted Splurge's reaction.

"So you sent a message to Wilkins through telepathy?" Splurge had heard of such a thing, and though it often puzzled him how it was done, he was not over surprised.

Mysterio nodded, grudgingly. "If you like, but here we call it zooming. We zoom into other minds. It's the best way with Quargs. And they prefer it like that. They have never been creatures to take direct orders. Something else you must learn if you are to work with them."

Splurge scratched his head in bewilderment. "How can I do that. I have enough difficulty in talking to them as it is."

Mysterio chuckled. "I shouldn't worry too much. Now you have your mind contruded you will find it much easier."

"But how do I send messages to them – to zoom into their minds, as you call it?"

"Now this will take some practice and I suspect that you will find it difficult to concentrate for any length of time."

For a moment he thought that Mysterio had read his mind. His teachers at school had told him that often enough. The trouble was that his head kept getting filled with all sorts of other things instead of what it was supposed to be filled with.

"First you must empty your mind of anything that is not to do with the task in hand. Then you must fix an image in your mind of what you want, whether it be a person or thing." He allowed himself another sly grin. "I daresay you might find such a gift quite useful in the outworld."

Splurge grinned in return. Mysterio was right about that. He could just imagine the effect it would have on Dash and Blip, if he could implant his thoughts into their heads.

"If you are ready, we will begin our practice," said Mysterio.

"If I can do this mind zooming thing, will I then be able to leave here?" Splurge was beginning to feel the effects of this abnormally long afternoon. The play in the main theatre surely must have finished by now, and his class would have left to go home. Who knows what trouble he had caused by his truancy, which he regretted more and more as time went on.

Mysterio didn't answer at once. Instead he frowned, a dark, threatening frown, which made his face look like an ominous thundercloud. Then it disappeared as quickly as it had appeared, to be replaced by a beaming smile. "Of course," he said.

Splurge wasn't so sure. He couldn't altogether trust this magician. That smile was a little too slick for his liking. But before he could challenge Mysterio, a tremendous noise erupted from the darkness at the side of the stage.

Coloured smoke was emanating from the gloom, punctuated by small flashes of light. Then, with a sudden, resounding crash a figure landed on the stage in front of Splurge and Mysterio. The figure picked himself up and, after a brief, contemptuous glance at Splurge, strode right up to Mysterio.

It was Broga.

Instinctively, Splurge stepped back a pace or two, not wanting to get involved in the conflict, which was surely about to erupt between these two magicians.

"Where is the green Quarg called Meela?" Broga screeched. "You promised no interference, Mysterio." Broga shook a long, threatening finger at the master magician, which Mysterio calmly pushed to one side.

"Before you get too worked up about it, I should tell you that it is no longer my concern. It is for the new Master to decide."

Broga was on the point of uttering another screech of accusation, but paused and slowly turned to Splurge. A crooked smile creased his face as the significance of Mysterio's words sank in. "So," he said, "this young outworlder is to be the new Master." Broga approached Splurge, his eyes glittering with a mixture of delight and fury. Now was the time that Splurge really wished he hadn't decided to play truant.

Chapter Twelve – Broga Declares War

Splurge wanted to run; to get away from Broga; and away from this stage and this theatre. In fact he wanted to be anywhere but here.

Broga seemed to read Splurge's fear because his expression had changed to one of triumph. "So the new Master is afraid me already. And I haven't even given you the benefit of my magical arts." He chuckled and slowly withdrew a wand from inside his cloak and advanced menacingly.

It was then that Splurge realised he had allowed Broga to read his mind. He was determined that he wasn't going to let this lumpy, dirty purple creature get the better of him without a fight. With a click of his fingers, Splurge concentrated.

It must have worked because Broga suddenly stopped and a puzzled look crossed his misshapen features.

"So, the outworlder has learned something." Broga sounded almost pleased that Splurge wasn't going to be that easy to defeat. "What else has he learned, I wonder?" He turned to Mysterio, with a leer. "Or perhaps it is you, Mysterio, who still pulls the strings."

Mysterio remained impassive, and just stood looking in front of him, as if he hadn't heard Broga.

Though his fear hadn't entirely left him, Splurge felt a little more confident. Perhaps now would be a good time to try and put some of his thoughts into Broga. The trouble was that he couldn't remember exactly what Mysterio had said.

It had something to do with concentrating really hard. Before he had a chance, however, Broga had stepped up close and peered up into Splurge's face, with a twisted smile on his lips.

"I want Meela," he said softly, in a cracked voice, thick with menace. "If you interfere, so much the worse for you."

Splurge couldn't help but be fascinated by the large, bulbous eyes, which stared at him, and the lumpy face, which contorted and twisted with every word that Broga uttered.

"Did you hear what I said, outworlder? No interference!" He snapped out the last words with a snarl, which was close to being a shriek.

He looked just like a bad-tempered child, thought Splurge, except he was much more ugly. It was difficult to take him seriously and he didn't see why such a creature should get his own way.

"Why do you want Meela?" Splurge asked in as pleasant a tone as he could summon up. After all, he didn't want to offend this magician, unnecessarily.

But Broga didn't recognise Splurge's friendly gesture and merely stamped his foot in annoyance.

"Because she belongs to me, as all the Quargs belong to me."

Splurge looked at Mysterio, who surely should have said something to Broga about this outrageous claim. But the master magician remained quite unmoved, almost as though it was none of his business. For a moment, Splurge was baffled and might have ignored Broga, if this strange, purple magician had not suddenly prodded him in the midriff.

Now Splurge didn't like being prodded at the best of times. If either Dash or Blip had prodded him the way this Broga had, he would have retaliated, as he did now. Before he had realised what he was doing, Splurge gave the tiny figure a shove, which sent him sprawling to the floor of the stage. "That's what you get for being rude," Splurge said, and was about to turn away, when he suddenly felt himself in a vice-like grip.

Broga had regained his feet, though not his composure, and he was screaming all sorts of insults, at least Splurge assumed they were insults. The actual words were indecipherable. He fumbled for his wand, which had become entangled within his cloak, and was wildly brandishing it about as if conjuring up some kind of curse upon Splurge.

When he looked, Splurge could see that he was not bound by rope or any other kind of restraint, yet he could neither move his arms nor his legs. He looked across at Mysterio, who said nothing but gave him a wink. Splurge could only interpret that wink as some sort of sign that he, Mysterio, had put a spell on Splurge. But why would he do that?

Then he noticed that Broga too had stopped moving although his shrill voice was still echoing around the theatre. Perhaps Mysterio had bewitched them both. He remembered once during a scuffle at school between two boys, how a teacher had separated them.

Then just as suddenly the vice-like grip disappeared.

"Up to your tricks again, Mysterio," Broga shouted. "No interference. You promised me. Those were your terms not mine."

"This outworlder," Mysterio nodded at Splurge, "is not part of our agreement, and I want no interference with him."

Mysterio spoke in slow deliberate tones as he advanced on Broga and held out his arm as though he were going to do something drastic to the Quarg magician. "Go! Go before I do something that you might regret."

Splurge could tell from the way that Mysterio spoke that he wasn't joking.

Broga seemed to realise the same thing because he took a step or two backwards and slowly lowered his wand. But he wasn't overawed by Mysterio's threat. "One day, Mysterio," he hissed, "you or your lackey there," he pointed at Splurge, "will be in my territory and then you will see whether you like the boot on the other foot."

Mysterio laughed, one of his loud echoing laughs, which made the small theatre tremble with the sound.

Splurge didn't feel like laughing, however. This Broga was beginning to annoy him. Always threatening him whenever he couldn't get at Mysterio. "Why don't you just go away," he shouted. "You're not going to get Meela or any other Quarg."

For a moment there was an uneasy silence.

Splurge had not intended to say so much but before he could realise the importance of what he had said, Broga let out a shuddering shriek.

"This is war!" he screamed. "You realise that, Mysterio. And it will be between me and that outworlder." Without another word he suddenly disappeared in a cloud of dark smoke, which left both Splurge and Mysterio spluttering and coughing.

"He could never get that one right," Mysterio gasped in between coughs. When he had managed to get his breath back he turned to Splurge with an amused smile on his face. "Well, you certainly ruffled his feathers. I suppose you have a plan?" He raised his eyebrows into question marks. "Because if you haven't, I don't think much of your chances. He's a mean one, who will show no mercy."

"But..but..but," Splurge stammered. "I didn't mean to..to..."

"Too late now," Mysterio said and calmly walked off the stage, leaving Splurge to ponder on what had happened.

Chapter Thirteen – Splurge's Dilemma

When he had defied Broga, Splurge hadn't felt particularly brave, though he had certainly felt some anger, but that was now wearing off. Had he done the right thing, he wondered? It had sounded fine at the time but it hadn't taken long for the doubts to set in. He knew that he couldn't possibly defeat Broga, with his limited knowledge of magic. Though Broga was definitely not in the same class as Mysterio, he knew more than enough to cause Splurge plenty of misery, to say nothing of embarrassment and humiliation.

Why did he have to get involved? It was nothing to do with him. In fact none of it was anything to do with him. He only wished - but what was the point. He was trapped, as much by his own stupidity as anything else. Never again would he play truant. That's something of which he could be dead certain.

As he was inwardly bemoaning his fate, Splurge had not noticed a small figure beside him. He was so engrossed in his problem that he began to walk off the stage in the direction that Mysterio had taken, not noticing that the tiny figure was following him, till he pulled up suddenly before the door of the Quarg workshop, and Hodges bumped into him.

Though startled, Splurge was glad that it was Hodges and not Meela. He would have had a hard time in explaining to her that she must go to Broga or it would be war.

"You have not finished your training," Hodges said in his usual, flat monotone.

"Eh?" said Splurge said, somewhat disconcerted by the remark. "What has training got to do with the mess that we... I.. you are in?" he stuttered. "Don't you know that it could be the end of the Quargs if Broga takes over from Mysterio, as seems very likely at the moment?"

"You must continue to learn. I will help you. Jonesy will help you." Hodges paused. "And the green one will help you."

Splurge thought he detected the timiest hint of change in Hodges features when he mentioned the 'green one'. Of course he meant Meela but somehow he could not mention her by name. Very odd, he thought. "Why don't you say Meela, if that's who you mean?"

"She is to go to Broga when she has finished with your training." Hodges features betrayed no further hint of emotion and he stared at Splurge with large, round unblinking eyes.

"Hmph. That's what you think. If there is going to be a war, I want no part of it. This is your theatre, your people and your war. I'm getting out of here and you can like it or lump it. It's not my concern." Splurge turned once more to the door to the workshop, in the hope that he could find Mysterio. He was the only one who could help him get out of this theatre. And he needed to get out now. At the same time, however, he did feel a little guilty at having spoken to Hodges like that. After all, perhaps it wouldn't have come to something as drastic as war if he hadn't annoyed Broga. He tried to explain. "I didn't ask to be in this place and I certainly don't want to be the next Master."

His explanation looked as though it was falling on deaf ears because Hodges turned and beckoned Splurge back onto the stage.

Splurge threw up his arms in exasperation. "You can never get through to these Quargs," he muttered angrily to himself. He was about to follow Hodges when he suddenly realised something. The Quarg had not read his mind; otherwise Hodges would have been sure to say something. The thought pleased Splurge and he wondered if he could start practising putting his own thoughts into the Quarg's head. He decided to give it a try, and with a supreme effort, which showed as he screwed up his face in concentration, he tried to make Hodges think about Broga. That should do it, he reckoned.

As Splurge stood there at the side of the stage, Hodges had walked out into the middle and picked up the dusty old top hat and carried it with all solemnity back to Splurge. "You will need this if you are to defeat Broga."

For one joyful moment, Splurge thought that he had succeeded in implanting his own thoughts into Hodges, but he couldn't be absolutely sure. He would try again later. It would have been nice, though, to have actually succeeded in doing something useful, even if it wasn't really magic. But there was no time to think about that now, because Hodges suddenly propelled him towards the centre of the stage and handed him the old wand, which must have fallen out of Splurge's pocket during his confrontation with Broga.

"Take this," he intoned. "You will need it. And don't forget about Jonesy, in the hat." He pointed to the battered old top hat that Splurge was holding, without even realising he had it.

"I thought you said that it was all arranged. That Meela had to go to Broga."

"Now war has been declared, it does not matter."

"What am I supposed to do? And what good will I be anyway? You saw Broga. You must know what he is like, especially as it seems that he is after you Quargs."

Splurge just tumbled out the words, hoping that they would stir Hodges into some kind of reaction, but the tiny Quarg registered nothing. He might as well have been talking to a brick wall.

"You must practise," said Hodges, who had ignored Splurge's outpourings. "If you are to fight Broga, you must learn more."

Splurge almost exploded. "F...fight Broga! You must be mad! Firstly, he is much too good for me, and secondly, and this is more important, it is not my fight – IT IS YOURS!" He shouted the last words so violently that the Quarg suddenly took a step back from him. "At last! Something does penetrate that thick skin of yours," Splurge muttered more to himself than to Hodges. Not that he was really bothered anymore whether it pleased the Quarg or not. He was past caring, so he may as well say what he felt. At the moment he felt angry, frustrated and fed up with the attitude of everybody he had come across in this theatre of magic.

"You must fight Broga. You are the only one. You are..will be the Master."

For one brief moment, Splurge fancied that Hodges was on the point of showing some real emotion, as his usually steady monotonous voice wavered - but only for a moment. It soon reverted to its normal tone.

"I will not be the Master," Splurge said defiantly. "You can put that in your pipe and smoke it. There is only one thing I want, and that is to get out of this theatre. And if none of you will help me, then I will have to help myself.

It's about time to show you what a trapped outworlder can do when he sets his mind to it."

Splurge hadn't intended to be so rude to Hodges as he was well aware of the power and strength of these Quargs, but it was pointless, as far as he could see, to be anything else. They were obviously not going to help him so the sooner they realised that he was determined to get out, the sooner they might possibly relent. He was certainly not going to fight this Broga. And something else had struck Splurge. He was hungry and thirsty.

"Is there anything to eat in this place?" He half glanced around in case something had materialised without him knowing it. But again the Quarg had not read his mind. That pleased him.

Hodges stared at him unblinking.

Perhaps he didn't understand, and Splurge mimed eating motions with his hands.

Still the Quarg stared.

"Maybe I should try intruding you," Splurge muttered softly to himself and began to concentrate hard on putting the thought of food into the Quarg's head.

Hodges continued to stare with only the occasional blink of his eyes.

Splurge was annoyed, with himself as much as this emotionless Quarg standing before him and showing no sign that he had understood. He should be looking for Mysterio and concentrate on finding a way out of here. Once again he turned towards the side of the stage and made for the door to the Quarg workshop.

Hodges suddenly spoke "You can leave here."

Splurge wheeled about and looked at the Quarg. "What did you say?"

"You can leave here but first you must fight Broga."

"I've already told you, I am not fighting Broga. That is your fight, not mine. I just want to leave. I'm tired and hungry and most of all I'm fed up with all this magic rubbish."

"You will not leave unless you... fight... Broga." For a moment, Hodges usual toneless voice faltered.

Splurge was quick to notice that the Quarg was not quite so sure of himself. Maybe this was his chance to press home his advantage. He folded his arms and looked at Hodges with a slight smile on his lips. "What would happen if I don't fight Broga?"

The tiny Quarg rolled his eyes as though trying to come up with a suitable answer to Splurge's question, and he began to turn a darker shade of blue. That was a sure sign that Hodges was exhibiting some sort of emotion.

"Well?" Splurge remained staring at the Quarg with arms still folded and feeling slightly pleased with himself that he had set the Quarg a puzzle that he was obviously unwilling, or unable, to solve. His smugness was soon to be shattered.

"If you do not fight, Broga will take Meela. He will then take every other Quarg one by one till none are left. I will be taken and Wilkins will be taken. The Master will have no Quargs to serve him. Without the Quargs there will be no magic. Without magic there will be no theatre. Broga does not think about the Quargs and will destroy them all. He hates the Master." Hodges put no emphasis on his words and he sounded as though he was reading a weather forecast.

Splurge found it hard to believe that Hodges could be so cold-blooded when he was talking about the possible destruction of his species. However, he wasn't sure that he cared enough about the theatre, Mysterio, or the Quargs, to get involved in a war.

"We shall help you if you do this for the Quargs and the Master," Hodges said, as though to add weight to his plea, even if it sounded nothing like an appeal for help.

Splurge was tempted, but could he trust the Quargs? He could fight their battle for them and maybe even win, but would they help him to escape afterwards? He would have to give the matter a lot of thought. "Why do you not fight him yourselves? You know plenty of magic. If you all joined together you could easily defeat Broga. Each one of you is a much better magician than I'll ever be."

With a slight flicker of the eyelids Hodges spoke in a strange, grating voice, very unlike his usual tone. "We cannot fight our own kind. It is against our laws and our nature."

"Even if he means to make slaves out of you, or destroy you?"

"We cannot. We cannot. We cannot," Hodges's voice became even harsher as he repeated his statement.

Splurge didn't understand.

"That is why you are the only one who can fight Broga. If you do, we can show you the way out of the theatre." Hodges's voice had resumed its normal flat emotionless tone.

Whilst he did feel a little sorry for the Quargs and this problem with the renegade Broga, he felt more sorry for himself, trapped in this strange little theatre. At the moment, though, he was too hungry and thirsty to concentrate on the problem. Perhaps if he had something to eat and drink he might be able to think this thing out and find a way that would suit everybody. Mostly, he needed to speak to Mysterio. But where was he?

There was a sudden loud booming sound of a drum and onto the stage strode a strange assortment of

Quargs. The one banging the drum was very like the one he had seen when he had first arrived in this theatre. The others were a mixture, in costume if not in colours. He could now distinguish between the greens and blues, but because they all had similar features he couldn't recognise anyone in particular. He had half hoped that Meela might be amongst them.

The noise was deafening and at each thump on the drum one or two Quargs would leap out and perform some acrobatic trick in front of Splurge.

He pretended to be impressed but he couldn't see what all this fuss and noise was about. Before he could question Hodges, the tiny Quarg had stepped up to the performing group and held up his hands.

The noise immediately stopped and the Quarg reception, if that's what it was, became motionless and they just stared back at Hodges. For a while noone spoke.

Hodges turned to Splurge. "You must choose what you wish to do. But you cannot leave until the Quargs are safe from Broga."

'Hobson's choice', thought Splurge, (Miss Eddison, his English teacher, had explained the meaning to the class). "I'll need to think about it." He didn't really need to think about it because he knew that he was already trapped here. If there were the slightest chance that he could get away he would take it- but fighting Broga – that was something else. There was no doubt about it, he was in a tight spot. Perhaps he could somehow play for time until an opportunity presented itself.

"We must have your decision now," Hodges snapped out, and his words were accompanied by a sudden thumping of the drum and a series of twirls and somersaults by the other Quargs.

"Decision now! Decision now!" they all chanted in their strange, high-pitched voices.

Splurge put his hands over his ears to drown out the noise. "Alright! Alright!" he shouted. "If you'll keep quiet, I will tell you what I've decided."

Chapter Fourteen – The Quarg Corum

"You will help me, won't you? You promised," said Splurge, trying to pin down the Quarg to a definite answer.

"We will help you," Hodges intoned.

For some reason, he couldn't quite fathom, Splurge was not wholly comforted by the Quarg's promise of help in his fight against Broga. There was something lurking at the back of his mind that made his own promise to help the Quargs seem to be a foolhardy thing to do. 'Never volunteer, son', his father had always said. Now he wondered if he had, in fact, made the right decision, even it was the only decision open to him.

Splurge didn't like the feeling that he had been manipulated, or worse, that he was being bullied into doing something that he felt was totally wrong and dangerous. But while he was contemplating his next move, he felt a tug on his arm. It was Meela.

"I have come to help you," she said.

Splurge didn't know whether to be glad or concerned. He didn't like the feeling that everything depended on him. Hodges hadn't said as much but he sensed that they needed him, and needed him badly.

He sighed. The best he could do was to try, he supposed. He picked up the battered top hat and put the shabby wand into his trouser pocket.

The Quargs watched in silence, which was some sort of blessing. Their noise could be quite unbearable. He looked at Meela and then at Hodges. "Well what's the next step? Shouldn't I – we go into training or something?" He looked directly at Meela, but she said nothing and just hung her head slightly. He then turned to Hodges, who began to roll his eyes. "Well? What am I supposed to do?"

Neither Quarg spoke, although the small group of Quarg performers began to shuffle about, and Splurge fancied he heard some sort of whispering noise. It was never easy to tell with Quargs, as he had never heard them whisper before.

"I don't want to stand here all day while you make your minds up. I'm thirsty and hungry, AND I WANT TO GET OUT OF HERE!" He shouted the last words and it had the effect of making Meela jump away from him in alarm.

"That is your weapon," a small, sharp voice rasped.

At first, Splurge thought that it was Hodges, who had spoken, but then he remembered the hat. He looked inside and there he could see two eyes peering up at him. He had forgotten all about Jonesy. "What weapon? I still don't understand."

"You have to understand the Quargs. They cannot shout or get angry. You may have noticed that they can hardly express any sort of feeling. But you - you are an outworlder and all outworlders, to my mind, get angry very easily. This upsets Quargs and it will upset Broga."

Splurge still found it difficult to talk to a hat and he was glad that none of his friends were here to see him do it. He could just imagine Dash and Blip having a good laugh at his expense. "B..but how will that help? I thought the idea was to beat him not make him angry." He half whispered the words into the hat feeling distinctly silly as he did so. Perhaps it was the presence of so many Quargs that made him nervous.

It made no difference to Jonesy, for he answered in an even louder, and more rasping voice. "Speak up! Why are you whispering?"

"Sorry," Splurge mumbled. "Why should I make him angry?" He shouted the words into the hat, which vibrated so much that he almost dropped it.

"I can hear you," the voice from inside the hat snarled. "No need to shout."

Could never tell what pleases these odd creatures, thought Splurge.

"Quargs don't like violence of any sort, especially violent noise."

That's rich, reckoned Splurge, after all the noise he had heard coming from them, with that drum and their weird wailing sounds.

"Violence upsets their concentration and their special magic goes wrong," said Jonesy, supplying the answer to Splurge's unspoken question.

"So all I have to do is to shout at Broga?"

"Not quite, but it is a useful weapon to start with. That's all the help I'm going to give you. The rest you must work out for yourself." The voice stopped abruptly, leaving a strange silence all around the theatre.

Splurge looked into the hat but now it appeared to be empty. Jonesy had somehow disappeared. He looked at Hodges and then at Meela. Both of them were staring wide-eyed at him. They must have heard what Jonesy said, and perhaps they were a little afraid of him now he knew their weakness.

The other Quargs, who had come out onto the stage with such a flourish of noise and movement, began to slip back into the wings one by one, trying hard not to be noticed.

Splurge did notice and he was not sure that he liked the feeling of people being afraid of him. It was good in one way maybe, especially when he thought of the coming battle with Broga. Then he wondered if he needed to bother with all that. If he just got angry with the Quargs — really angry, then maybe they would let him go.

After all he was a typical boy, and typical boys knew only too well how to create mayhem and chaos, at least enough to make the Quargs regret capturing him. He wouldn't really want to hurt them, now he had got to know them a bit better. He grinned. It felt good to have such a weapon and already he was beginning to feel less afraid of the Quargs and the prospect of doing battle with Broga.

While he was musing on the possibilities of having such a weapon at his command, Meela had approached him and tugged at the sleeve of his jacket.

"Master," she said in an unusually soft voice, "will it please you to come to the Quarg Corum?"

Splurge, not wishing to alarm Meela, smiled. "If you tell me what the Quarg Corum is, then I might consider it." He spoke pleasantly enough but sudden knowledge of his power mad him feel a little superior to these strange little creatures.

But that moment of superiority was soon punctured when Hodges strode up to him and took him by the arm.

"Ouch!" Splurge cried out. "That hurts!"

"You must come to the Corum. The green one did not make it clear. It is not an invitation but a command from the High Factor. He wishes to see you."

Momentarily taken aback, Splurge could only allow himself to be led by Hodges whose grip was as firm and rough as those Quargs who had first dragged him onto the stage. He also sensed that Hodges was displeased with Meela, though he couldn't see why he should be. "Why do you always call Meela, the green one? She has a name. You should use it."

Hodges made no reply but Splurge felt the grip on his arm tighten a little.

If he thought he was going into the workshop again, Splurge was mistaken, for he found himself being pulled along towards the side of the stage and to a small door, which he had not noticed before. He had never had much opportunity to really look around this stage, or any other part of the theatre. There were still lots of mysterious places that needed exploring, and this looked like one of them.

The door was surprisingly small and, though large enough for a Quarg to enter quite easily, Splurge had to almost bend himself in two to get through. Once inside, he could see that it was a large, spacious room, even by his own standards, more like a school assembly hall. To the Quargs it must have seemed enormous. The room was filled with them, both blue and green, ranged in a huge semi-circle, going up in tiers towards the ceiling. It was like a Roman amphitheatre, Splurge decided. His history teacher had described such a thing, and he thought that this place fitted the description.

There wasn't exactly any chattering, as might be expected in such a large crowd. Splurge supposed that Quargs didn't waste their breath on unnecessary talk, but he did detect a kind of subdued whispering sound, like insects rustling their wings or rubbing their legs together. For a moment he could imagine that a host of enormous glittering beetles encircled him. The idea made him shudder.

The rustling stopped as soon as Splurge entered, and he could sense hundreds of large, round eyes all staring at him, as though he were some strange creature on a laboratory table, to be probed and examined.

"You will wait there." Hodges pointed to a small platform on which Splurge was supposed to stand, about a foot high.

In accordance with Hodge's direction, Splurge stood on the platform. It may have been large enough for a Quarg, but he had some concern that he may fall off. Already his feet protruded over the edge. The fall would have been nothing but Splurge didn't want to appear foolish before all those staring eyes.

He then noticed that Meela had followed him into this hall and stood next to him. The small platform made him that much taller and the tiny, female Quarg barely came up to his kneecaps.

She looked up and him and flickered her eyes.

Splurge was certain that she had smiled but he still couldn't be sure with these Quargs.

Hodges positioned himself in front of Splurge and faced the crowd of Quargs, which unlike most crowds in the outworld, showed no signs of anticipation, impatience or any desire to be obtrusive.

For the first time since he had arrived in this strange theatre, Splurge was hearing the true Quarg language, for Hodges was addressing the crowd in what seemed to be gobbledegook. It sounded like nothing he had ever heard before and he had heard plenty of foreign languages from the television. But then, Splurge would be the first to admit that he didn't have much of an ear for language.

When Hodges had finished talking to the assembled crowd, he turned to Splurge. "I have spoken to the Corum and told them that you will fight Broga, but if you fail, the green one," he pointed at Meela, "will have to go to him."

"Who is the Corum?" Splurge asked nervously.

"They are the Corum." Hodges pointed at the assembled crowd with a flourish, as a sort of pride showed through his usual expressionless face.

"W.w.what am I supposed to do now," Splurge stammered. He was beginning to feel somewhat foolish standing on this small platform in front of such an intimidating crowd.

"You will tell them that you are the new Master and that you will banish Broga forever."

Splurge was dumbfounded.

"I can't tell them that!" he hissed.

But Hodges had turned away and walked towards the first row of the seated Quargs.

Splurge looked at the rows of blue and green faces, with their large, round eyes all staring in expectation at him. What was he supposed to do now? What could he tell them? He was no magician, not like Mysterio, and he knew that it was going to take a lot more knowledge of magic than he had to fight someone like Broga. He turned to look at Meela, who still stood close by. But she didn't give any sign that she would help him. He gave a heavy sigh. "Here goes," he muttered under his breath and stepped off the small platform.

Before he could utter a word, there was a loud explosion.

For one agonising moment, Splurge thought that Broga had appeared. That was all he needed.

Then a voice spoke, a loud booming voice that made even this large hall vibrate with the sound.

Splurge inwardly groaned. That voice could belong to only one person, and he turned round to confront Mysterio - but there was noone there. He looked around the hall, for even among such a crowd, Mysterio would surely stand out. But he couldn't spot him.

"Behind you," the voice said, more quietly.

Splurge looked at the small platform and there, gently bobbing up and down like a balloon, was the head of Mysterio.

"Remember this one?"

The head suddenly shot upwards towards the ceiling, where it hovered for a while before descending just as rapidly.

Splurge found these magical gymnastics quite disconcerting and wished that Mysterio would stop playing about like that.

The head spoke again. "That's good. I couldn't read your mind, but I could guess at what you were thinking." Then the head winked. "I have to put on some sort of show, for them," he said quietly. At the same time an arm suddenly appeared and waved at the assembled Quargs. "They expect it from me, as they will expect it from you."

"B..b.but I can't do that," Splurge spluttered. "I can't do anything. I'm not a magician."

It was bad enough that he had to have a conversation with just a head and an arm, but when that head expected him to perform the same sort of tricks, it was just too much for Splurge.

"I'm getting out of here!" he yelled and started to walk towards the entrance.

Immediately there was a strange whirring sound, which came from the Quargs. At first it was a like the noise some sort of engine might make, but much quieter.

Splurge paused and looked at the rows of Quargs, who were gently rocking back and forth as if they were playing some sort of game. They did not look at him but just stared in front at the small platform.

Mysterio was gone.

Splurge turned back towards the door and as he did so the humming noise grew louder and increased with each step he took. He couldn't stand it any longer. "What do you expect me to do?" he shouted at them.

There was no response. The Quarg Corum continued with their weird humming sound and stared into space.

Splurge was by now, frustrated, angry and generally fed up. "Oh..Oh." he stammered, as he tried to think of something suitable to yell at them. "Oh, go to sleep, the lot of you!"

It was if someone had turned all the lights out, for suddenly everything went dark and the humming stopped.

Splurge was mystified and a little nervous. What now, he wondered?

"Well done! I knew you could do it if you tried."

The voice, from somewhere in the dark, startled Splurge. Then he realised that it must be Mysterio but he couldn't see him. In fact he couldn't see anything because of the dark. "What do I do now?" he yelled.

"You know what to do." Mysterio's voice gave no hint that he was prepared to step in and help Splurge.

"What? What?" Splurge was becoming frustrated and he wasn't altogether sure that he had been the one that had caused the darkness. Somehow he had a feeling that it had something to do with the Quargs, or perhaps Broga. He didn't like to think of that possibility, however.

Mysterio's voice continued. "You made it dark, now make it light."

"How do I do that? I don't even know how I made it go dark."

Splurge was getting more and more frustrated. Firstly, he couldn't see anything, not even a way out; and secondly he was irritated at the casual way Mysterio seemed to be taking this situation.

"Try to remember what you did before it went dark."

Splurge pondered for a moment. He couldn't recall that he did anything special. "I just told the Quargs to go to sleep, that's all. I was a bit annoyed at them because they kept making that silly noise."

"And then it went dark?"

"Yes, I suppose so. I wasn't really thinking about it. I thought you had done it, or..or maybe Broga."

There was a low chuckle from somewhere in the dark. "Oh no. Broga can't get in here. If he could, he would have been running things from the start. The Quarg Corum banned him long ago, and it certainly wasn't me that put the lights out. No. It was your own special magic. You wanted something badly enough and you made it happen. Magic sometimes works like that. Besides, you have something the Quargs don't have, something that only outworlders possess."

"You said that before, didn't you? Or was it Jonesy? I can't remember now. But noone would tell me exactly what it was. "Is it something to do with getting angry and shouting?"

Msysterio chuckled. "Partly," he murmured. "The rest you will have to find out for yourself."

There was a slight popping sound, and Splurge knew that Mysterio had gone. What to do now, he wondered? And what did outworlders possess that the Quargs didn't. He couldn't really believe that being angry would make him a magician. If only he could remember what he did to make it go dark. He screwed up his features in thought as he tried to re-trace his actions. It must be something so obvious and ordinary that he just wasn't seeing it. The darkness made it difficult for him to think properly. All this business had begun in the dark and looked like it was going to end that way. He couldn't hear the Quargs anymore and supposed that they really must be asleep. Asleep! That's it! He had sent them to sleep and that's why it was now dark. All he had to do was to wake them up. The thought excited him because at last he was beginning to see what Mysterio meant. But his excitement was short-lived because he wasn't sure how he had put them to sleep in the first place. As far as he could remember he had just told them to go to sleep. Maybe if he told them to wake up, then they would.

"Wake up you lot!" he suddenly shouted. But there was no change. It was still dark. Another try, he thought. "Wake up!" he shouted again, but still no change. He was getting angry and frustrated again. "One more try," he muttered, "then I'm packing it in. Wake up!" he yelled fiercely.

Splurge couldn't have been more surprised if Mysterio's head had suddenly exploded. Once more the hall was bathed in light.

The Quargs, seemingly unaffected by the darkness, were nodding and making some sort of clicking noise. They were paying no attention to him. He might have been invisible for all they cared. For one horrible moment, he wondered if he was invisible. With all this magic about, he could never be certain about anything. The idea of being invisible did have its advantages, however, and he idly wondered if he could achieve such a thing. It might be possible. After all, he had apparently been able to work some sort of magic with the light, though he still didn't know how he had done it, so why not other stuff.

While he had been dwelling on the more intriguing aspects of being invisible, Splurge had failed to notice that Meela was standing next to him. A tug on his sleeve soon woke him from his fleeting vision.

"You must talk to them now. They will listen." She spoke in a normal Quarg monotone, which revealed no sort of pleasure or surprise at the fact that Splurge could now perform some sort of serious magic. "The High Factor has arrived and is waiting for you to explain."

"Explain what? The High Factor! Who is he? And what am I supposed to explain?" Splurge spluttered out his words. He had forgotten all about this High Factor person. Suddenly there was another thing to worry about.

Splurge didn't have any difficulty in picking out the High Factor from among the crowd of Quargs because he was entirely different from the rest of them and appeared to be seated on some sort of throne. This High Factor was obviously a Quarg but most unlike any one he had seen thus far, and that included the purple, warty Broga.

He had the same doll-like features as the average Quarg except that he was a sort of metallic silver in colour, with an ornate, flowing costume, also silver, to suit his station.

Splurge was reminded again of a mechanical doll. He had thought this when he had first encountered the Quargs. The appearance of the High Factor seemed to confirm his suspicions that they were not real people at all, but some sort of robots. What was he supposed to say to this important Quarg? And what should he call him? Sir - Your Highness - Your Majesty, or perhaps none of these. On reflection, he decided that he would just speak to the crowd as if he hadn't noticed the presence of the High Factor. But what should he say?

While Splurge was trying to summon up courage and some idea of what to say, he felt another tug on his arm. It was Meela again.

"You must say something to them," she said quietly.

"What? They wanted to see me." He gestured to the assembled crowd. "I don't know what to say. It's all a waste of time if you ask me." He scowled at Meela, as if to blame her for his predicament.

Meela appeared to take no notice of Splurge's irritation and just stared at him.

"Tell me what to say and I will say it."

"The female Quarg has already told you once. How many more times must you be told?"

The rasping voice made Splurge jump. He had completely forgotten Jonesy; neither had he realised that he was still holding the top hat. That was odd because he didn't remember holding it a few moments ago. Not wanting the Quargs to see him talking into a hat, he turned his back on his audience.

"What am I supposed to say?" He whispered fiercely, feeling his annoyance growing again.

"As the green one has already said," Jonesy rasped.

Splurge turned to Meela.

"You are the new Master. You will banish Broga forever." She spoke the words as though reciting a poem.

Splurge shrugged. "If that's what you want," he muttered, and turned and faced the assembled Quargs. "I am the new Master. I will banish Broga." Though he had shouted the words, they somehow sounded feeble and silly. At first, he wondered if all of the Quargs had heard him, but a slight ripple of movement along the rows of the tiny creatures was evidence that they had heard. Whether they believed him was another matter.

As he wondered what to do next, there was the familiar rustling sound, (again Splurge was reminded of beetles), and all the Quargs stood. At first, he thought it was for himself till he saw coming towards him from his throne-like position at the back of the hall, the figure of the High Factor. The Quargs made a pathway for him as he approached Splurge.

Splurge was nervous. He had never met anyone important before, and this dignified, silver Quarg certainly looked important.

As the High Factor got closer, which seemed to take ages, Splurge noted that apart from his colour, he was not quite the same as the other Quargs in other ways. For a start, he moved very slowly, like an old man. He had never thought of Quargs as being old, but supposed they must grow old eventually. In fact he had never given much thought about the lives of the Quargs, or what they did when they were not working away at preparing magical gadgets. He had been much too intrigued by their appearance and their magical skills.

At last the High Factor stood in front of him, and Splurge wondered if he should kneel or something. Then he remembered that Mysterio was often in the habit of bowing when whenever he spoke to Wilkins or Hodges. So he made a short bow to the small, silver Quarg, hoping that was sufficient, because he felt funny bowing to one of these creatures. He was not in the habit of bowing to anyone – not that he had ever had much cause to do so in his own small village of Wolverton. Maybe if he had done it more often, the Quargs might have been more sympathetic to his plight, though he somehow doubted it. But what should he do now – say something or wait for the High Factor to speak first? It would be polite, he supposed. He certainly didn't want to upset this particular Quarg, who was obviously looked upon as someone extremely important to the Quargs. He also noticed that Meela, who had been standing beside him, knelt down as if to receive a blessing from the High Factor. So he decided to wait for the silver Quarg to open the conversation.

As Splurge waited patiently, he began to notice some odd things about the High Factor. For a start, now he was close up, he could see that he must be very old, because all his movements were slow and jerky. At first, when he had seen the High Factor approach so slowly, he had taken it for some sort of royal march, like kings and queens in a procession. Also, Splurge could see that his skin wasn't exactly silver but more of a light grey colour, and it was wrinkled. Definitely very old, he decided. But the most noticeable difference between the High Factor and other Quargs Splurge had come across, were his eyes. Unlike most Quargs, whose eyes were large and round, his eyes were half closed, and he seemed to be looking at Splurge through tiny slits. In fact, Splurge couldn't remember ever having seen anyone who looked as old, not even the librarian's mother, who was reputed to be at least ninety.

As Splurge was trying to make some sort of estimation of his age, the High Factor spoke.

"I am Kanu. Are you the new Master?" He spoke slowly and in a faraway voice, as though it belonged to someone else.

Splurge nodded and was about to say something, he wasn't sure what, when the High Factor spoke again. It was in that same faraway voice, which sounded a little spooky to Splurge.

"And you will banish – Broga?"

Although he had put it as a question, Splurge had the uncomfortable feeling that he was now definitely committed to the task. What else could he do? He couldn't say 'no' to this silver Quarg, who looked so important, and so old. He still wondered how old he actually was. Must be close to a hundred, he reckoned.

"I will sit." The High Factor made a slight gesture with his hand and immediately a chair appeared. It was no ordinary chair, but a highly decorated one, more like a throne. Slowly he lowered himself into it.

For Splurge, it seemed that everything about the High Factor was in slow motion, and it gave him a chance to study this important silver Quarg at more leisure. To his surprise, however, the wrinkles and sagging cheeks, he had noticed only a few moments ago, had gone. Had the High Factor used magic to get rid of them? Or had he been deceived? Splurge realised that in this place, things were not always as they appeared. Perhaps Kanu was vain and concerned with his looks. Who knows? He could be so old that he is probably nothing more than a skeleton and uses his magic to make himself look younger. After all, as the High Factor he would know a lot more magic than the other Quargs, maybe more than Mysterio himself. The other big thing that he noticed, that made the High Factor different from the other Quargs, was his skin.

Despite their colours, all the Quargs he had seen had certain lustre to their skin, and made them look as though they had been highly polished. It was odd that he had never really thought about it before. He had automatically assumed that all Quargs were the same. But the grey skin of the High factor was without any kind of sheen, as though it had worn off with time. And what about the colour? He had become used to the idea of blue Quargs, who were male, and green Quargs who were female – but what about a silver Quarg? Maybe his colour changed when he became High Factor. Then there was Broga – he was a dirty purple. None of it made any sense to Splurge.

"You are wondering why I am silver, instead of blue or green," murmured Kanu, without even glancing at Splurge.

"Er – yes." Splurge was at a loss. How could the Quarg read his mind if he was now contruded? He looked hard at the High Factor trying to ensure that no more thoughts would be read by him.

Kanu peered at him in turn and it was then that Splurge really noticed his eyes. Now they were opened, he could see that they were not large and round as he had expected them to be, but much more like human eyes, and they looked very tired.

Splurge felt a little sorry for Kanu, who reminded him of a grandfather or a very old uncle. Nor did he seem to be as cold and unemotional as the average Quarg. He detected something more in Kanu, who appeared to convey emotion in his eyes. 'Funny', he thought to himself, 'I don't feel afraid of this Quarg.' He had to admit that all those Quargs he had met so far, made him feel a little uneasy. That first meeting was still vivid in his mind, and he remembered the bruises when two of them had dragged him onto the stage. Subconsciously, he rubbed his arms. Kanu, however, didn't look as though he had the strength to walk, let alone throw people about. On the other hand it did seem that that he could perform some serious magic. Maybe that's why he was the High Factor. "Why are you silver?" The question slipped out before Splurge had realised. He hadn't intended to ask it, although of course he really did want to know.

Kanu didn't reply straightaway, but merely looked at Splurge through half-closed, grandfather eyes and then surprisingly – winked.

Splurge wasn't sure that he had seen it. So unlike a Quarg to show any kind of humour, that he was taken by surprise.

"I am silver because I am the High Factor," Kanu said, in that faraway voice.

Splurge was puzzled but before he could ask a further question, Kanu continued.

"Once in a thousand years a Quarg is born silver in colour and it is a sign that that Quarg is destined to be High Factor."

"You must be very old," said Splurge with awe.

Kanu nodded tiredly. "Three hundred and twenty five of your years I have been High Factor, and I expect to live for another two hundred years at least."

"Wow!" was all Splurge could say. He supposed it must be true. He already knew that Quargs lived a long time, but over five hundred years – didn't seem possible.

"Oh, it is possible. We do not live at the same pace as you outworlders, so we do not wear out so quickly," he paused as if to regain his breath but suddenly stood. Though only slightly taller than the average Quarg, he seemed to grow in stature, and his eyes were now fully open. He gave Splurge a fierce look and a long, crooked finger pointed at him. "You must destroy Broga." His voice, no longer faraway, sounded strong and stern.

If he had any misgivings or reluctance about taking on such job before, Splurge knew a command when he heard one and felt obliged to obey it. (It was exactly the way his headmaster used to speak when he addressed the school at Assembly).

There had been several times during this strange adventure when Splurge thought that he must be dreaming – this was one of them. He couldn't really believe that he was now being asked, or rather ordered, to go to war on behalf of these strange little creatures. Nor could he believe that he was still in a small, magical theatre, where everything happens so fast. Most of all, he couldn't believe that he was now part of this bizarre world. He closed his eyes and hoped that it would all be gone when he opened them. No such luck. He was still in this large room, with a crowd of Quargs, all waiting patiently for him to do or say something special. And there was Kanu, the High Factor, enthroned like a king – also waiting.

"But how do I destroy Broga? Splurge asked. "I'm not a great magician like Mysterio." He turned towards the tiny green Quarg who was still kneeling before Kanu. "I'm not even as good as Meela."

Meela raised her head a little to give Splurge the merest hint of a smile.

"You have power and knowledge enough to complete your task. You must not be afraid." Kanu's voice had lost some of its faraway quality and now it sounded cracked and wheezy. "I will bestow one gift upon you," he continued. "Use it wisely because it can only be used in times of extreme danger."

There was a low hum from the assembled Quargs, as he said this, and Splurge realised, with nervous anticipation, that he was to be privileged like no other outworlder. He wondered what sort of gift it would be, and how would he recognise it?

Chapter Fifteen – Kanu's Gift

Before Splurge could give more thought to what Kanu, the High Factor of the Quargs, had bestowed upon him, a wild commotion had suddenly broken out at the back of the hall. Quargs were unceremoniously and savagely thrust in all directions, like so many rag dolls.

At first, Splurge couldn't see what had caused such a commotion but he was not left in doubt for long.

Striding towards him, like a misshapen, angry troll, was Broga. With eyes blazing and arms waving like flails, he swept away the remaining Quargs in the front rows till he stood before Splurge. He had ignored the presence of Kanu, who just glanced at him, with half-closed eyes, as if he were no more than a troublesome insect.

"So!" Broga snarled at Splurge. "You have ignored my warning and decided to interfere in my business, after all. So much the worse for you." His eyes bulged and the lumps on his hands and face pulsated, as though there was something trying to get out of his skin.

Splurge was startled and afraid, but mostly he was disgusted by Broga's appearance, which was worse than ever. He couldn't remember ever having seen anything so ugly. He turned to Kanu, half expecting the High Factor to do something about this obnoxious intruder, but the silver Quarg remained seated and unconcerned.

"Aren't you going to do anything about this?" Splurge whispered fiercely.

The High Factor opened his eyes and gave a slight shake of the head.

Broga gave a loud cackling laugh. "He won't help you," he said with a sneer. "He won't even help himself." He turned to face the assembled Quargs, most of whom had now regained their seats, but made no sound or outcry at the disruption, and disrespect shown to the High Factor. They just sat with eyes fixed on Broga and Splurge. Broga laughed again and pointed to Kanu. "His time is over! A new High Factor will take his place – ME!"

There was a soft clicking sound like the running of some electric motor in the distance. From what he had seen of them, Splurge guessed that the Quargs were not terribly pleased at the prospect of a new High Factor. He heard a faint sound behind him and turned to see Meela on her knees, quivering and making small movements with her fingers.

"Don't be afraid, Meela." Splurge tried to reassure her but he needed just as much reassurance for himself because at the moment he didn't have a clue as to how he was going to deal with Broga.

With a smirk on his face, Broga turned to Splurge and then looked at the trembling figure of Meela on the floor. "I think you had better come with me now," he rasped.

Meela didn't respond but bowed her head till it was nearly touching the floor.

Broga saw this as an act of defiance and strode up to the tiny green Quarg and roughly grabbed her arm. "I said, you will come with me," he growled and pulled her to her feet.

Meela gave a slight whimper.

Splurge had never heard a Quarg make a sound like that, or express any real feeling of pain or happiness.

The idea of this small female Quarg being so brutally handled made him angry – so angry that he didn't care what this Broga might do. With a sudden lunge, he lashed out and caught Broga on the side of the head. "Leave her alone!" he yelled, and at the same time made a grab for Meela.

Broga was so surprised at this onslaught that he let go of Meela, who quickly scurried behind Splurge. He soon recovered his wits, however, and turned on his attacker with a savage cry. "How dare you interfere? You miserable outworlder will wish that you had never met me, Broga – Lord of all the Quargs, and rightful heir to the Theatre of Magic." He paused in his outburst to gather more strength. "Give me the green one! She is mine, as they will all be mine!" His voice had risen to a rasping screech, which made Splurge's ears ring with the sound.

The more Broga ranted, the more Splurge's determination hardened. He wasn't going to let this lumpy, warty Quarg get his own way.

"Keep behind me, Meela.He won't touch you. He has to get past me first." Though he sounded brave and calm, Splurge was anything but calm inside. In fact he felt distinctly scared and could feel his heart thumping wildly. He hadn't intended to get involved, but he couldn't just stand by and see Broga hurt Meela.

Broga was a bully, and Splurge hated all bullies. He had met them before, at school, always picking on someone smaller or weaker than themselves. At heart, he knew that they were cowards and would run away when their bullying tactics were challenged. It was the same with Broga – at least he hoped it was. Now was the time he could do with some help. Where was Mysterio? He always seemed to pop up when he didn't need him. Now he wanted him, he was nowhere to be seen. He couldn't even ask Jonesy what to do. The battered top hat was lying on the floor but too far away to make a grab for it. Splurge knew, however, that he needed more than advice. He needed magic, and powerful magic at that.

Broga had stopped screeching and eyed Splurge with a venomous sneer on his warty face. "Give me the green one or it will be the worse for you," he said quietly, but with unmistakable menace in his voice. As he spoke, he took a step forward and a long, crooked arm reached towards Meela.

What happened next was as much of a surprise to Splurge as it was to anyone else – especially Broga.

As Broga was about to lay his hand on Meela, Splurge instinctively put out his hand to ward him off. He had no idea what he had done, but the effect on Broga was immediate.

There was a flash of bluish light and Broga was instantly frozen in his tracks. He could neither move nor speak, his features still contorted into a mask of hate and surprise.

For a while, Splurge was unsure what had happened, till he remembered that Mysterio had done the same thing in the foyer of the theatre when accosted by Broga. He couldn't believe that somehow he had the same power. It just wasn't possible. Then he realised that it couldn't have been him. It must have been Mysterio. Splurge glanced quickly about but he was nowhere in sight. Then another thought struck him – it must have been Kanu. But when he looked towards the place where the High Factor had been sitting, there was no-one there. Kanu had completely vanished. That seemed to be proof enough for Splurge. One thing was certain, and that was he knew he couldn't have done it.

"Master?"

A small voice at his elbow roused Splurge from his bewilderment and speculation. It was Meela, who was no longer hiding behind him, but instead now knelt in front of him, her large, round eyes, looking up with a sort of reverence, though he could never tell with Quargs.

"It is safe now, Master. You have the power," she said.

"Don't call me Master, and don't kneel down. I'm not a god. What do you mean? I have the power. And where has Kanu gone? And what has happened to him?" He pointed at Broga, who still remained frozen like some ugly gargoyle.

Meela stood up. "You ask many questions, master. Is that the way of outworlders?

Splurge was confused and found it difficult to look Meela in the eye. He wanted some answers but was half afraid of hearing them because he had an uneasy feeling that he already knew what they would be.

"The High Factor is gone to his rest," said Meela, with unblinking eyes. "You are the new Master. The other Master will go back to the outworld, where he will perform great magic." She spoke with a mixture of awe and certainty, as though pronouncing a great truth.

Then it hit Splurge, like a light going on inside his head. "It's the gift!" he exclaimed. "The gift of Kanu. I..I do have the power," he stammered, not quite believing it could be true. He grinned at the realisation at what the gift meant. No more problems with Broga, for a start. But the grin soon faded when he thought of what else the 'gift' meant. He could see that he was now completely trapped in this theatre, not by the Quargs, but by his own sense of responsibility. Little by little he had been drawn into this strange world and its problems. All he had ever wanted was to escape back to the real theatre and his friends. He wasn't even afraid of the trouble he would surely be in for playing truant. It was just as certain that noone would believe his story for he hardly believed it himself.

As if reading his thoughts, Meela picked up the battered top hat and held it out to Splurge. "The Quargs will help you, and Jonesy will help you," she said.

Splurge didn't take much notice of the odd look that Meela gave him as she spoke. He was torn between this new sense of responsibility (totally alien to him), and his continuing desire to get away from here. The more he became involved in the affairs of the Quargs, the more likely he would be trapped forever. The prospect scared him more than the idea of fighting Broga. He looked at the motionless figure of the purple Quarg, still stuck in his grotesque pose, and wondered what he should do with him. Splurge was not entirely sure how he had managed to stop Broga like that. It must have had something to do with the waving of his arms, yet it made no sense to him. He only wished he could remember what he had done, when he had performed such feats of magic before. It would be a great help on future occasions, though he hoped that there would be few of those. He remembered the changing of the light with the waving of his arm, but it couldn't be as simple as that. He was tempted to try again but not in front of everybody.

Then he suddenly he realised that he was supposed to say something to the Quarg Corum. They had been expecting some sort of pronouncement from him and with all the comings and goings of Kanu and Broga, he had entirely forgotten them.

Now he could feel hundreds of large round eyes staring at him. He had that uncomfortable feeling again, like a specimen under a microscope. "What shall I say to them?" he whispered to Meela.

"Ask Jonesy," she said simply, and indicated the battered top hat.

Splurge hesitated. He wasn't happy about talking into a hat in front of so many staring eyes. "What shall I say to them?" He asked nervously, hoping that the Quargs did not notice what he was doing. He really did feel foolish.

"Tell them what they want to hear," the voice inside the hat growled. "It'll make no difference. They think you are the new Master, so they will believe you."

"But..but I'm not..." Splurge spluttered.

"Just tell them anything. Then get rid of Broga."

Splurge detected a sign of impatience from within the darkness of the hat, which only made him feel more foolish, and slightly annoyed. It was all very well for Jonesy to issue these instructions. He wasn't the one who was going to have to carry them out. Splurge sighed. He gave the hat back to Meela. "Here goes," he muttered to himself. He then turned to the rows of assembled Quargs. "I -", he halted, as he struggled for the right words. Clearing his throat he began again.

"I will get rid of Broga, and you will have no more trouble from him." He was shaking with nerves as he spoke. Never having spoken before in public, his voice sounded small and insignificant. 'Louder', he thought to himself. "I will be the new Master and get rid of Broga for you." He paused for he had an idea. "I will get rid of Broga for you – only if I am allowed to leave the Theatre of Magic and go back to the outworld." Splurge held his breath. Would they accept such a condition, he wondered – or had he said too much?

There was that familiar rustling noise again, and after a few moments, one Quarg stood up. It was Hodges.

"You are the Master. Once you have defeated Broga, then you may do as you wish."

Splurge had a feeling that Hodges didn't really want him to leave, although the Quarg hadn't said as much. It was something in his tone that unsettled Splurge, but he decided that he would work that out later.

"I thought that I had already defeated Broga. Look at him." He pointed to the immobile figure of the grotesque purple Quarg.

"He is not defeated. He only waits for your magic to weaken. Then he will have twice the power."

Hodges words suddenly filled Splurge with a sense of foreboding. He really had thought that he had trapped Broga for keeps. He frowned in puzzlement. His magic wasn't that good after all, and all his previous doubts and fears came sweeping back. Without thinking, he raised his arms in a gesture of hopelessness, and to his amazement, there was a tremendous flash of light, quickly followed by an eruption of black smoke — and Broga was gone.

So much for the High Factor's gift, thought Splurge.

Chapter Sixteen – Splurge Makes A Decision

After Broga had so spectacularly vanished from the hall, the Quarg Corum began to break up, and Quargs slipped away in groups. Soon Splurge was left on his own, with only Meela for company. She held the battered top hat, which she handed to him.

"Just you and me." Splurge gave a wry grin. "And Jonesy, I suppose," he said, as he gave a cursory glance into the hat. "What do I do now?" Though he muttered the words to himself, Meela answered him.

"You must fight and defeat Broga, Master."

"Don't call me Master. I'm not the Master. I'll never be the Master!" Splurge yelled. He was feeling particularly bad-tempered at the moment and was fed up with everyone thinking of him as Mysterio's successor. Now, more than ever, he wanted to be out of this place.

Meela ignored Splurge's outburst and just looked at him with unblinking eyes. Her features were even more Quarg-like – impassive and expressionless. Then she spoke. "You are the Master, whether you like it or not. We are Quargs, whether we like it or not. The Master must protect the Quargs."

Her voice sounded harsher than before, more like the way Hodges would have spoken.

"Why must I?" retorted, still angry.

"Because there is no one else who will protect us from Broga." Meela, in the usual Quarg way, did not emphasise her plight but spoke in a calm, unemotional way.

It made Splurge realise that he had been unfair to the tiny green Quarg by taking his frustration out on her. After all, she was the only one who had stayed with him. "Sorry," he mumbled, feeling himself go red. Girls always had that effect on him. "I shouldn't have shouted at you. It's not your fault." The truth was that he was feeling sorry for himself. After all, he didn't ask to come here. He gave a heavy sigh. Apart from being hungry and thirsty he was really tired. All this magic and the trouble with Broga were too much for him. He sighed again.

"Why does the Master make those sounds?" Meela looked at Splurge, her head slightly tilted to one side and her large round eyes staring at him with a look of enquiry.

Splurge was confused for a moment, till he realised that Meela was referring to his sighing. "Oh," he stammered, going red again, "it's just something that outworlders do when we're sad or fed up."

Meela looked at him for a while as she digested this piece of information. "What is 'fed up'?"

Splurge could fell himself getting irritated again but he forced himself to smile and tried to explain. "It's like all this trouble with Broga and being here in this theatre. I didn't wish to be here. I really want to be somewhere else. That's what I mean by being 'fed up'."

"I understand," Meela said. "It is the same with me and the other Quargs. We do not want Broga to take us. We too are – 'fed up'."

Splurge studied the small green Quarg, trying to determine whether she showed any sign with her features that she did indeed feel the same as he did. But her face registered nothing, neither sadness nor frustration. "Why do not Quargs laugh or cry?" he suddenly asked.

"We do not laugh or cry. We do not know how to." Meela gave Splurge that same enquiring look, as if expecting him to explain why it should be.

Splurge had never given much thought to the plight of the Quargs, most of the time being too concerned with his own plight. He hadn't thought much about the Quargs in any respect, seeing them only as strange, tiny, workers, whose sole ambition seemed to be to provide Mysterio (and now himself) with all the apparatus of magic. Maybe it was about time that he learnt something more about them.

"What do Quargs do when they are not making magic things? Where do you live? And where are all the children?"

Splurge fired off his questions one after the other in the manner of most boys who want all the answers at once, and for a brief moment, he thought that he detected a slight change in Meela. It seemed to him that she had gone a slightly darker shade of green, and he wondered if he had struck a vulnerable spot.

Meela hung her head. "Master asks many questions," she said quietly. "I cannot answer you because I am – forbidden."

Splurge sensed something almost sinister in her reply and wanted to know more. Had the tiny green Quarg more knowledge of outworlders like Splurge, she would soon have realised that boys always wanted to know more, specially if there was a mystery or even a hint of danger. Boys of Splurge's age (he was now twelve) were always looking for an opportunity for adventure, dangerous or not.

"Why are you forbidden, and by whom?" Splurge was not giving up so easily. "Besides, if I am to banish Broga, I need to know as much as possible about you Quargs. After all, Broga is a Quarg – isn't he?"

For a while, Meela was silent, and Splurge wondered if she hadn't heard or understood him. He was about to repeat the question when another voice forestalled him.

"Quargs cannot destroy Quargs," the voice rasped. "You should know that by now."

Splurge didn't need to ask who had spoken. "But I can, I suppose," he muttered resentfully.

"Of course. You are the new Master," Jonesy continued. "You have a gift and all the magic you could wish for."

Splurge wanted to contradict that voice coming from the top hat. He wasn't sure about possessing all the magic he could wish for. If he had, he would have got himself out of this mess. "How do I do it then? I am not in the habit of destroying people, you know," he said with a heavy touch of sarcasm.

There was no reply and Splurge peered into the hat. Had Jonesy disappeared again, he wondered? That was the trouble with that Gromilly, always giving advice but never actually explaining how to carry it out. He sighed.

"Are you 'fed up' again, Master?" Meela asked in a soft voice.

Splurge looked at Meela and nodded. "I seem to have been given a job to do but I am not quite sure what the job is, let alone how to do it."

"I will help you," said Meela, and then looked down at the floor as if ashamed of what she had said.

"I'm sure you will. But won't it cause trouble for you, and maybe the other Quargs?"

Meela raised her head and looked at Splurge. It was another of those odd sorts of looks and Splurge was disturbed by it.

"You are the Master," she said at length, "and you will protect me."

"I was afraid of that," muttered Splurge to himself. How would Mysterio have managed, he wondered? And where was he? Whenever he was needed, he was nowhere in sight. It seemed that all that Mysterio could do was to show off and do silly bits of magic. Splurge was beginning to lose confidence in that master magician. It meant that the only person he could rely on was Meela, and he didn't fancy his chances. Then an idea struck him.

"Meela," he said loudly, startling the tiny green Quarg, "how about showing me where you and the other Quargs live?" He didn't know whether this was the proper thing to ask but a sort of plan was beginning to form in his mind.

Meela just stared.

Splurge couldn't tell from her expression if she was surprised or angry with him for asking such a question. In any case, he didn't have much time, because he always had that nagging feeling at the back of his mind that Broga might strike at any time. From what he had seen of that lumpy Quarg, he wouldn't be too particular what he did. This Broga would have no compunction about destroying other Quargs if it suited his purpose. In a kind of way, Splurge was relying on this fact, for that might well suit his own purpose. But it all depended on the Quargs. He repeated his question to Meela. "Well? Will you show me?"

"No outworlder has ever been to where the Quargs live."

"Where do you live?"

"The crystal caves," she replied in a very quiet voice.

"And not even Mysterio has visited them?"

Meela shook her head and flickered her eyes. "Not even Mysterio."

Splurge wondered if he should put his idea to her, about the possible danger the Quargs might be in if Broga really turns nasty, but he didn't want to frighten her. After all his idea might not work, and he didn't want the Quargs to become his enemy as well. He tried to sound casual. "Are the crystal caves here, in this theatre?" he asked like one who wasn't really interested. Anyway, he reasoned, he was pretty certain that they weren't here. He had been amazed enough at the size of the rooms he had already seen. Surely the Quargs wouldn't be able to find space for something so large as caves in this small theatre. But then, he was forgetting that the Quargs were a very unusual people.

"I will take you, Master, but you must be prepared."

"Prepared for what? And how?"

Splurge received no answer, for suddenly Meela had taken him by the hand and pulled him towards the door.

"Where are we going?" he gasped, as Meela began to hurry, so quickly that Splurge was soon out of breath.

"I am taking you to the crystal caves – the home of the Quargs, That's where you want to go, isn't it?"

Splurge had enough breath to mumble 'yes'. It was a good job that these Quargs were much smaller than him, because he would never have been able to keep up, if Meela was anything to go by. He was surprised at her speed. Something else had been learned about the Quargs. They could move very quickly when they wanted to.

He wasn't taking much notice of the route that Meela was guiding (or rather dragging) him along. Once out of the hall, they proceeded through a series of passages, some of which, Splurge thought were vaguely familiar. He had expected, however, that they would be going downwards at some point, as he didn't see how any kind of caves could exist on the same level as the theatre.

If Splurge had been puzzled by the contradiction of these facts, he was even more puzzled when Meela suddenly stopped before a large, and rather solid-looking wooden door, banded with great metal strips.

The tiny green Quarg then made a strange high-pitched humming sound.

What he might have expected, Splurge couldn't even guess, the journey had been too rushed for him to have any thoughts about it, and he was still trying to get his breath back. Again, however, he was surprised at the size of the door, which he presumed was the entrance to the crystal caves. It must be huge inside. How could this be, he wondered? And what was Meela doing? It sounded as though she was paying a kind of homage to some awful thing the other side of that door.

Splurge could feel his skin prickle and he shivered as his mind began to race through a series of possibilities – none of them pleasant.

Chapter Seventeen – The Guardians

Meela's strange, ear-piercing noise must have been some sort of signal to who or what was on the other side for the door began to swing inwards, slowly and silently. As it did so, Splurge was conscious of a coldness, which emanated from the opening. He gave a sudden shiver, but it was not from the cold. It was something else. Though he stared hard through the gateway, a greenish mist swirled about inside, obscuring any detail. It certainly looked mysterious and foreboding.

Despite the fact that his imagination had prepared him for almost anything, he wasn't prepared for what now had materialised out of the mist. At first it just looked like a shape, huge and lumbering. But, as it slowly moved towards him, with great deliberate strides, the shape began to resolve itself into the form of some monstrous dragon-like creature,

Splurge stood petrified, and all his earlier ideas about visiting the Quargs had completely evaporated from his mind. His only thought now was to run, and to run fast. Never mind Broga; never mind the plight of the Quargs; never mind anything, except getting away from here. Though he desperately wanted to run, he found that he couldn't. He was rooted to the spot and could only guess that Meela must have used some sort of magic on him.

The creature appeared to be moving slowly towards the doorway, its head swaying and its large, saucer eyes blazing like fiery coals. Then it opened its mouth. Two rows of long, gleaming teeth were too much for Splurge. With a supreme effort he managed to free himself and began to edge away.

"Don't leave," said Meela. "It is really nothing to be afraid of."

Splurge paused and to his horror he could now see the outline of another monster, moving up behind the first one. "How many – of- these - things are there?" he stammered.

"There are several guardians," Meela replied in her usual monotone voice, as if it were the most natural thing to be confronted by two enormous and terrifying beasts.

Splurge was definitely not reassured. 'Several' echoed in his mind. One was more than enough for him. "You don't really expect us to get past these things?" He pointed at the nearest one and again began to think seriously about making a dash for it.

Meela walked up to him and took his hand. Her touch might have been pleasant in other circumstances, but it had no effect in calming him down. Seeing that he was reluctant to walk through the doorway, she tightened her grip and began to pull him towards the doorway. "They will not harm you if you are with a with a Quarg."

She sounded so certain that that Splurge was tempted to believe her, though he was still reluctant to move his feet in the direction of those monstrous beasts. He didn't have much choice, however, because like all Quargs, Meela had a powerful grip, despite her size, and great strength for a female.

Slowly, Meela dragged Splurge through the doorway till they were over the threshold. Then, suddenly, the door quickly closed behind him with a loud, resounding thump.

Splurge had never felt so trapped in his life. Nor had he ever been so defenceless. Even if he possessed all the magic in the universe, he couldn't see how he could ever overpower these creatures. The second creature had come closer, and he fancied that he saw the vague outline of yet another one lumbering up behind them.

Now he was much nearer to them, Splurge could see that they were enormous in size and towered over Meela and himself like tall skyscrapers, except that these weren't buildings but living, moving, monstrous things which could crush them both without even being aware that they had done so. Being so close, he could see their slobbering mouths opening and closing as they leaned forward about to devour them.

Splurge was mesmerised by the sight and would have remained in this trance-like state had not Meela suddenly given him a tug.

"Come. They will not harm you. They know that you are the Master, and will do whatever you ask." Again she spoke in that matter-of-fact tone, as if there was nothing to worry about.

"Wh...wha...what," Splurge stuttered, trying to find the right words. His mouth was dry and he could feel the perspiration trickling down the back of his neck. He was both hot and cold at the same time. He cleared his throat. "What do I have to say to them?" he asked in a hoarse whisper, not wishing the creatures to overhear him.

"You don't have to say anything. You have the High Factor's gift. Use it."

"I thought that it could only be used in times of great danger, and I've already used it to stop Broga," Splurge said anxiously.

Meela shook her head. "That was not the gift. You did that on your own. You have always had that power."

Splurge was confused. "I don't understand. What is the High Factor's gift and how do I use it?"

"You will find out," said Meela.

Splurge tried to remember what he had done when he had confronted Broga. It had only been a short while ago but the pressure of trying to think with these creatures towering over him, ready to pounce, made his head swim. All he could think about were those gleaming white teeth and baleful red eyes. The best he could do in such a situation was to stand transfixed and totally terrified.

Meela looked at him. "You must use your gift, Master, or we shall not be able to enter the crystal caves."

"It's not easy to think with those great brutes around," Splurge muttered. He felt annoyed at his own incompetence, and a little silly. He would never be a magician like Mysterio. He just didn't have the flair for it. "I've forgotten what I did to Broga. I stopped him but I don't know how I did it."

"Hurry, Master."

For Splurge, it sounded as though Meela was pleading with him to do something. That was new, he thought. After all, she was a female and he felt it was his duty to protect her.

Then he had a horrible thought.

Suppose he had already used up the High factor's gift without knowing it then he couldn't use it again. Not much a gift really. Firstly he didn't know what it was, and secondly he was not sure whether he had already used it. If someone would only explain things to him, then he might be able do something. It was at times like this that he wished he was back in his classroom and could just put his hand up and ask the teacher to explain. But he wasn't in his classroom. He was in some weird place in this theatre of magic with two monstrous creatures breathing down his neck. He had never felt so useless, and it hadn't been for Meela, and his own curiosity to see where the Quargs lived, he would have turned tail and run like mad. But now he couldn't. For a start those beasts might suddenly take it into their heads to bound after him.

While Splurge was debating with himself what to do, Meela made a dash forward. He made a grab for her, but she was too quick, and soon was vanishing into the green swirling mist.

The two gigantic dragons had made no attempts to reach out to her, concentrating solely on Splurge, who they continued to regard as a prospective meal.

Perhaps they weren't very fast, he thought. They had certainly lumbered up to the doorway very slowly. He began to have a glimmer of hope, but it was soon dispelled when the nearest of the beasts leaned forward, its mouth gaping wide.

Whether it was his own shout of terror, or the noise of the two monsters, Splurge couldn't tell. All he knew that as the nearest one leaned forward to take hold of him, there was a rush of sound like a howling wind.

Splurge looked in disbelief.

What he had thought to be two of the scariest monsters he could have imagined suddenly began to shrivel up before his eyes. At first they began to sway as though drunk, and then like balloons which had been pricked, they became smaller and smaller. As they did so the sound grew less.

Splurge would have laughed had he not been so frightened. It took some minutes before his heart resumed its normal beating, and not like some great steam hammer in his chest. It had taken hardly any time at all before the two creatures, or whatever they were, had completely disappeared. Cautiously he stepped closer. Where they had stood so menacing only a little while before, there was now - nothing. Not the slightest trace had been left behind, in the green, swirling mist.

How it had happened, Splurge couldn't tell. He wasn't aware that he had used any special gift. It might have been when he shouted. But that wasn't deliberate. More like an instinctive yell of terror.

Still reeling from astonishment, and at the same time, slightly mystified, Splurge peered into the mist, wandering if there were more of these creatures lurking somewhere beyond his vision, creatures which would not be so easily deflateable. He was undecided what to do. If he had learned anything in this theatre, it was to expect the unexpected.

As he pondered on his best course of action, he suddenly remembered Meela. She should be all right, he reasoned. After all, she was a Quarg and this was her home. One thing was certain. He could not stay here forever. Though very much tempted to turn back and call the whole thing off, he knew that he would never get out of this theatre till he had, at least, made some sort of attempt to defeat Broga, and to do that he needed the Quargs.

Slowly, he took a tentative step forward into the green mist, his eyes darting about, looking for the slightest sign of anything that might be dangerous, though he could see very little. It was like walking in a fog and he was half expecting to bump into something at any moment.

He had taken only a few steps more before he did bump into something.

Chapter Eighteen – The Crystal Caves

At first wasn't sure what he had bumped into. It wasn't very large and it moved slightly, as he struck it. He also thought he heard something that sounded like a small whimper.

It was Meela.

"Master. It is you. I have been waiting. I knew that the guardians would be no trouble to a great magician like yourself."

Splurge wasn't sure whether the tiny Quarg was making fun of him or not. He knew very well that he was no great magician. He was also beginning to doubt whether those dragon creatures were real after all. They were likely some kind of illusion to scare away unwanted visitors. They certainly scared him, but here, wherever here was, (he could no longer believe that they were in the theatre, or that they were not underground), the presence of this green mist made everything look weird.

"I'm…sorry. Hope I didn't hurt you," he mumbled.

Meela ignored Splurge's attempt at an apology and took him by the hand and led him forward deeper into the mist.

Splurge was glad that at least one of them knew where they were going, because he couldn't see a thing. He allowed Meela to guide him through this strange, silent world, hoping that their journey wouldn't be too long, because he was feeling distinctly tired, besides being hungry and thirsty.

They had not gone far when the mist began to thin out and it was only a matter of a few paces more before it had entirely disappeared. Now, at last, Splurge could get some idea of his surroundings. "The crystal caves," he whispered in awe.

"This is not a crystal cave. We have not yet arrived at the crystal caves," said Meela. "This place is only for the gathering."

Splurge wasn't interested in Meela's explanation. He could only look in wonderment at the enormous cave in which they now stood. How it had been formed, he couldn't guess and of what type of rock, he hadn't a clue. He was just struck by the size of it and the glistening walls, which sparkled and shone with thousands of tiny coloured lights. He was reminded of the lights on a Christmas tree but no electric light could produce this kind of brightness. "I must look at this," he said, and without waiting for Meela's approval, he strolled over to the nearest wall for a closer examination. "Wow!" he exclaimed excitedly. "They're jewels! All sorts of jewels!" He looked around the cave, noting that even the roof was lit up in the same twinkling brightness. "They must be valuable. The whole place must be worth millions, like Aladdin's cave."

"I do not know valuable and I do not know Aladdin," said Meela in her best Quarg manner. "We do not have time to stay here. We must go to the crystal caves, before it is too late."

Splurge wondered what she meant by this, because he hadn't realised that there was any time limit on his visit. "Why don't we have much time, then?" he asked as he sprinted after the retreating figure of Meela, who had somehow appeared on the other side of the cave.

Before he could receive an answer, a loud chiming sound echoed around the cave, taking Splurge by surprise and caused him to hesitate for a moment. That hesitation was almost his undoing.

He could see that Meela had made for a darker recess in the cavern, and when he had caught up with her, he saw that it was a passageway, along which the tiny Quarg was hurrying as fast as she could.

Splurge had never seen a Quarg move so quickly. When he heard the chiming sound, he had paused at the opening and immediately heard another sound. This time it was a harsh grating noise from somewhere above his head and he saw to his horror a huge slab of rock descending at some speed. It was going to land on top of him, but if he acted quickly he could get out of the way. However, he wasn't sure on which side he wanted to be. All sorts of thoughts raced through his mind. Already trapped in a theatre, with no means of escape, he suddenly saw himself being trapped inside this passageway. If he stayed outside, at least he could get back to the theatre. He didn't fancy being doubly trapped. If he had not heard a small muffled cry from inside the passage, he would likely have stood there and allowed the slab of rock to crash down thus keeping him from following Meela. In a flash he decided and scrambled through the narrowing opening. He had barely tumbled into the passage, when the huge rock crashed into place. The ground rumbled for a second or two with the impact.

Splurge was breathing hard, not so much from the exertion, but because he realised with a dreadful certainty that now he would never escape. He stood for a while, contemplating the barrier of rock, which had with a dreadful finality, cut him off, not only from his own world, but also from the Theatre of Magic.

He pushed against the rock, just in case it could be moved. It might have been some sort of illusion like the dragon creatures. They had turned out not to be real, so why not this gateway - but no such luck. His question had been answered. It was solid alright, and unless there was some special way of opening it, he was doomed to stay here forever.

Resigned to his fate, he turned and peered along the passage trying to get a glimpse of Meela, who must be somewhere ahead. He had expected it to be quite gloomy but the path was lit by the same kind of light, which had illuminated the large outer cave. He was tempted once more to examine the sparkling jewels but a sound in the distance caught his attention. It was Meela.

Somewhat reluctantly, he tore himself away from the lights and hurried down the passage. It was a long passage, and at first he couldn't see anything. "I'm coming," he shouted. He hoped that she hadn't taken some hidden turning and would wait for him. The sparkling lights made it difficult for him to distinguish anything ahead. "Wait there!" he called out as he ran. "Let me catch up to you." He hoped Meela would hear him and not go darting off in some other direction.

The passage seemed endless and Splurge ran quickly, ignoring the distraction of the sparkling light, which tended to confuse him. In fact, he hadn't gone far when he saw her. She was standing at what looked at first sight a glass door, the sort he had seen in the big stores in Traffield.

"Are all outworlders as slow as you?" was Meela's greeting.

Splurge was tempted to make some rude retort but he was still concerned about that slab of rock which had sealed them in. "We…I…we are trapped. A huge rock.." he tried to explain in between gasps.

Meela didn't respond but merely went up to the glass door, which opened at a touch, and she strode through.

Splurge followed closely, not wanting to be left behind a second time. "These are the crystal caves," said Meela.

Splurge was constantly being amazed since his arrival in the Theatre of Magic. The jewel encrusted outer cavern had been something special, but he was even more astonished at the new world he had stepped into. Much lighter than the outer cave and much larger, it was difficult to tell whether it was one big cave or a series of smaller ones. Light glowed brightly from scores of these smaller caves, except that they were not really caves. Ranged around this huge cavern like some sort of niches for statues, (Splurge had seen such things in the museum), they looked as though they had been carved out of solid crystal. The openings shimmered with reflected light though he could not pinpoint the source. As he moved towards them, the lights danced about and changed colours.

Although these small caves were cut out of the side, there was still little space in the centre of the large cave as most of it was taken up with huge constructions made out of glass. Splurge supposed that these were buildings of sorts. They were not very wide but they did reach high into the ceiling. He couldn't tell how high they were as they seemed to disappear somewhere above, beyond his vision. At first, he thought that these strange shaped buildings were monuments of some kind, till he saw an occasional Quarg appear to walk out of them. Though made of glass, in a variety of hues, they were not transparent. This puzzled him for a moment, till he remembered that this was all part of the Theatre of Magic, though how something so large could possibly exist inside the small theatre was totally beyond his comprehension. He had learned to accept most things in this weird world. The crystal caves were definitely among the more magical.

While Splurge had been engrossed in the sights of this new world, he had not noticed that Meela had once more slipped away and was again lost to his sight. He had turned to talk to her and when he discovered that she had gone, he suffered a moment of panic. It may be a strangely, wonderful crystal world into which he had been tumbled, but he had no desire to be permanently imprisoned within all this glass. It may be alright for a while, but that shut-in feeling was creeping on him again. Perhaps that's what it is like to be a goldfish. He wondered what he should do now. Perhaps if he tried to get inside one of these buildings he might meet a Quarg who could direct him. Cautiously, he approached the nearest of these, which was a pale green in colour, at least he thought so, till he got close and discovered it was quite transparent like ordinary glass. He searched for an opening but all he could find was a wall of continuous glass. How did the Quargs get in and out of these places? He was getting quite irritated and in his frustration he slapped the side of the building. Immediately there was a dull booming sound, which echoed all around him. He jumped back in alarm, expecting something terrifying to happen. But there was nothing. Maybe the Quargs were asleep. They had to sleep sometime, he supposed, but that didn't help him.

"Where have you been?"

Splurge gave a start, but relaxed when he saw that it was Meela. "Where have you been?" he retorted. "One minute you were here, then you were gone."

Meela looked at him and blinked her eyes. She seemed to be on the point of saying something but instead took his hand and led him away from the building and towards the side of the cavern. "I will take you to the crystal caves now," she said solemnly.

Splurge would have said more, but what was the point. Quargs wouldn't understand. At least, he was being taken somewhere definite, and this time he was not going to let Meela out of his sight. The hunger pangs were returning and the thought of food made him wonder what the Quargs ate or drank, and would they offer him something? He tried to think of what he would most like, though at the moment almost anything would have a tremendous appeal.

"Here."

Meela had suddenly stopped before one of the crystal openings.

Splurge received another surprise, for what he had at first thought to be a cave cut out from the larger one, was no more than an elaborate doorway, some sort of fancy screen.

Meela touched something and immediately, like a huge shutter, the door or gate, shot upwards with a great swish.

Splurge had the impression that the whole place was like a rabbit warren, with all sorts of weird openings. He tried to work out in his head how these doors, or screens operated, whether mechanical or magical. But he had no time to work it out as Meela had pulled him into what was another extraordinary place.

Meela let go of his hand and made a low trilling sound, which for Splurge was like the chirruping of a grasshopper.

Immediately there was a metallic rustling noise, which reminded him of a small clockwork toy. (The idea of robots was still in his head). Apart from the rustling noise, however, there was nothing else.

While he waited for Meela to do whatever she was doing, Splurge looked around this smaller cave. It was not lit up with the same brightness of the larger outer cavern, so he couldn't tell how large it might be. There was light enough to see that it was indeed a proper cave, though not made from ordinary dull rock of which caves are usually made. The walls seemed to glow with some sort of hidden light, and he was close enough to tell that there were no jewels here. Instead, it looked as though the walls were covered with a rich, silken material, like a golden moss, something like one of those Christmas grottoes he had seen in big stores in Traffield. He wondered if the other smaller caves were the same. He would have liked to explore further but the glow just faded into the darkness at the back of the cave.

"What are we waiting for?" he asked after exhausting his curiosity about the nature of this cave.

"You will see, Master," said Meela, and chirruped again.

Splurge wasn't sure that he wanted to wait. This entire journey had been one of waiting or hurrying. Hurrying when he wanted to wait, like when he wanted to examine those jewels in the outer cave, and waiting when he could have been getting a move on.

After a while, and more chirruping sounds from Meela, Splurge began to get bored and was about to ask her again what they were waiting for when suddenly the air was filled with odd, fluttering and buzzing noises. At first, he couldn't tell what it was but then he noticed that scores of small flying insects were darting about. They looked like butterflies at first then bees, till he realised that there were several kinds of insects whirring through the air. They were much larger and more solid looking than those he was used to seeing around his village of

Wolverton. The most surprising thing, however, was that they were all the same colour – golden.

As they fluttered and buzzed, mostly around Meela, like pets, she joined with them in their strange chirruping song.

One or two fluttered close to Splurge, but he waved his arms about trying to keep them away, then one landed on his arm. Tempted to brush it off, he paused and noticed with some wonder that it was not only golden in colour, but also actually made of gold. They couldn't be real, he thought to himself. They must be some kind of clever clockwork toys, which the Quargs had manufactured for their own amusement. He wanted a closer look, so slowly and carefully he cupped his hand around the insect, which had the appearance of a butterfly. There was no wild, fluttering as with a normal butterfly, but a gentle, almost soothing, vibration. He opened his hand slowly, half expecting it to fly of but it remained in his palm, its wings motionless, although it still gave off a soft vibration.

"It likes you. That is because you are the Master." Meela had approached Splurge and on her arm was an insect, which looked like a golden cricket. On her shoulders were several other insects, which Splurge guessed were bees or moths. It was difficult to tell because being golden they did not exactly fit the shape of real insects that he was used to seeing.

Splurge wanted to ask questions or express some sort of surprise but he was tongue-tied by the wonder of these tiny creatures. It was something beyond his imagination.

The butterfly suddenly took of and for a brief moment, he felt a keen sense of disappointment, till almost immediately another insect replaced it, this time a bee, on his upturned palm. Normally, he would have been quick to dash from his hand such an unpredictable creature, fearing it might sting him. Bees had stung him before and it wasn't very pleasant. However, like the butterfly, it had a strange, soothing effect on him and he was certain it would cause him no harm. But unlike the butterfly, this insect throbbed, and it was as if Splurge could feel its heartbeat. Both insects were definitely heavier than their normal counterparts in the outworld, probably because they were made of solid gold. It didn't occur to him to question how they could fly being so heavy or that they might be in some way sophisticated toys. They were real. There was no doubt in his mind. One by one, different insects settled on his hand or arm, as he held them out. "This is great," he whispered to Meela, half afraid that the sound of his voice might drive them away.

Meela seemed pleased for Splurge, and her eyelids flickered several times.

"You nearly smiled then," said Splurge quietly, not wanting to lose the insects.

It was odd, how all of a sudden, he felt that these insects somehow belonged to him, and he was strangely reluctant at any thought of leaving them. Somewhere at the back of his mind he knew that he must leave them sooner or later. "Where do they come from? Do they live in the crystal caves? Can I keep one?" Splurge was so excited that he had forgotten about his habit of throwing a series of questions at Meela.

She looked at him steadily. "You still ask many questions. There are no answers to such questions. Augs just are."

Splurge frowned. "Augs? They looked liked insects to me, butterflies and bees and so on, except they are really made of gold."

"Augs are the keepers of all that is pleasing to the Quargs, and it seems so to outworlders also. They exist in our thoughts and hopes, and in our dreams."

Splurge was a little puzzled. It wasn't like Meela to talk in that way. It wasn't like any Quarg to talk like that. A more matter-of-fact, stony bunch he had yet to meet. For people who expressed little or no emotion it was strange to hear one talking of such things. Even so, he thought he understood and he felt happy about the answer, even if it sounded odd coming from a Quarg. "Are there any more strange things – creatures – you know, in these caves? For one brief moment, he wondered if he had just seen the good stuff and that there might be something much nastier hiding somewhere in the dark depths of the cave.

No sooner had he thought that, there was a sudden wild fluttering and whirring as all the insects began to fly off, back to the darkness. When the tiny creature on his hand had left him, Splurge knew that he had let the wrong thoughts come into his mind, and could have kicked himself for being an idiot.

"You must be careful, Master. The Augs know things that we do not, and they are a source of powerful magic, magic that neither we Quargs or Mysterio can perform."

Splurge felt in some way that he had been admonished by Meela, though she hadn't said as much. He knew that she was right and only hoped that he would have the chance to see these mysterious insects again. "I'm hungry," he said suddenly, "and thirsty." He spoke to himself and it reminded him that he was here in these caves, the home of the Quargs, for a reason. The sooner he could speak to the Quarg people and settle this matter with Broga, the sooner he could get out. That was the important thing – to get out of here and get out of the Theatre of Magic.

"You must now come with me, Master. I will now take you to the home of the Quargs." Without waiting for him, Meela went back to the opening of the cave and opened the screen.

Splurge, unwilling to be left behind, hurried after her. "Where are we going now?"

Meela said nothing, but strode purposefully back to the centre of the larger cave, and went up to the tallest glass building and stood still.

Splurge did likewise, though he couldn't see the purpose, because there was no obvious way in, just glass, all the way up. But he had, perhaps a little grudgingly, learned to trust the Quargs, particularly Meela, who seemed as though she genuinely wanted to help. So he stood beside her and waited patiently.

It was not a long wait, for without warning; there was a dazzling series of reflections as the smooth, glass wall in front of them, suddenly became some sort of revolving door. Meela quickly stepped into the dazzling light, followed, more nervously, by Splurge.

He wasn't exactly sure what had happened, for he closed his eyes when stepping into the flickering lights. He half thought that all this revolving glass would slice through him but he felt only a slight tingling sensation. When he opened his eyes, he saw that he was in some sort of entrance hall like they have in big, posh hotels. Unlike hotels, the place was packed with hundreds of Quargs, even more than he had seen at the Corum. They were scurrying in all directions, although they appeared to be going nowhere. They were like a lot of large insects, thought Splurge, and all looking very busy, but not actually doing anything. He wondered if it was some kind of recreation area, where they exercised. They probably needed to after all the hours they must have spent in their workshop.

"This is the Quarg centum," said Meela, in answer to Splurge's unspoken question, and waved her arm to indicate the whole building.

"Centum?" Splurge frowned. "What's that?"

"This is where the Quargs live." Meela looked at Splurge. "You have another word in the outworld?"

"I suppose – a city or town. Something like that."

"What is a city?"

"The same as town, only bigger. It is where a lot of outworlders live together in buildings."

Meela nodded in understanding. "Centum is our town," she said solemnly. If you wish to talk to all Quargs, this is the place."

"Do you have shops here? I have some money and I would like to buy something." He rattled some coins in his trouser pocket.

Meela put her head to one side, a habit Splurge had noticed, whenever she was puzzled or didn't understand something.

"How to explain things?" he murmured to himself. He kept forgetting that Quargs were not like humans. Though they could speak his language, there was obviously still much that neither understood about the other. "Shops are where you buy things, like food, in exchange for money," he said slowly and slightly louder than he had intended. It always happened like that.

Like many outworlders, Splurge confused puzzlement for stupidity or deafness.

"Master does not have to shout. Outworlders are strange beings, I have decided. They seem to think that it is important to make a noise. There is much noise already. More noise will intrude the mind."

Splurge knew that she was right but he couldn't help being an outworlder, no more than he could help being hungry. In a further effort to explain, he took some money out of his pocket and showed Meela, trying to mime buying food and drink. This action, however, brought about an unforeseen consequence.

Chapter Nineteen – The Quarg Centum

Splurge had no sooner taken a handful of coins out of his pocket, than Quargs immediately surrounded him. He had never experienced anything like it before. They were like children in their eagerness to see what he held in his hand, and they didn't mind jostling and pushing each other in order to get a good look. Apart from a slight clicking noise, they were not noisy or boisterous, like a crowd of children might be. Splurge was puzzled more than surprised. If he had learned anything about the Quargs it was that they rarely, if ever, expressed any kind of feeling, like joy, sadness, or even anger. The action of the small crowd now surrounding him seemed to indicate that maybe they were different in their own surroundings.

Meela attempted to shoo away the nearest Quargs, who stared with large, round eyes at the coins in Splurge's hand, not sure whether to reach out and touch them. She wasn't very successful as others joined the growing throng around Splurge.

Splurge himself was slightly bemused at their curiosity and put some coins into his other hand so that more of them might see. He sensed their longing to reach out and touch the coins, although they betrayed hardly any expression of wanting to do so on their faces.

"Haven't they seen money before?" he said to Meela.

"We do not know money," she replied, in what sounded like an offhand tone, which made Splurge think that she wasn't pleased with his display.

"The Quargs believe that you are the Master, and that what you have produced in your hands is some kind of powerful magic."

"Magic? Money?" Splurge exclaimed, then thought about it for a while. "Maybe it is sometimes. I know it can be extremely useful in the outworld."

"These are not clever Quargs. They did not serve Mysterio, nor will they serve you."

"I thought that all Quargs were clever, and had all kinds of magic. They're probably cleverer than me anyway. They are certainly nosy," he added quietly to himself.

"Broga takes the clever ones, those who do the real magic and he teaches them his ways. He teaches them the...," she paused.

"Teaches them what?"

"He teaches them the forbidden magic," she said and flickered her eyes at the same time.

"What is the forbidden magic?" Splurge asked eagerly. He felt that he ought to know as much as possible about such stuff if he was to do battle with Broga.

"I am not allowed to tell you," Meela said, "but I can tell you that there are only a few clever ones left."

"Like Hodges and Wilkins, I suppose - and you." Splurge thought he detected Meela turning a slightly darker shade of emerald. He grinned to himself. He was beginning to understand the ways of the Quargs. They may express little by way of any facial change, but he was certain that they understood such things as praise. Suddenly he jumped back in alarm. One of the jostling group, (a blue Quarg) unable to suppress his desire any longer, had reached out to touch the coins. Instead of the coins, however, his tiny hand accidentally touched Splurge's hand.

Splurge felt a sharp tingle, almost like a small electric shock, the sort that he had experienced with static electricity. At first he thought that's what it was, till several other Quargs, encouraged by the first one, also reached out to touch the coins. Although none of them touched his hand, he still felt a peculiar buzzing-like sensation as they made contact with the coins.

Splurge quickly closed his hands and put the coins back in his pocket. The Quargs, however, still jostled around him, uttering a series of clicking noises. He looked at Meela for an explanation.

"They think you have performed some sort of magic. I told you that they were not clever."

Splurge examined the palms of his hands and rubbed them together. He could still feel a slight tingle, like having been stung by nettles.

Meela noticed Splurge's discomfort. "They have not yet learned to control their touch. Sometimes it is even difficult for clever Quargs."

Splurge was again reminded, more forcibly than before, of the idea that Quargs were some sort of robots. He would have to keep a very sharp eye on them, specially here, in their own centum.

After a while, the crowding Quargs began to drift away and soon Splurge and Meela were left on their own. The experience hadn't helped Splurge to satisfy his hunger or thirst. He would have to try something different. "Meela, when do Quargs eat? And what do they eat?" He mimed the motion of eating, because he had an idea that there was a lot that the Quargs did not understand, about such ordinary things as shopping for example.

"Quargs eat and drink when it is time," Meela said in her most solemn tone, which sounded to Splurge like a parent telling a child what was good for them.

"Do you understand being hungry or thirsty? It is now time for me." He emphasised 'time' to show that he understood her.

"We shall both eat and drink later. First, we have to see the High Factor. It is proper."

Splurge shrugged. If he was going to be fed at last, he supposed that he could afford to spend some time with the High Factor. It might be a good opportunity to ask him about the gift he was supposed to have been given. If he knew exactly what it was, it might help him to plan a campaign against Broga, though he wasn't in the mood for thinking about that just now. However, it did remind him of why he wanted to come to the crystal caves in the first place, the home of the Quargs. He needed them, though his opinion of their magical powers was considerably lowered by their display with the coins. He hadn't stopped to think that Quargs might not all be the same. A chat with Kanu could be useful though.

Meela took his hand and began to lead him through the milling throng of Quargs. "Do not let go, Master, else you will become lost again."

Splurge grunted. Meela was beginning to sound like his mother. On the other hand, he didn't fancy getting lost among a crowd of Quargs, who were sure to detain him one way or another.

In her usual, swift manner, Meela sped through the milling throng of Quargs on a direct path to a large staircase, which Splurge had only just noticed. He was sure that it hadn't been there a few moments ago. Maybe it had appeared when he was showing the coins to the Quargs. He shook his head in puzzlement. There was no doubt that these Quargs could arrange some surprising things. He had tried, more than once, to fathom out how they managed without machinery of any kind. It just wasn't possible, unless it was hidden of course. He would like to have known something of the working of all these doors and suchlike, but he supposed that the Quargs wouldn't let him in on the secret.

The staircase, like everything else around them, was made of glass, cleverly tinted in a variety of hues, like the colours of the rainbow, but much more subtle. As he stood on the first step, he saw that the colour changed, and it was the same with every step. Another piece of magic, he thought, but one of which he definitely approved. How far these steps went, he had no idea. It was significant, however, that he had seen no other Quargs on the staircase, going up or down. "Is this a special staircase for us?" he asked Meela. "I don't see anyone else using it."

Meela didn't reply, but relentlessly dragged him up the stairs, still holding his hand, though Splurge didn't really see the need for it. He could hardly get lost here.

The steps themselves were narrow and small, suitable for Quargs. Splurge could easily have bound up them, three at a time, but the continual changing of the colours fascinated him.

At last they reached the top, and when Splurge looked back down the staircase, to get an idea of how high they had climbed, he could no longer see them. It was as if they had somehow been magically transported up to what now looked like a platform. Another strange thing was that he could no longer see any Quargs below, as he would have expected. It was almost like being in a lift. He wanted to ask Meela how such a thing could have happened, but he probably wouldn't have got any answer. She never answered his questions about anything to do with the Quarg world. It didn't occur to him that perhaps she didn't know the answers.

Soon they were in a room. However, it was not an ordinary room, but the kind one might expect to find in a palace, a glass palace. Everything in it was made of glass, and though it was quite beautiful and decorative, Splurge thought it was rather cold and impersonal. It had no character - a bit like the Quargs themselves. Maybe that's why they never showed any emotion. In any case he didn't particularly like it. There was too much glass and nothing else.

"Wait here," Meela said, and went darting off to the end of the room, through a door, which seemed to have magically appeared before her.

Splurge wondered if these sudden appearances and disappearances had anything to do with the fact that everything was made of glass. He had often heard the expression, 'it's all done with mirrors', and this place seemed to be a perfect example of this phrase.

Meela was back before Splurge had any opportunity to look around. What he had managed to see of it reminded him of the kind of room in a palace. He had seen such things when he had visited old places, like castles and big country mansions. The thing that had surprised him most about such places was how much room there was, probably because there was there was very little furniture. It was like that here, perhaps even less furniture, though with everything being made of glass, he couldn't really tell what was furniture and what wasn't. There were just pieces of strange, twisted glass shapes. They could be ornaments for all he knew.

"The High Factor will see you. He will explain about the gift," said Meela and stated to walk back towards the 'magical' door, her tiny legs moving like steam pistons.

Not wanting to be left behind at this stage, Splurge kept close to her.

It wasn't difficult to pass through the doors, as the glass parted to allow them to enter into a much larger room and one which was much more to Splurge's liking.

Chapter Twenty – The Book of Qualigor

Remembering the esteem with which the High Factor was regarded by the Quargs, and the way he had carried himself, Splurge expected his room to be very regal and highly decorative. Though made of glass, he was surprised to find that the room was carpeted and there were large, comfortable-looking easy chairs, and pictures on the walls. There was even a long bookcase stacked with hundreds of books of all sizes. Splurge couldn't believe it. It was all so unQuarg-like. This was the first time that he had seen anything that might have resembled a room from the outworld, the world with which he was more familiar. It looked very rich and expensive and he could feel his feet sink into the deep, soft pile of the carpet. But even so, there were oddities about the place, such as a large bath in the corner, and right in very the middle of the room, a small tree in a pot. It looked like an apple tree to Splurge, and he was sure there was fruit on it.

Kanu himself was seated on a long, plush settee at the far end of the room. When he caught sight of Meela and Splurge, he motioned them to join him on the settee.

Splurge wasn't sure what all this was about. It didn't feel right. He had thought that Kanu's own place would somehow be different.

"How do you like my stateroom?" Kanu asked in a cracked voice. "I did some little research about your outworld. My people made these." He waved a tired arm around the room.

Splurge nodded enthusiastically. "Very good," he said, "but..." he paused as Kanu opened his eyes a little wider, "why the bath?" He pointed to the corner of the room where the bath was situated, but at closer quarters he could see that it was not even plumbed in. (His father had told him about such things when he tried to fill a new bath before it had been properly fixed).

"Is it not right?"

"Yes it is, but..." Splurge hesitated again, unwilling to say anything, which might upset the High Factor. "But it should have a room of its own."

Kanu nodded in understanding.

"It's very good though" Splurge repeated, "and very comfortable."

"We do not get everything right, for we have little experience of outworlders and their tastes." He gave a small sigh.

Splurge wanted to ask him about food. He was really hungry and his throat was so dry, that he could hear his voice crackling as he spoke.

"You might want to eat and drink. I had forgotten about that. We Quargs do not have the same needs as outworlders. We will do our best, however." His eyes narrowed into their usual slits and he appeared to have gone to sleep.

Splurge wondered if he should give him a nudge or something. He probably would have done but was forestalled by Meela, who suddenly stood and walked to the door, which opened before her.

She did not go through but waited. After a moment or two, another Quarg handed a large glass tray to her.

Carefully, she walked back to Splurge and laid the tray on a glass table, which had risen up in front of him.

He might have been astounded at such a piece of magic, but still preferred to think that there was some mechanical force at work. Probably the tray itself was also the table, with some sort of hidden device, which set the legs free. But explanations could wait for there was food and drink on the tray and he was unwilling to believe that magic had anything to do with that. A trick table, maybe, but that was all. He was also pleasantly surprised to see that it was the sort of food he was used to eating. There was a plate of chips and several freshly fried sausages on one plate and a large cream bun on another. Both plates were made of glass but not the usual sort of glass. It was something like the staircase, for they kept changing colour. If he hadn't been so hungry he could have spent some time in discovering just how that particular trick worked. To wash down the food there was a tall, glass tumbler of some fizzy drink, which also kept changing colour. He wondered if it was drinkable, and he took a sip to make sure. It was very tasty but an odd mixture of vanilla, strawberry and orange. Before he realised it, he had emptied the glass, and no sooner had he set it down than it began to refill itself. He paused as he was about to work out how such a trick was done, but he was too hungry to be bothered with finding an explanation at the moment, and those chips looked delicious.

As he munched away, he kept glancing at Kanu, who was watching him eat. The High Factor hadn't said anything, and waited patiently until Splurge had finished every last crumb and emptied another glass of fizzy drink. This time the glass didn't refill itself, somehow recognising the fact that Splurge's thirst had been assuaged.

"That was to your satisfaction?" the High Factor murmured.

"That was great. Thanks," said Splurge. "But how did you know what sort of food I liked? And is it the same sort of food the Quargs eat?"

Kanu didn't reply but merely put his hands together and nodded slightly, his expression being one of slight amusement.

Splurge reckoned that Quargs ate something entirely different. Neither Kanu nor Meela had eaten anything. Maybe their food was so strange and possibly horribly gruesome, that they didn't want to scare him in any way. For a second or two, he allowed his mind to wander on the various sorts of things that they might eat, from live slugs to crunchy spiders, or maybe fried worms. He was brought back to earth by a tug on his sleeve by Meela.

"The High Factor now wishes to speak to you," she said in a soft, almost reverential tone.

Splurge then remembered that he wanted to ask Kanu some questions but he would wait until the High Factor had spoken.

For a moment, Kanu said nothing but studied Splurge through his half closed eyes as though trying to decide something. Then suddenly, his eyes opened wide, and his voice, usually so thin and faraway, was strong and commanding.

"As High Factor, it is my duty to see that my people are kept safe and well cared for," he paused, and deep furrows creased his brow, even more so than the natural creases with which age had lined his face. "But now we face a time of great peril in the form of Broga. You have already met this Quarg, and because of you, he has declared war on all Quargs, including myself."

Splurge felt that it was unfair to blame him for Broga's attitude, but before he could protest, Kanu held up his hand.

"I do not say that to blame you, but it has long been foretold in the book of Qualigor, that the Quarg people would beset by one from within, and that the Quarg people would either be destroyed or enslaved." He paused and his eyes began to return to their usual narrow slits. "But it is also written that there would be one, a person from the outworld, who would come and make all safe for the Quargs.

"Me, I suppose," Splurge muttered. "But what about Mysterio? Surely he is more qualified and has great powers. He is more likely to succeed than me, and he is much better than Broga. I'm sure if you asked him he would get rid of Broga for you."

Somehow, Splurge knew that his pleas would fall on deaf ears, no matter how hard he tried to make a case for Mysterio carrying out this particularly unpleasant and somewhat dangerous mission.

"Mysterio is gone," said Meela quietly. "We can do nothing ourselves because we cannot cause harm to another Quarg, no matter how bad that Quarg is."

Kanu nodded. "What the green one says is true. Mysterio was a great power, second only to my own. He was the Master. But now he has gone. You are the new Master and you will help us."

"Why me?" gasped Splurge. That feeling of being manipulated and used was creeping up on him again, and made him angry.

The High Factor ignored Splurge's outburst. "Because it is written in the Qualigor," he said calmly.

"Are you sure that it said in your book that it had to be me?"

"You may look for yourself if you have any doubts. We want you to be sure." With a slight, almost imperceptible wave of his hand, the door opened and two Quargs walked in, carrying what looked like an enormous book.

Splurge recognised the two Quargs as Hodges and Wilkins. He wanted to say something to them, but once he caught sight of the book, he knew that he had to examine it. He had seen old books and he had seen large books; and books both old and large; leather books and even books with locks on them, but nothing could compare with the magnificent volume, which the two Quargs placed upon a glass lectern which had mysteriously sprang up from the floor. Another mechanical trick, he guessed.

Hodges and Wilkins stepped away from the book and stood either side of the High Factor, who indicated with a casual wave of his hand that Splurge should have a closer look at this impressive tome.

Splurge stepped up to the lectern and perused the outside of the book, which glittered and sparkled as though it had been sprinkled with gold dust. He hesitated to open it, for fear of damaging it in some way. Though large and sturdy looking, it was much too grand to actually handle. Splurge remembered the enormous bible he had seen in a great cathedral once on a school trip. He thought that was imposing enough at the time, but nothing compared to this book in front of him, which he supposed in some way, was like a Quarg bible. He tentatively reached out, but before he could touch it, the book slowly opened of its own accord as if anticipating Splurge's action. Nor did it open at the first page, as he reasonably expected it might do, but somewhere in the middle.

The pages glowed with a soft light and he could see all sorts of strange coloured designs and symbols, which looked as if very young children had drawn them. Although they looked interesting, they made no sense to Splurge. Perhaps he should turn a page, but again before he could do so, the book slowly closed only to open immediately at another page. This particular page did not glow. In fact it was the opposite, a velvety black with nothing written or drawn on it at all. He dared to touch the page to see if it was velvet or a similar material. As his finger touched the page, words began to etch themselves onto the paper in a flickering orange, like the sizzling of a small firework's blue touchpaper. He was sure that they made the same sound, as letter-by-letter words were burned onto the black velvet paper. Then he realised, with some surprise that these were words, which he could read and as they unfolded, he gasped in alarm.

There, shining up at him in bright gleaming letters, was his name, S.P.L.U.R.G.E. How could this be? But more followed, for the writing continued till the page was complete and it did indeed tell of an outworlder who would be the new Master and defeat Rogab. He couldn't believe it. It just wasn't possible, and he rubbed his eyes to make sure that he wasn't seeing things. It was at that moment that the lettering faded and the book slowly closed itself.

Splurge stepped back from the lectern, not quite sure whether to believe what he had just seen. Had his name really been inscribed in the Qualigor, the ancient book of the Quargs? And what had happened to the writing? It must have been an illusion, because the Quargs couldn't possibly know that it would be he who somehow ended up in this weird world. It could just as easily have been Blip or Dash. He felt a little more relieved at realising this, and concluded that it must have been another trick performed by the Quargs, or perhaps by The High Factor himself, a trick to persuade him into a fight with someone else. He turned to Kanu.

"It said that I am supposed to fight Rogab. Is he another enemy of the Quargs?

Kanu didn't answer but made a sign to Hodges and Wilkins, who then took the Qualigor from the lectern, which promptly disappeared. They then held it up before Kanu who laid his hands on it and murmured something, which Splurge couldn't hear. The two Quargs resumed their places beside the High Factor, with Wilkins having the honour of bearing the Qualigor, and looking as though he might drop it at any moment, for it was indeed a mighty volume for one so small.

Then Kanu spoke. "Rogab is another name for Broga," he said in that faraway voice, with just a hint of a smile on his lips.

Splurge was nonplussed. Firstly he couldn't believe what he had just read. It couldn't mean him. How could it? How did his name get into that Qualigor book? It made no sense. And then there was the question of what to do about Broga. He knew what he wanted to do – get out of here and out of the Theatre of Magic. But precisely how he was going to achieve his escape, he hadn't a clue. This fight with Broga was taking on all sorts of complications and he still hadn't the faintest idea of how best to do it. If the Quargs could only help in some sort of positive way, he might stand a chance. So far, however, they hadn't shown any indication that they would help. He felt that Kanu could solve the whole problem of Broga or Rogab, whoever he was, with just a wave of his arm.

Kanu's voice broke into Splurge's thoughts. "We who are chosen can do no more than accept our destiny with a good heart and a firm resolve. I did not choose to be

High Factor, but I was chosen, as you were chosen to be the new Master and do battle with Broga."

Though Splurge understood what the High Factor was saying, it didn't mean that he had to like it. "But how do I fight him? I don't have any magic, not real magic like you or Mysterio." He wanted to ask about the special gift that Kanu had bestowed on him earlier. Somehow it seemed inappropriate at the moment, as it might sound as though he was complaining and trying to get out of doing what he had been chosen for.

His question, however, was answered by the High Factor.

"My gift to you is not one that is easily perceived. Nor is it any magical device or incantation. It is a gift to be used sparingly and once used it becomes part of you and stays with you for as long as you wish."

Splurge suspected that the old Quarg was talking in riddles. Maybe he was going ga-ga. It certainly didn't make any sense as far as he could tell.

"Magic is not something that is performed in a theatre." Kanu had opened his eyes wide and his voice became strong and certain. "Magic is you. You now have the gift. If you do not use it will disappear."

"But what is it?" Splurge asked, the impatience showing in his voice.

Kanu had gone back to his more usual faraway voice and his eyes had become slits again. "That is all I can tell you." He sighed in a tired voice. "The rest you must discover for yourself."

Splurge was annoyed, with himself more than with Kanu, because he should have known better. The Quargs weren't going to hand him everything on a plate. He realised that only too well. He would have to work most things out for himself. Perhaps Kanu was right not to explain about his gift. He remembered once, when he had been much younger, how much fun he had, when he had worked out how to ride a bicycle by himself. He had nursed a tiny hope that in meeting Kanu again, he might learn something that could be of use to him, but no such luck. It looked as though he was going to be on his own in this fight against Broga, despite all the promises of the Quargs.

"Will the Quargs help me?" he asked. "They don't have to fight. I know your custom about Quargs being unable to harm other Quargs, but they could still help me to fight Broga."

The High Factor appeared not to hear for he said nothing for a while, then, as Splurge was about to repeat his question, he pointed to Hodges and Wilkins. "They will help you," he said in a tired, cracked voice. Then, to signify that the interview was at an end, he rose from his chair and slowly walked towards a door at the other end of the room. As he was about to pass through it, he turned and looked at Splurge. "You will succeed." The words came out as a mere whisper, but to Splurge they sounded strangely comforting.

Hodges and Wilkins, who had stood immobile in the presence of the High Factor, now moved with surprising speed. First, Wilkins put the Qualigor back onto the lectern which had magically appeared once more (Splurge was sure that there was something mechanical involved), then he and Hodges took hold of Splurge's arms and propelled towards the door by which he had originally entered. Meela followed behind them.

"Where are we going now?" Splurge bellowed. The firmness of their grips of his arms reminded him of the first time he had met these tiny, strange people. They had been rough with him then and they were no less rough now. "You don't know your own strength," he muttered, not wanting to show any kind of weakness in front of them.

Once out of the room, however, the Quargs released their grip and stood in front of him with heads bowed. Meela, who had followed them, also bowed her head.

Splurge was puzzled. What now, he thought? Was this another sort of ritual he was to take part in. He turned to get Meela to look at him, but she didn't look like moving. "What am I supposed to do now?" he asked.

Wilkins slowly looked up and blinked his eyes. "Your name is in the Qualigor, which means that you are the Great One, the one who has been chosen."

"Greater than the Master," echoed Hodges.

"Command us and we will do all that is in our power," said Wilkins in the usual flat tone of the Quargs.

Splurge pondered for a moment on what Wilkins and Hodges had said. It sounded too good to be true. He knew that he wasn't the 'Great One', and there was a niggling suspicion at the back of his mind that these two Quargs had some other reason for all this lavish praise. Perhaps he was being too suspicious. The fact that his name had appeared in the Qualigor had obviously impressed them. After all, the High Factor had promised their help but Splurge's problem was how to make the best of such help. He needed a plan. His original idea was to somehow get the Quargs as a whole to back him up in any fight against Broga, but he couldn't see that happening.

While Splurge was lost in thought, he hadn't noticed Meela, who now tugged his arm and pointed to the battered top hat.

That was odd. He didn't recall that she had brought it with her and he was somewhat perplexed when she handed it to him.

"Jonesy wants to speak to you," she said.

"Where...?" he was about to ask how she had managed the top hat but he decided not to bother. He wouldn't get a straight answer anyway.

He cautiously peered into the hat, expecting to see a pair of bright, beady eyes staring back at him, but it was completely empty. "Where is he?"

"I'm here, if you care to look properly," a familiar voice barked out.

"I couldn't see you," Splurge muttered, feeling that he was being messed about again.

"Because you don't see a thing, doesn't mean that it isn't there. You should have learned that by now," Jonesy rasped.

Splurge grunted. "Well? What do you want to speak to me about?"

"I want to give you a warning. Though you may have all that you need to defeat Broga, beware."

There was a dull silence and Splurge wasn't sure that Jonesy had finished speaking.

"Beware of what?" he said at length.

There was another long pause and Splurge felt the hat tremble. "I'm not afraid of this Broga, even if the rest of you are," he said raising his voice.

There came the sound of muttering and cackling from the hat. "Beware, I said, and that's what I meant. Do you really think that Broga will be on his own? He has many followers, each as bad-tempered and quarrelsome as he. You will likely have to subdue them all. But..." he paused, "Broga has all kinds of followers. Remember – he is a Quarg himself."

The battered top hat trembled once more and then was still. Splurge peered inside but could see nothing. Splurge would have turned it upside down. That would have shaken up the irascible Gromilly. He resisted the urge. Instead he tried to make sense of what Jonesy had said, but like everything else in this place it sounded like some sort of double talk. There were warnings and gifts but nobody would actually get down to the business of explaining things in detail. He was seriously considering in calling the whole thing off. If this Broga had a whole lot of followers the same as he, Splurge couldn't see that he would have much chance, without help from the Quargs, proper help, not just advice. "And where is Mysterio?" he suddenly said aloud.

"Mysterio is gone into the outworld," Hodges intoned.

"He will not return," said Wilkins in the same flat tone.

"You are now the Master," said Meela.

"Hmph," was all Splurge could reply. He looked at each Quarg in turn but could detect no hint of a solution in their bland, impassive stares. He uttered another 'Hmph'. His brow creased in thought as his mind raced over a variety of possibilities, none of which were remotely attractive,. They ranged from seeing himself being blasted into a thousand pieces to being trapped in this place forever. He was torn between fear and anger. Then he had an idea. He looked at Wilkins. "Will the Quargs come with me, when I meet Broga?"

Wilkins turned to Hodges and both looked at Meela.

"Quargs cannot harm other Quargs," said Meela.

Splurge grimaced. "I know that. I'm not asking you to fight. I'm not asking anyone to fight. What I want to know is wether the Quargs will come with me – be there?"

Again the three Quargs looked at each other as though not understanding Splurge's questions.

"Well? Will they?" Splurge said loudly. He was getting angry and frustrated by the evasiveness of these Quargs.

First Wilkins nodded somewhat grudgingly, followed by Hodges and Meela, as though they were being asked to jump into a stream of molten lava.

Splurge shook his head in exasperation. "Like getting blood from a stone," he muttered to himself. "Come on then. Let's get cracking. I want to get out of this place, and the sooner the better." He strode from the room followed by the three Quargs, who were making clicking sounds.

"Wait, Master," Meela called out. "You will need this." She held out the battered top hat.

Splurge hesitated then shook his head. "No use to me. All he does is to give me useless advice. I'm better on my own."

"Where are you going, Master?" asked Hodges, who sounded less like the Hodges of old, being more subdued and uncertain.

"I'm going to arrange a battle. If you're interested, you'd better come along." Splurge didn't wait for any response but strode purposefully towards the giant staircase.

Chapter Twenty One – Mysterio's Gift

Splurge wasn't particularly bothered whether the Quargs came with him or not. They had never shown any kind of desire to give him any proper help. It didn't matter anyway. He had already decided that it was probably best if he tackled Broga on his own. That way he wouldn't have to worry about what the Quargs were doing and whether they needed his protection. He was fed up with all the run-around he had been given by everybody, including Mysterio. Splurge blamed him the most for his trouble because he could have helped, but it didn't seem as though he was much interested in Splurge's dilemma.

As he raced down the staircase and into the grand, imposing foyer, he wondered if he would ever see Mysterio again. It didn't really matter, because he had decided on a plan and, as he pushed through the milling crowd of Quargs, he tried to work out the details. It was difficult to think and hurry at the same time, especially when he wasn't sure of the direction he should be taking.

"Master. You are going the wrong way."

Meela had caught up with him and began to tug at his arm.

"Well, show me the right way then," Splurge said brusquely. "I don't have much time and I want to get this business over and done with quickly."

Meela did not show that she was upset by Splurge's manner, but continued to tug at his arm. "Where do you wish to go, Master?"

Splurge stopped. It was true. He had no idea of how to get out of this place and he could be blundering about for ages. "We need to get back to the Theatre of Magic. That's where I shall fight Broga."

If Meela was alarmed at this prospect, she didn't show it, nor did Wilkins or Hodges, who had now caught up with them.

"It is all the Theatre of Magic, Master," said Meela.

"Even the Crystal Caves and those dragon monsters - the guardians? And all this?" He waved his arm around the Quarg centum.

Meela nodded and blinked her eyes.

Splurge was sure that these Quargs understood what he meant but they were still playing their own game with him. He didn't care anyway. It had taken a while, but at last it was beginning to sink in, that the Quargs would no offer no help even though they continually said that they would. He wasn't too upset at the prospect of standing alone against Broga. After all, he had stopped him once, and would do it again. If he really was the new Master, then he must have some special powers, which he himself didn't know about. He would soon see.

Once out of the Quarg centum, Meela led the way to the long sparkling passageway.

Splurge suddenly remembered that slab crashing down and sealing him inside this Quarg world of crystal caves. But he shouldn't have been too surprised when, at a touch from Meela, the massive stone slab slid upwards and allowed them to pass through into the large outer cave.

For a brief moment, Splurge was tempted to go across and explore the cave where he had seen those strange, golden insects. He pushed the idea from his head and followed Meela into the green mist, which swirled around the entrance to the Quarg world. He slowed down as he remembered the guardians, those terrible looking monsters. Would they now prevent him from getting out?

Meela walked directly into the mist without any hesitation, as did the other two Quargs, Hodges and Wilkins. Splurge followed more cautiously, keeping a sharp eye on the eddying mist. He had a weird fancy that the mist could twist itself into strange and terrifying shapes and become once more those monstrous guardians. Several times he thought he saw a shape materialise and come towards him, but it always turned out to be just mist.

At last they were through the gateway with the crystal caves behind them, for which Splurge was thankful.

"Quick!" Splurge urged. "The Theatre of Magic. The sooner we get there, the sooner the battle can begin." He wasn't sure why he said that, for he had never felt less like a battle in his life. Already his heart was pounding with fear and excitement, though any excitement he might have felt was fast being replaced by total fear. Yet he knew that if he was to have any chance against Broga, the theatre itself was right place to have such a confrontation. It would be his battleground, a place where at least he had some familiarity; he only wished he knew what he was going to do.

The three Quargs sensed Splurge's urgency and hurried along passages and through doors as fast as their tiny legs would carry them. Splurge himself was soon out of breath. He would never understand how these creatures could move so quickly considering their size.

They were soon back on the stage in the Theatre of Magic.

Splurge paused to get his breath back, while the Quargs stood around him, apparently unaffected by the mad dash from the crystal caves.

"Ah, you're back," a voice boomed out from somewhere in the theatre.

Splurge was startled by at the sound. "Mysterio?" he called out, as he looked around the stage and into the auditorium.

"Here."

Splurge jumped again, for the voice boomed out just behind him. He turned and saw the familiar face of Mysterio – just the face, for the rest of his body was invisible.

"I wish you wouldn't do that," muttered Splurge. "Try something else for a change."

"Like this, you mean." With a loud popping sound and a small flash of light, Mysterio had somehow become a television set, with his face beaming out at him from the screen.

Splurge sighed. "Why can't you just be normal?"

"What is normal? This is the Theatre of Magic, where all things are normal, or unusual, depending on your point of view."

Splurge didn't have the time or the inclination to argue the point with him. "I have to prepare to meet Broga, so I thought that you might like to help me, or at the very least offer some sort of advice."

"Oh, I can't help you," Mysterio said solemnly. "You are now the new Master. You must do as you think fit. But you will succeed. I'm sure of it."

Mysterio's words and tone didn't fill Splurge with much confidence. "Well, I'm not so sure. Besides, I thought you had left for the outworld."

"I have. I have," Mysterio purred. "I returned to give you something. It might help - or it might not."

Suddenly, the screen of the television set swung outwards like a cupboard door, and floating out came a black cape and a top hat.

"Those are for you now. They will make you look the part if nothing else. I know that appearances are not everything, but they can be very useful. You will soon be in a war, and that cape and hat will be your battle-dress."

The screen closed with a snap, leaving Splurge clutching Mysterio's cape, and a brand new shiny hat.

Splurge was slightly disappointed. "So you are definitely not staying to help me or the Quargs?"

Mysterio chuckled. "I have helped you. You will see."

The screen went blank, and Splurge found himself staring at a fuzzy whiteness. Mysterio had gone – almost.

"Just a few parting words, which you may also find useful. Remember – what the heart desires, the mind can achieve – but you must want it enough. Now I have to go out there, into the outworld, where they need my magic. You are from this moment officially my successor."

"Must I stay here forever?" Splurge was confused. "The Quargs said I could leave if I defeated Broga."

Mysterio chuckled again. "Quargs. What would we do without them, eh?" When you find a successor, you will leave, but I warn you, it will not be so easy to leave your magic behind. What you have learned, you must pass on, either here, in the Theatre of Magic, or in the outworld. Use it, else it will die – then the world will die."

With another loud pop and a flash of light, the television set vanished.

For a moment, Splurge could only stare at the vacant space where Mysterio had appeared. He thought it an overwhelming thing for the Master Magician to say, about magic and the world dying without it. He wasn't altogether sure that he believed him, but then he was Mysterio, the powerful and all knowing. He should know if anyone should. Now that he was finally gone, Splurge felt a curious sense of loss, yet he did have the master magician's cape and top hat.

The three Quargs had remained motionless during the conversation between Mysterio and Splurge, almost trance-like and not seeming to be interested. After Mysterio's departure, however, they were suddenly full of bustle and activity.

Wilkins ran up to Splurge and took the hat and cape from him, while Meela ran to the side of the stage and closed the curtains. Hodges meanwhile was assembling a pile of magical gadgets and contraptions, which were being deposited on the stage by a team of Quargs, who had mysteriously appeared from the darkness at the rear.

As Splurge watched in wonderment, Wilkins was draping the cape over his shoulders, and tying it up with some sort of fancy cord. He then handed Splurge the top hat, indicating that he should try it.

Splurge felt a little self conscious at wearing Mysterio's cape and hat. At first he was not sure that they would fit him. Strangely enough they did. More of Mysterio's magic, he reckoned. But would they give him the same powers as the master magician himself? He somehow doubted it. Even so, he did sense that something was different. He wished he had a mirror so that he could properly judge the effect.

"Master, it is as you wished."

Meela was standing before him with a full-length mirror. She blinked her eyes before coming to stand beside him.

Splurge was half afraid to look in the mirror, because he was sure to appear ridiculous. Nevertheless, he did look and to his surprise, and some relief, his reflection was of a suave, debonair magician. It was like seeing a smaller version of Mysterio himself, except it was Splurge's face, beneath the elegant top hat. He decided that at least he looked the part if nothing else. Somehow, he didn't mind appearing before an audience now. The cape and top hat had, in some way, suddenly given him more confidence, though he was still aware that it would take very much more to overcome Broga. He turned to Meela. "How do I look?"

"Master looks like..." Meela hesitated. "Master looks like Master."

"You mean I look like Mysterio."

"No. You look like yourself – the Master."

Splurge still wasn't sure what she meant exactly, but he was content with the fact that she hadn't mentioned anything about him looking ridiculous. On the other hand, perhaps Quargs, who had thus far shown him little or no sign of emotion, didn't understand the idea of appearance. They themselves didn't dress in a particularly trendy manner, except for the High Factor, of course. Though he felt much better, in an odd sort of way, he still wasn't sure about the best way to tackle Broga. Then there were his followers to consider. He remembered what Jonesy had said about them, not that he had really said that much, just that there were lots of them and all as mean as Broga himself. He hadn't said as much, but Jonesy had hinted that they could be Quargs, though after what he had learned about these tiny creatures he wasn't so sure that any of them would side with such an obnoxious character. If his followers were some kind of renegade Quargs, then they would possess almost as much magic as Broga himself, a magic that Splurge didn't have. For a moment he had a vision of being manhandled by hundreds of tiny purple Quargs, all as ugly looking as Broga. He subconsciously rubbed his arm where he had been so roughly handled by the Quargs when he had first arrived in the this theatre. Maybe Broga's followers wouldn't be so strong, though he somehow doubted it.

While Splurge had been admiring himself in the mirror and thinking about the contest, Hodges and Wilkins had been busy laying out all manner of gadgets and magical devices on long tables, one on each side of the stage.

Splurge recognised some of the gadgets as being similar to those he had used in his first performance. It now seemed so long ago, and it was with a kind of affection that he gazed at the boxes and balls, which were changing colours even as he stared. The boxes also were unfolding and reassembling into a variety of shapes and colour. A bit like runners limbering up for a race, thought Splurge, almost as if they had a life of their own and knew that there was to be some sort of performance.

Performance!

That was not what Splurge had originally envisaged. A battle or contest in his mind was something much more dramatic, involving the possibility of physical danger, than merely the performing magic tricks. He somehow didn't think that Broga would be performing. Everything he had seen of him so far indicated that the renegade Quarg would do something much more drastic.

Splurge called out to Hodges. "Why are you arranging those things? Broga isn't interested in magic tricks."

Wilkins walked across to Splurge and looked up at him in his usual solemn Quarg manner. "Oh. But this is how Broga will fight."

"He always uses magic when he fights," Hodges intoned.

Splurge was puzzled. He found it difficult to believe that Broga would not want to use something more destructive. Immediately his mind raced over a number of horrific possibilities, including knives, guns and bombs. "Magic tricks?" he asked in surprise.

The two Quargs were silent and just stared at him, their large round eyes betraying nothing.

"Well, maybe I can manage a bit of magic," said Splurge, not only reassured, but also feeling more confident than he had for some time. Already he was anticipating the prospect of getting out of this place. Finding a successor should not be too difficult. He would just appoint one of the Quargs, Hodges or Wilkins. With Broga gone, they should manage well enough. He clapped his hands in delight, causing the three Quargs to flinch at the suddenness of the sound. "Right. Let's get organised." He strode across to the tables and examined the various objects laid for his use. There were a few strange ones he hadn't seen before, such as a ball of string, or something similar, which unravelled itself and then began to pirouette like a dancer, before rolling itself back into a ball. He wished he had more time to discover the magical properties of all these objects, but he had to concentrate on the forthcoming encounter with Broga. He wasn't particularly worried, however, as that feeling of confidence was growing. It was odd, he thought, that he could now actually look forward to the approaching battle.

He turned to the three Quargs, who had stood motionless, as though awaiting further orders. Splurge grinned. "Are you sure that you are not robots?" he couldn't help asking. Somehow the idea amused him, though he didn't know why it should. He felt totally different about everything in this strange little theatre, including the Quargs. He could even forgive Mysterio for leaving him in the lurch like this. Then it struck him.

"The cape and the hat!" he exclaimed.

He took the hat from his head and examined it. It was not at all like the shabby one, which housed the Gromilly, Jonesy. This one was so brand new and glossy. He couldn't really see Mysterio wearing anything but the newest and the best. Then the idea crept into his head that Mysterio had somehow put a sort of magic into these items, something of himself very likely. "That's what it is," he murmured. "It's this cape and hat." He wasn't sure whether he liked the idea or not, but he reasoned that he would need all the help he could get. If by giving him his cape and top hat, Mysterio had helped, Splurge wasn't going to say no. Besides, it felt good to be wearing them. At the same time he tried to remember what Mysterio had told him, but it had all become jumbled up in his head, though he had an idea that it something about magic being important. He also wondered about the gift that Kanu had bestowed on him. Whatever it was, he could only hope that it would also prove useful, and that he would recognise it. But he couldn't worry about any of that now. The most important thing on his mind at the moment was getting ready for the meeting with Broga. He glanced at the items on the tables to see if they were identical, though he could be assured that Hodges would have seen to that. Quargs, he had learned, were very thorough. It didn't really matter that much, he supposed, if the contest was only going to be the performance of magic.

"When do we start?" Splurge had turned to Hodges and Wilkins, but they were gone. "They have gone to get some tricks?" he asked Meela.

She shook her head. "No Master. They have gone because...because..." she stammered in a most un-Quarg-like manner.

"Because what?"

"Because they are afraid." Meela practically whispered the words, again most un-Quarg-like.

Splurge laughed. "Why should they be afraid? They are not fighting Broga. I am."

Meela looked down at the floor and didn't answer.

"Are you afraid, Meela?"

She nodded but would not look up at him.

"I don't understand. Broga might be better at magic than me but I know a few things now. I have learnt a lot since I arrived here. Besides, I have Kanu's gift and Mysterio's cape and hat. How can I lose?"

Meela raised her head and looked directly at Splurge. "I am afraid, Master, but I will stay with you when Broga comes."

"Then I think that you are very brave, Meela."

"I do not know what 'brave' is. I only know that I have to stay here with you."

"You don't have to," said Splurge, hoping that she would stay anyway. He was going to need some help. That was certain. Since Hodges and Wilkins had run off, there was only Meela he could turn to.

"Why are Hodges and Wilkins afraid. They must be as clever as he is, and between them, between the three of you, you should be able to do something."

Meela looked at Splurge, her large, round eyes blinking and rolling as though she would rather not answer. "Hodges and Wilkins say that Broga will defeat you and that I must stay here, so that I will go with him when you are no more."

Though Meela's words sent a momentary shiver down his back, he felt a little annoyed at the defeatist attitude of these Quargs.

"Why do they say that? I think we ought to wait until this fight is over, because I aim to give this Broga a good run for his money."

"You will not win, Master," Meela said quietly.

Splurge looked at the tiny, green Quarg and shook his head. "You must really have more faith, Meela. Nothing is lost until it is over." (He had heard some football commentator say something like that once, and he thought it would be a good thing to say now). "If you are afraid, you can always stand behind me."

"But you will not win, Master, despite Kanu's gift." Meela sounded almost tearful as she spoke, though she did not weep. Quargs were not in the habit of expressing such emotions.

"Why do you keep saying that? I know that Quargs cannot fight other Quargs, but I thought that you could at least, give me some support."

"You will not win, Master because..." and her face became a duller shade of emerald. "You will not win because Broga will use forbidden magic."

"Forbidden magic?" echoed Splurge. "What is 'forbidden magic'? If you can tell me quickly what it is, then at least it will not come as a surprise and I might be able to prepare for it."

Chapter Twenty Two - Forbidden Magic

Meela shook her head. "You cannot prepare. Forbidden magic is in the mind of Broga, or whoever may use it."

"So it has been used before then?"

"I do not know. There is no Quarg who has a memory of such a thing. Maybe the High Factor knows, but forbidden magic was banished centuries ago. It nearly destroyed the Quargs, but Broga doesn't care. Mysterio stopped him from using the magic. But Mysterio is now gone, and there is no-one to stop Broga."

"Hmph. I thought that I was the new Master. If I am, then I must have the same power over Broga." He looked enquiringly at Meela, expecting her to agree with him.

However, she gave no indication that what he said was true. She just blinked her eyes.

It was a fine time thought Splurge, to suddenly be told, that although he was the Master, he didn't really have any power at all. "What about Hodges and Wilkins? Would they know about the forbidden magic?"

"I do not know, Master. I will ask them but it will be no good, because Broga doesn't care. I will fetch Hodges and Wilkins. You can ask them yourself about the forbidden magic. She turned towards the darkened rear of the stage and was gone.

Splurge wondered why she had disappeared like that when she could easily have summoned the other two Quargs by means of her telepathic powers, which Quargs were always doing he had noticed.

He sighed. Another problem for him to cope with, and for a moment felt a twinge of anxiety. The news of this forbidden magic had somehow sapped all the newfound confidence from him. He wondered if there really was such a thing, then he remembered that Mysterio had mentioned something about it. Why 'forbidden', he wondered and the thought began to gnaw at him. Magic was magic and anything was possible, so it would be pretty difficult to prevent so-called forbidden magic. He was saved the trouble of trying to work out what such a thing might entail, by the return of the three Quargs.

"The Master is asking the green one about forbidden magic?" Hodges made the question sound like an accusation, as though Splurge shouldn't have asked about such a thing.

Splurge was annoyed with Hodges, who was always saying what couldn't be done and never offered any encouragement. Nor did he much like the way that Hodges always referred to Meela as the 'green one'. Very rude, he thought.

"What about the forbidden magic? What is it - exactly?" Splurge adopted his best Master voice and tone, and tried to sound as much like Mysterio as possible. He wasn't going to be put off with evasions. Quargs seemed to have a habit of not answering direct questions. Not this time, however, and if necessary, he would shout and yell till he got one. He knew that such behaviour frightened the Quargs.

Hodges and Wilkins looked at each other as though to make up their minds whether an outworlder like Splurge was worthy of their confidence.

Although they betrayed no emotion in their faces, Splurge could sense that they did not trust him with such important information. Their attitude irritated him. "Im fighting Broga for you!" he suddenly yelled, stamping his foot at the same time. "TELL ME WHAT YOU KNOW ABOUT FORBIDDEN MAGIC!"

The three Quargs jumped back at the sound of Splurge's voice and Meela covered her ears. Then all three suddenly dropped to the floor and began to writhe about and twitch like stricken, giant insects.

Splurge couldn't believe his eyes. He hadn't realised how effective his use of shouting could be, and he hoped that he hadn't overdone it.

"Ha! Ha! Ha!"

The sound of harsh laughter from the other side of the curtains, somewhere in the theatre could mean only one thing.

Broga was here.

Splurge was about to have his first taste of forbidden magic, armed only with Mysterio's cape and top hat, and the mysterious gift, which Kanu had bestowed upon him.

Chapter Twenty Three – Splurge's Challenge

With a sudden swish, the curtains flew open and there, as expected, was Broga. This time, however, he was not alone.

Every seat in the tiny theatre was filled. Even the gangways were crowded with Quargs, but Quargs the like of which, Splurge could never have imagined. At first sight, they looked like skeletons, except they had bulbous heads and bulging eyes. He also noticed that they were of a variety of dirty looking colours, which he managed to identify as brown, yellow, red and purple. They were definitely much smaller than the average Quarg. Broga himself stood at least a head taller than the tallest of them. Like Broga, they appeared to be covered in sores and boils, which gave these creatures a most hideous appearance. Their clothes were ragged and as dirty as they themselves were. Splurge reckoned that they would have made good scarecrows. They certainly gave him the shivers.

Such was Broga's army, and this time it looked as though the warty, purple Quarg meant business.

Splurge could only gape at the crowd before him, and his heart sank, as he understood why the Quargs were afraid. He could see no way that he could tackle Broga and his repulsive followers, without getting seriously hurt. The only thing to do at the moment was to put on a brave face and try to bluff his way out. Though there seemed little likelihood of that.

"Where is he?" screeched Broga, as he strutted up to the stage. "Where is Mysterio? Is he afraid to meet me?" He gave another harsh, screeching laugh, and the crowd behind him cackled in chorus.

Splurge, his heart now beating wildly, felt that he ought to do or say something, if only to give himself time to think. He glanced briefly at the three Quargs, who had stopped writhing and were now quivering on the floor. They would be no use to him. He was completely on his own.

"Mysterio is gone to the outworld. He will not return," said Splurge, in what he thought was his best authoritative voice.

Broga and his minions just looked baffled for a moment, and then burst into a frenzy of wild laughter.

"I am the new Master," proclaimed Splurge, with as much pomp as he could muster.

Broga pointed a long, scabby finger at Splurge. "You, the new Master? Don't make me laugh – but you do make me laugh. I can't help it." Broga began to make a sound like someone choking. "You the Master?" he repeated and unable to contain himself any longer, he burst into another bout of raucous laughter, which again was echoed by the discordant cackle of his followers.

Splurge was not to be put off, however, and had decided that he wasn't going to let Broga win the war of words. He knew he could, at least, match him in that. He strode to the centre of the stage, folded his arms and glared at Broga.

"If you don't stop that noise," he said in as loud a voice as his nervousness would permit, "I shall have to silence you, as I did before. And I shall make it permanent." As he spoke, he raised his right arm in an appropriate threatening gesture.

Broga ceased his laughter and glared back at Splurge. He was on the point of making some sort of gesture himself, but changed his mind. "You are not the Master, despite what the miserable Quargs tell you. Mysterio was the only Master, and not much of one at that." With a sudden bound, which took Splurge by surprise, Broga had leapt onto the stage.

Splurge had never thought of Broga as possessing such a degree of agility. He had always seemed too ungainly in his movements whenever they had met on previous occasions, but despite his appearance, he was still a Quarg, and Quargs, he had discovered, were capable of surprising feats.

Broga strode up to Splurge and pointed a long, crooked finger at him, a finger Splurge noted, that was scabbier than before. His face also seemed to have sprouted more boils, all of which looked to be on the verge of bursting open.

For this reason, Splurge took a step backward, as he didn't fancy being in the path of anything that might explode from Broga's face.

"I warned you," Broga snarled at him, "and you have not heeded my warning." He looked at the cowering figures of Hodges, Wilkins and Meela. "They will have to pay."

"You won't take Meela. Not if I can help it." Splurge sounded confident but inside he was shaking.

Broga permitted himself a short, throaty chuckle. "I no longer want the green one. I no longer want any of them. I already have enough." He turned to the crowded auditorium and waved his arm.

Immediately there was a renewal of the hideous, cackling, silenced only when Broga turned back to

Splurge. "You see, with Mysterio gone, I can now do as I like, and you haven't yet seen what I can do. There is no one to stop me. You," he sneered, "will present no problem."

Splurge didn't like the way Broga said that, and while it was still a war of words, he was determined to regain the initiative.

"It seems, Broga, that whatever you think you are going to do, you will still have to get past me first." Splurge knew it was a bold statement, but he had to get Broga off his guard. He also had an uncomfortable feeling that what Broga planned for the Quargs wasn't going to be very pleasant.

Broga gave another sneering laugh. "Ha! You will not stop me, outworlder. No one will stop me now."

This was the moment, thought Splurge, to do something unexpected. "I challenge you, Broga, to single combat." (He had read about such things in the olden days, and he had seen all the films). "Of course, if you are afraid to accept my challenge, I shall understand. After all, it is not every day that you can cross swords with the Master, with only a slight chance of winning." As he spoke he indicated the array of gadgets on the tables.

Splurge wondered if he had said too much. He didn't want Broga to lose his temper and start making magic that he couldn't possibly match. It was necessary to keep it simple. In that way he had some chance.

Broga rolled his eyes and licked his warty lips. "This will be easy," he sniggered. He then walked up to the tables and began to pore over the various magical items arrayed. "You expect to fight me using these toys?" He shook his head and gave another laugh. "I propose something much more exciting and worthy of a battle between us. Not that it will be much of a battle."

Splurge reckoned that he had gone too far, for he had hoped that he could lure Broga into making it a contest of magical tricks. At least, that way, he would have had some chance, especially if the Quargs decided to help him. However, it looked as though Broga had something quite different in mind. It made him nervous just to think about it, even though he didn't know what it involved. There was only one way to find out. He would have to put a bold face on it, and brazen it out with Broga.

"Do your worst, Broga. I'm not afraid you or your..." He paused and waved at the cackling, jabbering throng who were eagerly awaiting their master's performance.

"Querks," Broga cut in, with another sneer. "I don't suppose you have seen their like before. Well, you are going to see plenty of them from now on."

Suddenly there was a bright flash followed immediately by an explosion of orange smoke. When the smoke had cleared, Splurge could see that there were now a dozen or so of these Querks on the stage, all prancing about Broga, and making horrible chirruping sounds. At closer quarters, their appearance was even more revolting. If Splurge had thought that Broga was ugly, with his blotchy skin and disgusting protuberances, he was even more sickened at the appearance of these cavorting Querks. What he thought to be sores were in fact patches of inflamed skin, which heaved and throbbed with an independent life of their own. Their bulging eyes and oddly shaped heads, gave him the impression of some sort of deformed goblins. He had seen enough pictures in books to make a fairly close comparison. They were ugly creatures and no two were alike, some having the red blotches on their bald heads, others having larger heads than others. But it was their eyes which repulsed him the most, much larger than the Quargs, they rolled around in their heads like marbles in a jar. There were enough similarities, however, to make Splurge wonder if once they used to look like Quargs.

One of them came up close to Splurge and he stepped backwards as long, wrinkled, bony fingers began pointing and probing him. He shuddered at the touch but he wanted to show no weakness in front of these creatures Soon the inquisitive Querk was joined by two or three of his equally repulsive companions.

This was too much for Splurge, and with a violent sweep of his arms, he hurled them away, sending them flying all over the stage. "Get away!" he shouted. His voice reverberated loud in the small theatre, just as Mysterio's had done. It didn't make the stage tremble, however, but it was enough for Splurge to realise that Mysterio had left him with another useful weapon – or maybe it was all part of wearing his hat and cape. It didn't matter which, as far as Splurge was concerned. He was just glad that it happened, because immediately the Querks ran to Broga and grouped themselves around him like a pack of frightened hounds around their master. Even Broga himself looked a little perturbed.

"I see you've learned another of Mysterio's tricks," said Broga, his eyes narrowing as he surveyed Splurge with a mixture of loathing and caution. "It matters very little what you have learned because I have special powers that not even Mysyterio himself dare use." He came up close to Splurge and leered. "But I dare," he hissed. "And you will see the futility of opposing me." He cackled and turned to his group of Querks on the stage. "Fetch me the Qualigor."

The Querks scuttled from the stage to do their master's bidding and returned at once with a large book, which Broga placed on a lectern, which had mysteriously appeared in front of him.

Splurge was puzzled. Broga couldn't have the Qualigor. That was the book of the Quargs, in which his own name was written. It was too well protected for Broga to be able to get hold of it. Then he realised that this book wasn't the Qualigor, though it resembled the one he had seen in Kanu's place. Once opened, Splurge could see that the pages were of a murky green hue. This Qualigor was obviously some kind of twin of the other, and he wondered what other differences there might be apart from the colour of the pages. He had an uneasy feeling that this book was going to be the opposite of the one in the possession of the Quargs, and he was reminded of a film he had seen once on late night television. It had been about black magic. Perhaps that's what the Quargs meant when they spoke of forbidden magic. Splurge knew that he had no answer to all that weird stuff.

As Broga turned page after page, he would occasionally pause and mutter to himself, at the same time casting malevolent glances at Splurge. The Querks surrounding him were making all sorts of strange faces and gestures, though they still feared to venture from the lectern.

The Querks no longer worried Splurge, now that he had discovered how to render them impotent. He also noticed that those in the auditorium were not so noisy and their cackle was more infrequent and that was mostly muted. Even so, Splurge felt distinctly uncomfortable watching Broga turn the pages as though he were the subject of some diabolic recipe, a bit like the way a turkey must feel before Christmas, he supposed.

With a loud snap, which startled the Querks around the lectern, Broga closed the book and handed it to one of them. "Keep it close. I may need it again, though I somehow doubt it." Once more he walked up to Splurge.

"So you want a contest do you? I accept your pathetic challenge, outworlder. I think you are forgetting that I have already declared my intention of crushing you and your miserable Quarg friends." He walked towards Hodges, Wilkins and Meela, who had not moved since Broga appeared. "I will destroy you and all your kind," he said, his eyes shining with demonic anticipation.

The three Quargs showed no emotion at Broga's threat, but it was noticeable Hodges and Wilkins had turned a slightly paler shade of blue. Meela, on the other hand, showed no sign that she was cowed by Broga's words, and even made a comment of her own. "The Master will defeat you, and all your Querks," she said.

Broga ignored her and returned to Splurge. He smiled, although it was difficult to tell the difference between his smile and scowl. To Splurge he always seemed to be scowling. "So let me challenge you," he said mockingly, "and I will give you a lesson in real magic."

"From that book, I suppose," Splurge muttered aloud.

"The book has nothing to do with my magic," Broga snarled. As if to prove the point, he indicated the nearest table and immediately an object flew towards Splurge, which would have struck him full in the face, had he not ducked. As it was, it still caught him a glancing blow on the side of the head, causing him to stagger.

Splurge was slightly dazed by the effects of the blow and rubbed his head, only to discover that he was bleeding. On the floor lay a heavy metal frying pan.

Broga thought it was funny and gave one of his grating laughs, to be imitated by the group of Querks around him. The audience also thought it was funny, and discordant cheers and catcalls resounded throughout the theatre.

"I think I shall try that again," said Brogal, with a malevolent leer.

Though it had not been a bad cut, just enough to break the skin, Splurge could see that Broga meant to do him some real physical harm. This was going to be no contest of magical skill. Broga was out to hurt him, maybe even kill him. The idea had not entered his head before and he suddenly felt scared. What would be the best way to protect himself, he wondered? Or maybe he should go on the attack – but how? He feverishly looked about the stage. Broga was closer to the tables so he couldn't get at any of the gadgets, which might help him. He thought of making a quick dash for it. But what was the point? There were too many of them and they would soon catch him. And what about the Quargs? He looked at Hodges and Wilkins, who seemed rooted to the spot, either unwilling or unable to help him. However, when the frying pan struck Splurge, Meela did provide a cloth for him to mop his bleeding. But he guessed that was about all the help he was going to get from the Quargs.

Broga, not allowing Splurge to recover, began to hurl an assortment of objects through the air at him. Some were not so bad, like the boxes and balls, but amongst them was the occasional heavy object, which caused him to grunt with pain when it struck him.

All of Splurge's resolve to stand up to Broga began to weaken under this onslaught and he found himself ducking and weaving about, in a most undignified manner. Not at all like the Master should do. Splurge hadn't noticed, but Meela suddenly ran off and returned at once and handed him something. Without thinking, Splurge took it from her and would not have bothered to look at it, so intent was he on trying to avoid some serious injury from all the flying objects. It was only when a sharp, rasping voice sounded nearby, that he realised that Meela had given him the old, battered top hat.

"Tell him to stop," Jonesy's voice called out from within its depths.

Splurge wasn't sure that he had heard correctly. It was somewhat tricky trying to listen to a voice in a hat, while at the same time trying to dodge all manner of missiles. A loud clang on the floor caused him to jump back. Another frying pan had come hurtling at him, and missed only by a few inches. Broga was now starting on the other table. (Both tables had identical objects on the assumption that it would be a fair fight).

"What did you say?" Splurge shouted into the hat.

"Tell him to stop," Jonesy repeated.

Splurge couldn't see that such advice was going to help much. It would be like telling a volcano to stop spouting lava. Nevertheless, he would give it a try, in between fending off the less lethal objects, which were still flying through the air in an endless stream. At the same time he would keep a sharp look out for anything that looked really dangerous.

"Stop!" he shouted.

Nothing happened except that Splurge took another whack on the side of the head. Not as heavy as the frying pan, but he could feel something trickling down his face and into his mouth. He was bleeding again.

"Say it louder, and as if you meant it," snapped the voice from inside the hat.

Splurge might have taken exception to the way that Jonesy always spoke to him, if he had not been in such a desperate situation. Risking receiving further blows, he stopped weaving about and shouted as loud as he could.

"STOP!"

The effect was remarkable. It was more than remarkable. It was magical. Splurge couldn't believe what he saw.

Suspended in mid-air, were a dozen or so objects, stretching like a string back to the table from which they set out. Not only were they frozen in space, like a still photograph, but also Broga himself was caught in the act of waving his arm, with an evil grin fixed on his face. His gang around him were also transfixed in a variety of grotesque poses, which made them look like cathedral gargoyles.

Splurge was not only relieved that he had thwarted Broga, but was pleasantly surprised that he had managed to perform some sort of magic.

Meela tugged his arm. "Master, you will now defeat Broga. But you must act quickly because he will soon find a way out of the puzzle."

Splurge was pleased with what he had achieved but he remembered that Broga had broken out of a similar situation before. "How long will he stay like that?"

"As long as you can hold the thought, Master. But it is difficult to keep such magic happening for a long time. It will soon wear off." Meela sounded downhearted as she spoke but didn't show it in her face.

Splurge came to a quick decision. "Meela, collect all the objects and take them back to the workshop. Hodges and Wilkins will help you."

It was strange to see her pick the different objects out of the air and hand them to a group of Quargs, who had suddenly appeared on the stage. In no time, everything had been taken away, including those, which had been thrown at Splurge.

While the Quargs were getting rid of the magical contraptions, and Broga and his gang were still immobile, Splurge took a few minutes to examine his cuts and bruises. He felt sore in the places where objects had struck him, but nothing serious as far as he could make out. The cuts on his face and head had stopped bleeding, but the bumps were still painful, though it could have been worse. Already, that renegade Quarg had a lot to answer for. He walked up to Broga, stuck like a fly in a spider's web. With mouth agape and his misshapen limbs sticking out like the sails of a broken windmill, he looked anything but dangerous. His henchmen, grouped around him, all twisted and contorted into grotesque attitudes, like withered trees, also seemed harmless enough. He was surprised when he looked out at the audience and noted that they were also stricken in the same way. How long would they stay like that, Splurge wondered? He also wondered how he had managed to stop them. Had it been the High Factor's gift or was it the wearing of Mysterio's cape and hat? It was also something of a mystery how the hat hadn't been knocked of his head considering the number of objects that had been thrown at him. But still the immediate question was how long Broga and his followers would remain frozen?

Round one to Splurge.

What was he to do next? Splurge was fully aware that Broga would not be caught like that again. He could imagine that he would do something equally, if not more unpleasant. He now realised that Broga did not care about magic in the same way as did the Quargs. To him it was a weapon to create havoc and misery.

Though Splurge had learned that he had at least one weapon to protect himself and the Quargs, he was still very much concerned about that forbidden magic. When would Broga use it and what form would it take? He was sure that this ugly, purple Quarg would soon tire of throwing things, and resort to something much nastier.

Again, a whole range of thoughts ran through his head, as he tried to anticipate the sort of thing that Broga might do. He had to give it up as he realised the possibilities were endless. If only he could get the Quargs to help him but he wasn't too hopeful. He had seen how helpless Hodges and Wilkins had been in the face of Broga's antics. They would likely run away if anything more dangerous occurred. Meela might still help him, of course. And then there was Jonesy, though what a Gromilly, who resided in a battered top hat could do, Splurge couldn't imagine. Nevertheless, he had given him some good advice. That was an idea. Perhaps he ought to ask Jonesy about the forbidden magic and get him to explain exactly what it was.

"Meel..." Before he could complete her name the tiny green Quarg was standing before him. At first, he wondered if she had read his mind, then he remembered what Mysterio had said about sending thoughts to others. Maybe he had inherited the gift, along with the hat and cape. He couldn't be sure, but he would try again later, on Hodges or Wilkins.

"Meela, do you have..?" Again before he could finish, she had held out the hat for him. He murmured a 'thank you' and gave her a small bow. He did not know why he did that, except that it seemed the right thing to do. That was Mysterio's doing, he was sure of it. While wearing his top hat and cape, he would undoubtedly take on some of Mysterio's habits.

Meela flickered her eyes and Splurge was certain that she turned a slighlty brighter shade of emerald. "Jonesy is not there," she said, as Splurge was about to peer into the hat.

Nevertheless, Splurge did look into the hat. It appeared to be empty and to make sure, he turned it upside down. "Where has he gone?" He asked the question in exasperation, rather than actually wanting an answer. "He seems to have a sixth sense when I want some important information. I shouldn't be surprised if he doesn't know and it his way of avoiding awkward questions."

"What is 'sixth sense', Master?" asked Meela, as she took the hat back from Splurge.

Splurge shrugged his shoulders. "It is difficult to explain. It's like knowing a thing without any proof that it is there – I think." It was the best explanation he could offer at the moment because his mind was focussed on his present predicament. He didn't really have time for answering questions. It was his questions, which needed answers. What would Broga do next? That was the most important one.

But Splurge received his answer rather more quickly than he had anticipated. A loud explosion, accompanied by a flash of blue light, and suddenly the stage was enveloped in a foul-smelling black smoke.

Broga had broken free!

Chapter Twenty Four – Jonesy's Advice

When the smoke had dispersed, there was no sign of Broga or his followers. The entire theatre was empty, except for Splurge and the Quargs on the stage.

Splurge was under no illusion that Broga would be back, and would probably come along prepared to use every dirty trick he had at his disposal. That was what worried Splurge. What sort of tricks would he come up with next time? The idea of forbidden magic kept running through his mind. In some strange way, Splurge wished he would use it, then at least he would know what it was exactly. He turned once more to the faithful Meela.

"Tell me, Meela, what is the forbidden magic? I must know if I am to have any chance of fighting it."

Meela stared up at Splurge, her large, round eyes betraying nothing. "I do not know, Master," she said quietly. "Ask Jonesy again." She held the old, battered top hat out to Splurge. "He might give you an answer this time."

The way that she spoke made Splurge think that perhaps she knew more about Jonesy's habits than she had confided. He had noticed that she was always popping up with the hat whenever he had a problem. As he took the hat, he murmured his thanks and gave her a small bow. This bowing business was getting to be a habit, he decided and he wondered if he would ignore it when he took off Mysterio's hat and cape.

He peered into the hat, and sure enough, two bright pinpoints were peering back at him from its depths. This was always unnerving to Splurge, a bit like looking at a giant tarantula lodged there, except that he could never distinguish anything other than Jonesy's eyes.

"Well?" rasped Jonesy. "I see you managed well enough, so what do you want now? I can't be spending all of my time answering your questions, and getting you out of trouble."

Splurge had become used to Jonesy's tone by now, although he was often tempted to reply in the same manner. But he didn't have time to banter with him. "What is the forbidden magic? I must know before Broga returns."

"Don't want much, do you?" Jonesy grunted. Then for a while there was silence and Splurge thought that he had forgotten or gone back to sleep. He gave the hat a slight shake.

"Alright! Alright!" Jonesy's voice grated. "I'm thinking. It's a complicated question and the answer is equally complicated. I must give it some thought."

Splurge wished he would hurry up. Already he was becoming nervous and could sense that Broga's return would be imminent, by the pricking on the back of his neck. He quickly looked around the stage and out into the theatre. There was no-one there, but he sensed that something was not quite right. Then the curtains shook slightly and he felt a distinct draught. He shivered.

"Forbidden magic is magic which is forbidden," the voice from the battered hat said at length.

Splurged sighed with annoyance. "I know that. I want to know what it is," becoming irritated at Jonesy's obtuseness.

"I'm coming to that," Jonesy snarled. "Forbidden magic is the kind that does not create. It merely destroys. It can be anything, depending on the user and the person upon which it used, and it can be mental, physical, psychological or even emotional."

The hat gave a slight shudder and for a moment Splurge thought that Jonesy had finished. "Is that all there is? It doesn't tell me much." A waste of time, he thought.

"Don't be so impatient. I'm coming to the important part and I want you to take careful note of what I tell you, because it cannot be repeated."

Splurge waited. He could still feel that pricking down his spine. Broga definitely must be around somewhere.

"Forbidden magic is the magic you fear most – not only to receive but to perform. It can destroy the user as easily as those it is used against. It is your own fear that you will fear most of all. There! Now you know." The eyes disappeared and the hat trembled slightly.

Once again Splurge was nonplussed. He had been hoping, and expecting, that Jonesy would have come up with a better explanation than that. It didn't make sense. He shivered again as he felt a draught and he noticed that the curtains were moving. The pricking sensation had also returned. Broga must be back, he thought and hiding somewhere. Yet the stage was empty, with just himself and Meela. The other Quargs had disappeared. He pointed to the curtains. "Did you see that?" he whispered.

Meela said nothing but walked towards one side of the stage and then the other. "There is nothing there, Master. If it is Broga you are expecting, he has not yet arrived. I will know when he is here."

"Aren't you afraid, Meela?" said Splurge in a low voice, fearing that he may be overheard.

Meela shook her head. "You are the Master. You will defeat Broga."

"You keep saying that, but I still haven't a clue how I'm going to do it."

Without warning the curtains suddenly closed, making Splurge jump in alarm. "Wh... who did that?" he stammered. He looked at Meela, thinking that it might have been one of her magical tricks, but she just stared at him as though she hadn't heard the question.

Splurge took her silence to mean that it wasn't she who had closed the curtains. He shivered. There was that draught again.

"He's here. I know it. Playing games."

Splurge had no sooner spoken, than the two tables, which had not yet been taken away by the Quargs, began to rock about as though invisible hands were moving them.

"You'll have to do better than that, Broga," Splurge called out and his voice echoed around the stage getting fainter at each echo till it faded altogether. There was no doubt in his mind that Broga was about somewhere and trying new tactics.

"What next, Master?" Hodges and Wilkins had returned and both waited at attention, like troops awaiting further orders.

"I... er... don't know," said Splurge absently and started to look around the stage, and then peering through the curtains to see if anyone was in the theatre. Noone. The lights were still on but all the seats were empty.

Suddenly all the lights went out, including those on the stage. Everything was in pitch darkness. Splurge could feel that draught again. "Why are the lights out? What's happened to the lights?" he shouted. He was puzzled, annoyed and scared all at the same time. "Are you there, Meela? Hodges? Wilkins?"

There was no reply. Now Splurge was really becoming scared. He couldn't think of a worse predicament, alone in the dark, in a place he didn't want to be, with a mad Quarg on the loose and intent on destroying him. He was sure that it would come down to a battle of magical skills. Broga was out to finish him one way or another.

The something touched him!

It was a light touch, like some insect. Splurge immediately thought of spiders. He hated spiders, and began to imagine hordes of them creeping out of cracks in the walls, and the floorboards. He was sure that he could hear them rustling, and creeping towards him, big and hairy, with gleaming eyes and champing jaws. They were huge, he was sure of it. The fact that he couldn't see anything made it worse, for his imagination was now racing.

"Where is everybody?" he called out.

Splurge took a couple of tentative steps, but didn't dare to go too far in case he fell off the edge of the stage. Holding his hands before him, trying to feel his way like a blind man, he felt something soft and furry. "Ow!" he yelled in alarm and jumped back, till he realised that it was only the curtain his hand had brushed. He reached out again to make sure, running his hand down the length of the curtain till he touched the floor. At least he knew where the edge of the stage was. All he had to do was to walk in the opposite direction. Slowly he walked towards where he judged the back of the stage to be, trying at the same time to remember if there had been anything else on the stage at the moment the lights went out. He felt sure that there was nothing and he was a little more confident. If he could reach the back wall, he might be able to feel his way to the Quarg workshop. There was bound to be someone there. Quargs were always working.

The silence was eerie, and together with the darkness, and those spiders, Splurge could hardly walk a straight line, he was trembling so much. He hadn't felt this scared, since he felt out of his bedroom window once. He believed that he had been pushed, though he was alone in his room at the time. It was strange that he should remember that episode now. He had never thought about it before. In fact he....

His thoughts were suddenly swamped by the sound of a footstep. At least, he thought it was a footstep, somewhere in front of him. Fresh fears and fancies began to overtake him.

"Who's there?" he called out.

There was no reply.

Maybe it wasn't a footstep after all. Then his mind began to take off once more as he began to conjure up all sorts of possibilities. A one-legged spider definitely didn't make sense, though he wouldn't put anything past Broga. Perhaps something had fallen. But what, and from where? The stage had been completely empty when the lights went out. It must be someone stalking him. The thought frightened him but he was consoled by the fact that, whoever or whatever it was, would have some difficulty because it was pitch black, with not even a hint of light. On the other hand, it could be some sort of creature, which could see in the dark, or had some other means of finding its way about, like bats. He wished he hadn't thought of that because now he could imagine them flying about his head and swooping down on him, to bite and suck his blood.

The momentary panic at this thought was soon dispelled, when his common sense came to the rescue and told him that bats had not yet learned to make a solid footstep.

Clunk! Clunk! There it was again! There was definitely somebody out there in the darkness. "Who is it?" he yelled, at the same time frantically waving his arms about, trying to catch whoever it was in front of him. He didn't care who it was as long as it was somebody solid. Splurge was becoming really scared. Anybody, even Broga, would be a relief.

Clunk! Clunk! There was the sound of footsteps again, but no nearer. Perhaps they weren't footsteps but something else. Once more, his imagination began to work overtime, trying to put a form to these sounds. He wasn't sure whether to move towards them, or let them come to him. Convinced that, whatever it was, would sooner or later find him, he thought that it might be better to wait, rather than go stumbling into the blackness. At the same time, he wondered what had happened to the Quargs. Had Broga conjured up this blackness to ensnare him and keep him here while he went after the Quargs?

"Meela! Hodges! Wilkins!" Splurge called their names out one at a time, but there was no reply. "Where is everybody?"

There was still no reply.

His voice seemed to be swallowed up by the darkness. "Come on somebody. I know it's you, Broga, so you can stop playing these silly games." Splurge tried to sound bold, but his fear was greater than his anger, and his voice wavered.

He was pretty certain that it was Broga causing all this trouble, but it wasn't like that renegade Quarg not to strut and show how clever he was. But what if it wasn't Broga? Maybe it was something else – something worse.

The images of spiders and other creatures began to invade his thoughts again.

"What was that?" he suddenly yelled, as he definitely felt something brush his face. Desperately waving his arms about, he tried to swat away whatever had touched him, but he felt nothing as he flailed the empty air. He was now really scared and could feel his heart thumping loudly. The only thing to do was to get out of this place as quickly as possible. He walked a few stumbling paces, anticipating at any moment that he would bump into something, which he did. But it was not what he expected. Something soft, smooth and slightly furry had wrapped itself around him and he found himself struggling with an unknown monster.

Splurge had never been so terrified and could feel himself being smothered and finding it difficult to breathe. He tried to fight back and delivered blows in all directions, relying more on luck than anything else that he might get this thing to relax its grip on him. But there was nothing solid and, after a while, he was too exhausted to continue. As he paused, he felt the thing loose its grip. Strange, he thought, but it did seem as though the creature, if it was a creature, had suddenly gone. He was only partly relieved, because, not being able to see anything in this darkness, he suspected that the thing was lurking somewhere close by waiting to pounce again. So he waited, ready to do battle again.

Maybe, in some fashion he had hurt this thing, though he didn't see how. It didn't seem to have a solid body and offered no real resistance, so he reckoned it couldn't have been because of his own efforts to free himself from its clutches. He decided that he would wait a while to see if it resumed its attack. The silence and the darkness were closing in on him, threatening to smother him. The only sound was his own heavy breathing and the wild thumping of his heart.

As the seconds passed and became minutes, Splurge began to relax once more. Whatever that thing was, seemed to have given up. Perhaps now was the time to make a determined effort to get to the back of the stage and find a door to somewhere. Anywhere would do at the moment. So he stumbled forward, feeling his way as best he could. He slid each foot slowly along the wooden boards, the scuffing noise sounding loud. At the same time, he reached out with his hands, hoping he might feel something solid that he could use as a guide.

Then he heard another noise.

This time it was not the heavy sound of footsteps, but something much lighter and more rapid.

"Who's there?" he called out, feeling a shiver run down his spine.

Broga had sent something else, he was sure of it.

Then the lights came on.

"You called, Master?"

Splurge stared in surprise. He had been certain that he was walking towards the rear of the stage, but now he could see, he discovered that he was only a couple of feet away from the edge. He realised, that in the darkness, he had totally lost his sense of direction. A few more steps and he would have tumbled through the curtains and onto the floor of the theatre and probably broken something.

Then it dawned on him. The curtains! That was the mysterious creature, which had wrapped itself around him. He reached out and touched them, feeling the soft, fur-like material brush his fingers He would have laughed at his own stupidity had he not felt an enormous sense of relief.

"What happened to the lights? Where have you been? Didn't you hear me call? And where is Broga?" Splurge fired off his questions with such speed, that the tiny, green Quarg could only blink.

"Master, you ask many questions, but I cannot give you any answers. The lights are as they have always been. I did hear you call, and I have been here beside you. And Broga is not here." Meela answered the questions one by one in the cool manner of the Quargs, without emphasis or emotion.

Splurge was bewildered. He didn't believe that Quargs would lie just to fool him. If he had learned anything about these tiny people, it was that they did not waste their words on saying something, which was not true. That being the case, he could only assume that something must have happened to him. He tried to work it out in his mind. Perhaps there had been some sort of time slip.(He had heard of such things from watching science fiction stories on television). If that was the case, then another question came into his head. Why just him and what was the purpose?

He couldn't help thinking that Broga was somehow behind it all, but then something like time was not part of the special world of the Quargs. They depended upon magical contrivances. What had happened to him was entirely different and a little spooky. It made him shudder to think about his experience of stumbling around in the dark, on his own, and beset by all sorts of dangers, real and imagined. He sometimes wished that he didn't have such a vivid imagination.

Then like a flash of lightning it struck him.

"Forbidden magic!" he exclaimed aloud, causing Meela to jump back in alarm.

"Don't you see? What Jonesy said made sense. Forbidden magic can be anything. 'It is your own fear that you must fear most of all'" He repeated Jonesy's words, beginning at last to understand what had happened to him. His own imagination had been turned against him and almost brought disaster. "Broga must be somewhere near." Splurge had no sooner uttered these words than there was the noise of familiar, raucous laughter from the other side of the curtains.

"Open the curtains, Meela."

Meela went to the side of the stage and made some sort of pass with her hand and immediately the curtains swished open.

There, in the centre of the theatre, sat Broga.

Splurge strode to the front of the stage and glared at the dirty, purple Quarg. "Where's your army, Broga. You wouldn't have the courage to come here without them."

Broga continued to laugh and the sound of his harsh cackle reverberated around the tiny theatre, till it reached an almost unbearable pitch.

Splurge was sorely tempted to clap his hands over his ears to shut out the sound, but resisted because he wasn't going to give Broga the satisfaction of knowing that he had annoyed him.

Broga stood up, still quietly cackling. "How did you like that, oh Master?" He made an elaborate bow, but coming from Broga, it looked more like a severe spasm in his back. "There is magic and then there is – MAGIC." He grinned as at some private joke. "I have the knowledge and can perform my 'magic' whenever I choose. Next time, it will be something different, but just as interesting." He lingered over his words and then leered at Splurge and then pointed a crooked finger. "You have a choice," he suddenly snarled. "Stand aside and I may ignore you. Interfere and I will surely destroy you – after I've had a little pleasure, at your expense, of course."

Splurge was defiant. "You can do what you like, Broga. I'm no longer interested in your magic, let alone frightened by it. Do your worst and see what happens." He waved his hand and the curtains suddenly swished closed.

Splurge hadn't really expected that to happen. He was never quite sure what the waving of a hand did. It was something different each time he did it, and he had a sneaking suspicion that Meela had arranged for the curtains to close like that. In any case, he was sure that it would annoy Broga, who was now left on the other side of them.

Now at last, he was beginning to understand what this forbidden magic was all about, and he was less apprehensive. Whether or not he could use it himself, he didn't know, but he recalled Jonesy's words about such magic rebounding on the user. It seemed to Splurge that forbidden magic was some sort of mental thing that had nothing to do with ordinary magic. It had been his own fears, which had created the darkness and led him to imagine all sorts of terrors. But why was it forbidden? Perhaps the Quargs had the kind of minds, which could not cope with it. The more he thought about it, the more he wondered how Broga had managed it.

But he didn't have time to worry about all that now. He had to prepare for the next attack, which he was certain would come – and soon. He turned to Meela, who had been waiting patiently while Splurge had tried to organise his thoughts.

"Broga will come soon, Meela, and we must prepare..." Splurge hesitated.

"Yes, Master," she said solemnly without the slightest flicker of emotion to show that she was concerned. "How shall we prepare, Master?"

"That's the trouble. I don't know." Splurge frowned. "The Quargs know Broga better than I do. What sort of magic is he likely to perform?"

"Broga is a bad Quarg. He has done many bad things and has promised many times that when Mysterio is gone, he would use the forbidden magic to make slaves of the Quargs, so that we make magic only for him." Meela slowly shook her head and it seemed to Splurge that her eyes had grown moist, as though she was about to cry. "Once, long ago," she said quietly, "some Quargs said that they did not want to be Broga's slaves. That made Broga angry and he killed those Quargs and sent their bodies into the crystal caves. You saw them."

Splurge struggled to understand. "I didn't see any dead Quargs."

"The golden insects, the Augs, were once Quargs. Broga would make us all golden insects, if he could." Meela lowered her eyes and stared at the floor.

Splurge felt genuinely sorry for her. Her explanation, bizarre though it was, did make a sort of sense. The Quargs had no knowledge of money, as he had already discovered, but maybe Broga, at least, understood that gold was important, specially in the outworld.

Then suddenly he could see the whole of Broga's plan, and only now did he realise how important it was to stop him. No longer was it a question of saving the Quargs, for a much bigger task awaited him.

Broga wanted to get into the outworld.

In the outworld, gold mattered and somehow Broga had learned that. Splurge didn't like to think of the damage that the renegade Quarg could do once he got out of the Theatre of Magic.

"It is worse than I thought, Meela. We must stop Broga in whatever way we can. I need the Quargs to be strong. We must all fight him because he is going to do something so terrible that we will all be destroyed."

"I do not understand, Master." Meela looked at Splurge. Her head was held slightly to one side, which was her way of expressing puzzlement.

"I can't explain it all to you now, but you must believe me when I say that it is important for all Quargs and those who live in the outworld."

Meela still held her head to one side and blinked her eyes.

"Can you get Hodges and Wilkins for me?" He had no sooner made his request than the two Quargs were standing before him. If he didn't know better, he would have thought that they had read his mind, but since he had been contruded, he knew that it was no longer possible. He wondered instead, if he had at last managed to convey his thoughts to them. Mysterio was able to do it and he might have inherited some of that power. But he didn't have time to ponder on it. "I need to see the High Factor, urgently. I don't think it would be a good idea to visit him myself, not with Broga lurking about. So I want you two to take a message to him."

The two Quargs said nothing but merely stared at Splurge with unblinking eyes, till at length Hodges spoke.

"There is no need for any message to be sent to the High Factor. You are the Master. You can intrude his mind."

"The High Factor can also has the power to intrude your mind," added Wilkins.

Splurge was both pleased and disconcerted. "I see," he said thoughtfully. "So we have a telepathic link. Do I have to do anything special?"

"Just make your thoughts go to him and he will answer you," said Hodges.

"Sounds simple," said Splurge, thinking that it was anything but simple. But he would give it a try.

The two Quargs watched as Splurge closed his eyes and screwed up his face in an attitude of thought and concentration. He knew what he wanted to ask Kanu and it would also be easier this way to explain about the real threat, which Broga represented. Kanu was sure to understand and appreciate its importance.

Splurge didn't know what to expect and was shaken when he heard the voice of Kanu inside his head. It was so real and clear that he must be somewhere nearby, but when he looked at the faces of the Quargs, he could tell that they had heard nothing.

'WE RECOGNISE THIS DANGER, AND THOUGH QUARGS CANNOT HARM OTHER QUARGS, THEY CAN FIGHT. I WILL INSTRUCT THEM TO FOLLOW YOUR COMMANDS. I PLACE GREAT TRUST IN YOU AND YOUR SPECIAL POWERS. LOOK AFTER MY CHILDREN WELL.'

Splurge was relieved to hear the words of the High Factor and felt a surge of confidence. Though he trusted Kanu to keep his word, he was not so sure how the rest of the Quargs would react to obeying Splurge's orders, not that he had any particular orders at the moment. He looked at the three Quargs and thought it best to get it over with now. They may not like it but they must obey the High Factor, though he couldn't see how he would communicate with them.

He needn't have worried.

It was Wilkins who spoke first. "We have been informed by the High Factor that we are to fight." His thin, piping voice sounded subdued, as though the order didn't please him.

"But not to destroy," added Hodges, who spoke more forcefully.

"You will be our Master and we shall obey your commands," said Meela, who went a deeper shade of emerald as she spoke.

Splurge understood their fears and concerns, and he hoped that he wouldn't have to call upon the Quarg community to help him. He much preferred to do battle with Broga on his own. But it was good to know that he had a second line of defence if things got out of hand. With Broga that was practically a certainty.

"I will not ask you to fight but I may need your help in other ways. We shall wait and see what Broga does."

"We shall help the Master." The three Quargs spoke in unison, sounding like a chorus.

Splurge grinned. He definitely felt a lot better, especially after that scary business with the lights and the curtains. Now he could look back and laugh at his fears, although they were real enough at the time. There was only one question, which now remained. When would Broga reappear?

His question was answered almost immediately.

A loud crash echoed around the whole theatre. The stage shuddered under the impact of something huge, which must have landed in the theatre. The reverberations resounded for a while and above the receding echoes a loud, coarse laugh was heard.

Broga was back.

Chapter Twenty Five - Broga Plays Dirty

"Stand by, here we go," muttered Splurge to the Quargs. "Let's see what surprises he has in store for us this time." He strode towards the curtains and waved an arm. Immediately, they flew open with a violent swish. He had no idea how it happened, but he felt that they would open. It was as Mysterio had said, if he wanted anything strongly enough, it would happen. After the trauma of the dark, he now had a new found confidence, and with Kanu's backing, he was certain that he could match anything Broga could do.

Broga was alone, sitting in the middle of the theatre. There was no sign of his band of followers. "So you have recovered from your experience," he sneered. "Well, I have more delights to show you, which you will find much more interesting." His face twisted in a crooked smile, causing the bumps and protuberances on his face to throb with a life of their own. At the same time he threw something at Splurge.

At first, Splurge couldn't identify what Broga had thrown till it landed. It looked like a stick and he was about to pick it up and throw it back, when the stick moved.

Suddenly, he was surrounded by Quargs. One of them picked up the stick, which twisted and writhed like a snake in the tiny hand. Then, with a loud 'pop', it exploded into a shower of coloured paper.

"Broga stole that magic from me," the Quarg muttered and returned to the group.

"Bravo! Bravo!" Broga cried out and clapped his hands. As he did so, another 'stick' flew towards the stage. Another Quarg came forward and grabbed the stick, which was making strange noises. It then divided into smaller pieces, each one writhing and twisting about on the floor.

But the Quarg was equal to the sudden change and instead of picking it up, merely stamped upon the several pieces, which with a series of popping explosions disappeared entirely.

"You are clever little Quargs," said Broga contemptuously. "How about this then?"

This time he did not throw anything but took a deep breath and blew hard.

Suddenly the stage was enveloped in a thick blue mist, which swirled and sparkled.

At first, Splurge thought it was a feeble effort, till he discovered the sparkle was caused by hundreds of tiny needles which swam around in a random manner, making it difficult for anyone on the stage to move without being severely scratched.

This time, it was Meela who came forward, and with a sweep of her tiny arms, somehow gathered up all the sparkling needles and then crushed them into a powder, which she threw at Broga. Immediately the blue mist vanished. She looked at Splurge for a moment.

He was sure that she smiled.

"Was that one of your tricks that he stole?" he said quietly.

Meela nodded. "Broga stole many things from the Quargs. That is why he thinks he is powerful and clever.

But it is only the forbidden magic that makes him powerful."

Broga didn't seem too upset that the Quargs had thwarted his magic.

"Is that the best you can do, Broga?" said Splurge. "You have to use someone else's magic. Don't you have any of your own?" Splurge further taunted.

Broga scowled and his warty face turned a dark purple. "I can see that I will have to do something special," he snarled, and rushed from his seat and out through the back of the theatre.

At first, Splurge was surprised that Broga had given up so easily, but almost immediately he had returned. With him came a horde of his followers, leaping and scrambling over seats till the theatre was completely full. Broga himself strode to the front and confronted Splurge.

"Now you will see. So far I have been indulging in games. Let me see how you manage with this one."

As he spoke he made some strangely awkward movements with his arms, which reminded Splurge of a wooden puppet. He then glared at Splurge and began to rub his hands togetheras if moulding a ball of clay. It wasn't clay – it was a ball of fire.

"Take that," he hissed. At the same time he threw the ball of fire, which travelled very slowly towards Splurge.

"Beware, Master. That is not one of our tricks," Hodges called out. "It is the forbidden magic."

There was a scuffing of tiny feet, as the rest of the Quargs retreated to the back of the stage, only Meela and Hodges remained by his side.

Splurge was shaken, but was determined not to show it. The ball of fire was getting closer and already Splurge could feel the heat. This was real and not in his imagination. Should he run or stay and bluff it out? It could destroy the whole theatre. He couldn't believe that even a twisted person like Broga would actually let such a thing happen.

The ball of fire was getting ever closer and he could feel beads of perspiration breaking out on his forehead. He turned to the Quargs whose faces now glowed orange in the light from the approaching bundle of writhing flames. He didn't want to let them down and to run would definitely show weakness.

"Tell it to stop, Master." Meela's voice was calm and steady, though it sounded a little higher than usual.

Why not? Thought Splurge. He had had some success with his new hand passes and it was about time to give them a real test. If it didn't work, he and the Quargs could still run.

"Here goes," he muttered to himself. He then held up both hands and with the loudest voice he could muster, he yelled, "STOP!"

The effect was truly magical.

The ball of fire was halted in mid-air and hovered above the edge of the stage. The heat was quite strong and for a moment he thought that the curtains might catch fire. Then he had a crazy idea. If he could stop it, maybe he could make it go back. Thinking hard, he held up both hands and yelled "GO BACK!"

At first, nothing seemed to happen, so he yelled again, even louder.

This time the effect was even more astonishing, for the ball of fire began to retreat even quicker than it had approached.

Broga stared wildly at the ball of fire as it now began to rebound back to him. His eyes rolled and he tried to scream but nothing came out of his mouth. He frantically waved his arms but no effect. Then he tried to move out of its the path, but the swirling flames just changed direction to follow him.

Splurge noticed that the ball was growing smaller as it got nearer to Broga, till with a final surge it had returned to its sender.

Broga opened his mouth wide and swallowed and the last of the fire was gone, leaving only wisps of smoke coming out his nostrils and ears. His body, almost black in colour, twisted and writhed violently as he struggled to contain the fire now inside him. For a moment it seemed as though he would erupt in flame.

Broga's followers nearest to him, quickly scrambled away, fearing that their leader was about to explode and rain fire over them.

Broga struggled to speak but could frame no words as his mouth continued to belch smoke and small tongues of flame.

Splurge was transfixed by the sight. He had not intended that Broga should be destroyed in this way but perhaps it served him right. After all, it was Broga who had started it. Splurge would have been quite content to expel the renegade Quarg, without incinerating him.

Broga's contortions became less, and soon he had managed to control the ball of fire, and his normal colour began to return. A few more minutes and he had returned to his usual state. He glared at Splurge and tried to speak, but though his mouth framed words, still no sound came out, just small puffs of smoke.

If it hadn't been so serious, Splurge would have been unable to suppress a chuckle at seeing this dirty, purple Quarg, trying hard not to open his mouth for fear of belching out more smoke.

Despite the fact that Broga appeared to be incapacitated, it would only be for a short time, and when he got himself together, Splurge was certain that he would be back with more dirty tricks - and forbidden magic.

Broga pointed at Splurge and tried to speak, but his voice was harsh and grating, and no proper words came out, just a series of throaty growls interspersed with wisps of smoke. In his frustration, he began to stamp his feet and wave his arms about, as if to conjure up more magic. Finally, with a baleful glare at Splurge and the Quargs, he made a grand sweeping gesture with his arms. With a loud crack and a flash of light, he was gone, leaving only a thick pall of black smoke above where he had been standing.

As the smoke cleared, Splurge could see that Broga's followers had also disappeared, though quite how he wasn't sure. He assumed that they had scurried away like rats, or insects, into cracks and crevices around the theatre itself. As far as he was concerned, it was good riddance. Though he was certain that Broga would return, he couldn't afford to worry about it now. He would just have to wait and see what sort of tricks Broga would get up to next time before he started making plans. He turned to the three Quargs, who had stood motionless throughout the encounter.

"Thank you for your help. I didn't know that he had stolen your magic, though I should have guessed. It's the sort of thing he would do."

"We shall continue to help the Master," said Wilkins, who had suddenly reappeared. "But we created much magic and Broga has taken what we do not use."

"Our magic will not harm you, but Broga will use it to disguise the forbidden magic," added Hodges in a subdued tone.

"You don't think that I can beat Broga, do you?"

Hodges blinked but avoided Splurge's question. "The Master now has much magic, but it may not be enough.

Now Broga has opened the Black Qualigor, he can use much forbidden magic. Magic that Quargs do not know."

For a moment, it seemed to Splurge, that Hodges actually sounded disconsolate. He repeated his question.

"You really don't think I can win, do you?"

The tiny Quarg shook his head. "Forbidden magic is too great for Quargs. It will be too great for the Master."

"Well, if it is too much for the Master, how did Mysterio manage to get it banned?"

"He didn't," Meela said. "The High Factor forbade all magic that can harm or hurt Quargs, and gave the Black Qualigor to Mysterio to keep safe. But Broga stole it."

Meela hung her head as if ashamed of what she had just said.

Splurge was not too dismayed by what the Quargs had said. He had already learned the sort of things that forbidden magic could do, and realised that Jonesy was right when he said that it could destroy the user as well as those it was used against. But did Broga know of the dangers in using such magic? He somehow doubted it.

Another thing Splurge had learned was that the Quargs were really quite afraid of Broga, and because of his use of forbidden magic, he could see them giving in before he had a chance to really fight this renegade Quarg. He couldn't afford for them to run away, which they might easily do, despite the High Factor's command. He remembered how most of them had run off the stage when Broga had hurled his fireball. What they needed was some sort of encouragement; a rallying speech like a general might give to his army. Splurge felt he was like a general. But would he be a good general? He hoped he would, because if he lost the bulk of the Quargs, then he couldn't see himself lasting too long in any battle.

"Listen to me. Quargs have great strength and great magical skill. I know my magic is only borrowed, but we outworlders possess other kinds of powers. One of them is not to be afraid. You must not be afraid. I will protect you from Broga, but I can only do that with your help. Get all the Quargs to make new magical tricks, ones, which Broga will know nothing about. You must also tell me when he is using one of the stolen tricks." He paused and looked for some reaction to what he had said but their faces remained impassive.

He wondered if they had understood him, and if they had, would they do as he asked? Their frozen looks made him think about robots again. He wished he could read their minds. Being able to contrude was a great help to him but he really needed to put his own thoughts into their heads. Without knowing how to intrude, he couldn't see how he could do it. It was now that he began to understand his teachers who must have felt what he did now – frustration.

He tried again and this time spoke only to Meela, who had always expressed a sort of sympathy with him. "Meela, do you understand what I am saying, and how important it is for us to stick together?"

Meela said nothing but stared up at him with her large, round eyes quite unblinking

Splurge felt a slight annoyance. Even if the Quargs were not robots, they were certainly acting like them – completely switched off.

He sighed and Meela came to life.

"Master is 'fed up'," she said, blinking her eyes, which she tended to do whenever she expressed any kind of feeling.

Splurge nodded. "Yes, Meela. Did you not hear what I said just now, about making new magical tricks which Broga cannot take from you?"

"Yes. We are always making new magical things. It is our job. You may use them, if you wish. I will help you like before."

"We will all help you. We have promised." Hodges suddenly spoke up. "Do not judge us by the other Quargs. They are not the clever ones. They do not know of forbidden magic, and they afraid when they see it. We know about such things so we are not afraid."

"We have promised. We will help you," intoned Wilkins, as though reciting a piece of poetry.

Splurge was a little puzzled. "I thought all Quargs were clever, but what you are saying is that only you three have any real knowledge."

"There were others but Broga took them and now they follow him," said Meela, her voice betraying no emotion, which seemed odd to Splurge. To be a traitor was about the worst thing a person could be in the outworld – his world.

"Broga is the most clever of all Quargs, that is why he took all the Quigs, so he can teach them his ways." Wilkins shuffled his feet as though he had said too much and was uncomfortable with what he had disclosed.

Splurge knew that Quargs were very secretive about their world and he remembered Mysterio telling him something about Quigs, and not to ask about them. It didn't seem to matter now that one of the Quargs had brought up the subject.

"What are Quigs?" he asked, pretending that he had never heard of them before.

The three Quargs looked at each other, none of them wanting to be the one to betray such secrets. It was finally left to Meela.

"The High Factor has commanded us to tell you of the deep secret, because it might help you to understand." She paused and looked at the other two Quargs, who showed no sign that they approved or disapproved of what Meela was about to say. Quigs are the very young ones," she said quietly. "Many years ago there was a great fight and Broga, the most powerful Quarg next to the High Factor, wanted to rule all the Quargs. But he was banished by the High Factor, and his revenge was to take many of the young ones. Quargs became afraid that he would take all the Quigs, so we have hidden them, where no-one, not even Mysterio or yourself, Master, can ever find them."

"The Quigs are our future," Hodges said solemnly. "They are important, more important than making magical things. We must guard them. That is why the other Quargs ran when they saw the forbidden magic being made."

"But don't they want to get the their children back?"

"Children? We do not know 'children', said Meela.

"Young ones. Quigs. Do you want to get them back?"

"We want those who were taken to be returned, but many Quargs are afraid that they will be destroyed - if Broga does not defeat you, Master." Meela spoke the last words so quietly that Splurge had to strain to hear them.

"Does 'not' defeat me. I do not understand"

The three Quargs were definitely uncomfortable. They looked at each other and began to shuffle their feet in a most unQuarg-like manner.

Splurge could well understand their difficulties, for the Quarg children were effectively hostages for the good behaviour of all the Quargs. He pondered for a while and it was at times like this that he could do with some advice from Mysterio, even Jonesy. "Meela? Where is the hat? I want to speak to Jonesy."

Meela blinked. "You do not need Jonesy, Master. You have become a great magician. He cannot help you any more."

Splurge grinned. "I don't want his help – just his advice."

Immediately the battered top hat was in Meela's hand.

How she always managed that, Splurge could never fathom. He took the hat from her and moved a few paces to the back of the stage. This conversation needed to be out of earshot of the Quargs. He looked into the hat but could see nothing. "Are you there, Jonesy?" he whispered. "I need to speak to you. It's important." There was no immediate response but then Splurge felt a slight movement within the hat.

"Don't I get any peace?" a voice growled. "We Gromillys need our rest like anyone else. What is it now? I thought you had sorted out that business with the forbidden magic."

Splurge was sure that Jonesy would have continued to grumble had he not interrupted.

"Well, yes, I did eventually but that isn't the problem. It is the Quargs." He spoke as quietly as he could for fear of arousing the curiosity of the three Quargs. He glanced towards them and was unnerved to see that they had turned in his direction. Did they suspect, he wondered?

"Come on, don't whisper – and hurry up. I have to get back to my rest."

Whenever Splurge needed to speak quietly with the Gromilly, Jonesy always perversely spoke loudly so that all around could hear.

"I have to whisper because I do not want the Quargs to hear, and I would take it as a special favour if you didn't answer so – so loudly."

"Hmph. Setting conditions now are we? Give him a bit of magic and it goes to his head," Jonesy muttered to himself. "Come on then, get it over with. What do you want now?"

"Advice mostly. You know about the Quigs and what happened to them. Well, I want to release them, because while Broga holds them, the Quargs will not really help me. They are afraid of him more than I thought. Now I know why they want Broga to defeat me. What should I do?"

"What do you want to do?" the voice in the hat growled quietly.

"Like I said. Rescue them. But I can't till I know where they are being kept and what sort of danger I might be putting them in. That's why I need you advice."

There was silence for a while and Splurge wondered if Jonesy had gone to sleep. He peered into the hat and saw two pinpoints staring back at him.

Then Jonesy spoke. "It is a difficult problem. Magic I can solve, but this is something different. This is where your own gift will be useful, not the one Mysterio gave you, or the one the High Factor gave you, but the one that you brought with you into the Theatre of Magic. That will be your best weapon but..," Jonesy paused and the hat trembled in Splurge's hands. "I'm coming with you and we shall talk again."

The hat stopped trembling. Jonesy had finished speaking.

Splurge supposed that if Jonesy said he was coming with him, then it must mean that he approved of the idea of rescuing the Quigs. He felt a lot better for having someone, albeit such an odd creature, agreeing with him. It didn't help him, however, with any plan of how to accomplish what was obviously going to be a dangerous mission. First, he would have to find out where the

Quigs were being kept, and he wondered if the Quargs would be willing to tell him. Maybe if he could show them that he was stronger than Broga, they might be prepared to give him more trust. He decided that he wouldn't wait to be attacked but take the fight to Broga. That would be his first step.

Splurge walked back to the Quargs and handed the battered top hat to Meela. "You are to look after Jonesy. I know you can do more but it is more important that nothing happens to the hat."

Meela took the hat and looked up at Splurge, her large, round eyes staring into his as though to get him to change his mind and not go ahead with his plan.

Splurge was confident that the Quargs could no longer read his thoughts, though it was possible that the High Factor might have communicated the information to other Quargs. He seemed to know everything, though he doubted that Kanu would do such a thing without first telling him.

Anyway, he would he would tell them himself soon enough, meanwhile he had to find Broga.

"Where does Broga live?" He looked at each of the three Quargs as he asked the question. All he received were blank stares. "You must have some idea. Does he live in the theatre or is there another place outside?" Splurge was determined to get something from the Quargs and he would nag them until he got an answer. Looking at each in turn, he tried hard to get into their minds. Nothing happened. Perhaps he ought to try harder. His brow wrinkled as he concentrated.

Suddenly Wilkins tottered unsteadily and collapsed onto the floor. The other two ignored him and continued to stare resolutely in front of them.

For a moment, Splurge was torn between helping the fallen Quarg, and continuing with his attempt to get into their minds. He needed the information, if he was to go after Broga, and that, in his view, was the more important thing at the moment. So he continued to probe the other two, but nothing was coming to him. He would have to try something else. Perhaps shouting or getting angry might work. The Quargs had always showed some alarm when he had shouted before.

"Where can I find Broga?" He didn't yell his loudest. It was just as well, because he was sure that he felt the stage tremble from the force of his voice.

There was still no response and Wilkins, who seemed to have recovered, got to his feet somewhat unsteadily, none the worse for his tumble, and it was he who broke the deadlock.

"Broga will come to us. He is not in the theatre." He spoke in the usual flat, unemotional Quarg manner.

His answer intrigued Splurge. He may not have discovered the secret of getting into their minds, but if he could get them talk, they might inadvertently give him a clue.

"How do you know that he is not in the theatre?"

Wilkins just stared blankly at Splurge.

It was not Splurge's nature to bully, but he was becoming exasperated with these Quargs, who seemed very unwilling to help him and themselves.

"Tell me," he insisted. "If Broga is not in the theatre, you must have some idea where he is likely to be." He had raised his voice again and saw at once that it had an effect on them.

The Quargs began to make strange clicking noises as though communicating with each other in their own language.

Splurge had always assumed that they had a language of their own, or what passed for a language. As far as he could tell, it was either in the form of a clicking or buzzing sound. He hadn't a clue how they had managed to learn English.

"Broga will be here soon," said Hodges, and the other two nodded in agreement.

"In that case," said Splurge, "I will capture him." He was sure that one of them gave a gasp when he made the statement, but he couldn't tell which one. "So you think that it is not possible. Well, like I said before, we outworlders also have powers, strange, mysterious powers, which we only use when we have to." He was bluffing, of course, but the Quargs were not to know, and sometimes he thought that they acted like small children. It was no wonder that a renegade like Broga could do almost as he liked with them. He reckoned if it had not been for Mysterio, and now himself, the Quargs would have had a rough time of it.

"Broga will come, but he will bring all his followers," said Meela. "Will you capture them also?" She looked at Splurge with something of hope in those large, round eyes.

Splurge grinned. "I don't have to. Without Broga, they are nothing, just sheep."

"What is 'sheep', Master?" Meela asked.

"Mindless followers, who only act on the word of their leader, in this case, Broga. They have no thoughts of their own." As he said this, Splurge was reminded of certain people he knew in the outworld, specially those bullies at school. "But I will need help from all of the Quargs. You three must tell the others how important it is." As he spoke a plan was beginning to take shape in his mind, and he tried to explain that he wanted them to distract Broga's followers by using their magical skills. "These will not harm them, but they might confuse. Once confused, even frightened, then I can deal with Broga. I don't want you to interfere because I don't think he would mind destroying any Quarg who got in his way." He looked at the three of them, hoping that they understood. "Is that clear?"

They nodded, but not with any great show of enthusiasm, though in truth, Splurge didn't think that Quargs could show enthusiasm if they tried. He would have to be enthusiastic for all of them. "One last thing. Do you have any idea when Broga will return?"

"We cannot tell such things," said Hodges, "but we always know when he is in the Theatre of Magic, even though sometimes he cannot be seen."

Fair enough, thought Splurge. He would just have to be on his guard and not let himself be caught napping like he was with the lights. Expect anything, he decided, and be as determined and ruthless as Broga. At least he would give it a good try.

"One more thing," he said as he addressed the three Quargs. "Whatever time we have, Hodges and Wilkins, you will get ready your own magical tricks. You can do what you like and you can hide them where you like. Meela, you stay with me and look after Jonesy."

Without further discussion the two blue Quargs trotted away to prepare, whilst Splurge looked around the stage for any kind of dark corner or secret door. He even stamped on the wooden boards. "Is there anything underneath the stage, Meela?" Most theatres he had heard about usually had a trap door out of which a wicked magician would usually spring with a flash of blue smoke or something. (He had remembered the pantomime but hadn't been that impressed). He certainly didn't want it happening for real, particularly with a magician like Broga. Nevertheless, he would like to get him on the stage, and the closer the better. "Meela, I will need a chair and some rope."

He had barely uttered the words before she had returned with both items. The rope looked strong enough and he gave a few hearty tugs to make sure it was real. He suspected that the more ordinary and straightforward his own props were, the more successful he was likely to be.

"What will the Master do now?" asked Meela.

"I will wait, and when Broga comes, I will capture him and tie him up." He smiled at her and sat on the chair with the spiral of rope on his lap. Exactly how he was going to accomplish such a feat, he hadn't quite worked out, but he felt strangely confident that he would manage one way or another. Anyway, it was best to appear confident in front of the Quargs, even though, privately, he had to admit to a few nerves. At least, this time it was more because of anticipation than fear. The hat and cloak of Mysterio had certainly worked for him. He idly wondered if he could do any of the things that Mysterio could do, like sending his head spinning upwards as he had done the first time they met. AS Splurge thought about it, he leaned back in the chair and looked up into the blackness above the stage.

That was his big mistake.

Chapter Twenty Six –
Splurge Captures a Querk

All Splurge could remember afterwards, was looking up into the darkness above the stage. Then it went black inside his head, as something hit him very hard.

When he eventually the blackness in his head had receded, he found himself still on the chair, but tightly bound with the rope with which he had hoped to secure Broga. He also had an aching head, and surely the biggest of bruises. It took him a few minutes for his head to clear and try to understand what had happened to him. He remembered looking up and then had a vague feeling that something fell on him. The only thought that kept flashing through his mind was that it must have been Broga up there. He was still dizzy from the effects of the blow and found it difficult to focus. Several misty shapes were moving around him and there was a distinct sound of some kind of jumbled chant ringing in his ears.

Gradually as he began to see more clearly, the shapes resolved themselves into groups of ugly, twisted followers of Broga, half Quarg, half something else. Splurge could only compare them to some sort of doll-like creature, which had been smashed and put back together – badly. They pranced around the chair making strange throaty noises and occasionally daring to poke a scrawny finger into his ribs. Broga was nowhere in sight.

Splurge guessed that he had left his creatures as guards, and he wondered how effective they were. He struggled to break free but only enough to realise that the rope was really tight and it would require either great strength to break free or he had to get help from somewhere. Then it struck him. What had happened to the three Quargs? Where was Meela? Had Broga taken her? For a wild moment, all sorts of possibilities rushed through his mind, none of which he really wanted to think about. He cursed himself for being an idiot and letting Broga creep up on him like that. It would be all his fault if anything happened to the Quargs. He remembered that Meela was particularly vulnerable, as she had already been promised to Broga.

When his head had finally cleared, Splurge began to think of ways out of this predicament. The circling group of Querks had so far done no more than chant and make an occasional jab. Perhaps they were still a little afraid of his powers and were unwilling to risk doing anything more in case he retaliated. He wondered how Mysterio would have got himself out of this mess. Wouldn't have got in it in the first place, Splurge supposed. He made another attempt to free himself from the rope. No luck. Could magic get him out of this chair, he wondered? Obviously, whoever had bound him, was aware of the new power that he now possessed, for they had made sure that his arms, in particular, were so tightly bound that there was no possibility of him wrenching even one of them free.

He wondered how long he had been unconscious. Time enough probably for Broga to accomplish whatever he had set out to do. It seemed that he was once more trapped within a trap. How he wished that he had now gone into the main theatre with the rest of his class.

Ignoring the cavorting figures, which continued to prance around him, he tried to turn his chair so that he could look about the stage. He couldn't see into the main body of the theatre because the curtains were closed. The stage was empty. There was nothing he could use and nothing that he could do to get out of this mess. Maybe some magic might work if only he could free his arms.

As he was trying to work out some plan of escape, one of the prancing creatures, more daring than the others, reached out and ruffled Splurge's hair, which was not particularly tidy at the best of times. It was the sort of hair, which couldn't make up its mind whether to be curly, frizzy, or straight. Mostly it sat in an untidy bundle on his head. His mother was always telling him to run a comb through it, but he never bothered half the time. Nevertheless, there was one thing he hated, and that was to have his hair ruffled. His uncles were always doing it and he had to grit his teeth when they did. He had, as far back as he could remember, felt that it was a bit of an intrusion. His hair was his business and when this ugly creature had the nerve to do the same thing, Splurge lost his temper.

"Gerroff!" he yelled angrily.

The effect was instantaneous.

Immediately the group of creatures surrounding him, not only stopped dancing, but also scuttled off to all the darker corners of the stage, like frightened mice.

Splurge grinned. At least, there was something he could do. But how could he get this rope unravelled. Now the creatures were no longer hovering about him, he could concentrate on the problem. Perhaps if he shouted for one of the Quargs, Hodges or Wilkins, they might be able to help. It should be no problem to untie him. They had strong fingers, as he was well aware from his earlier experience. However, he was a little puzzled that none of them had shown up. Broga wasn't around, so they had nothing to fear. And where was Meela? He was strangely worried and had a premonition that something horrible had happened to her. But it was no use worrying until he could get out of this predicament. Perhaps if he could somehow twist the chair so that it fell sideways onto the floor of the stage, he might be better able to loosen the rope, which bound him. So he began rocking backwards and forwards. It didn't take long for him to overbalance and fall to the floor with a heavy thump. He had forgotten that he had only recently received a heavy blow on the head, and the fall made his head ache afresh. It took a minute or two for the throbbing to cease. Nevertheless, he had been right about it being easier to get out of this entanglement on the floor, as he could exert more leverage by lying on his side and pushing hard against the chair. Soon he could feel the ropes sliding up, and in no time he was free. He stood and flexed his arms, which had gone to sleep, having been pinioned for so long. After more rubbing of chafed limbs he felt ready to resume his battle with Broga. But where was Broga? And where were the Quargs? The place was eerily silent. He waved his arms and the curtains swished open. The theatre was empty and just as silent. There was something peculiar going on and he meant to find out.

Time had little relevance for Splurge, ever since he realised that he was not getting out of this place. The play, which the rest of his classmates had been watching, must have been over hours ago. Everyone would have gone home. Blip and Dash would have missed him and he wondered what excuse they would have invented to explain his absence. In an odd sort of way it didn't seem to matter to him any more. Speed was the only thing that was important now, as the longer he did nothing, the greater the danger for Meela and the others. He had to hurry.

He dashed to the back of the stage looking for the door, which led to the Quarg workshop. It was so gloomy that it was some moments before he found it. But it wasn't of much use, because when he opened it, he saw to his horror that the place had been totally wrecked. Previously, where there had been scores of Quargs working at producing an endless supply of magical gadgets, there was noone. The long tables and the floor were strewn with tattered remnants of magical tricks. Pieces of metal, wood, and paper were scattered everywhere. As he walked along the lines of tables, he tried to work out the reason behind this vandalism. He could only think that Broga was behind it and had ordered his gang to go on the rampage. They hadn't quite managed to destroy everything, however, because Splurge noticed that the coloured balls were bouncing about in a haphazard fashion but still changing colour at each bounce.

On another table, a partially destroyed box was busily trying to reassemble itself, but with so much of it damaged, it looked rather odd, with pieces balancing on end, trying to form something it no longer could. Splurge wondered how long these magical contrivances would keep on working. He also noticed another object still moving, struggling to assemble itself. Upon a closer look, he saw that it was a mask of some sort, and despite his need to hurry, he could not help but be fascinated at the way it tried to change its features. The mouth twitched and stretched, while the eyes opened and closed alternately. He wished he could have seen it before, as it looked as though it might have been quite interesting. Now it just looked grotesque and frightening. He shuddered and hurried on, determined to ignore anything else that might delay him.

It was a much larger place than Splurge had at first thought, and though he ran along the rows, avoiding the worst of the debris, it took him a while before he was satisfied that there was no-one here.

Out of breath and more than a little worried, he paused at the top of the steps leading back to the stage, and surveyed the scene. Apart from the odd item that still made some movement, there was nothing. Everything had been destroyed.

Then he saw it.

He should have remembered the table at which Meela had been working, but couldn't tell at first which one it was among all this mess. But he did see something, which gave him hope. He dashed back down the steps and there on Meela's bench was the battered top hat, which the tiny female Quarg had been looking after for him. He eagerly grabbed it, hoping that it had escaped the mayhem, and peered inside. He couldn't see anything and for one awful moment thought that Jonesy had gone for good. He turned the hat upside down and then gave it a shake at the same time.

"Careful!" a familiar voice rasped. "Whenever I want some rest, it seems that someone is ready to see that I don't get it."

Splurge could have laughed with relief. At last he had a chance. "Sorry about that, but I need you now more than ever." In as few words as he could manage, he recounted all the events that had taken place, but rattling out his story at such a pace that he had to pause for breath.

"Not so fast. Try to be a little slower when you speak, and tell me exactly what has happened. The Quargs are gone, you say?" For once, Jonesy's voice sounded unsure, even a little concerned.

Splurge told his story from the time he had last spoken to Jonesy, trying hard to contain his impatience. After he had finished, he waited for the Gromilly's advice. "What should I do now?" he finally gasped

There was no immediate reply from the hat and Splurge wondered if Jonesy had understood what he had said. He looked into the hat and sure enough he saw the two pinpoint eyes staring back. "Well? We don't have much time."

"First, try not to be impatient," the voice in the hat, growled. "You will have enough time."

"But I don't know where to start. I'm sure that the Quargs know where Broga lives, but they won't tell me."

"Quargs are strange creatures. They have much power, but you now have greater power. Use it!"

If Splurge was expecting more details on what he should do, he was to be disappointed, because the hat went silent. Jonesy had said all he was going to say.

With hat in hand, he rushed up the steps and back onto the stage, in time to catch a glimpse of several of Broga's creatures scramble from the hiding places and rush towards the exit at the back of the theatre, knocking over seats and tumbling over each other in their haste.

Splurge waved his arms and shouted at the retreating figures. "Stop!" He hadn't been sure that it would work, but he guessed that Jonesy knew a thing or two, and there was no harm in trying. Besides, he was beginning to get used to this power he had so recently acquired. Nevertheless, he was still surprised at the effect he had on the fleeing group.

As if struck by an invisible hand, they suddenly became totally still like statues and presented an odd sight with some caught in the act of running or climbing over seats. It was almost comical the way their twisted bodies had become even more repulsive. But Splurge was not bothered how they looked. He wanted them, as they could lead him to Broga.

Splurge jumped from the stage and ran up to the nearest one, which was draped over a seat in an almost impossible pose. He had not really taken in much detail of these creatures before, being intent only on getting away from them. This one looked like a scarecrow, and an untidy one at that, with legs and arms protruding from a bundle of dirty rags. Its long, bony hands were poised in mid air like a hurdler about to leap. The grisly looking face, like Broga's, was warty and covered in lumps, with its large, round eyes wide open. Its head was round and bald, much like a Quarg, except the naked skull was covered in scabs. Altogether an ugly looking creature, Splurge decided, and he wondered if they were some kind of deformed version of a Quarg. He glanced at the others and saw that they were all similar in appearance and dressed in much the same way, though dressed would be an overstatement. Each had the same scrawny scarecrow look about them, only differing in where the lumps on the faces and hands were situated. One of them, he noticed, had a very nasty looking lump on the end of its nose, which appeared to glow red, making it stand out from its greyish skin. Splurge shuddered. "What an ugly bunch you are," he muttered to himself. "But what to do now?"

"Do what you intended to do," a voice rasped out, causing Splurge to turn around in alarm.

Then he saw it. On the stage was the battered old top hat. He relaxed but frowned. "I don't remember picking it up," he murmured.

"Well. Get on with it," the voice growled. "Now you've got prisoners, use them."

Splurge agreed with the idea but how was he to do it? Firstly, he would have to unfreeze them, or at least one of them. Though he was not completely sure how he had managed to render these creatures stationary in the first place, he was pretty sure that if he waved his arms again he would unfreeze them. So he waved his arms and then wished he hadn't.

The motionless scarecrow figures suddenly came to life and immediately resumed their efforts to, seemingly oblivious of the fact that they had been suspended in time.

In an automatic reaction to stop them, Splurge reached out to grab the nearest one. He missed getting a good grasp, but his fingers caught hold of some ragged cloth and surprisingly, this was enough to halt the fleeing creature, which paused in its flight to see what had got hold of it.

It turned and looked at Splurge, its large bloodshot eyes staring in a mixture of astonishment and terror. It could still have run away, for Splurge was only clutching at some sort of ragged coat, which threatened to disintegrate if any further force was used. However, it remained transfixed, like a rabbit caught in the headlights of a car.

Splurge was quick to take advantage. He needed some sort of guide and a hostage. This one would do, though he didn't fancy manhandling such a dirty, misshapen figure. "Stay!" he said in his best commanding tone.

The creature stopped struggling and became rigid once more.

Splurge wiped his hands against his trousers. Could never tell where these creatures had been. He went back to the stage and fetched the piece of rope with which he himself had so recently been bound. It took only a few moments to secure his prisoner around the thin bony hands. "You're coming with me," he muttered. He gave a tug on the rope and the creature stumbled forward a few paces. "Now take me to Broga," Splurge commanded.

The creature rolled its eyes and uttered some sort of humming sound but made no attempt to move.

Splurge gave another tug on the rope and the creature allowed itself to be pulled forward, but offered no hint at which direction to take, despite Splurge's command. "Come with me," Splurge muttered angrily, and pulled the unresisting creature up the steps to the stage. There he picked up the shabby top hat. He peered inside. "I have a prisoner, but it doesn't seem to understand what I want. Do these creatures understand anything?"

"Querks." The voice from the hat spoke.

"I know they are called Querks but what are they exactly?"

"They used to be Quargs, but have become so depraved by Broga, that they are scarcely anything now, except as you see them. But they will respond if you know how."

There was silence again.

Splurge wished that Jonesy didn't have this habit of suddenly saying nothing when there was obviously more to be said. He could never really tell whether he had finished talking or not.

"Well? How?" Splurge enquired, as politely as he could. He knew that Jonesy could be quite irritable if asked too many questions.

"How many more times must I tell you? You have the power. Use it."

From his tone, Splurge guessed that Jonesy was not going to say any more. It meant that he would have to work things out for himself. He studied the pathetic looking creature he held by the rope. Maybe, just maybe, he could intrude into its mind, if it had one. It was worth a try anyway. Staring into the sorrowful round eyes of the Querk, he concentrated hard.

At first, he tried to find out the whereabouts of Broga, but there was no response from the creature. It merely continued to stare at Splurge, showing no emotion or desire to do anything.

"Perhaps you don't have a mind of your own," Splurge murmured to himself. He would have to try something else – letting the Querk go perhaps, and then follow it. But he dismissed that idea. It would prove too risky as the Querk could easily escape and then he would have nothing. There had to be another way. "Go to Broga," he said aloud.

Immediately the Querk, swivelled about and made for the door at the end of the theatre, but was pulled up short by the rope tied to his hands. That did not prevent the creature from struggling towards the exit and Splurge was surprised at the strength of this Querk, for he felt himself being pulled along behind the creature. It was like having a large, excitable dog on a leash.

Splurge pulled back on the rope and reached for the battered top hat. He may need Jonesy again before he was finished, so he couldn't afford to leave it behind.

Now he was ready to find Meela and the other Quargs.

Holding the battered top hat in one hand and the rope in the other, Splurge allowed the struggling Querk to head for the exit.

Splurge was about to take yet another excursion into an unknown section of this magical theatre, an excursion which could lead him anywhere, very likely into danger. Overall he was excited but there was always a lingering fear at the back of his mind that he may already be too late to save Meela and the other Quargs, to say nothing of saving the Quigs. It was a tall order but he had no other choice.

Chapter Twenty Seven – Broga's World

Splurge had no idea where this Querk was leading him, for once through the rear door of the theatre, he was plunged into gloom. It was some kind of passageway but not like any of the others along which he had already travelled. He had long ceased to be surprised at the enlarged space, somehow conjured up within this Theatre of Magic.

This passage had a distinct smell, something between dead leaves and drains. It was odd now he came to think of it, because he had not really come across any distinctive smells since he arrived in this place. The passage was damp as well and he could feel the dampness clinging like a wet coat. He suspected that he wasn't being taken anywhere magnificent or even pleasant like the crystal caves.

The Querk was wasting no time and it scurried along the passageway like some skeletal rat looking for food. Splurge heard it slither and splash as it lurched along the passage. Then he felt something wet against his feet. They were virtually paddling through ankle deep water, which smelled like a sewer. He fervently hoped it wasn't a sewer. Already he was finding the stench unbearable. Fortunately it did not last long and his feet soon trod on drier and more solid ground. He only wished that he could see something of where he was going. In the murkiness he could barely make out the twisted shape of the Querk, which continued to scramble onward without pausing.

How wide or long was the passage, Splurge had no way of knowing. He just had to rely on his prisoner and hoped that the journey was not going to be another long trek through interminable passages. His feet were wet and uncomfortable, and he could hear them squelch at every step.

Suddenly the Querk gave a quick leap forward as it scrambled wildly towards a glimmer of light, which shone from somewhere ahead. Splurge could only hope that it was the end of the dark, smelly passage. Gripping the battered top hat firmly, he gave the rope a tug to slow down his captive. He didn't fancy being yanked into some dangerous place before he was ready. He preferred to approach with some degree of caution. After all, it could be a trap. Anything could be waiting for him at the end of this corridor, and he wouldn't put it past Broga to have something ready for him - something nasty.

The Querk suddenly stopped and then crouched down as though looking for something on the ground, causing Splurge to bump into it. The light was quite close now, only a matter of a few yards Splurge reckoned.

The Querk straightened up and though it was somewhat murky, Splurge could see that it was holding something in its hand. Whether it was a weapon or some sort of key, he couldn't tell, but he was taking no chances. He kept a close watch on his prisoner as it stumbled forward and prodded at something in front of it. It was clearly a door of some kind, for there was a grating sound. A surge of light flooded the passage and the Querk pulled Splurge through the opening.

If he thought he was about to enter a bright, colourful world, similar to the crystal caves, Splurge was quickly disillusioned.

Apart from the light at the entrance, which came from a glowing ball suspended in mid-air, everywhere else was quite gloomy, only slightly brighter than the passage through which Splurge had just emerged. He found it difficult to make out any detail of this place to which the Querk had led him. Vague outlines suggested a straggling arrangement of ramshackle buildings. For the moment, he wasn't interested in such details, for there, in the centre of a large open space, stood Broga.

"At last, you are here. I wondered how long it would take you."

The Querk, which had acted as Splurge's guide, immediately ran towards its master and crouched beside him.

Splurge released the rope, allowing the Querk to slip it from its wrists. He glared at Broga. "You were not difficult to find, Broga. I just followed the smell."

Broga ignored the insult and laughed, a loud raucous laugh. "Why do you think that I left some of my creatures behind? If you had any wits, I was sure that you would use them to find me."

Though Splurge should have guessed that had been Broga's intention, he wasn't going to give this dirty purple Quarg the satisfaction of thinking that he had gained an advantage over him. "Did you not think that I hadn't worked that out for myself. I wanted to be here, Broga, so that I could, once and for all, send you to where you belong."

"And where is that, precisely?" Broga sneered.

Splurge, of course, had no idea, but while he could keep Broga talking, he was taking in as much detail of this dingy place as he could. As he became used to the dim light, he was casting his eyes about for likely places where the Quargs could have been hidden.

"Ask him about the Quargs," a familiar voice growled from within the top hat, which Splurge still had gripped in his hand. "Get him to take you to them."

Splurge wondered if Broga had heard Jonesy. But he showed no sign that he had. Maybe Jonesy was right and he should ask directly about the Quargs. He certainly wasn't going to find out by just standing here and hoping that something would happen.

"WHERE ARE THE QUARGS YOU TOOK?" he demanded in the loudest voice he could muster. The sound echoed and resounded with the same force and in the same way as when Mysterio boomed. For a moment it seemed that this space (he wasn't sure whether it was a room or not), and all the buildings surrounding it, would collapse under the vibrations of his voice. Bits of wood and chunks of dirty plaster-like material fell from the roof and walls.

Even Splurge himself was surprised at his own power.

Broga was visibly alarmed by Splurge's yell, and he stepped back a pace or two, glancing fearfully around him as though expecting everything to disintegrate about his ears. Once the trembling had stopped, however, he soon resumed his arrogant pose.

"You want the Quargs, do you? Well, young Master," he snarled. "You won't get them. You can shout and bawl all you like but it won't do you any good, and it certainly won't do them any good," he added with a sinister leer.

Slowly, Splurge put the battered top hat on the ground, trusting Jonesy to look after himself for a while, and advanced on Broga in the most menacing manner he could muster with arms held out, ready to perform some great feat of magic. He hoped it looked imposing because he really had no idea what to do, but he wanted to see how Broga would react and then take it from there. Broga was a bully and like all bullies he was a coward Splurge believed and, if necessary, he would have to do some bullying himself.

Unfortunately for Splurge, Broga wasn't in the mood to be bullied or cowed. Firstly, he was much too confident in his own ability; more important, however, was the fact that at the moment he held all the advantages.

"You think that with your puny skill, you can get your way. Mysterio never could, so I don't see you doing it. Besides, did it not strike you as strange at how easy it was for me to take the Quargs?" He gave a half leering grin and his face shone with some knowledge, which he was tantalisingly dangling before Splurge. "I could have destroyed you!" he suddenly screeched and his face became of mask of hatred. Then as suddenly, he changed as his eyes glittered and shone brightly in the gloom. He chuckled to himself at some secret knowledge. "Do you want to see where I keep them?"

Splurge couldn't keep up with this ugly purple Quarg. He had the distinct impression that Broga was toying with him and he had an uncomfortable feeling that he was not going to like what the purple Quarg would show him.

"Just show me where they are," said Splurge grimly, "and cut out this cat and mouse game."

"Cat and mouse game," Broga mimicked, in a curious high, rasping voice. "Is that some outworld sport?" He chuckled again, a loud guttural sound, like a wild animal about to devour its prey. It made Splurge shiver.

While Broga had been talking, Splurge kept glancing about, trying to judge the most likely place that any captives might be held. He couldn't see that much because of the gloom.

"No, they're not here," Broga gave a wheezy chuckle. "But I can show you where they are." He smiled, a crooked smile, as though daring Splurge to take him up on his offer. Splurge naturally suspected everything Broga did or said, and was hesitant to follow this twisted Quarg. Yet he had little choice if he wanted to find the Quargs.

Broga shuffled towards an extra dark place behind him and tugged at something.

It was obviously a door of some sort, for immediately there was a squealing sound, which ended in a sudden crash as the door or gateway came off its hinges, sending a shower of dust and small bits of debris into the air.

Splurge was not surprised, for everything in this gloomy place looked as though it was about to fall apart.

"Come," Broga rasped. "Come and see my world." He went through the opening, barely visible in the deep gloom, closely followed by the Querk, which had been crouching at his feet.

Coughing and spluttering, Splurge picked up the battered top hat, now even dirtier than before, and walked cautiously after Broga. His feet crunched on the remnants of the doorway, which disintegrated even further, and stepped into what appeared to be a dark alley. There was a loud crash behind him, and he could only guess that some other building had gone the same way as the door.

Splurge couldn't be sure whether he was still in the theatre or outside of it, because the alleyway in which he found himself, looked like a main road through a village or small town. It was lined with buildings, but not real buildings made of brick or stone. As far as he could tell in the gloom, they were more like ramshackle sheds, ready to collapse at the slightest breath of wind. Everywhere was damp, and the smell of decay was overpowering. Splurge would have held his nose but one hand firmly gripped the battered top hat, and the other he wanted free in case he needed to use it in a hurry. In this clogging atmosphere, he expected anything at any time and needed to keep his wits about him. Even if Broga had some other plan for him, he didn't trust his followers, the Querks, to keeping their distance. They were such an ugly, weird lot that he believed that they were capable of anything.

As his eyes grew accustomed to the murkiness, he could now see more clearly that the buildings, which he at first thought were sheds, were in fact no more than lumps of wood roughly put together to make some sort of makeshift shelters. Anything could be lurking in those hovels, and he hurried after the sound of Broga's footsteps, half expecting that one of those creatures might spring out from their murky corners. Querks he could deal with, but there might be other, more terrifying things in this dark world of Broga.

The path through the tangle of hutches, twisted and turned, making it difficult for Splurge to keep up with Broga. It continued to surprise him that such a place, as this could exist within the tiny theatre. He would like to know how space could be stretched in such a way. For the moment, however, he must concentrate on following Broga through the untidy, decaying mess of this dark, dismal world.

The footsteps ahead of him had stopped, and Splurge hurried forward and saw that the alleyway had opened into a wide space, with Broga strutting about like some sort of king. It looked like a cave but Splurge couldn't really tell because everything was so gloomy.

Broga stopped his strutting when he saw Splurge and gave a wave of his hand.

Splurge, thinking that he was about to produce some more forbidden magic, raised his own hand, ready to ward off any possible attack. But it turned out to be a signal for his followers, for dozens of the scrawny figures came scuttling out of the darkness to crouch around Broga.

They were like dogs waiting to receive some reward, thought Splurge, though on second thoughts, perhaps rats was a better description.

"This is my place," Broga said proudly.

What he had to be proud of, Splurge couldn't imagine. The place was dark, dirty and devoid of any kind of furniture or trappings which would make it special. It was as unlike the crystal caves as was possible.

"It may not be much to you, outworlder, but it is mine." He practically snarled the words. "I rule here and soon I shall rule the entire Theatre of Magic." Broga's eyes blazed with a frightening intensity.

Splurge was quite sure that he meant what he said.

"You can keep your world," Splurge said contemptuously. "From what I've seen, it doesn't look much. Your world? Huh - more like your mess." He wasn't bothered whether he upset Broga or not. He was not going to be bullied or persuaded to believe that Broga was right. "Where are they, then? You said that you would show me the Quargs you had taken." He decided not to mention the Quigs till he had discovered more about Broga's kingdom.

Broga laughed, his usual loud, rasping laugh, and clapped his hands at the same time. There was a bright flash accompanied by a cloud of thick blue smoke. When the smoke had cleared, a group of Quargs were assembled in a row behind Broga.

Splurge waited, expecting Broga to produce more Quargs, but there were none. "Where are the others?" he called out brusquely.

There was no Meela, Hodges or Wilkins among them. Splurge scrutinised them one by one to make sure, as he had by now become sufficiently used to the Quargs, that he could easily recognise those three. He wondered if Broga was toying with him. If he had all the Quargs, why did he not produce them?

Splurge felt that Broga was up to something, and it wouldn't be anything pleasant. What should he do next? Perhaps now would be a good time to have a word with Jonesy, or he could just charge straight in and battle it out with the renegade Quarg. Before he could decide anything, however, Broga clapped his hands once more, but this time there was no flash and no smoke. Instead, two Quargs appeared from the deeper gloom.

Broga smiled, or maybe he scowled.

Splurge couldn't really tell which, as his face was a perpetual mask of ugliness.

"You see I have all the Quargs, including this green one." He pushed at something with his feet and Splurge saw to his horror that it was Meela. It looked as though she had been roughly handled because her features were all blotchy and her clothes tattered and dirty.

Splurge felt his anger rising. He wanted to do something savage to the smirking Broga. Teach him a lesson he wouldn't forget. But he couldn't take the risk while Meela was so completely in his power.

"You see I have the green one. She was promised to me and now she has been delivered."

"What do mean, delivered?"

Broga chuckled. "You should be more careful who you take as friends. The green one was promised and the Quargs cannot help but keep their promises." As he spoke, he pointed towards the gloom and two more Quargs appeared – Hodges and Wilkins.

Splurge had a feeling that he wasn't going to like what was coming, and he was right.

"These two Quargs were my spies. It was they who arranged the delivery."

Though Splurge was unwilling to believe Broga, he knew that Hodges, at least, was always prepared to surrender Meela, thinking that it would safeguard the Quargs. "Did you arrange this?" he asked Hodges.

Hodges blinked but said nothing.

"What about you, Wilkins? Were you a traitor to your people as well?"

"Broga will protect the Quargs, if the green one is given to him," Wilkins replied in the usual flat, unemotional manner of the Quargs, which seemed to irritate Splurge more than the actual betrayal.

"Once Mysterio was gone, it was easy," said Broga, who was plainly enjoying Splurge's discomfort at the revelation. "The Quargs will do anything for an easy life."

"So, I suppose that you think that you can now go marching into the crystal caves and become the new High Factor." Splurge taunted the misshapen Quarg with the idea, because he knew that no matter what Broga and the treacherous Quargs did, Kanu was never going to allow someone like him to enter the crystal caves and take over the centum of the Quargs.

"Become High Factor," Broga repeated slowly, as if savouring the idea. He chuckled. "No. I want to be more than that. Now I want to possess the whole of the Theatre of Magic – and beyond." His eyes glittered wildly and the warts on his face began to throb as though they might at any moment erupt. "I am already High Factor," he screeched. "See!" He pointed to the huddled figure of

Meela on the floor. "I have his Quig. To you outworlder, that means I have his offspring."

"I know what a Quig is," muttered Splurge grimly. He tried not to show his surprise at the revelation, but it did explain why this warped, purple Quarg could have such grand ambitions. For if he had Kanu's daughter, then he had Kanu himself. He would then, indeed, become greater than the High Factor. Worse, however, was Broga's dark suggestion that his ambition would stretch beyond the Theatre of Magic. He would definitely have to do something about that, but what, he couldn't fathom.

Broga then strode up to Splurge and glared at him. "You have two choices, outworlder. You can leave here and I will see that you get out of the Theatre of Magic, or you can stay and see the Quargs destroyed one by one. Then it will be your turn."

Broga spat out the last words with such venom that Splurge was momentarily startled and stepped back a pace from him.

On the face of it, Splurge knew that he should be sensible and take the first of Broga's choices. After all, he had been waiting to get out of this theatre ever since he had landed here. But Splurge was a boy and boys are rarely sensible. Despite his natural desire to get out, he knew that he would choose to stay and fight Broga, and by the look on the purple Quarg's face, he reckoned it would be to the death. The idea should have frightened him. Yet strangely enough, as the thought passed through his mind, Splurge felt no fear or dread of such an outcome. In some odd way, he knew that it would turn out all right, though he couldn't understand why. It might have had something to do with Mysterio's hat and cape, which had somehow imparted a new confidence in him; or it might have been Kanu's gift, which must be the special power to intrude into minds; or it might just be because there was still a tiny, niggling doubt in the furthest recess of his mind, that any of it was real.

Whatever the reason, Splurge knew what he wanted to do. "You will have to fight me, Broga. You will have to fight me all the way. If you thought that Mysterio could harm you, it will be nothing to what I shall do. I give you fair warning. Get back to your world and leave the Quargs to theirs or I will..." Splurge paused. He was sounding like an avenging angel or something. Those were not his thoughts, his aims or ambitions. He wasn't like that. The thought of fighting Broga, or anyone, was not usually his first course of action. He much preferred to settle things peacefully. On the other hand, if he was attacked, that was a different matter. He would feel no compunction in defending himself in any way he could. At the moment his thoughts and feelings were very confused.

This confusion must have shown in his face, because Broga approached and spoke quietly to Splurge. "Why bother with these Quargs? It is not your fight, not your responsibility." He spoke in a confidential tone, trying hard to control his natural instinct for snarling and shouting his words. "They're not worth bothering with." He turned and glanced at the Quargs lined up behind him. "If they can not only betray you, but betray their own, are they really worth fighting for?" He looked at Splurge with an expectant leer on his face, confident that his words would have some effect.

Splurge well knew that Broga had a point, however much he distrusted him. It was true, he didn't owe the Quargs anything, and his only real ambition had been to get out of this place. Why shouldn't he take Broga's offer?

As Splurge debated the logic of the situation with himself, Broga turned to look back at the Quargs once more. "I will be their protector from now on, so you don't have to worry any more about them." He supplemented his words with what he probably thought was a smile, but it turned out to be more of a scowling leer.

That was enough for Splurge to make up his mind. Moreover, he was curious as to why Broga should make him such an offer. If he was as powerful as he had boasted, there was no way he would be offering such terms unless – unless he believed that Splurge could really prevent from carrying out his aims.

"Can't help you, I'm afraid," said Splurge tersely. "I shall do my best to stop you by whatever means I can."

Broga scowled and stamped his feet. He looked as though he was on the verge of doing some wild, frenzied dance, when, with a sudden movement, he rushed towards the line of Quargs and pointed at one of them, uttering a strange sound as he did so.

Immediately, the Quarg, which had been chosen, collapsed in a heap. Broga then signalled to two of his followers, who picked up the lifeless Quarg and carried it away into the darkness. He then turned back to Splurge, eyes blazing and arms waving as though he was about to repeat his actions.

Splurge was taking no chances and he gave a loud yell. "STOP!"

Broga was halted in his tracks, but unlike before, he wasn't struck dumb. "Your magic tricks won't prevail here. This is my world and here I am the Master," he screamed and waved his arms towards the Quargs. "They are mine, whatever you say or do. And I will do with them as I please. If I want to destroy them, I will."

"Then you will have nobody," said Splurge, who was unmoved by Broga's ranting.

"There are always more Quargs," Broga sneered. "And I have all the Quigs."

Splurge was unsure what his next step ought to be. The wrong word or action could cause Broga to go completely out of control, and he wasn't far from it at the moment. Then there was Meela, still lying there all crumpled, and for all he knew she might be dead. Though Hodges and Wilkins had let themselves be bullied by Broga, he could understand their motives, for giving her up. He sighed. Whatever he did was sure to put more Quargs in danger and he didn't want that.

The awful realisation was beginning to dawn on him that he would have to get rid of Broga completely but the idea of just walking away was still very appealing. "What should I do for the best?" He spoke his thoughts aloud, not realising that he was till holding the battered top hat.

"You know very well what you must do. The longer you delay, the worse it will be." Jonesy's voice was strangely soft and muted.

"That's the trouble," said Splurge. "I don't really know."

"You are the Master. You must act like the Master."

"What would Mysterio have done?"

"He is not here, so the question is irrelevant." Jonesy's voice had resumed his usual rasping tone. "You know what you must do, so do it. You have the power – now have the courage."

Splurge thought about what Jonesy had said. He knew that the Gromilly was right but he was still undecided and would likely have debated with himself indefinitely, had not Broga done something, which settled the matter.

Splurge and the Theatre of Magic

Chapter Twenty Eight – The Duel

Whether Splurge was getting used to the gloom of Broga's world, or whether it was in fact a little lighter than before, he couldn't tell. He was now able to see further into the dark recesses of this cavern, for that's what it now looked like. It was also much larger than he had at first supposed, much larger than any of the crystal caves. If the situation had not been so dangerous, he might have found time to marvel at how something so large could possibly exist in such a tiny theatre. For now, however, he had to concentrate on rescuing the Quargs.

Broga strutted around this large space like some sort of ringmaster in a circus. He paused in his strutting to summon two Querks, who produced a large black book. It was the same one he had used earlier – the Black Qualigor

There was to be more forbidden magic.

Splurge became tense as he realised what Broga was up to, and he prepared himself for another onslaught. But it never came. Instead, Broga went to the huddled figure of Meela and pulled her to her feet. She offered no resistance and stood like a battered rag doll, waiting without complaint whatever fate Broga would decree for her.

Splurge wanted to snatch her from Broga's clutches, but doubted it would be that easy. The twisted, purple Quarg was sure to have some plan to lure him into a false move. So he waited. And then wished he hadn't.

Broga pulled the unresisting Meela nearer to Splurge, just a few paces away. He stared hard at Splurge, his eyes glowing with hate and malevolence. "See this Quarg," his lip curling as he spoke, "she is mine, as they are all mine. You cannot save them." He suddenly pulled Meela away. She stumbled and almost fell.

Before Splurge could intervene, Broga pointed a finger at Meela and made some sort of sound. Immediately, to Splurge's consternation, something began to rise from the floor of the arena.

Splurge had never been able to discover whether the ground was stone, earth, rock or even wooden boards. Whatever it was suddenly began to shudder, as though something was about to erupt, but only around the figure of Meela.

For the first time since he had come in contact with them, Splurge could now see a definite emotion being registered on the face of a Quarg. Meela looked scared and seemed as if she was about to cry out. Before she could do so, however, long metal bars had arisen from the floor of the cave to form a cage around her. So narrow were the spaces between the bars that she could scarcely thrust her tiny hand through them, though she tried.

Before Splurge could protest or do anything to help Meela, Broga had conjured up a large cloth, which draped itself over the cage. Then, with a typical magician's flourish, he immediately withdrew the cloth to reveal the cage to be empty. With an equally dramatically series of flourishes, he repeated the manoeuvres with the cloth to show that the cage itself had now disappeared.

Though Splurge was concerned for Meela, he could recognise a magician's trick when he saw one. If Broga was only going to rely on such magic, then he reckoned that he might have a chance.

"So you are trying to show me how clever you are, Broga. Well done." He gave an ironical clap.

Broga scowled. "Perhaps you would like to see something more daring. Something that the Master might appreciate?" he said and gave a mocking bow. As he straightened up, he suddenly hurled the cloth, still in his hand, towards Splurge, except that it was no longer a cloth but a large, screeching falcon.

With gleaming orange eyes and outstretched talons as sharp as razors, it was making directly for Splurge's face.

Though feeling distinctly scared, Splurge held his nerve until the bird was almost upon him, then he raised his right hand as though to ward it off and at the same time shouted, "RETURN!" Immediately, and much to his relief, and some astonishment, the fierce looking falcon had become a cloth again, which fluttered harmlessly to the ground.

Broga was not dismayed to see that his effort had been thwarted. Instead, he grabbed the nearest Quarg and hurled the unresisting figure into the air. Before landing, with what Splurge thought might be a fatal crunch; Broga had conjured up a tub of water, into which the hapless Quarg fell with a great splash. Looking dejected and very wet, he was hauled out by Broga, who proceeded to give a large, expansive bow, accompanied by a sudden loud noise, which echoed and resounded around the arena, like the roar of a thousand cheering voices.

Splurge wondered what had happened till he realised that it was just another trick, much like the kind that Mysterio would practise.

"If that was to impress me, you failed," said Splurge, trying hard not to show his nervousness. "Is that the best you can do?"

Broga glowered but said nothing. The Quarg, which had suffered a drenching, waddled back into line with the others, showing no sort of fear, anger, or any kind of emotion.

Splurge decided that Quargs were a funny lot, but if he wanted to get just one of them back, or achieve anything in this dark, dismal place, he should show Broga some of his own magic. Without the Quargs, he didn't really know what to do. He needed something big and spectacular – something perhaps that would frighten Broga or at the very least give him something to think about. His face screwed up in thought but nothing came into his head. Maybe if he shouted. That always seemed to produce some sort of effect. Then a strange thing happened.

A small circle of mist arose out of the battered top hat to form a sort of screen and a quite voice began to speak from the mist. At first he thought it was Jonesy, but it sounded nothing like the irascible Gromilly, even at his mildest. This voice was in his head and then he realised it was Kanu, the High Factor. As the realisation dawned on him, Kanu's face materialised in the patch of mist like someone on an old television set, all blurred and snowy. He spoke.

"Use the gift I have bestowed."

Splurge was puzzled. He hadn't yet fathomed out what this gift was, and what form it would take. He tried to tell this to the High Factor but found that he could not speak. Yet the answer came back immediately.

"You have the gift of fire. Just wish it and it will flow for you."

The voice, which Splurge was not sure was in his head or coming out of the misty screen, continued in its serene manner.

"Broga also has the same gift. But Broga has the forbidden magic because he stole it. He took the Black Qualigor. The magic in that book was forbidden, because I forbade it. If the book is not returned then that magic will rebound on its user."

Though Kanu's words were soft spoken, they made Splurge shiver. "What about my gift? If I use it then it will rebound on me."

The ancient Quarg allowed his face to crease into something resembling a smile, though it was difficult to tell from the misty screen. "Yours is a gift – not stolen. I am sure that you will use it wisely."

With that the mist suddenly disappeared.

Splurge shook his head in disbelief. Had Kanu really appeared, or had it all been in his mind? He looked at Broga and at the Quargs, but they showed no sign that they had seen or heard anything. He only hoped that he was not having hallucinations or some sort of brainstorm. If the gift worked then it was a powerful weapon, but would he dare use it, he wondered? He ought really to give this gift a little try out, just to test that it really worked. He would have to think of a way of testing it without arousing Broga's suspicions. Fire! That could be dangerous thought Splurge. Perhaps after all, he would be better off not testing it just yet. He wasn't at all sure that he could bring himself to use such a dangerous gift. But then he thought of Meela's crumpled body and knew that he would use it, if that was the only way to rescue her and the others.

As it happened, Splurge need not have worried, for while he had been talking to Kanu, Broga had been busy.

Several Querks had wheeled into the arena what looked like a cage, similar to the one he had caused to erupt and ensnare Meela. Broga seemed quite excited at what he was about to perform, for he kept prancing about the cage and gleefully chuckling to himself. Occasionally he would cast a baleful look at Splurge.

Whatever it was that Broga was going to do, Splurge realised that this time he must get in the first shot. He tried to imagine how Mysterio would deal with such a situation, but quickly dismissed the thought from his head. Anyway, he didn't necessarily agree with everything that Mysterio had done. Now he had the chance to do what he wanted to do.

"Here goes," he muttered to himself.

Flicking the cape back to give his arms as much freedom as possible, he pointed at an area around Broga's feet and said, "fire." Though he wasn't sure what would happen, he more than taken aback at what happened.

A string of flame shot from his forefinger and hit the ground in front of Broga. As it did so it bounced into the air, sending a shower of dazzling sparks cascading down onto the purple Quarg, who was now hopping about in frenzy, trying to avoid them.

Splurge couldn't help grinning. The blotchy, renegade Quarg looked quite funny, doing what looked like some strange dance routine gone wrong. At another time, he might have laughed out loud but he remembered Meela and the other Quargs. He lowered his arms and the string of flame disappeared.

Broga was still being peppered with the last of the sparks and strove desperately to avoid them, though whichever way he turned, they seemed to follow and cause him to hop and shriek out in pain and anger.

Splurge wasn't one bit sorry. "Now you know what it's like, Broga, to be tormented. Do you want more?"

The sparks had finished, though Broga continued to flinch and shudder every few seconds. At length realised that the fiery sparks were finished and he looked at Splurge with a face full of hate and fear. But his hate was stronger. "You have used the forbidden magic. Mysterio would never have used such tricks. He even forbade me to use it." He screeched his words and began to dribble in his rage.

"You stole the Black Qualigor. Its magic is forbidden to you, Broga. For me it is a gift and I will use this gift as often as I like. You know what you have to do if you want me to stop." Splurge was hoping that Broga would take the hint. He wasn't really in favour of using violence to get what he wanted, and he couldn't think of anything more violent than fire. He also realised that if he pushed Broga too far, the twisted mind of his, might just take out his rage on the Quargs, especially Meela.

It seemed that Broga had read Splurge's thoughts for, with a wave of his hand, he produced a large, silk cloth, and with a flourish, accompanied by a bright flash of orange light, Meela appeared.

She looked so tiny and frail as she crouched before Broga, who gave her a kick, which sent her sprawling to the floor.

Splurge wanted to do something, but he knew that he had to be careful for fear of harming Meela. He could feel himself getting really angry and for a moment he wanted nothing more than to completely obliterate Broga.

Meela struggled to her feet and stared at Splurge, her large, round eyes now definitely sad-looking. Broga pulled her in front of him.

"Now do your worst," Broga sneered. "Or are you too squeamish to watch your Quarg friend being destroyed?" As he spoke, he suddenly hurled something towards Splurge, being careful at the same time to keep Meela in front of him.

Because of the general gloom of this place, Splurge wasn't sure what Broga had hurled at him. At first, he thought that the purple Quarg might have retaliated with fire, but it looked more like a large, round object, something like a football. He soon learned that it wasn't a football. As the object landed in front of him, it burst open and to his horror hundreds, maybe thousands, of spiders came scurrying towards him, growing in size, as they got closer. Splurge had a morbid fear of spiders and his fear was always magnified in the darkness. The nearest spider, a large hairy thing, with bright pinpoint eyes was almost upon him. He quickly jumped back, trying not to show any panic. He hated spiders and probably would have just stamped on them, but there were too many. Soon they would be all over him, touching, feeling, and biting. He wanted to scream but realised that he must keep his head. "Go back," he said and pointed at the scurrying mass, but nothing happened.

Then the first spider touched him and started to climb up his leg. It was one of the larger spiders, and as its hairy legs, carefully and deliberately, propelled the creature upwards, Splurge let out a yell. "Gerroff!" he shouted. It was purely instinctive but it had the desired effect. Immediately the spider dropped to the ground and began to scuttle back towards Broga, followed by hordes of its brethren.

Though mightily relieved, Splurge wondered how he had managed to get rid of them by just shouting. Then he realised. He had already given the command to go back. It just needed reinforcing. He must remember to shout his commands, whatever the situation, else he may not get the chance next time.

As the hundreds of spiders neared him, Broga gave a wave of his hand and they suddenly exploded with a thousand pops of sound, sending a shower of sparkling confetti into the air.

Splurge hoped that would be the last of the spiders, but he was at least heartened by the fact that he knew how to get rid of them, or any other loathsome creature which Broga might send against him. He watched closely, as the renegade Quarg, still shielded by Meela, began to sidle up to the large cage-like contraption. Whatever Broga was going to do next required some preparation, and Splurge couldn't help trying to anticipate the sort of thing it might be. He would dearly have liked to attack Broga, but couldn't risk it while Meela was still in his clutches. The other Quargs, he noticed, had barely moved or shown any sign of interest at the recent exchanges between himself and Broga. It was as though they had been put in a trance. But he could never tell with Quargs, their normal state was little better than a trance.

Broga signalled to two of the Quargs, Hodges and Wilkins, who dutifully came running up to him.

Splurge couldn't quite hear, but was sure that Broga was issuing some sort of instruction to them. How he would like to have known what it was, not that he would have understood, anyway, because they spoke in their own language.

But his guess had been a good one, for Hodges immediately went to the huge cage and began to raise the bars at one end, obviously some sort of entrance, but not really visible from where Splurge stood. At the same time, Wilkins went to the line of Quargs and began to lead them towards the cage. Hodges had stood back to allow them to enter, which they seemed to do, if not willingly, certainly without any objection, as far as Splurge could tell. He would like to have known what Wilkins said to get them to go into the cage, which even the least clever of the Quargs must suspect as a trap. When all had entered, Hodges lowered the gate and went back to stand with Wilkins next to Broga.

Splurge was sickened at the thought that Hodges and Wilkins were actually helping Broga to destroy their own people. They had already done nothing to help Meela, not even by way of protest, though he had been aware, that for some reason best known to himself, Hodges had always expressed a certain distaste for the 'green one' as he would describe Meela. He was going to make sure that both Hodges and Wilkins fully explained their treacherous behaviour, but for the moment he was concerned more with what Broga had planned for the hapless Quargs.

Trying to interpret Broga's thoughts was not easy, but so far, Splurge reckoned that the purple Quarg hadn't been too imaginative in his magic, and that he might be about to repeat himself. Yet he couldn't help thinking that the Quargs in the cage were doomed. But worse was the fact that he couldn't do anything to help them. He must get Broga to attack him and not the Quargs.

"Have you given up then, Broga, or have you forgotten how this trick is supposed to work?" Splurge laughed, hoping that Broga would take the bait and turn his attention to himself.

Broga was apparently unconcerned at Splurge's sarcasm or laughter, for he merely walked up to the cage and made pretence of checking that the bars were secure. He also wanted Splurge to see that the Quargs could not get out. Nor had he forgotten to drag Meela along with him, thus still keeping Splurge at a distance.

Splurge wished he could have spoken to her. Told her not to give up hope, and that he would rescue her, or something like that. He certainly wasn't going to shout those sentiments in front of Broga, for him to sneer at. In fact he was surprised that Broga hadn't used Meela in some way to threaten him, though he had an uneasy feeling that that he wouldn't hesitate if nothing else worked.

It didn't look too good for the Quargs in the cage and Splurge was trying hard to think of a counter attack before Broga decided on his move.

"So, are you ready outworlder? Are you prepared to watch and see how a real Master makes his magic?" Broga's raucous laugh echoed and reverberated around the arena, and again there was a loud cheering response from an invisible crowd.

"BEHOLD!" Broga pushed Meela from him and held up his arms.

A huge ball of light descended from somewhere above and settled between his hands. After a few mocking flourishes, he suddenly hurled the ball of light at the cage, where it shattered in a huge roar of flame. A raging fire suddenly enveloped the caged prisoners, who had no possible hope of getting out.

Broga stood back and laughed, a loud, demonic laugh, which echoed even above the roar and crackle of the flames, which were seeping between the bars of the cage.

Splurge watched horrified and tried to think of something, anything that could save the helpless Quargs. This was no magical fire, he was sure of it, because he could feel the heat from where he was standing. He also noted that Broga took great care to step further away from his gruesome handiwork, as did Hodges and Wilkns. Splurge was as much disgusted at their demeanour as he was at Broga's actions, for they stood by quite impassively while watching their own people burn.

Then Splurge had an idea.

He would have to act quickly, though he had no idea whether his plan would work. But it was a chance he would have to take.

"Come to me!" he yelled, as he moved closer to the blaze and stretched out his arms.

It was total guesswork, but he had the thought that his 'gift' might work in reverse. There was not much time, for it would take only a few minutes before every Quarg in the cage was burnt to a cinder. He yelled again, even louder. "COME TO ME!"

Broga watched with an amused leer on his face. "You are too late, outworlder. You do not have the power. My forbidden magic is stronger than your puny efforts. I will be the Master. And when I have finished with the Quargs, I will deal with you." He ended his threat with another hideous laugh and began his crooked dance, prancing about like some demented demon. In the flickering firelight, his shadows romped about the edges of the arena like so many imps from hell.

BUT IT DID WORK!

Slowly but surely the flames began to dwindle and soon they had come together to form a large ball of fire which began to roll towards Splurge.

Surprised and a little scared, he backed further away, trying to give himself as much space and time as possible, to carry out the next part of his plan. He would have to judge it very carefully, for all the while that

Broga had literally been playing with fire, Meela was still by his side.

When the ball of fire was far enough away to do no more harm to the caged Quargs, he called out again. "STOP!"

He wasn't sure that this part of his plan would work, and he could feel his heart thumping as he began to realise the danger in which he had placed himself. The ball of fire continued to roll towards him. Now he could feel the heat of it and the sweat was beginning to trickle down his neck. The ball of fire rolled every closer. "STOP THERE!" Splurge yelled again. This time much louder, till his voice resounded like a booming gong, all around the arena. He held his breath.

At last the ball of fire came to a halt.

"Now Meela, run to me – quickly." He called across to the tiny, green female Quarg, hoping that she would realise what he was trying to do. "Run! Run!" he repeated.

While Hodges, Wilkins had been staring at the inferno, seemingly unaffected by the fact that fellow Quargs were being roasted alive, Meela was constantly fidgeting and her eyes rolled wildly.

"Run, Meela!" Splurge called out again.

As though coming out of a trance Meela suddenly moved with a swiftness, which took her captor by surprise. In a second or two she was beside Splurge. She looked up at him and gave him a Quarg smile.

Splurge grinned. He felt a lot better now that he didn't have to worry about the daughter the High Factor.

Meanwhile, the ball of fire, now paused between Splurge and Broga, still crackled and roared, spewing out shoots of flame like a miniature sun.

Splurge knew that he couldn't wait much longer. "GO BACK TO BROGA!"

The ball of fire shuddered and then slowly it began to roll away from Splurge, making directly for Broga, who not only showed surprise in his bloodshot eyes but also fear. The ball gathered speed as it made for its creator.

Splurge remembered what Jonesy had said about forbidden magic rebounding on the one who used it.

As the ball of fire reached Broga, who had been trying, in vain, to make it change direction, he gave a loud screech and ran in a wild panic from the arena into the darker gloom of what Splurge now recognised as an enormous cave.

The ball of fire suddenly halted and then with a great roar exploded into thousands of tongues of flame over the spot, which Broga had so recently stood. Then, with a series of small popping sounds, these tongues of flame were extinguished.

Splurge had watched in awe and relief. He would never have believed that he could have done it and was grateful to the High Factor for bestowing such a useful gift on him. Furthermore, he realised that it was not just being able to conjure up fire that was important, but to have the nerve and ability to use it well and wisely. He put that down to wearing Mysterio's hat and cape, which magically seemed to have imparted some of the Master magician's knowledge.

"Come. Meela. Let's see how those Quargs are." Though he had done his best, he feared that his help must have come too late to save them.

They ran towards the cage and could see that they were still there.

Splurge couldn't see that any had been burnt or even singed, as he had feared that they would have been. As he and Meela came near, the trapped Quargs grabbed at the bars of the cage and one or two even attempted to reach out to them.

The Quargs looked none the worse for their ordeal, though they did remind him of animals in a pet shop. They looked so forlorn and they continually blinked their eyes, which seemed to be the limit of their reaction.

Meela went up to the bars of the cage and touched the hands, which pushed out, making some sort of clicking noise as she did so.

"Are they alright, Meela?" Splurge asked, half afraid that there may be an incinerated body or two among them.

Meela looked at Splurge, her face showing definite signs of sadness. She held out her hands, which were cupped together. "Two, Master," she said.

"Where? I don't see any bodies." Splurge was quickly scanning the group of Quargs for some sign.

"Quargs do not completely die, Master, as I told you before." She opened her hands and to his surprise, he saw two golden insects, which appeared to be crickets or grasshoppers, nestling in her tiny palms, chirruping away and very much alive.

"So... they are now – dead?" he said haltingly, not really sure what had happened to them.

Meela shook her head. "As I have said, Master, Quargs become these when they have finished being Quargs. Then they will go to the crystal caves."

Splurge nodded. He thought he understood, but the idea, of dying, or rather not dying, and becoming insects seemed rather at odds with what he had been led to believe in the outworld. But then, why shouldn't it be different here? So many things were different, so why not the idea of dying. "Will you take them to the crystal caves?"

"No. They will make their own way there." She lifted her hands and the two golden insects leapt into the air and began to sail away with a series of whirring and chirruping sounds. Soon they were lost in the gloom, and only a faint whirring sound could be heard till that faded into nothingness.

Splurge didn't know whether to feel happy or sad at the loss of two Quargs. He did recall with some pleasure, his visit to the crystal caves and the various insects, which he had seen, and those that had landed on him. Maybe dying wasn't so bad after all. But he couldn't get rid of the feeling that he had let the Quargs down by not stopping Broga. The twisted, purple Quarg had to be stopped before more Quargs were harmed.

"Let's get them out, Meela." He strode to the cage and checked the end where he had seen Hodges raise the gate. It proved simple enough to open and he wondered why the Quargs inside had not thought to open it themselves, or at least try. Soon he had it open and the Quargs stumbled out to line up beside Meela.

"They could have got out by themselves," said Splurge. "Why didn't they?"

"They are not clever Quargs," said Meela quietly, "and they would do whatever Hodges or Wilkins asked them to do."

"Hm. Those two have got a lot to answer for," said Splurge grimly. "Where are they? And where is Broga?" He had been too concerned with the plight of the trapped Quargs to notice anything else, but he knew that Broga wasn't finished and was sure to return with more devilish tricks from his book of forbidden magic. He must somehow prevent him from taking more vengeance upon the Quargs, as in Splurge's mind, he was sure to do, if only make up for that fireball, which had rebounded on him. He must find that twisted, purple Quarg before he had the chance to make more mischief.

"I must go after Broga. Where do you think he has gone?" He turned to Meela for an answer but she only shook her head.

"You must not put yourself in more danger, Master. Broga is a clever magician and though you defeated him once, he will return with even more powerful magic."

There was a time when Splurge would have heeded Meela's advice, but after seeing how Broga had treated her and the other Quargs, he was not so sure that her advice was proffered to save him. He was beginning to see that the Quargs, though they had plenty of magic, had no will to fight, or even stand up for themselves. If he was to be a true Master, he must take on the responsibility. He didn't really fancy the idea but there was not much else he could do.

"If I am now the Master, you must learn to trust me, Meela. You do not have to come with me, but I do not see myself leaving your world till I get this job finished. Just tell me where I can find him and I will do what I have to do."

Though he knew the words sounded very fine and brave, inside Splurge felt anything but courageous. The thought of even following Broga through the filthy tunnels and alleyways of this world filled him with dread. But now he had said it, he would have to carry it through. Anyway he was still annoyed and disgusted at the attitude of Hodges and Wilkins, who he regarded as nothing more than traitors to the Quargs.

"I will come with you, Master," said Meela meekly, "and so will these Quargs." She pointed to the survivors of the fire, all of who looked anything but willing followers.

"Thank you, Meela, but I think it would be best if you led them back to their homes. They have been through enough already. I will take Jonesy with me." He picked up the battered top hat and took a quick glance inside. It seemed to be empty. "Just point me in the right direction."

"No, Master. I must come with you. These Quargs will find their own way back to the centum." As she spoke, the group of tiny Quargs scuttled off somewhere into the gloom.

"What about Broga's followers, the Querks. Won't they try and stop them?"

"Meela shook her head. "No, Master. The Querks have no magic of their own. Even Quargs who are not clever ones, have some magic."

Splurge was undecided. "I'm not sure. It will be very dangerous, specially for you, because Broga will be sure to try and capture you again."

"You do not know the way. I shall lead you, besides..."

Meela hesitated.

"Besides what?"

"Broga has to get to the place where he keeps the Quigs." Meela spoke quietly and hung her head.

Splurge suspected that something was not quite right. "What's the problem, Meela. You do not have to go. I've already told you that. You give me the general direction and I'm sure that I will find it."

"We Quargs are not supposed to see the Quigs. It is our law."

Splurge was puzzled. "I don't understand. I thought that the Quigs were the young ones, the children if you like. Why would there be a law against seeing them. It doesn't make sense."

Meela still hung her head and then shuffled her feet.

Her actions reminded Splurge of somebody caught out doing something that they were not supposed to do. He could think of plenty of similar occasions, some even involving himself. He could recognise the signs of guilt.

"The Quigs are the young ones, it is true but.." she hesitated again. "They are not Quargs. They come from the outworld, like yourself."

Splurge was even more baffled. "I still don't understand. Are you trying to tell me that Quigs are young ones who have come from the outworld?"

She nodded her head.

"And are they really young, or about my age?" Splurge was beginning to have a nasty feeling about this but he needed to know more. "Tell me. Meela, it is important. Are they outworlders like myself?"

"The green one has already told you," a voice rasped from the battered top hand in Splurge's hand. "They are inquisitive outworlders like yourself, who came to the Theatre of magic as you did."

"What happened to them?"

"Ask Mysterio. He knows. That's all I'm saying." The hat shuddered for a moment, and then was still. Jonesy would say no more.

"Huh! Mysterio has gone, so how am I going to find out. I don't like mysteries and it looks like that you have all been keeping a very big secret from me." Splurge was becoming irritated. He hated it when the Quargs gave him enough information to intrigue him but wouldn't give him a full explanation. "Well, I'm going to get some answers from somebody. Broga must know and I will get it out of him."

Splurge had a vague uneasy feeling about the Quigs and he remembered what Mysterio had said to him when he first arrived, about not mentioning them to the Quargs. The sooner he got after Broga, the sooner he could get to the bottom of this particular mystery.

"Right, Meela," he said with a determined look on his face. "Show me the way."

"You should not go, Master. It is a very bad place and Broga will do many bad things." Meela looked up at Splurge and blinked her eyes.

Though he felt sorry for the tiny, green female Quarg, who had been through quite a lot, he was not about to be persuaded from chasing Broga. He suspected that the warty purple Quarg was the only one likely to give him all the answers.

"Sorry, Meela. I want to get out of this place and you Quargs have promised, that I could leave once I have banished Broga. That I intend to do." Though he sounded determined, Splurge hadn't any idea how he was going to do such a thing. He grinned. "After all, I am the Master. So anything is possible."

Chapter Twenty Nine – The Black Tower

The dreary gloom of the arena was not the most inspiring atmosphere and Splurge felt his confidence beginning to ebb away. But he knew that he must seek out Broga. If he had been uncertain before, his mind was now definitely made up by what Meela had said about the Quigs. Moreover, he couldn't really believe that Mysterio would have allowed such a thing to happen.

"You take Jonesy." He handed the battered top hat to Meela. "And keep behind me, regardless of anything that Broga might do." He gave her a grin of reassurance, though it was as much for himself as for Meela. "Let's get cracking then." He peered into the gloom hoping he could spot a likely way out.

"Get cracking, Master? What is that?"

"Get a move on, hurry. We don't want to give him too much time to prepare." Splurge already suspected that Broga would try and lay a trap for him. In fact he expected a whole string of dirty tricks from that warty Quarg.

"This way, Master." Meela suddenly went scurrying away into the gloomiest part of the arena.

Splurge, almost taken by surprise, hurried after her. "Be careful, Meela!" he called out, but she seemed not to hear him. "Females," he muttered aloud. He had come to the conclusion they never seemed to take notice of anything. The more dangerous it was, the less notice they took. It looked like it was the same with Quargs as it was in the outworld. At least, that's how he saw it.

Splurge could hear the tiny feet pattering somewhere ahead of him. "Slow down, Meela. We don't want to go charging into a trap. Ouch!" He had stumbled on something and felt himself falling. Instinctively he put out his arms to steady himself and felt something like a body, then realised it was Meela. "You didn't have to stop so suddenly. I hope I didn't hurt you." He felt a little embarrassed, though he didn't know why he should. Females always had that effect on him.

Meela, however, seemed not notice.

Splurge could barely see her in the murkiness. "Where are we? Is it a passage of some sort? It's so hard to tell. Ouch!" He had bumped into something else, this time quite solid and not so yielding as Meela.

"There are many obstacles in Broga's world. He is an untidy Quarg," said Meela.

Splurge tried to discover what he had stumbled into, and had caused what was sure to be a substantial bruise on his shin. He felt around cautiously and with some trepidation. The object appeared to be some kind of box, quite a large one. As his fingers ran along its edge, he suddenly had a nasty feeling that it could be a booby trap. "Keep away, Meela. I think I have found one of Broga's surprises." He didn't know why he thought this but it would be the sort of thing that he might do himself if he was on the run. "Ah! I've found something."

It was a catch of some kind and gingerly he flicked it back. Nothing happened. Perhaps he was mistaken. He half expected a Jack-in-the-box creature to spring out at him. If he wanted to find out what it was, he would have to raise the lid, but was unsure about doing that. He gritted his teeth. It was best that he knew what sort of thing that Broga was likely to do. Slowly he raised the lid, but nothing sprang out at them. In an odd sort of way, Splurge was disappointed. If it hadn't been so dark, he might have put his hand inside the box to see if there was anything there. Who knows what it could contain – spiders, snakes or something equally scary? As soon he began to think about such things, he wished he hadn't. Visions of snakes crawling up his legs suddenly came into his head. He quickly let the lid fall with a thud. "I don't think it was anything, just an empty box. You are right, Meela. Broga is an untidy Quarg. But it is best to take no chances. Keep close to me, and walk slower."

"It is not far now," said Meela, in a strange wavering voice.

Splurge recognised that she was afraid of something and he did not want to have to worry about her as well as himself.

He had hardly taken half dozen steps when a loud, squealing noise, like broken bagpipes, from behind caused him to turn quickly. All his thoughts about a trap had suddenly come to life. But he could see nothing, nor was the noise repeated.

"Not to worry, Meela," he said to the tiny Quarg who had come running back and gripped his arm. "Nothing to be frightened of, just one of Broga's jokes. To scare us very likely." Though Splurge didn't think it was much of a joke. "We'll have to keep our eyes open. There'll probably be other things that he has planted to slow us down."

Slowly, they made their way among the litter of Broga's world towards their destination, wherever that was. Splurge had no idea where they were going and relied completely on the tiny Quarg, who was now holding him by the hand, to lead him in the right direction. He sighed.

He would be glad to get out of this theatre to somewhere that he recognised and where there was some light. But they had gone only a few steps more when another box barred their path, slightly larger and giving off a greenish glow.

Splurge paused and he felt Meela's grip tighten.

"Wait here, while I have a closer look." After disentangling himself from the nervous Meela, he cautiously approached the box. As he got closer, he could see that though it was square it did not have the solid looking appearance of the first box. In fact, it crossed his mind that this may be some sort of illusion. It was doing nothing except glowing, though he suspected that there was something more to it, especially if Broga had left it there. "We could go round it, I suppose," he murmured to himself. He knelt down and tentatively stretched out a hand. There was no heat from the glow, and he could feel something wooden, or even cardboard. He stood and beckoned Meela. "We'll go round it. No point in disturbing whatever it is." As they began to move cautiously around the glowing obstacle, so the box moved, and like a sentinel, it was back in front of them barring their way. Whichever way they turned, so did the box and always ended up in front of them.

He was a little afraid to do anything too drastic, but Splurge could feel his frustration building up. He wanted to kick it to one side, but wasn't sure what terror he might unleash by doing so. He felt a tug on his arm.

"Master. You have the wand."

For a moment, Splurge wondered what Meela was talking about. "The wand?" He was about to say that he hadn't got such a thing when he remembered. "Of course. Hodges gave it to me with the hat. I had forgotten. I didn't think it was important." He felt in his jacket pocket, and sure enough the wand was still there. He took it out and gave it a disparaging glance. "It's not what I would call a wand. It looks more like an old stick."

"If Hodges gave it to you, it must have some magic," said Meela, in a usual solemn Quarg manner.

"Okay. I'll give it a try, but what do I have to do exactly? I've never used a wand before." Secretly, Splurge had always believed that the stage magicians in the outworld only used a wand to distract the audience.

"Point it at the light," said Meela and then stood behind Splurge.

"Why are you hiding behind me? You are not expecting anything nasty are you?" Splurge was a little suspicious, but then he had to make allowances for the tiny Quarg. She had been through a lot recently and she was bound to be scared. "Here goes," he muttered, and pointed the tatty looking wand at the glowing light. He then understood why Meela had hidden behind him,

A blinding flash of light suddenly lit up everything, and the brightness was so sharp that Splurge was temporarily blinded, giving him no chance to study his surroundings.

Rubbing his eyes, Splurge stumbled around for a while, till once more he had become used to the gloominess.

The box had gone.

"Do you see anything else, Meela? Any more of those things?" He pointed at the spot where the green glowing box had been.

"There are more of such things, Master. I will guide you to them. I do not need such light." She took hold of Splurge's hand once more and gently led him forward.

Splurge was grateful for Meela's guidance, as he was still seeing stars, and resolved to be extra careful with any more of Broga's surprises, though he would rather avoid them if he could.

"Here is another one, Master." Meela stopped and pointed.

Splurge, his vision almost back to normal, could make out what appeared to be a large round urn. What could he expect now? It had the look of something more sinister than the previous obstacles. It was quite tall, almost the same height as Meela, and he suspected that it could be hiding something or someone, a Querk possibly, or even Broga himself. He dismissed the latter idea, as he couldn't see Broga wasting an opportunity to taunt or threaten him. It seemed that he enjoyed that as much as performing whatever unpleasant act came into his lumpy head. "Stand well away from it, Meela. I am going to smash it." He took out the tatty wand once more and pointed it at the urn, willing it to smash as he did so.

Nothing seemed to work on some obstacles as Splurge had expected or hoped. Whatever he did seemed to make them either dangerous or frightening. But nothing happened with this one.

Just as he was beginning to think that perhaps this one was a dud, he heard a strange gurgling sound coming from it, soft but definite. Suddenly he had visions of something slimy and loathsome about to slither out. A cold shiver ran down his neck and already he was imagining some horrible serpent-like creature about to slide its head over the rim. He waited, trying to work out what he should do if his worst fears were confirmed.

After what seemed an age, with nothing happening, it struck him that Broga was once again was using some of that forbidden magic to play about with his mind. Fear was a great weapon, even in small quantities, and Broga had been clever enough to sense Splurge's weakness in this respect. He looked at Meela, who had not moved or spoken, but who's large, round eyes were focussed with a strange intensity on the urn.

"What do you think, Meela?"

As if coming out of a trance, the tiny Quarg shook her head from side to side. "It is nothing, Master. Broga is a clever Quarg. He plays games with us."

"I think that you are right about that. Let's not waste any more time." Splurge felt better now that problem had been solved, and they continued their journey. It was strange, he thought, how each of the obstacles they had encountered had only reacted when he had tried to do something to them. Perhaps with the next one, he should test his theory by totally ignoring it.

Though he kept peering hard into the gloom, he could discern no more obstacles, and after only a short distance further, they stopped.

Meela pointed. Sure enough, ahead of them, only a matter of a few yards, a light seemed to be coming up from the ground. It was a much greater light than anything they had seen so far in this gloomy world of Broga.

Splurge was sure that he could also hear voices, but sort of vague and jumbled.

Meela put her fingers to her lips and slowly went forward towards the light, almost crawling as she did so.

Splurge was quick to imitate her action and began to crouch as he moved towards the light. The ground was hard and more than once he grazed himself on the uneven surface. Although he had never had a good sight of this world of Broga, he guessed that it was much the same in construction as the Quarg world, and was carved out of rock. He winced every time he rubbed against some stony protrusion. His trousers and sleeves of is jacket must be in a real mess. He could imagine his mother's face when he eventually got home and looking as though he had been in a fight. He gave an inward sigh, as he knew that he was never going to be able to explain how he had got into such a state.

"Master must be quiet. Broga will hear," Meela cautioned.

Splurge didn't much care about Broga, or what he thought, but he agreed that for the moment it might be a good idea not to go barging in to wherever it was. Then he saw it.

It was another place that was as magical and impossible as any he had seen in this strange realm of the Theatre of Magic.

He and Meela were now perched on the edge of what looked to be the rim of an enormous hole. It was so wide that he couldn't see much of the other side, despite the extra height. How the hole, which was more like a crater, had come to be here, he had no idea. It looked as though it had been scooped out of the ground, but he was less interested in its origin than what he saw before him.

Hundreds of tiny pinpricks of light sparkled from numerous buildings of varying sizes. It was a bit like having a bird's eye view of a city at night. (Not that Splurge had seen many cities at night, but he had seen such things on television). There was a great deal of movement among the buildings, but Splurge could detect no detail and could only guess that the tiny, moving figures were Querks. But what really caught his eye was one building, which protruded far above the rest, a dark, sombre, brooding edifice, which seemed to be cut out of the rock itself. From his position on the edge of the crater it looked to be very rough and misshapen. If it was Broga's headquarters, it well suited his character, he thought.

Splurge was so engrossed in studying the dark building that he gave a start when Meela touched him on the arm and pointed. Following the direction in which she had pointed, Splurge noticed another unusual feature. At first he thought it was another hole, but from his lofty position, it could have been anything. Nevertheless it seemed so out of place and he could only suppose that it was for some special purpose.

"We must get down there, Meela. I can't see Broga from this distance and I can't see any Quargs." Splurge stood and moved back from the edge of the crater, his eyes searching for a means of getting down there.

Meela said nothing but hung her head in the same manner she had done earlier, like someone caught out doing something forbidden.

"What's the matter, Meela?"

"Master must not go down there. He will see things. Meela will go to Broga and the Master will be safe."

"You are talking in riddles, Meela. What do you mean?" Splurge had often thought that Quargs were somewhat reluctant to communicate too much when they spoke. He could never tell whether it was part of their manner, or whether it was deliberate.

"I do not know riddles," Meela answered meekly, still hanging her head.

Splurge wondered if Meela's attitude had something to do with the Quigs. He still wasn't absolutely sure what a Quig was and the only way to find out was to see for himself. There lurked somewhere at the back of his mind an idea that he ought to know, or at least be able to guess the truth about the Quigs.

"Riddles are when you make more questions than answers. The only way I am going to find out anything is to get down there. I need to get to Broga before he does any serious harm to anyone." He had decided that if the worst came to the worst, he would climb down. It didn't look too steep and he was sure that he could manage. "You stay here, Meela. I don't want Broga getting hold of you again." With that he began to ease himself over the edge of the crater.

"No Master!" Meela gave a sudden cry. "You must not do that. It will be dangerous." She paused and then, with a strange look on her face, she continued. "If you must go to the dark place, Mela will show you the way, but I may not come with you."

Splurge scrambled back. He much preferred his way down to be as trouble free as possible, as he was he was sure to get plenty of trouble when he got there.

"Where?"

Meela led him a little way further along the rim and then pointed. "There, Master. Those steps will take to the dark world."

Splurge was surprised to see a set of stone steps, at least he supposed that they were stone. The whole place looked as though it had been carved out of solid rock, though somehow he couldn't see Broga taking such trouble. He wondered how he had managed to miss them. Maybe it was just a question of angles. He hoped that they were not too ragged, otherwise it would be no different to scaling his own way down.

"Right. I shall go down, but you wait for me here," he said to Meela, sounding very much like a big brother. "Now, have I got everything?" He checked his jacket pocket for the wand – still there. But he was not sure what to do about the battered top hat with Jonesy inside. It might be useful, he thought, and before he could ask Meela, she was holding it out for him. He gave her a reassuring grin and began his descent into Broga's stronghold.

The steps were solid enough, even if a little uneven, and though from the edge of the giant crater he had seemed to be quite high up, there were not many steps to negotiate. When he had reached the last one, he saw why.

What had looked like a small town was indeed a small town. The buildings were tiny. Only the black one was of any size, standing out like a huge, threatening monument above all the others. Splurge, of course, was forgetting the size of Querks, who were no bigger than the Quargs themselves. An optical illusion he guessed.

He was also puzzled by the fact that he could see no obvious source of light, which seemed to be cast down from somewhere above, perhaps from some hidden floodlights. But that couldn't be, because he would have seen it when he was at the top of the crater. Perhaps it was another optical illusion. Anyway, Broga wouldn't use such ordinary gadgets. He probably had his own magical method of making light.

But where was Broga?

Slowly and cautiously, Splurge began to thread his way through the tangle of small buildings, making for that tall black building, which he assumed was the place that Broga himself would use. It was looking more formidable and menacing as he drew closer, which didn't take long as the buildings down here were much more organised and neatly laid out, almost in a sort of street pattern.

Then he was there, staring up at the tall, black building, which towered over every other, monstrous and threatening. Splurge couldn't help giving a shudder when he looked at it, but he wasn't surprised – it was so like Broga.

If this fortress was made of rock, it was surprisingly smooth and neatly cut out, although a little uneven in its proportions, no one wall being the same size as another. The whole building looked as though it might topple over at the slightest nudge. The doors, of which there were several, also had that same lopsided look. Splurge could see no windows, though he did notice several dark recesses, which he supposed were outlets of a sort, but no glass. In other circumstances, this crooked building might have caused him some amusement. It was not so much weird as grotesque and Splurge felt shivers run down his spine by just looking at it. What should he do now, he wondered? Go inside? That was where Broga was sure to be. Yet it was odd that the evil Quarg was not here to greet him. That would be Broga's style, he reckoned. But there was noone. In fact the whole town, what he had seen of it, appeared to be deserted. From up above he had seen much activity among the Querks, but they seemed to have all disappeared. Maybe they were in hiding, because they were afraid of him, though he didn't think that likely. And what about that pit? It must be somewhere around here but, before he could begin searching for it he must find Broga.

As Splurge was about to was about to move towards the crooked building, he was startled by a loud booming sound, which echoed and reverberated with such intensity that he was forced to put his hands over his ears. It was like the tolling of an enormous bell, with him in the bell chamber, so loud was it. Then it stopped as suddenly as it had started. For a moment there was a deathly silence, broken by a strange whispering. At first it sounded like a gathering of Quargs. Something made him turn round and there behind him were scores, maybe hundreds of Querks, all slowly advancing upon him.

If Splurge had though them ugly before, in such large numbers they were even more hideous, at first looking like a mob of angry scarecrows, but gradually beginning to resemble skeletal bodies which had just climbed out of their graves. Their humming was interspersed with odd whirring sounds, which made him think of mechanical toys somehow come to life. He should have been afraid, but after the last encounter with these creatures, he was confident that he could deal with them.

The Querks kept moving forward, at the same time forming a circle around him. Now was the time for the wand and another dose of Kanu's gift. He took the scruffy looking stick out of his pocket and pointed it at the nearest of these creatures.

It worked. Immediately they all came to a halt as though suddenly switched off. Their faces showed no sign of fear or panic, though it was difficult to tell, because their features were so distorted and twisted anyway.

Splurge pondered how long they would remain like that. He had used no magic, nor had he shouted as he usually did. Perhaps they were afraid of what he might do. Nevertheless, he would keep a careful lookout for any sign that that they might suddenly decide to rush at him. Though he had stopped them, he wasn't sure what to do next.

The question was answered for him.

A loud, raucous laugh caused him to turn back to the black building. Standing there in front of it, on some sort of pedestal, which had magically arisen from the ground, was Broga. It was the same ugly, warty Quarg, but now wrapped in a deep purple cloak, making him look like a giant bat.

"So, you avoided my little surprises. Good. They were small tricks of mine to give you something to think about. I thought I would have a little amusement before we got down to the serious business."

Though his face was screwed up in a crooked smile, there was something decidedly unpleasant about the sound of Broga's words. Splurge was reminded of a vampire about to take over his prey. (He had seen several films about vampires, so he knew).

Splurge was not far wrong, for with a quick flourish, Broga suddenly unfurled his cloak and there within its folds were the cowering figures of Hodges and Wilkins.

Splurge struggled to understand, for Broga appeared to have grown and was now about the same size as he was, unless the Quargs had somehow been reduced in size. More forbidden magic, he supposed, or it could all be an illusion. He could never tell with this place, though he had a strong suspicion that machinery came into it somewhere. Even Broga, who now assumed an arrogant pose with the two Quargs quivering beside him, could be the work of some clever mechanic. Yet he doubted it. Broga was too loathsome to be a machine or a robot.

But, whatever Broga was, one thing was certain and that was his intention to inflict more misery on the Quargs.

"So this is where you are hiding, Broga," Splurge called out, using his best sarcastic manner. He had to get the purple Quarg down from that pedestal. At first he had considered using Kanu's gift once more, but decided that the situation wasn't that dangerous. Also he was afraid of hurting Hodges or Wilkins, although he didn't have too much sympathy for them, after the way they had betrayed him and their fellow Quargs. "I don't think much of your castle, if that's what it's supposed to be."

Broga glowered. "Castle? I do not know castle," he snarled. "This is my domain, and you would do well to remember that, outworlder." He practically screeched out the words.

Splurge forced a laugh. "Your domain? Not much of one, is it? Why don't you come down and met me on equal terms, if you understand 'equal', or if you dare."

Broga continued to glower and his eyes bore into Splurge, like some demented sprite.

Splurge could not make up his mind about this renegade Quarg. Sometimes he acted like a spoilt child and at others he would both look and act like a vicious imp from hell. As far as Splurge was concerned, he possessed no redeeming features, either in looks or manner, and his deeds so far had been anything but pleasant. At the moment, however, he looked like a bird of prey waiting to swoop upon some luckless victim. Splurge was going to make sure that he wasn't going to be that victim, but he needed Broga on the ground where it would be easier to fight him, as fight him he must.

Though it didn't look as though Broga was to be persuaded or taunted into coming off that pedestal. Splurge would have to think of something else. Perhaps he could use some other form of magic but, unfortunately, he didn't know much. What magic he did have he had so far been using by instinct or accident. He had been lucky and he was afraid that at any moment his luck would run out.

As Splurge eyed the malevolent, purple Quarg, trying to think of a way to lure him from his perch, there was a rustling sound behind him. As he turned to face what he thought would be an advancing circle of Querks, there was a loud explosion only a few feet away from him.

Black smoke erupted from the spot and within the smoke Splurge could see tiny flashes of light.

Without warning, Broga had struck.

Suddenly, Splurge began to writhe in agony as he felt hundreds of small, sharp stabbing pains all over his body. As he strove to brush off whatever had struck him, he realised that these flashing lights were in fact very tiny daggers. There were so many that he was having difficulty removing them. He was sure that his face and head would be pouring with blood, but worse was the thought that the Querks would now close in and finish him off. He was endeavouring not to panic. Despite the desperate situation, he had to think straight. If he could just get at his wand, he might be able to do something. But just as he managed to get his hand into his jacket pocket, he felt something pull at him. Dozens of long, bony hands began to grab at him, pulling and pinching as if to tear off his flesh. He could no longer feel the pain of those tiny daggers because the new pain was much more damaging. As he struggled with all his strength he fancied he could hear Broga laughing.

The smell of these creatures, as they strove to pull him to pieces, was enough to make him vomit. He could stand it no longer. "GERROFF ME!" he shouted as loud as possible.

The effect was immediate as it was magical.

There was a sudden, wild scampering as the encircling Querks retreated, as though they had been scalded. The black smoke had now dispersed and Splurge could see that most of the Querks had run off. Only one or two lingered, hiding behind their tiny buildings, occasionally poking out a misshapen head to stare at Splurge, with wide, fearful eyes,

Broga too was gone. As Splurge glanced up at the pedestal, he could see only the two crouching figures of the Quargs - Hodges and Wilkins. As he dusted himself down and removed the last of the daggers, he was surprised to find that they hadn't caused much harm to him after all. And there was no blood streaming down his face, as he had been sure there would be. For a moment, he wondered if he had imagined it, because Broga did have this nasty habit of using one's own fears to cause uncertainty and confusion.

"That's what forbidden magic is all about," he murmured to himself, as he was sure that's how Broga would use it. If only he could do the same to the twisted Quarg, though he was sure that Jonesy had mentioned something about it rebounding on the user. If ever he was going to defeat Broga that was the way to do it – but how?

Splurge didn't have much time to think about it, however, because his thoughts were interrupted by the roaring voice of Broga, who had reappeared upon the pedestal.

"So you are still here?" Broga grimaced. "I thought my loyal guard would have had you in the pit by now. You are lucky, outworlder. But your luck is about to run out." With a violent thrust he toppled the two Quargs from the pedestal, where they plummeted to the ground with sickening thuds.

Splurge was sure that was the end of them, though he did detect slight movements from the crumpled bodies. He wanted to go to them and see if he could help in any way, but daren't let himself be exposed to the wiles of Broga.

"That's how I will deal with you!" Broga screamed, and pointed at the two inert Quargs on the ground. With a complete change of manner, he allowed himself a smile, though to Spluge it was more like a smirk. "I may let you live," he said slowly, "but only on condition that you acknowledge me as the one and only true Master. I have the forbidden magic – all of it, and nothing can stop me, so you may as well give in now and save yourself more pain." As he spoke, he pointed, and a beam of light shone from his hand, aimed directly at Splurge's head.

Instantly, Splurge raised his own hand to ward off the light. It struck him on the forearm, and rebounded at a right angles to shoot away and explode somewhere in a ball of flame, demolishing several Querk dwellings.

If Broga was disappointed or discouraged by his lack of success, he didn't show it, but continued to fire further beams at Splurge, one after the other.

Splurge found it relatively easy to deal with them in the same manner and soon there were many more dwellings on fire or totally destroyed. The unfortunate occupants of any such building scrambled into an adjoining one, which almost immediately would be blown up.

But even Broga tired of the game when he saw how easily Splurge had dealt with the deadly beams of light.

Splurge himself, had no idea how he had managed, and it occurred to him that Broga was softening him for something much more deadly – or perhaps he didn't, after all, have much in that bag of tricks of his. On balance, he was inclined to think that something more lethal was likely, and that may not be quite so easy to handle.

Broga was still perched on his pedestal, looking down on Splurge in his usual arrogant posture. "Now you are about to learn what a real Master can do," he growled. With a quick movement, almost taking Splurge by surprise, he unfurled his cloak and from within its folds scores of black winged creatures emerged.

They looked like huge flies till they were close to Splurge, when he recognised them as some sort of wasp, but not the usual striped variety. He also noticed that their stings were quite long in relation to their bodies.

Splurge shuddered.

They were dangerous looking specimens and he could almost feel their sharp stingers as they circled around him, getting closer and closer. Their buzzing was like a thousand tiny aeroplanes. Though he had expected something far worse, he would still have to take special care, as he was certain that they could cause him a lot of pain, maybe even death. (He had heard of people being stung to death by wasps). Once again he stretched out his hands in front of him and yelled as loud as he could. "GO BACK!"

This time, instead of returning to Broga, the horde of black wasps dropped to the ground where they immediately dissolved into tiny pools of dark, sticky liquid.

"When are you going to get tired of playing these games, Broga? You should know that I could deal with anything that you throw at me. You? The Master? Don't make me laugh." Splurge did a forced guffaw, as he tried to lure Broga from his pedestal. And it worked.

Broga stamped up and down, spitting and snarling like an angry cobra. In a sudden flash and a cloud of black smoke, he was gone, and so was the pedestal. But he reappeared just as quickly, this time in front of Splurge.

Splurge stepped back in alarm at the suddenness of Broga turning up like that. But now that he had his wish he could do nothing, for held tightly in his grasp was the figure of Meela, who looked as though Broga or his minions had beaten her again. Dark smears streaked her face and there were ugly marks and swellings around her eyes.

"What have you done to her, you coward?" Splurge was bursting with anger and he took a step towards Broga, ready to abandon all thoughts of any magical tricks and just give him one huge punch.

Broga, sensing Splurge's intention, stepped back a few paces, pulling the unresisting Meela with him. There was a strange glint in his eyes, as he suddenly realised that he had unexpectedly found his enemy's weak spot. "One more step and you will never see your precious Quarg again," Broga sneered with delight.

Splurge was not deterred by Broga's threats. He advanced upon the renegade Quarg, determined to get hold of his lumpy face and give it a good bashing. That was definitely in his mind and he would have taken his chances against any forbidden magic, which Broga might use. Then he heard a voice.

"Use your head, not your fists."

Splurge faltered, and then relaxed a little. It was Jonesy's voice, and sure enough at his feet was the battered top hat. How did it get here? He looked at Meela, who flickered her eyes, but appeared to be in no state to explain. In any case, Jonesy was right. He must use his wits against this evil Quarg, because he couldn't do anything while Meela was in his clutches.

"You want me, Broga, not that Quarg. Let's do a deal. Let her go and I will leave, go back to the outworld. Then you will be undisputed Master. How does that sound?" Splurge was trying hard to think of anything that would satisfy Broga and get him to release Meela. How she had let herself be taken was a bit of a mystery, but he would sort that out later.

Broga said nothing but slowly shook his head, his eyes glowing with a demonic sparkle.

"Well? What about it? Seems fair to me." Splurge didn't really expect Broga to agree but he had to try everything. With Meela being held hostage, however, he was hampered in what he could do.

"You can have this green one, but first you must come to the pit." Broga's eyes still shone and he slowly licked his lips, as if to anticipate some special delight in which he was about to partake.

"The pit? What do you mean?" Though Splurge had asked the question, he had already had a glimpse of some great hole, when on the rim of the crater. He was intrigued and he had to find out more and to do that he must continue the game of bartering with Broga.

"Come with me and I will show you. It will answer all your questions about the Quargs and me. Maybe you won't be so eager to help them when you learn the truth." He chuckled and gave a hearty tug on Meela's arm. She whimpered with the pain.

"I'll come with you, Broga, but first I must see if Hodges and Wilkins are still alive." He pointed to the foot of the pedestal, where the crumpled figures of the two Quargs still lay where Broga had thrown them.

"Don't trouble yourself, outworlder. My people will bring them." He motioned with his free hand and at once a dozen Querks appeared and scurried towards the two figures and dragged them upright. They appeared to be alive, for which Splurge was thankful, but they looked to be in worse shape than Meela, and staggered very unsteadily as they were prodded and pulled by the Querks. Neither of them looked at Splurge or Meela, but both looked so miserable that even Splurge was feeling a little sorry for them.

"You will follow us. If you decide to change your mind and go back to the outworld, you can do so anytime you like. But you will not see these Quargs again. Abruptly he turned from Splurge and strode away, pulling Meela along behind him.

Though angry at Broga, Splurge knew there was nothing he could do yet and could only wait for a suitable opportunity, though he was a little uneasy at visiting the pit. Broga had hinted strongly at some funny business and Splurge himself had again let his imagination work overtime. It was, therefore, with some misgivings that he allowed himself to be conducted to this pit, which Broga seemed to think would answer all his questions.

However, instead of walking towards the great dark hole, which Splurge had seen from the rim of the crater, Broga turned towards the black fortress and disappeared through one of its dark portals.

A little puzzled, Splurge had no option but to follow.

The inside of Broga's castle was just as disjointed as it had appeared from the outside. Everything was cut from the same black stone, which shone like highly polished marble. There were numerous twisting passageways and winding staircases but nothing to show where one room began and another ended. Also there was no sign of any kind of furniture or adornments and the polished floor echoed the sound of their footsteps.

Splurge was reminded of the Quarg centum, except that everything was in reverse as in a photographic negative. There appeared to be no obvious source of light that Splurge could see, though a strange dull orange glow oozed from the walls.

Querks were everywhere, hiding in the darker corners or scuttling like rats across the smooth floor, and Splurge was constantly on his guard, expecting that they might launch an attack at any moment. A distinctly creepy place, he reckoned.

Broga stopped before two massive doors, which were definitely hung in an odd crooked way.

Splurge suddenly had a moment of panic as he remembered the entrance to the crystal caves and those monstrous guardians. If Broga had anything like that, then they were sure to be much worse.

With a wave of his free hand, the doors swung open, creaking and groaning as though not used very often. To Splurge's relief, there were no guardians, nor was there any mist. The doors had opened into nothing more than a great hall at the end of which was a wide staircase. It seemed to lead up to the ceiling but where it stopped, Splurge couldn't tell. This room was much less crooked than the rest of the building. In fact he could see nothing wrong with it, except that it was all black marble. Splurge shivered. It was cold in here.

Broga stomped his way to the foot of the staircase and clicked his fingers. Immediately dozens of Querks appeared. He thrust Meela towards them and several of them began to drag her up the steps. Others were doing the same to Hodges and Wilkins.

For the first time since he had been catapulted into this strange world of the Theatre of Magic, Splurge heard Quargs cry out. Whether it was in pain or rage, he couldn't tell, but Meela began to struggle and was making a keening sound, like a bird in distress. Then she called out to him.

"Master! Master! You must stop them!"

Hodges and Wilkins were making similar noises, but did not call to him, though they also struggled against their captors.

Splurge was a little surprised that they were unable to break free because he knew how strong Quargs could be. He remembered his own manhandling and the bruises they had caused when he had first found himself in this theatre. These Querks were no more than skeletons, only half his size, yet they must possess great strength to be able to handle the Quargs. It had never struck him before, but perhaps Broga was using some sort of magic to help the Querks to drag their prisoners along with such ease.

Meela continued to call out as she was forced up the steps and her cries sounded so pitiful that Splurge was strongly tempted to use his 'gift'. But maybe the old fashioned way was best in this case.

Before Broga, or any of the Querks, could stop him, Splurge had bounded up the steps three at a time till he was beside the struggling figure of Meela. He immediately lashed out at the Querks holding her, but they proved too strong and awkward for him. "LET HER GO!" he shouted, but they ignored him. Not loud enough, he thought. "LET HER GO!" he yelled at the top of his voice. At the very least his voice should have echoed and re-echoed, as it usually did, but it sounded no more than a feeble growl. The Querks holding Meela merely grinned, and continued to pull her up the steps, easily repelling any attempts by Splurge to release her.

Why hadn't it worked? Splurge was perplexed, and suddenly felt a distinct vulnerability. It looked as though he had lost one of his major weapons. What could he do now? He turned to Broga, who stood at the foot of the staircase and was laughing, a loud, coarse laugh which filled the whole of the hall, and reverberated throughout his black castle.

"You have no power here, outworlder – and soon you will have precious little else." As he spoke, he hobbled up the steps till he was face to face with Splurge. "You cannot save the green one, nor can you save the others. Mysterio is gone and now I have the hat."

To his dismay, Splurge saw that Broga was holding the battered top hat in which Jonesy was hiding. Now he knew that he was totally alone – except for Kanu's gift. Dare he use it – and would it work? Or was Broga bluffing? He looked into the watery bloodshot eyes of the dirty, purple Quarg, and then looked up the stairs to the struggling figure of Meela. He didn't know whether to risk it.

"Come, outworlder, let me show you what fate awaits those miserable Quargs."

Before he could resist, Broga had taken hold of Splurge's arm in a vice-like grip. He had forgotten that Broga himself was a Quarg and Quargs of course were possessed of great strength. Broga was now acting as though he had nothing to fear from Splurge.

"I must show you my finest creation. You will appreciate it, I'm sure." He chuckled at some private joke. "You will also learn something about these Quargs." He leered at Splurge.

Splurge didn't react to Broga's forceful invitation, though he was sure that he could have broken away, if he had tried, but he wanted to see where Meela and the others had been taken. He still couldn't understand why she had so easily let herself be taken. Meanwhile he noticed that the Querks had disappeared up the staircase, which seemed to go on forever.

Without warning the staircase ended, and in front of them was another large hall or it might have been a landing. Splurge couldn't really tell, but his attention was caught by a dull humming sound, which came from somewhere ahead. At the same time he could see crowds of Querks, all standing in a circle.

"Come! Come!" Broga pulled him forward to the edge of this circle and there a strange and horrifying sight met his eyes.

Splurge and the Theatre of Magic

Chapter Thirty – The Pit

At first, Splurge couldn't believe what he was seeing. He had long suspected that Broga had some sort of dark, sinister place where he kept his prisoners, but nothing so wide and deep as this pit into which he was now staring. Like a huge cauldron it heaved and throbbed. Countless bodies of Quargs writhed and twitched in one horrid tangle.

Broga hopped about like a mad goblin to see the look on Splurge's face. How do you like my brew?" He cackled and waved his hand towards the struggling mass. Immediately a shower of objects, which looked like chunks of rock, rained down on the hapless victims, causing them to writhe about even more.

Splurge was sickened at the sight. How long had those Quargs been kept prisoner, he wondered. He was sure that many of them must have been trampled to death.

"Don't feel pity for them, outworlder," Broga snarled. "They are nothing. They are there for punishment and training."

"Training?" Splurge asked. "Training for what?"

"They are training to be Quigs."

Broga's explanation didn't make sense. "Why should they train to be children?"

Broga laughed aloud. "You have been fooled, interfering outworlder. The Quargs are very good at not revealing the truth. Quigs are my slaves. They help to work my magic, which soon will be so strong that even that old man, Kanu, will have to acknowledge me as the one true Master. All will be mine." He laughed his usual raucous laugh, which, this time was echoed by the numerous Querks gathered around the pit. It made a terrifying sound as if scores of screeching gulls were wheeling about overhead. Broga paused in his merriment to give Splurge a cold, calculating look. "Beware outworlder." He pointed a long bony finger. "When I have taken control here, I may come to your outworld and make magic there."

"Over my dead body," Splurge retorted, feeling anger rising within him.

"That can also be arranged," Broga said with a crooked smile. He motioned several Querks, who advanced on Splurge. "How would you like to join them?" He pointed to the writhing mass in the pit.

"NO!" Splurge let out a yell as the first Querk touched him.

The Querk jumped back in alarm, and the others hesitated, waiting to see what Splurge would do next.

"So you can frighten my feeble followers." Broga chuckled. "They are not much but they have proved useful. Maybe their time has also come, as it has for this Quarg here." He went towards Meela, still being held on the edge of the pit, and pulled her roughly towards him.

Meela whimpered and looked at Splurge. She said nothing, but her large round eyes implored him to do something to save her.

Splurge was still tormented by the thought of whatever he did, might easily cause her and the other Quargs to be harmed or even destroyed.

"Do you really think it is worthwhile for you to be concerned with these creatures? They are weak and spineless. They do not tell the truth and worse – they have betrayed you. Those two," he pointed at Hodges and Wilkins, "have been particularly useful to me. They have arranged for an endless supply of Quargs for my pit and the mines, where they work once they are trained."

"You are a Quarg yourself, Broga," Splurge said hotly. "It is you have betrayed your own kind. You have used their unwillingness to harm other Quargs to blackmail them into doing your dirty work."

"I am not a Quarg!" Broga suddenly screeched, stamping his feet at the same time. "Do I look like one of those?" He indicated the squirming bodies in the pit.

"If you looked in a mirror, you would see what an ugly creature you are, Quarg or not. And it's about time that someone stopped you."

"You, I suppose," sniggered Broga. "You have neither the power nor the wit to match me, let alone stop me." He gave a wide toothy grin, though with few teeth it looked anything but a grin. "Besides, you wouldn't want anything to happen to this green one." He pulled Meela towards the edge of the pit, threatening to throw her in.

"You are not only ugly and a poor magician, but you are also a coward," Splurge said, his disgust and anger building up to boiling point. He wanted to smash this Broga into a million pieces, obliterate him. "I'm surprised that Mysterio didn't deal with you."

"He did. He did." Broga said gleefully. "But his power is no good down here, as your power is no good down here. Nobody's power but mine can succeed." He screamed the last words, and with a violent fling, threw the battered old top hat into the pit.

Splurge watched the hat plummet into the mass of bodies, to be lost from sight at once. His heart sank.

Jonesy was gone. There was no more help to be had from that quarter and he could only hope that the Gromilly had somehow had managed to escape or do something, but what, he couldn't imagine.

"And that's how this green one will go." Though he was not much bigger than Meela, Broga lifted her into the air and was on the point of throwing her into the pit, when Splurge, in a sudden wild dash, charged. He knew that he was taking a tremendous risk, but he had to do something.

Splurge hit Broga with such force that the three of them fell to the ground, and only inches from the edge of the pit.

Winded but unhurt, Splurge quickly scrambled to his feet. Broga was less nimble and it took him a moment or two before he managed to stand upright. It was enough time for Splurge to reach into his jacket pocket for his wand. It was not a moment too soon, for as soon as Broga was upright, he unleashed a ball of fire and hurled it into the pit, where it exploded, sending up a shower of bright tongues of flame.

Splurge could only gape in horror. All the Quargs in the pit must have been killed, murdered by Broga, who now turned to Splurge and was preparing to do something similar to him.

"Your turn, meddling outworlder." Broga spat out the words, his face twisted into a mask of hate. "And then that green one." He pointed at Meela, who tried to scramble further away but was prevented by the ring of Querks. "The green one first, I think." He sneered at Splurge and hurled another fireball at Meela.

"NOOOOOOO!" Splurge gave a prolonged shout and, pointed his wand at the ball of flame, which was suddenly halted in mid-air. For a brief second it paused before swerving around towards himself. As he was a step further away, he had a fraction more time to think and plan what to do. Now he had to protect himself. He pointed the wand at the mass of roaring flames as it sped straight at him. "BACK!" he yelled.

But nothing happened. The ball of fire was almost upon him. Soon he would be engulfed like those Quargs in the pit. There was only one thing to do. He dropped his wand and stretched out his arms towards Broga, who was just visible beyond the flame, skipping and dancing in a wild delight. Splurge knew that he was taking a chance on Kanu's gift taking effect through flame, but he would have to try. The heat was unbearable as he strove to concentrate, and he hoped that Broga wouldn't have time to prepare a defence.

Then it happened.

He felt a sharp tingle in his right arm and a white light shot out from the ends of his fingers. The beam cut through the flame, dissolving it into nothing, before turning towards Broga.

Splurge could never be absolutely sure whether he had intended for it to happen or not, but when the beam of light struck Broga, his whole body convulsed into a sheet of light, which seemed to leap and dance about. No sound came from the purple Quarg, and though it took only a second or two, it seemed to Splurge that Boga was dancing in agony for ages.

Then it was over.

The beam of light flowing from the ends of Slurge's fingers stopped, leaving him with a strange emptiness. He looked across at Broga, who was lying on the edge of the pit, not moving. Cautiously he approached the crumpled form of the renegade Quarg. There was no movement and Splurge could see that he was dead, though in his last moments, it looked as if Broga had tried to speak or make some sound for his mouth was all twisted out of shape and wide open.

Now it was done, Splurge felt no sense of achievement or satisfaction. He would much have preferred for Broga to simply vanish without all this killing.

"It couldn't be otherwise."

Splurge almost jumped out of his skin, for standing before him was the figure of Kanu, the High Factor and with him, Mysterio.

Splurge could only gape in astonishment. "But..but..," he stuttered and pointed to the lifeless form of Broga. For some reason he suddenly felt very sad for this ugly purple Quarg, as well as for all the other Quargs who had been killed.

"You must not feel sorry," Kanu said in his faraway voice. "You were brought here to destroy Broga, but we had to make it so that you were angry enough to destroy. We knew what Broga was capable of and what he could do." The High Factor paused as though trying to gain his breath. "We cannot kill our own, but we have discovered that outworlders seem not to mind killing their own, and seek out many different ways to do so. We do not understand such things."

Splurge, his sadness now replaced by feeling of bitterness. "So you brought me here to do your dirty work for you." He glowered at the High Factor, daring him to contradict, but Kanu merely nodded in understanding of Splurge's resentment at being used.

Mysterio took Splurge by the arm and led him away from the pit. "You must understand the Quargs," he said quietly. "You may have noticed that they are not particularly brave. They don't have what you might call 'backbone'." Mysterio's dark eyes twinkled and he clapped Splurge on the shoulder, almost sending him crashing to the ground. "You supplied that, as I knew you would."

"But..I thought that you were gone," Splurge stammered.

Mysterio laughed, a reverberating laugh, which sounded oddly out of place in the grim surroundings of Broga's world. "Come, let's get back to the theatre," he boomed. "My hat and cape if you please."

Before Splurge could blink, the hat and cape were back with Mysterio.

"What about the Quargs?" Splurge indicated the pit. "Shouldn't they be buried or something? And what about Broga? You are not just going to leave him there, are you? And what about Meela?" He looked at the tiny green Quarg, who seemed not to notice him as she was kneeling before Kanu. Splurge felt that he ought to say something to her but he had no idea what to say. "And shouldn't we do something about the Quigs?"

"Qigs?" Mysterio gave a slight chuckle. "It was as Broga said. They were his slaves, Querks in training so to speak. It was the Quargs' idea to suggest that they might be something more in order to feed your determination to fight Broga. Very shrewd these Quargs."

"So what happens to them now? Splurge nodded in the direction of the pit.

"Don't worry about all that. The High Factor will sort it out." Mysterio gave him a friendly pat on the back. "We have to get you back to the outworld."

In a daze, Splurge found himself being shepherded back through the dark city of Broga and the Querks, who were strangely noticeable by their absence. He was taking little interest in his surroundings, however, as his mind was still full of visions of the burning Quargs and the death of Broga. They were images he wanted to forget but he couldn't help repeating in his mind everything that had happened here, over and over again. Before he knew it, he was back in the tiny theatre, almost as though they walked through a door and there it was. Splurge suspected that Mysterio had produced some sort of magic, but he was beyond wondering about all that stuff now. He just wanted to get back to his own world.

Soon he was treading the boards of the very stage on which he had given his first performance. It seemed so very long ago, and so much had happened.

"Do I get to go back to the outworld now?" Splurge asked wearily.

Mysterio knit his brow and gave him a strange look. "Are you sure that is what you want. You did a good job."

"Huh. I wouldn't have had to do it if you hadn't decided to leave." Splurge still bore some resentment at being manipulated. "You said you were going for good, and I thought that you had."

"I should have told you earlier, perhaps, but I couldn't do anything about Broga. I am not allowed to interfere in the lives of the Quargs. I have the power it is true, more power maybe than Kanu realises, but I may neither use it to help nor hinder the Quargs, or anyone else for that matter."

"You interfered in my life," Splurge retorted. "I didn't want to fight Broga, let alone kill him."

"Hmm." Mysterio stroked his beard. "Maybe you are right, but someone had to do it and you were the perfect choice."

"Why me?"

"Because you are an outworlder. Whatever you may feel, you will always do what you believe is the best. That's why you were chosen."

Splurge was bemused once more. He felt that Mysterio was trying to avoid his responsibility. "But you are an outworlder – aren't you? And what about Jonesy? He was destroyed in the pit – or was he?"

Mysterio had said nothing but listened to Splurge's attempt to make sense of it all, with an amused look on his face.

Suddenly Splurge had a blinding flash. He didn't know why he hadn't thought of it before. Not once in all his wanderings and dangers had he seen Mysterio and Jonesy together. Neither had been present when the other was there.

"You – you and Jonesy are...," he began, when Mysterio, with a wave of his hand and a bright flash of light suddenly disappeared from the stage. The curtains swished open to reveal him reclining in one of the small seats in the theatre. It was much too small for him, of course, but somehow he seemed to fit into it without any difficulty.

What now, Splurge wondered?

A strange noise began to fill the theatre and hundreds of Quargs trooped in to fill the remaining seats, leaving Mysterio like a large, black rock in the middle of a sea of blue and green.

"And now for our finale," Mysterio boomed and waved towards the stage, "with a full cast."

Lights blazed on the stage as they dimmed in the audience. Then, from somewhere at the back of the stage, a colourful Quarg marched out banging a big drum. As before, at each thump on the drum another Quarg would step from behind the drummer till a whole line of Quargs stood before him. The line parted as several other Quargs came down the stage towards him.

Splurge gasped in astonishment. The first of them was Wilkins, who came up to him, bowed and murmured "Master" and stepped back. The next Quarg went up to Splurge and bowed. It was Hodges, who also murmured "Master", before he too stepped back into the line.

Splurge looked out into the audience to see if Mysterio could offer any explanation, but it was too dark to see. He turned back when he felt a tug on his arm. It was Meela, who did not bow, but instead handed him a battered old top hat. "You are the true Master," she said. Then to Splurge's astonishment – she smiled, a proper, full blown smile. He gave her a grin in return and was about to say something to her when she too retreated back to the line of Quargs.

The line of Quargs then began to march about the stage to the throbbing beat of the drum till they had all disappeared somewhere in the darkness at the back of the stage. As the last Quarg disappeared, the lights came on in the theatre and another surprise awaited Splurge. All the audience were standing and clapping, making strange humming sounds at the same time. Mysterio was also applauding and shouting 'bravo', above the hum of the assembled Quargs.

Splurge felt embarrassed and a little foolish. The whole thing in the Theatre of Magic had been a performance – with himself taking the lead role. The clapping and Mysterio's 'bravos' continued, till he thought it best if he bowed a few times, to acknowledge the applause. As soon as he bowed, there was silence. The curtains closed with a sudden swish and opened almost immediately to reveal an empty theatre, apart from Mysterio, who had now left his seat and was back on the stage.

"I don't understand," said Splurge, shaking his head in bafflement. "Was it for real – Broga - Jonesy – the crystal caves?"

Mysterio grinned. "It's as real as you want it to be. You should remember that this is the Theatre of Magic. Even out there in your world, what you see in the theatre is not real. This being a magic theatre is even less real." Mysterio's eyes twinkled as he spoke, as though enjoying a private joke.

Splurge felt relief, but he also felt deflated. Ever since he had arrived in this theatre, events had been boiling up to a confrontation with Broga and now he couldn't even be sure whether he actually did anything. "Is, or was, Broga real?"

Mysterio looked steadily at Splurge. "There are Brogas everywhere. They too have to be defeated as you defeated your Broga. That should be enough for you." His eyes twinkled again. "The rest is merely trimming," he said with a casual wave of his hand. "Now you have earned the right to leave. One of the Quargs will show you the way out."

"Er – thanks," was all Splurge could say. The whole time he had been in the Theatre of Magic, he had fretted about getting out, and now he was actually getting his wish, he couldn't understand why he wasn't more excited about it.

Suddenly there was a bright flash of light followed by a cloud of billowing blue smoke, out of which stepped Meela.

"As this Quarg has shown a special attachment to you, I though you might like her to do the final honours of escorting you from the premises." Mysterio gave Splurge a short bow, and was about to walk towards the back of the stage when he paused and came back. "Remember, my young friend, what I have told you before. You have learnt much here, and you will take it into the outworld with you. Use the knowledge well and make sure that you pass it on — else it will die. Remember - without magic the whole world will die."

Splurge thought that it was an overwhelming thing to say, but then he was - Mysterio the all-powerful — the all knowing. He should know if anyone should.

With a twitch of his cape and a slight tilt of his hat, Mysterio smiled, and with a loud crack, was gone.

"Come, Master. It is time for you to return to the outworld, where you will perform great magic. I know it." Meela took his hand, and for a moment he felt a slight tingling, but not unpleasant.

Splurge wanted to say something to Meela, but wasn't sure what. 'Goodbye' somehow didn't seem enough. And how was he actually going to get out? He needn't have worried for Meela led him into the darkness at the back of the stage, with the same sureness she had led him into all sorts of strange places, till they reached some sort of door, barely visible in the dark.

Meela let go of his hand. "Go though that door. Goodbye, Master." She turned and walked away, the sound of her footsteps receding till there was just darkness and silence.

Splurge pushed the door and walked through into daylight.

Chapter Thirty One – The Magic Shop

Splurge looked around and saw that he was standing in front of a shop and staring into the window. It was one of the several in the alley next to the theatre. He didn't know how long he had been standing here, but it seemed like ages. Dash and Blip must have gone into the town but he had been much too fascinated by this shop to follow. There were all sorts of strange things in the window, but he couldn't tell whether it was a toyshop or some kind of magic shop. In the window he could see coloured balls, boxes of all shapes and sizes, which looked as though they fitted into each other. There were a whole variety of rubber masks of all the usual monsters. It must be the kind of shop that supplied costumes for the theatre, he decided. There were other things too which looked like dolls but not exactly. There was something strangely familiar about them. Then he remembered.

He looked over his shoulder and there was the blank wall of the theatre behind him. He felt sure that there should have been a doorway somewhere there. Perhaps he had imagined it.

The shop didn't have any sign, just a name - MR.E.O.JONES. That was odd in itself, Splurge thought because it was not very often, if at all, that he had seen 'MR.' in front of a name on a shop. Anyway, it looked interesting and he felt in his pocket to see how much money he had in case he wanted to buy something, though he wouldn't really know till he got inside and had a look around. He supposed he really ought to go after his friends, who would by now have reached the shopping mall. It surprised him that they should have given this particular shop a miss. It was the kind of weird place that usually intrigued them.

As he stood there, trying to make up his mind, whether to stay or follow his friends, he caught sight of something strange. One of the dolls winked!

For a moment, Splurge wondered if he had imagined it but no – there it was again. He peered closely through the window at the doll-like puppet. Its eyes were large and were now wide open. Maybe it was some sort of mechanical doll, which blinked and moved its arms when wound up. He would like a closer look.

Splurge wasn't sure why, but he felt a slight nervous twinge as he turned the handle of the door and went inside. (Of course, it could have been a guilty conscience for playing truant).

At first he couldn't see much as it was quite dim, and smelled funny - musty and old. As he became used to the gloomy atmosphere, he could see that the shop was packed with all sorts of things. There were rows and rows of costumes of all kinds, from clowns to gorillas. Every type of hat was on display, with one whole shelf devoted to silky, shiny top hats, the sort that magicians wore. There were the usual, wizards' and witches' hats painted and decorated with stars and moons. It was the masks, however, which were the most eye-catching, and every kind imaginable were hanging from all sorts of places, and all seemed to be staring down at him, and Splurge had this feeling that they were watching him, and he was definitely sure that one hanging behind the counter swivelled its eyes around.

"Well, young man, what can I do for you?"

Splurge almost jumped out of his skin. The eyes, which had been following him belonged to a tall man, with a small, black beard and dark eyebrows to match. For some strange reason, Splurge thought that he had seen him before, but he couldn't have done because he had never been to this shop before.

"Is... is this a magic shop?" Splurge stammered his question, being a little overawed by the imposing presence of the man behind the counter.

"Of course," the man boomed. "I am the owner and sole proprietor – Mister E. O. Jones – at your service." He came from behind the counter to give Splurge a mock bow.

Splurge had never seen anyone like him before. Dressed completely in black, he reminded him of a – of a – "Magician," he suddenly said aloud.

The man, Mr. Jones laughed, a low rumbling laugh, which seemed to echo around the musty, old shop. "Well? How can I be of service?"

Splurge was a little afraid of this tall, imposing figure and wasn't sure whether he should ask him about the doll. "I saw in your window that doll puppet." He pointed. "It blinked at me." As soon as he said it he knew that it was the wrong thing to say. It sounded so silly.

Mr. Jones merely raised an eyebrow and gave Splurge a strange knowing look. "We have no dolls or puppets. Our last consignment was unfortunately destroyed in a fire."

Splurge gave an involuntary shudder at those words, yet he didn't know why. "Oh," was all he could stammer.

"Look around," said Mr. Jones. "See if anything takes your fancy," he smiled." It's all for sale, and at knock down prices." He pulled Splurge nearer. "I'm having a clear out, you understand," he said in a low confidential tone. "Selling up."

Splurge murmured another 'oh' and wondered why the man should confide such a thing to him, unless it was to encourage him to buy something.

"I have to go back, you see," the man said, more to himself than Splurge.

Splurge was tempted to ask him where he had to go back to, but something at the back of his mind told him that it would be unwise to ask. Instead, he decided to wander around the shop, which was well stocked with all sorts of things. Apart from masks and costumes, there were the usual party things like balloons, streamers, funny noses, and false moustaches. There were even a few magic items. A bloodstained rubber axe caught his attention and while he was examining it, something else caught his eye, something intriguing. It was an ordinary blue box on the counter. He assumed it was a Jack-in-the-box and felt around for a catch, but couldn't find one. He would have asked the owner, but he was nowhere to be seen. He turned back to the box and thought he was seeing things, for the box had changed colour for it was now red. Of course, he could have been mistaken about the colour in the first place, but he was sure that it had been blue. With a shake of his head, Splurge continued his wandering. After all, it was a sort of magic shop, so there were bound to be a few unusual things. A selection of grisly objects on a shelf next caught his attention, eyeballs, several fingers, and an ear, even a severed hand, dripping blood. Splurge couldn't resist touching them. They turned out to be soft and rubbery, not too scary, after all - until the hand suddenly began to move.

At first, Splurge thought that he was hallucinating and he rubbed his eyes. But he wasn't seeing things; the hand was definitely moving and trying to feel its way off the shelf.

"Fascinating, isn't it?"

Splurge jumped in alarm at the voice behind him. It was the proprietor, Mr. Jones.

"It looks very real," the man murmured. "What do you think of this one, then?" Without warning he thrust a large ball at Splurge, which no sooner had he grasped than it became a bunch of flowers.

Splurge was impressed and thought that he might like something like that. It would also impress his friends, Dash and Blip. Perhaps not, he thought. It was a little corny after all. He handed the flowers back to the man, who somehow managed to convert them back into a ball.

Splurge wasn't sure what he wanted, if he wanted to buy anything at all, but it was fascinating just wandering about and looking at all of the ordinary and unusual items. He felt a little uneasy, however, at the presence of the man, who always seemed to pop up suddenly beside him. It was disconcerting to say the least, and somewhat unnerving. Moreover, time was running out. He had to catch up with Dash and Blip, so he had better settle on something quickly or forget it altogether. As he made his way back to the front door, through rows of costumes and dangling masks, he saw odd thing. He wondered why he had not noticed it before. There, one of the top shelves, where the brand new shiny top hats were laid out, he saw something completely out of place. He was about to reach up for it when he was halted by the man's voice.

"Sorry. That's not for sale. It shouldn't really be up there." He reached up and took down from the shelf a dusty and battered-looking top hat. "Don't know how it got there," he murmured, and disappeared with it somewhere at the back of the shop. He was soon back, smiling and hovering once more. "Everything is for sale. In fact the shop itself is for sale. I have to go back, you see." He paused and gave Splurge a strange look. "I don't suppose you would know of anyone who would like to take over."

Splurge shook his head. It could be fun, he imagined, to run such a place, but he wasn't sure that he would be good at selling. Playing perhaps, but not selling.

"Ah well, never mind," the man said in a regretful way. "Have you seen anything you like yet? No?" He looked at Splurge with one eyebrow raised. "I think I have something that just might suit you." Again he disappeared to the back of the shop and returned immediately carrying a small box, the sort that might contain a brooch or similar item of jewellery. He was about to hand it to Splurge, when he withdrew his hand. "This is not a sale, but a complimentary free gift." He then placed it in Splurge's hand. "But you must not open it till you are out of the shop. And you must tell all your friends about this place."

A strange request, thought Splurge, but he agreed. After all, a free gift is a free gift. As he was leaving the shop, the man, Mr. Jones, called out to him.

"Are you sure that you are not interested in owning this place," he said, with his eyes twinkling. "You could be the new master."

"No thanks," Splurge called out. "I've had enough of being a master for one day." It wasn't till he was outside the shop, that he wondered why he had said such a thing. But he soon forgot about that as he looked at the small box, wondering what the man had given him. As soon as he opened it, he knew. As he gently lifted the lid, he heard a familiar chirruping sound and there, nestling within, was a large golden cricket. "Wow!" was all he could say.

"Where did you get to then?" asked Dash."

"Yeah, it was great," mumbled Blip, through a mouthful of toffee or some sort of chewy sweet. "We saw this sweet shop. It - was – fantastic."

"We thought you were following just behind us," said Dash.

"I waited to make sure that Mr. Turnbull had gone in. You can never tell with teachers. He might have come looking for us."

"You could still have caught us up. We waited for ages." Dash looked at Blip and scowled. "Well, we waited as long as his stomach could hold out. So I guess we didn't wait very long," he said with a smirk.

"What you got there, Splurge?" Blip asked, his mouth now free of toffee and ignoring Dash's jibe.

"Something from that shop, there." He nodded towards the shop.

"Let's have a look then."

Splurge opened the box.

"Wow!" said Dash, suitably impressed.

"Wow!" echoed Blip. "What is it?"

"It's an Aug," said Splurge, though he didn't know how he knew that. The man in the shop hadn't told him. But he liked the name anyway.

"If it's really gold, it must be valuable," said Dash.

"How does it make that sound?" Blip tried to look into the small box and nearly succeeded in knocking out of Splurge's hands.

"Hey, careful! If you want one of your own, go in there. He might give you one."

"It's closed," said Blip, sounding disgruntled.

"Come on you two. It's late. We'd better get back and sneak in for the last bit of that play." Dash began to walk quickly back to the theatre.

"What if the teachers ask where we've been?" Blip gasped out, as he started to run.

"Tell them we went to get some popcorn or something. Knowing you, they'll believe that." Dash guffawed and ran on.

"Come on Splurge. We've just got time." Blip glanced at his watch as he called to Splurge.

Splurge was in no hurry. Carefully he closed the box and put it in his jacket pocket. Anyway, he had had enough of theatres for one day. Again, he wondered why he thought of that. It was altogether very strange. At least the day hadn't been entirely wasted – he did have his Aug.

For Your Future Reading Enjoyment

If the Theatre of Magic has enchanted you, then why not join Splurge in his next adventure?

In Splurge and the Hall of Mirrors, Splurge has to use all of his skills and daring to overcome the perils, which lie behind the mirrors.

Can he save his friends before they are lost forever? And what will happen is a mirror is smashed? Most important – who or what is Mister Dee?

Further Titles

Splurge and the Phantom of the Circus

Splurge and the Disappearing Village

Splurge and the Mystery of the Loch